TAMING LEO

A PARANORMAL ROMANCE

VALLEYWOOD BOOK

GIOVANNA REAVES

CONTENTS

Cover Design by EmCat Design

Editing by Contagious Edits

BLURB

Leo Devereux, the powerful CEO of Devereux Real Estate, Architecture & Design, isn't new to whirlwind flings that are hot, intense, and over before the sheets cool. However, one night left a mark. One gray-eyed stranger, one unforgettable connection... and then gone by morning. No name, no note. Just a memory Leo can't shake.

Jason Dupree never expected a one-night stand to follow him across continents. His friends thought it was hilarious to hire an escort for his birthday and going-away gift, a wild send-off before grad school in Singapore. He imagined it would be fun and drunken, with no strings attached. It was definitely not the start of something that would linger for years.

Six years later, Jason is back in Valleywood with a degree, accolades, and two clever, chaotic kids in tow. He has just landed a job at DRA&D and hopes to advance in his career. What he doesn't see coming? Running into the man who, unknowingly, fathered his children.

When Leo and Jason lock eyes again, the chemistry snaps back into place: instant, charged, and impossible to ignore. Both try to downplay it. However, when Leo makes a surprising request, Jason, a single father, agrees. What begins as a slow burn quickly turns into something neither of them can control: raw, real, and hard to walk away from.

But Leo is keeping a secret. One that could shake everything they are trying to build. If it comes out, it might tear them apart... or finally give them the family they never knew they were searching for.

ACKNOWLEDGMENTS

Thank you to everyone for their continued support. Shout out to all One-Night Temptation and Chance VIP members.

"You are mine. Mine, as I am yours."
–Diana Gabaldon, Outlander

CHAPTER 1
JASON

Jason stumbled through the hotel lobby, one hand pressed against the wall to steady himself. He was so drunk that he could barely see straight, his vision swimming with blurred lights and shifting colors. To celebrate their graduation from Valleywood University, he and his friends had gone all out, renting a private karaoke party room at Luxe Horizon Hotel, overflowing with top-shelf liquor, pulsing music, gourmet food, and lively hostesses who kept the energy high. It was a triple celebration; not only was he graduating, but it was also his birthday, and soon, he'd be heading to Singapore to further his studies in architecture.

As a going-away present, his friends had pooled their money to hire him a high-priced escort. Jason had no idea how they'd even managed it, considering that kind of service was exclusive to hotel members. But in his current state, the details didn't matter. If he were sober, he would have refused outright without a second thought. But right now? Right now, he wanted to be daring, to let go of his inhibitions, just this once.

Since being kicked out of his family at age eighteen, he had poured every waking moment into work and study, determined to graduate early. He had sacrificed sleep, relationships, and even the simplest joys just to reach this point.

So why the fuck not? I'm too young to live like an old man who has passed his partying and fucking prime.

He hadn't had sex since the night of his prom when he lost his virginity to a guy just as inexperienced as he was in a disappointing three seconds. He had timed it, caught up in the excitement of finally joining the ranks of those who had *done it*. So maybe sleeping with a stranger, someone who actually knew what they were doing, would take the awkwardness out of the equation.

It's just one night. What could it hurt?

Jason shuffled through the dimly lit corridor, squinting as he tried to make out the numbers on the room doors. Had Tracy said 609 or 906? He couldn't remember. Although he was tempted, knocking on every door to ask if they were the escort his friends had paid for was out of the question. That would be utterly humiliating. Just as he turned the corner, he collided face-first into something solid and unyielding, like a wall.

"Fuck," he groaned, his eyes stinging as tears blurred his already unsteady vision. Sharp pain radiated from his nose, the unfortunate casualty of the collision. Instinctively, he pressed his hands against the solid surface, trying to regain his balance, but his knees buckled the moment he stepped back. There was no stopping it; he was about to become very well acquainted with the floor.

But before he could crash down and form a painful bond with the ground, strong hands caught him by the waist, stopping his fall. In a dizzy blur, his world tilted, and before he could process what was happening, his back was pressed against an equally hard, unyielding surface.

When did walls get so warm...and grow arms? Jason wondered hazily, his drunken mind struggling to grasp reality. Before he could fully process what was happening, hot, wet lips collided with his, stealing his breath and eliciting a moan from deep within his chest.

Oh, fuck, whoever this is can kiss.

The rough scrape of a five o'clock shadow brushed against his skin, sending a shiver down his spine. He knew it was a man. He *should* have pushed him away, but his body refused to listen. It felt too good. Too right...and gods, he wanted this.

No, he *needed* this.

His muddled brain struggled to determine whether he was dreaming or still trapped in reality. But in the end, it didn't matter. All he knew was that his friends had arranged an escort for him, and somehow, they had found each other.

Jason whimpered against the demanding lips, his

breath ragged and his pulse pounding in his veins. He scarcely had a moment to catch his breath before an intoxicating aroma engulfed his senses: masculine, rich, and dark. Heat pooled beneath his skin, burning through him, forcing him to tug at his shirt in a desperate attempt to cool down. But before he could strip it off, strong fingers gripped his wrists, pinning his arms against the hard surface on either side of his head. Lips ghosted along his jaw, tracing a heated path down his neck, teasing the shell of his ear before sharp teeth sank into his skin, making Jason shudder.

A deep, raspy voice sliced through the haze of drunken desire.

"Are you willing?"

Of course I'm willing. Why else would I kiss you as if it were my last breath?

To prove it, he hooked a leg around the escort's waist, drawing him closer until their bodies aligned. A needy moan escaped as he ground his aching cock against the man's solid frame, craving more.

The escort chuckled, tightening his grip on Jason's wrists.

"Don't regret this in the morning."

The next thing he knew, he was being lifted off his feet, his body instinctively molding against the firm grip around him. They were moving, yet all Jason could focus on was the word regret echoing in his mind. He wouldn't regret this. Not when his body burned with desire, every nerve ignited with need, pleading for release. His omega slick soaked through his underwear, undeniable proof of just how badly he craved this.

As soon as his back hit the mattress, the escort was on him again, capturing his lips in a deep, breath-stealing kiss. Their hands moved with urgency, quickly stripping away clothes and tossing them aside carelessly. A nagging thought lingered in the back of Jason's mind: something important, something he should pay attention to. But then his legs were parted, and a thick finger slid inside his slick hole, obliterating all rational thought. He groaned, instinctively pressing down against the intrusion, his body yearning for more. The slow, deliberate drag of a single finger sent his brain spinning, his nerves tingling with anticipation for what lay ahead.

"More," he whimpered, his voice breathless with desire.

"Greedy little thing, aren't you?" the deep voice rumbled in his ear, rich with amusement.

"Too much talking, fuck me," Jason growled, crashing their mouths together.

The escort did not hesitate. Instead, he added another finger alongside the first, stretching Jason, keeping him teetering on the knife's edge between pain and pleasure. Jason rocked his hips, grinding his cock against the man's hard abs, his body silently begging for more.

A pleased shiver coursed through him, and it seemed that the escort had received the message. Then suddenly, the fingers disappeared. Before Jason could react, he was flipped onto his stomach. Strong hands gripped his waist, pulling him to his knees and spreading his legs open.

Jason buried his face in the pillow, a deep moan

ripping from his throat as a thick, hot cock pressed against his waiting entrance. A rough hand slid up his body, fingers tightening around his neck, pulling him flush against a firm, sweat-slicked chest.

"Let me hear you," the escort growled, driving in with a smooth, relentless stroke.

Jason howled, his body shaking violently from the sudden invasion. Pain and pleasure melded together, raw and overwhelming, yet he didn't pull away. He couldn't because it felt too good. A deep moan tore from his lips as he clenched around the thick length buried inside him, as if his body refused to let go. The escort didn't move right away. Instead, he rolled his hips slowly, grinding his pelvis against Jason's ass, stretching him further and forcing him to feel every inch.

"Fuck, you fit me like a glove," the deep voice murmured in his ear, laced with undeniable possessiveness.

Jason smirked through the haze of desire, rolling his hips in invitation. "Then take me."

A low growl rumbled in response, thick with challenge. "You're so fucking cocky. Let's see if you can keep up with me all night."

Jason didn't get a chance to respond. The escort took control, slamming into him with deep, unrelenting strokes, stretching him, claiming him, unraveling him piece by piece. His mind, body, and soul melted into the man's hands, shaped and molded however he pleased. The air thickened with sex, pheromones, and the lingering haze of alcohol, merging into a heady cocktail that made Jason feel drunk all over again. A dull discomfort flickered in his lower abdomen, yet he dismissed it. He was deeply lost. Too focused on the pleasure, consuming him whole.

"Oh, fuck yes," he moaned, spreading his legs wider, his back arching in complete surrender.

The fingers tightening around his throat didn't bring fear; instead, they unleashed raw, unfiltered ecstasy.

"Oh gods, please, oh gods, please," he whimpered, his fingers clawing at the sturdy headboard. He pushed back, meeting every thrust, chasing the pleasure that ignited inside him like wildfire. The burn. The stretch. It was an exquisite bliss. Too much...and yet not enough.

"No god can save you from me," his partner rasped, his voice thick with hunger, low and commanding. "Tonight, I am your only god."

Jason couldn't speak even if he wanted to.

His world shattered as the next thrust sent him spiraling into blissful oblivion. Pleasure detonated through him, his slick hole clenching as his orgasm tore through his body. His cum spurted onto the sheets beneath him, but his partner didn't stop. He fucked Jason through it, through the aftershocks, through the trembling weakness that overtook his limbs.

Jason barely noticed the sharp bite at the back of his neck, right where his omega knot lay hidden. A flicker of unease ignited deep within him, but it was overshadowed by his body's reaction to the thick knot tightening inside of him. He *should* have been worried. He should have recognized that something wasn't right.

But as wet heat flooded his insides, scorching him, igniting another wave of unbearable pleasure, his body betrayed him once more. His recently spent cock twitched, hardening again as his partner pulled him into another round.

And then another one followed until they both slipped into a blissful, exhausted sleep.

Jason nuzzled his face into the pillow, a soft and warm groan slipping from his lips at the discomfort. It was too firm, too unfamiliar. A dull, deep soreness settled into his muscles, the weight of exhaustion pressing down on him. Slowly, he pried open his heavy eyelids, waiting for the world to come into focus. A flicker of gold caught his gaze, the soft, golden hue of morning sunlight filtering through the curtains.

Where am I? This isn't my apartment.

Jason covered his face, his mind sluggish as he tried to piece together how he had ended up in someone else's bed. Then, like shards of glass slicing through the fog, the memories crashed into him, jagged, fragmented, and all too vivid. He froze, his breath catching. Behind his fingers, his eyes widened. Drinking, singing, and sex— lots of it. With a hooker...no, an escort. Slowly, he sat up, uncovering his face. The golden glow he had mistaken for sunlight was a man who was fast asleep.

Jason couldn't tell what he looked like because his long, curly, jet-black hair covered most of his face. He was tempted to pull it back but didn't want to tempt fate and wake the guy up.

Fuck, Tracy really knows how to pick an escort who is my body type.

Biting his bottom lip, he reached out a hand to gently pull some of the man's hair back so he could get a look at the face, but he froze and held his breath when the sleeping figure shifted but did not wake up. Jason let out a relieved breath and took it as his cue to get the hell out before the guy truly woke up. Jason had heard enough horror stories from his friends about awkward morning-after conversations, and he wasn't about to stick around for one of his own. Moving carefully, he slipped out of bed, biting back a wince as his body protested every movement.

He glared at the sleeping figure, silently cursing him to the high heavens. *Fuck, I feel like I was tossed around like a rag doll.*

Dragging on his clothes was an ordeal in itself, and every sore muscle was a throbbing reminder of what had happened last night. Only when he was fully dressed did his gaze flicker back to the man in bed.

Right. He's an escort. It's only fair that I leave a tip. Jason pulled out his wallet, thumbing through the bills before counting out a hundred dollars. He was about to set it down but hesitated. *I still need cash for later.* With a half-shrug, he took back half. Then hesitated again. Finally, with a quiet sigh, he placed the remaining bills on the nightstand and stepped back.

Then, as another wave of soreness rippled through his body, he reconsidered. "Learn to be gentler next time," he muttered under his breath, snatching back the fifty dollars. Peeling off a twenty, he let it flutter onto the guy's face before stuffing the rest back into his wallet.

It's not like I'll ever see this guy again.

With a final glance around the room to make sure he wasn't forgetting anything, Jason slipped out without a second look. He didn't stop, didn't hesitate, and just strode out of the hotel, leaving the past few *very* pleasurable hours behind. He couldn't deny it had been one hell of a send-off. And if nothing else, it was a fantastic way to kick off his future.

CHAPTER 2
LEO

L eo pried his heavy eyes open, blinking against the morning light. A frown tugged at his lips as he felt something stuck to his face. Reaching up, he peeled it away, his brows knitting together when he saw what it was.

A twenty-dollar bill.

What the hell...?

Leo sat up, pinching the bridge of his nose as hazy fragments of last night crashed into him. A sharp exhale escaped his lips, his chest rising and falling beneath the weight of memories. A lightly muscled, writhing body pressed against his breathless, broken moans—a sweet voice, raw with need, calling for him as if he were a god.

Heat flowed across his skin, so intense it sent a shiver down his spine.

It all started so simply. Leo had spent the evening finalizing a lucrative business deal with foreign dignitaries at the Luxe Horizon Hotel. The negotiations had been exhausting, extending late into the night, but the reward had been worth it. On his way out, he'd run into his friends Julien Ellis, the sharp-minded owner of Onyx Sentinel Cybersecurity, and Avery Shaw, the mastermind behind the Luxe Horizon Hotel and several of Valleywood's most elite restaurants. Both men were at the bar, celebrating their successes, with drinks flowing as freely as their laughter. They had coaxed him into staying, insisting *one* drink wouldn't kill him.

One became two. Then three. Then more.

The celebration moved to a private room, secluded from the rest of the hotel, illuminated by dim lighting and saturated with indulgence. The drinks kept flowing. And when several beautiful, flirtatious hostesses joined them, eager to keep the night going, Leo figured, why the hell not? That had been his first mistake. He had drunk too much, but that was precisely why he held a membership at the Luxe Horizon. Nights like this were expected. If things spiraled out of control, he had a safe place to sleep it off.

When he stood, his world tilted violently beneath him, and a wave of dizziness struck him hard and fast, sharp and disorienting. Instantly, heat surged through his veins, unnatural and all consuming. His body burned.

This wasn't the slow buzz of alcohol or the draw of exhaustion. This was something else—something *wrong*.

His pulse pounded in his ears. His limbs felt sluggish and heavy.

Then he realized someone had drugged him.

It must have happened when he wasn't paying attention, engrossed in conversation and laughing with his friends, completely unaware of the moment when his drink was tainted. His vision blurred. His skin felt overly hot and sensitive, while his thoughts slipped through his grasp like sand through his fingers. A familiar ache coiled deep within him, sharp and unyielding.

This was not merely a drug.

It was a potent and quick-acting aphrodisiac.

His body burned, every nerve ablaze with unbearable sensitivity. Each shift and every brush of fabric against his overheated skin sent electric shocks of sensation through him. His mind grew hazy, slipping further from his grasp as the need within him swelled, unrelenting and impossible to ignore.

"Are you alright, Leo?"

He recognized Julien's voice, steady yet tinged with concern.

"Yeah," he lied, his voice rougher than he had expected. *"I need to go."*

Julien didn't seem convinced, nor did Avery, who moved closer and pressed a hand to Leo's cheek. His gaze was piercing and searching.

"Did someone give you drugs?" Julain asked.

Leo exhaled sharply. *"Yeah, an aphrodisiac."*

A flicker of anger crossed Julien's face. *"Let's get you out of here."*

"No." He silenced them with a glance, his jaw clenched. *"I'll have*

Talos handle it. You two find out who did this."

Avery nodded, his expression becoming more resolute. "You got it. Get some rest."

Leo left the investigation to his friends and stumbled out of the lounge, his legs unsteady, his body burning from the inside out. He pressed his back against the cool marble wall, desperate for relief, but it wasn't enough. It wasn't what his body needed. His fingers trembled as he struggled to find his phone. His vision blurred, and his pulse thundered in his ears. He typed a single message to his special assistant with effort.

Get me an escort. Send them to my room.

The next thing he remembered was stumbling into his hotel room, fumbling with the lock, and then someone was in his arms. A lightly muscled, eager body pressed against him, molding to him so perfectly that it felt inevitable, as if they had been waiting for him. Their lips collided with his, desperate, consuming him as if he were sin itself. Leo couldn't recall if a single word passed between them. His booze-and-drug-clouded mind made sure of that. All he knew was that he couldn't resist. He wanted all of it: their touch, their lips, their body.

Immortal or not, he was still a man. And in that moment, all he wanted to do was *fuck*.

A low groan rumbled from his chest as he rubbed his temples, his head pounding from the effects of alcohol and mind-numbing sex. The memories were fragmented and incomplete. He recalled gray eyes, piercing and haunting. And a beauty mark that stood out even in the night's blur. But the rest? Gone.

Had they been beautiful? He could only hope. Leo blinked away the lingering haze of sleep, his gaze scanning the room. Empty. His companion had vanished without a trace as if they were nothing more than a fevered dream.

But it was real.

The faint scent of sex still clung to the air, a ghostly reminder of the night before. He wasn't sure if he was relieved or disappointed that the escort had left before he woke up. Frowning, he picked up the twenty dollars just as the door to his hotel room opened. From his vantage point, he watched Talos step inside, ever-efficient, with a steaming cup of coffee in one hand and a suit garment bag draped over the other.

"Sir, I brought a change of clothes," Talos said, hanging the garment bag over the back of the couch before stepping into the bedroom. "And coffee." He paused, his tone measured as always. "I also spoke with Mr. Shaw. He has identified the culprit, and they have been dealt with."

Leo nodded, refraining from asking further questions. He understood precisely what it meant when Avery took care of people. Setting the incident aside, he concentrated on the more urgent issue.

"Who was I with yesterday evening?"

Talos's expression remained impassive. "I am not certain, sir.

The young man who was sent to you reported that you never responded to the door."

Leo hummed, pondering that for a moment. "Find out who it was."

Talos nodded. "Yes, sir."

Leo reached for the crumpled bill beside him, holding it up between two fingers. "Oh, and when you do, return this."

Talos wore a frown. "What is that?"

A smirk played on Leo's lips. "My tip, I guess."

Talos approached, taking the bill from Leo's hand. He studied it for a beat before raising an eyebrow. "Is he saying you're only worth twenty dollars? Maybe you need to work on your technique."

Leo's gaze darkened ominously. "Do you want a smack?"

Talos grinned but quickly composed himself, tucking the bill away. "No, sir. I'll do as you instructed."

"Good."

With a lingering smirk, Talos turned and walked out of the room.

Leo exhaled and pushed the covers back, but when he moved to step out of bed, he suddenly froze. His gaze was fixated on a crimson stain against the pristine white sheets as his breath stilled and a torrent of unsettling thoughts flooded his mind, each one more disquieting than the last.

Was he a virgin? Was I too rough last night?

Leo ran a hand through his hair, trying to remember whether the man had shown any discomfort or hesitation. As far as he could recall, nothing had shouted danger. The man had moaned, begged, and clung to him, wanting more.

However, the red stain revealed a different story.

Leo prided himself on control, which was why he hated doing any kind of drugs. He knew he was well-endowed and was always careful with his partners. This involved using protection.

At that thought, his stomach sank.

He turned sharply, scanning the room, and his gaze fell on the trash can next to the bed.

Empty.

His pulse quickened. He got out of bed, his eyes scanning the floor for any signs of discarded wrappers. A condom. Anything.

Fuck. Nothing.

A slow, chilling realization crept over him, winding ice particles around his spine. His jaw clenched as urgency coiled tightly in his chest, twisting more and more with every passing second.

"I messed up." His voice emerged low and rough, laced with a hint of panic. Leo exhaled sharply, running his fingers through his hair once more, his mind racing.

"If he gets pregnant, I'll take responsibility."

And he meant it. However, he first needed to find him.

Leo set the thought aside for now. He couldn't do anything until Talos returned with the man's information. He made his way to the bathroom, attended to his morning needs, and used the extra toiletries provided by the hotel. The ordinary act centered him, calming his mind as he switched on the shower and stepped beneath the steaming spray. Heat seeped into his skin, easing the tension in his sore muscles, yet his mind didn't wander to last night. Instead, it drifted through the centuries that had shaped him.

Most regarded him as a man in his thirties. Few would suspect the truth that he was more than three thousand years old. Throughout the rise and fall of civilizations, Leo had lived under countless names, honing his skills as a master builder, painter, sculptor, inventor, and architect. However, one name resonated throughout history.

Daedalus.

A name he occasionally forgot. A name that belonged to a different lifetime.

But today, the world knew him as Leonides Devereux, the real estate tycoon, architect, and visionary he had chosen to be. When Leo first moved to Valleywood, years before Loki, the god of tricks, became mayor, he founded Devereux Real Estate, Architecture & Designs. He had always kept himself apart from divine gossip, especially after the trouble he had caused by defying the gods and aiding mortals in his past life.

However, those with true knowledge of the divine knew the truth.

Loki had lost his powers.

The once-mischievous god now lived as a human, though one possessing superhuman strength and intelligence. Leo had never put much stock in Loki. To him, the trickster was simply another chaotic force, more of a nuisance than a threat. Although Loki had angered the gods countless times with his schemes, the stunt that cost him his divinity was attempted murder when he already had blood on his hands. That irony was not lost on Leo. Loki had committed far worse offenses and survived divine wrath. For this to be his downfall was either a cosmic joke or Odin's plan all along to weave Loki's powers into the very fabric of Valleywood.

Time will tell.

Since becoming mayor, Loki had changed in ways that Leo hadn't expected. The reckless god he'd once heard tales of on Mount Olympus was nowhere to be seen. Though still sharptongued and irreverent, he carried himself with a quiet steadiness, a side of him few ever witnessed. In their business dealings, he was always direct, more measured than chaotic. There was something different about him now, something more controlled, as if he had finally learned when to wield his unpredictability and when to rein it in.

Leo didn't dwell on it; he had other things to focus on.

When he had just turned twenty, the goddess Athena took pity on him and adopted him in name, blood, and magic. She bestowed upon him the gift of immortality and extraordinary physical strength, as well as healing abilities, a bit of her knowledge and astuteness in battle, and the ability to manipulate runes. He had used that ability many times on objects, buildings, and even his blueprints, but never on people. Athena was convinced that his talents were too great to vanish with time. Leo was grateful for his mother's gift and took full advantage of everything life offered, but he also didn't flaunt his powers, choosing instead to live through his experiences.

Yet, even with all he had accomplished and built and gained, he couldn't deny a simple truth.

Something was missing.

Leo knew exactly what it was, but he would never say the word out loud. If he did, Athena would appear out of nowhere and start setting him up on blind dates, and that was a nightmare he wasn't ready to deal with.

Leo had never imagined the regal, battle-hardened Athena as a mother hen at heart, much less one who longed to be a grandmother. According to her, she had never married; neither god nor mortal had ever been worthy enough to be her lover. Thus, she had remained a virgin, choosing instead to adopt mortal children she considered exceptional, bestowing upon them immortality in acknowledgment of their talents and contributions to the world. Leo would never argue that his mother was selfish. However, in her defense, she never pretended to be anything else.

She had only one other child besides him: his younger sister, Ada Lovelace. A former duchess who was credited for being one of the first computer programmers.

Ada was an expert at getting under his skin. Despite being given not only a department but an entire company to lead the integration of artificial intelligence into the smart homes they were developing in Dragon City before expanding to the other districts, she still treated him like an old man stuck in the past.

Leo didn't care what she thought. She was barely two hundred and ten years old. *What the hell did she know?*

Shaking his head, Leo pushed thoughts of his sister

aside and finished his shower. He stepped out, wrapping a towel around his waist before reaching for another, rubbing it over his damp body and hair as he exited the bathroom, only to freeze mid-step. Sitting in the room and casually scanning through her phone was a stoic beauty with long, flowing platinum-blonde curls that reached her thighs. She looked no older than fifty, her sharp gaze locked on the screen before her.

Athena.

Leo had long since stopped trying to figure out how Athena always knew when he was thinking about her and how, without fail, she always appeared the moment he did.

"When will you stop indulging in these one-night flings and finally settle down?" Athena asked, her tone laced with the exhaustion of a battle she had fought too many times before.

Leo sighed, reaching for the coffee Talos had left for him. Thankfully, it was still hot—one of the small perks of living in a magical city where food and drinks were enchanted to maintain their ideal temperature.

"At least let me have a sip of my coffee before I answer." He took a deep, fortifying gulp, savoring the way the sweet bitterness grounded him.

"There. You've had your sip. Now, answer my question."

Leo barely had time to set the cup down before she pressed him again, her patience as thin as ever when it came to this subject.

"When I find the right one," he replied, his tone

steady, unwilling to let her pull him into this conversation any further than necessary.

"I thought you had found the right one long ago, but..."

"Don't mention him," Leo snapped. He didn't want to think about the one man he had given his heart to, who had imprisoned him. This was also the catalyst that led Athena to adopt him as her son.

"Daedalus..." Athena began.

"Mother, please," Leo interrupted. "Minos and I are in the way past."

Memories of his love affair with King Minos flashed in his mind, and he quickly shook his head, banishing them to the underworld.

"I heard he is making waves in Greece," she tsked. "He goes by the name Elias."

"Good, and let's hope he stays there."

"You really are over him?" Athena asked.

The word "yes" was on the tip of his tongue but was never said. Leo couldn't believe that after so many centuries, he still had some affection for the man.

"Fucking, Ishtar, I'm still trying to find out what she has on Minos and why he did what he did. But I know part of it is to spite me," Athena fumed. "It's not my fault she can't handle rejection."

The beef between Athena and Ishtar dated back thousands of years. However, it was primarily the Mesopotamian goddess of love and sex who had the issue. She's been infatuated with Athena and even tried to court her, but was rejected. As a matter of fact Athena wasn't interested in being with anyone even to this day.

Leo moisturized his skin as he listened to his mother's rant, then reached for the garment bag and pulled out the fresh pair of underwear Talos had packed. Keeping the towel loosely wrapped around his waist, he stepped into them, adjusting the waistband with a satisfied hum as the fabric conformed perfectly to his skin. Leo had recently developed a liking for the TS Fashion brand; the fit was seamless, the material breathable, and best of all, it didn't ride up throughout the day—a small but appreciated magical miracle.

Without a second thought, he yanked off the towel and tossed it onto the bed, continuing his morning routine. Athena remained completely unfazed, watching him with the patience of a goddess who had witnessed far worse in her time.

"When will that be?" she asked, her voice quieter this time. "Don't be like me, Daedalus."

A shadow flickered across her flawless features, brief but unmistakable—something close to regret.

Leo's expression softened. "It's not too late for you to fall in love, Mother. Gods as old as Odin are falling in love again."

"We're not talking about me," she deflected smoothly, stepping closer. Her fingers found his tie and adjusted it with the practiced ease of someone who had done it a thousand times before.

"Do you have a busy day planned?" she asked, her tone light, almost too casual.

Leo squinted. "The usual. Why?"

Leo knew better than to take his mother's questions at face value. When Athena asked something seemingly innocent, it meant she had something up her sleeve. She was the goddess of knowledge, after all, an expert at weaving words, shifting conversations, and leading people precisely where she wanted them to go. Even after all these years, she still had a knack for making him agree to things before he even realized it.

"Let's have breakfast together," she suggested smoothly. "We'll call Ada..."

Leo interrupted her. "You're hiding something from me."

Athena sighed, exasperated. "Why are you such a suspicious child?"

Leo raised an eyebrow. "I'm over three thousand years old. Hardly a child, Mother."

She smirked. "You'll always be one to me. Why, I still remember the day we met. You were just a young architect, so full of dreams—"

"Mom, please, let's not go down memory lane," Leo groaned. "And don't try to change the subject. What do you want me to do? Better yet, who the hell do you want me to meet?"

Athena's face brightened. "I met a wonderful young lady who would be perfect for you. She's—"

"No." Leo cut her off before she could continue.

She blinked. "Why not?"

Leo sighed. He had never cared whether his bed partners were men or women. Pleasure was pleasure, and satisfaction was what truly mattered.

"Mother, I'm busy. I don't need you finding me a date."

"But this young lady is perfect for you. And it would make me happy."

Leo rolled his eyes. Here comes the infamous Athena guilt trip. "Mother, I—" he began, but Talos interrupted.

"Sir, I have bad news," Talos interjected as he stepped into the room, his eyes focused on his tablet. "The hotel cameras were down last night and have only just come back up. I contacted Mr. Shaw for assistance, and he said he'd get back to me when he could. However, I did find out that a group of college graduates

were celebrating, and they ordered a..."

He trailed off when Athena cleared her throat.

Talos finally looked up, his eyes widening in shock before he straightened immediately. "Ah, madam. When did you arrive?"

Leo smirked, fully aware of what Talos truly wanted to ask: how the hell did she know he was here?

Talos was mortal. He knew shifters existed; his best friend was a cat shifter, something Leo had overheard him mention more than once. But gods? Talos believed they were nothing more than myths. He was human and remained blissfully unaware of the divine. To him, gods were simply ancient legends.

Athena smiled, completely at ease. "Young Talos, I've been trying to persuade my son to have breakfast with me. Tell me, what's his schedule?"

To his credit, Talos barely hesitated. "Um... Sir has a nine o'clock meeting with a new investor."

Behind Athena's back, Leo discreetly gave Talos a thumbs-up, making a mental note to add a thousand-dollar bonus to his paycheck; the man had earned it.

Athena hummed, clearly unconvinced. "Is that so?"

Before she could call Talos out, Leo jumped in. "Where's the meeting?"

Talos, catching on quickly, replied promptly. "At the office. If we don't leave now, we'll be late."

Athena's expression brightened. "Oh, that's perfect. We'll have lunch instead."

Leo felt as if his soul left his body when she leaned in and kissed his cheek.

"We will see you later, dear," she called over her shoulder, far too pleased with herself as she swept out of the room.

Leo turned, glaring at Talos. "Thanks a lot, Talos."

Talos frowned. "Sir?"

Leo crossed his arms. "You just lost your bonus for the month."

Talos blinked, truly perplexed. "But I just covered for you."

Leo sighed, rubbing his temples. "Forget it. Let's get to the office. And don't forget to keep searching for who I slept with last night."

His gaze flicked back to the bed. The red stain was now hidden, but that did little to ease the twisting in his gut. He still wasn't sure what to feel. Becoming a father had never been something he feared. However, he had always envisioned it happening when he was in love...again.

CHAPTER 3
JASON

Six Years Later

J ason navigated the bustling airport, one hand gripping a suitcase with an adorable five-year-old perched on top, while the other held onto a little boy who matched her in age and striking features. Five years ago, when he left Valleywood for Singapore, he thought he was carrying only his hopes, dreams, and luggage.

He had been wrong. Jason had found that he was almost three months pregnant.

After the initial shock wore off, he pulled himself

together and took responsibility. It wasn't the kids' fault that he hadn't realized he'd gone through his heat cycle, or that he'd missed his suppressants by a single day. The first two years were brutal. Juggling school, pregnancy, and newborns nearly broke him, but Jason refused to give up.

Once the twins were born, he'd hired a nanny to help during the day while he studied through the night. His babies became his purpose, his driving force. And if not for his grandfather granting him the first half of his inheritance, along with scholarships and competition winnings, he wouldn't have been able to afford the help he so desperately needed.

Having the twins only pushed him harder, making him more determined to succeed and ensuring they had a better upbringing than he ever had. His parents opposed everything he wanted, from his career choices to his move to Singapore. Being thrown out at eighteen had turned out to be a blessing in disguise. It forced him to understand his strengths and weaknesses on his own.

Jason had grown up in a home where competition wasn't just encouraged, it was expected. His father, a lawyer, and his mother, a pharmacologist, constantly pitted him and his siblings against each other. At first, it was all well and good. Until the rivalry turned violent and hospital visits became routine.

He was the one the doctors and nurses looked at with pity while they bandaged or operated on him. But no one ever called the authorities. Why would they? His mother was a well-regarded researcher at Valleywood General, and they were told he was a clumsy child, so his broken bones were his fault.

The strange thing was that the doctors did an excellent job of mending him because, as he matured, the scars seemed to fade away, as if everything that had happened to him during childhood and his teenage years existed solely in his mind. He believed it was because he was an unbound omega, but he knew he had not been born with the healing abilities that most had. His older brother, Ian, had followed in their mother's footsteps, becoming a scientist.

A researcher, to be exact. His sister, Willa, had done the same with their father, and worked for the same law firm, pursuing law as if it had been embedded in her DNA. They were business lawyers and known as the toughest father and daughter litigators winning their clients millions of dollars even if they are in the wrong. Jason wouldn't deny that out of his two siblings his sister was the most spoiled and annoying. From childhood, she would cause trouble and blame it on Jason, smirking whenever his parents scolded him or his brother beat him until he was bloody. She'd whine and bully her way to get what she wanted and no one would question things. Her ploys didn't just work on his parents, it included everyone in his family. It was as if she had cast a spell on them. Which was why they saw Jason as the black sheep of the family. Everyone in his family, including his grandparents, aunts, uncles, and cousins, was either a lawyer or a doctor.

Then, there was Jason.

Jason, the black sheep, the one who dared to dream

of becoming an architect, despite how hard they tried to change his mind. Sometimes, he wondered if it was because he was an unbound omega born with a knot at the base of his neck. Maybe they saw it as a weakness. Perhaps that was why his father and brother had spent years beating him down under the guise of making him strong.

Not that he had ever asked.

Because, honestly? Jason didn't want to know their twisted justifications. They had never cared about the things that mattered to him, so why should he care about their opinions? They had never recognized that being an architect was a respected career or congratulated him on the awards and achievements he'd won in college. Hell, he doubted they would even care that Ada, vice president of one of the most powerful real estate and architecture firms in Valleywood, had personally scouted him.

Jason would work for Arcadis Development, a division dedicated to preserving history while innovating for the future. The thought filled him with excitement; he was eager to learn, challenge himself, and create. The company had given him two weeks to settle in before his official start date, which was plenty of time to get his life in order. But before anything else, he needed to meet his best friend, who'd promised to pick him and the twins up from the airport.

Jason looked down at his children, a warm smile spreading across his lips.

They were his heart, his mischievous, brilliant little troublemakers who filled him with both pride and constant worry. Unlike the cutthroat competition of his childhood, Jason instilled one lesson in his twins above all else: stick together. Xander, or IcXander, had inherited a love for drawing and often stayed close when Jason worked at home. Even at five, the kid could already understand the basics of a blueprint.

Meanwhile, Sera was insatiably curious, never without her smartpad, and constantly absorbing information. But for all their brilliance, they were still five years old. They fussed when they were tired, cried when they needed their daddy, and, most importantly, had an imagination that kept him on his toes. Whether it was convincing Xander he couldn't jump off the table because gravity existed or explaining to Sera why she absolutely could not have a spear every day, it was an adventure.

But honestly? Jason wouldn't trade it for anything. They were his; he would protect them, give them everything their hearts desired, and ensure they never felt alone.

"Daddy, are we going to see Papa?" Xander's small voice interrupted Jason's thoughts.

Jason looked down and gave his tiny hand a gentle squeeze.

"Not today, Boebié. Your papa is busy."

The twins had not stopped asking about their father since they learned they were moving back to Valleywood. Jason, however, had not thought about that man in years.

Initially, he had considered tracking him down. But what was the point? There were too many what-ifs.

What if he didn't want children? What if he was married? What if that night had merely been a mistake to him? Jason had no desire to add more complications to his life. Besides, he could barely remember what the man looked like. He couldn't identify him in a police lineup, let alone track him down. His focus wasn't on the past; it was on the future. On his career. Maybe one day, he'd look for love. But until then, he had everything he needed.

"Daddy, are you sure he's busy?" Jason glanced at Sera, who was watching him far too closely. *What's with the suspicious look? I swear this kid was a reborn ancestor, but I don't know which one.* "Or do you just not want to look for him?" she asked, tilting her head suspiciously.

His stomach twisted. His baby girl was too smart for her own good. Jason sighed, shaking his head. *Who told me that explaining everything to them when they were two was a good idea?* He had assumed they wouldn't remember that their tiny toddler brains wouldn't hold onto the fact that they were the result of a one-night stand.

He had been very, very wrong.

"Don't worry, Daddy!" Xander declared. "I'll find Papa!"

Jason felt a sinking sensation in his stomach, and before he could respond, Xander yanked his hand away and sprinted through the airport.

Jason's mind froze.

No, no, he wouldn't run into the street!

"Xander, come back here!" he shouted.

Jason took off after his son without hesitation, dragging his luggage behind him and weaving through startled travelers. The little menace, Sera, laughed and cheered, clapping her hands as if this were a grand adventure. Jason barely dodged a woman with a stroller, muttering apologies as he sprinted after his devil of a child.

Fuck, why the hell is this kid so damn fast? And more importantly, *why the hell is he so mischievous?*

LEO STRODE through the underground parking garage on the far side of the airport, his long legs easily matching Talos's pace as the assistant read off the day's list of meetings. Fresh off a business trip to Las Vegas, Leo had just finalized a deal to build a new casino. Normally, he took his private plane, but it was a short trip.

"Today, you're meeting with Kyre Corporation's vice president, Thalara Ashthrone," Talos said.

Kyre Corporation was a new player in Valleywood, and Leo had been closely monitoring their movements. So far, nothing they had done raised any obvious red flags, but they had quietly acquired a significant amount of land, especially following that unusual blizzard last holiday season. The vice president served as the company's public face, but no one seemed to know who the CEO was.

Leo wasn't sure if it was mere coincidence or something more magical. He hadn't made up his mind.

"You also have dinner with Ms. Simpson tonight," Talos said, scrolling through the schedule on his tablet.

Leo's jaw tightened. "Cancel it," he said sharply, cutting him off before he could say more.

Mya Simpson was yet another of his mother's attempts to find him a "suitable companion." They'd been introduced six years ago, and despite Leo's complete lack of interest, Athena remained convinced Mya was perfect for him. Mya, of course, had taken that as encouragement.

Leo hadn't been with anyone since that one unforgettable night with the gray-eyed beauty. He'd searched for years, but it was as if the man had never existed—like a fever dream he couldn't wake from.

Much to his frustration, his workaholic habits had only worsened with time, giving Mya all the reason she needed to assume he was "waiting for the right woman." And the more active she was, the more he would see her as the woman for him.

Leo sighed. "Have—"

He didn't get the chance to finish. Something small suddenly latched onto his leg, gripping tightly. He stiffened, instinctively ready to shove whatever it was away, until a tiny voice shouted up at him.

"Papa!"

The single word hit him like a thunderclap. Leo's entire body tensed before slowly turning to Talos, who looked just as stunned. His assistant only shrugged, clearly as lost as he was. Leo's gaze dropped to the small arms wrapped tightly around his leg, the child clinging to him like he'd found something precious. Gently, Leo loosened the tiny fingers and guided the boy to stand in front of him. His breath caught. Those striking gray eyes were unmistakable. So was the messy mop of ink-black curls.

His stomach twisted. Was it possible? *Could this little boy be mine?*

Over the years, he'd occasionally wondered if the gray-eyed beauty had his child, but he'd never found him. Kneeling to meet the child's gaze, Leo felt something tighten in his chest.

"What did you call me?" he asked, his voice softer than usual. The kid grinned, his gray eyes bright with certainty. *"Papa."* Leo stared, and worry clashed inside him. *Is he mine?*

"Hey, little guy, you can't just go around calling strangers 'Papa,'" Talos said gently, folding his arms with a touch of exasperation.

The boy huffed, clearly offended, and pressed his forehead against Leo's with stubborn determination.

"I call him Papa 'cause he is my Papa! We look alike—see?"

Talos's gaze flicked between them, his expression shifting— first amused, then gradually settling into something more contemplative.

"Sir..." he said softly. "He does look a bit like you. Or... maybe

it's just the black hair. I'd say spitting image if his eyes were blue like yours."

Leo exhaled slowly, catching the faint smirk tugging at Talos's lips. His special assistant was definitely fucking with him, but despite the chaos in his mind, Leo felt strangely anchored in the moment.

"What's your name, little guy?" Talos asked, crouching slightly to meet the boy's eyes.

"It's IcXander!" the boy announced proudly. "Daddy wanted to name me Icarus, but I kept crying every time he said it, so he picked IcXander instead."

He turned his bright, eager gaze back to Leo. "Papa, do you like my name?"

Leo's chest tightened, not with confusion or disbelief, but with something far deeper.

He had always said that he would name him Icarus if he ever had a son. It was something that stuck with him all his years.

But the longer he looked at the kid, the less certain he was about the resemblance, and he couldn't decide if that brought him relief or something closer to disappointment.

"It's a nice name," Leo heard himself say, the words escaping before he could second-guess them.

Talos shot him a pointed look equal to curiosity and disbelief, but Leo ignored it.

Gently guiding the boy aside, Leo turned to his assistant. "And you," he muttered, "cut the nonsense."

He cleared his throat, refocusing. "Where are your parents, kid? Your mother or father?"

Before the boy could respond, a frantic voice echoed through the parking garage.

"IcXander!"

The voice rang out sharp and desperate, bouncing off

36

the concrete walls. The child froze, his little body tensing against Leo's leg.

"Uh-oh," he whispered, eyes wide.

A moment later, a man came rushing toward them, his face drawn tight with worry.

"IcXander Mathew Dupree! How dare you run off and scare me like that? How did you get here so fast?"

He scooped the child into his arms, holding him close. His voice was firm, but the tremor beneath it gave him away.

"Are you hurt?"

Leo straightened, watching silently as the man clutched the boy with palpable relief. He didn't need to ask. This was clearly the child's father. The resemblance was undeniable.

Same warm complexion. Same striking gray eyes. Delicate features, though the man's were more mature and refined. High cheekbones. A graceful jawline. A mouth that looked like it had forgotten how to smile.

The only difference was the hair: ink-black curls on the boy, straight golden blond on the man.

But it wasn't just the physical resemblance.

Leo saw it in the way the man held him. Protective. Desperate. Overflowing with love.

A knot formed in Leo's chest, heavy and unexpected. *Not mine*, he thought, as a quiet pang bloomed deep inside him.

He didn't speak often about wanting a family, but the ache had always been there. Quiet, steady, buried beneath work and duty. For one fleeting moment, he'd thought fate had cracked that door open. Just enough for him to feel what it might be like to have someone who was his. Someone to love. Someone who would love him back and never betray him.

Not like before.

He had given his heart once, trusted someone enough to imagine a future. But that trust had been shattered, leaving behind scars he rarely let anyone see. Since then, he had learned to want in silence. To dream quietly, without hope.

And yet, this child, this moment, had pulled that dream into the light, if only for a second.

But now he was watching someone else live it.

"Daddy, I'm fine. And guess what? I found Papa!" IcXander said excitedly.

The man, still kneeling, let out a heavy sigh. "Xander, we talked about this. Your papa is busy."

"No, he's not. He's right here." IcXander stepped away from his father and gripped Leo's hand with his tiny fingers.

The man finally looked up, and something shifted in Leo as his gaze trailed upward, locking onto his face. He watched as recognition flickered across the man's features. His eyes widened for the briefest moment before his expression settled into a guarded frown.

Leo wanted to hold on to whatever conclusion the man had just reached, wanted to chase the unspoken words behind that look, but the moment dissolved as soon as the man opened his mouth.

"Xander, come to Daddy," the man said quickly.

The child let out a small whine but didn't move. Instead, he looked up at Leo.

"Listen to your daddy," Leo said, his voice low but gentle.

Xander pouted but obeyed, slowly returning to his father's arms.

The man sighed again as he stood, adjusting his hold around his son. "I'm sorry about that."

Leo's jaw tightened. "Why are you apologizing? He didn't do anything."

Something churned in his chest, hot and irrational. Those beautiful gray eyes lingered in the back of his mind, refusing to leave, even as the sharpness in his own voice echoed between them.

"Word of advice. Don't teach your kid to think every man he sees is Papa. He could get kidnapped that way. Or is this some kind of scheme? See a rich guy, tell the kid to call him Papa, and hope he opens his wallet?"

His voice came out sharp, each word landing like a blow. He wanted to hurt this man, this stranger, even if he couldn't explain why.

For a split second, something flickered across the man's face.

Hurt, maybe.

Then it vanished.

His expression hardened, and he gently set his son down without a word.

"Boebié, cover your ears," the man murmured softly, stepping behind his son and gently pressing his hands over the boy's small ears.

Then his gaze snapped to Leo.

"Hey, asshole. What the fuck is your problem?"

Leo's body went taut. The man's gray eyes narrowed,

locking on to him with a heat that made Leo's pulse jump. For a brief second, he felt the urge to lick his lips but forced himself to stay still.

"You don't know me from a hole in the wall, yet you come at me like this? Who the fuck do you think you are, lecturing me about my kid?"

Something inside Leo twisted. The raw, intense fire in the man's eyes sent a ripple through him. It was unexpected, sharp, and electric. His body reacted before his mind could process it.

No one had ever dared to speak to him like that. Ever.

And to his surprise, he wasn't entirely angry.

He was intrigued. Maybe even excited.

That, at least, he could admit.

But the following words that came out were sharp and impossible to reel back.

"Then who's the kid's father?" Leo asked, his voice low and controlled, the challenge clear.

The man let out a bitter laugh, and as he tilted his head, Leo caught sight of a small beauty mark just below his jaw. It disappeared just as quickly. A trick of the light? Or had he really seen it?

"Why should I tell a stranger that?" the man snapped. His eyes flicked to his son, and something in his expression shifted. Hardened. "Oh, I get it. You're judging me because I'm a single father."

Leo didn't respond right away, too distracted by the man's mouth. Even now, while cursing him out, he found himself watching the movement of those lips, giving the man the space to vent without interruption.

"Listen up, fucker. My private life is none of your

damn business. And for your information, I would never teach my kid to call just anyone Papa."

He scoffed, the silver in his eyes flashing dark with fury. "What? Are you jealous he's not yours? You're just like every other alpha who thinks an omega needs them to survive. Well, guess what? You can go fuck yourself."

Leo's lips curled into a sharp smirk, his voice dripping with disdain. "As good-looking as you are, even if you were the last man on Earth, I wouldn't fuck you if my life depended on it."

He leaned in slightly, eyes narrowed, tone like a blade. "And while we're at it, get your judgmental head out of your ass. It's the twenty-first century. Newsflash, asshole. People fuck for fun, shit happens, and life goes on."

Then he pulled his hands away from his son's ears and lifted him into his arms.

"Now, I hope you have the day you deserve."

Without another word, he turned on his heel and walked away, his son waving at Leo over his father's shoulder.

Leo didn't move. Didn't breathe. Hell, he wasn't even sure he blinked as he stood there, rooted in place, watching the man disappear around the corner.

He had just been put in his place. No question about it.

And he couldn't figure out how to feel for the first time in a long time.

One thing was certain. His blood was on fire, and he didn't know what it would take to cool it. Sex, a cold shower, or punching someone square in the face, anything to help him make sense of whatever the hell that just was.

Behind him, Talos let out a low whistle. "Wow."

Leo's hands curled into fists. "Say another word, and you're fired."

"Not a word, sir." Talos mimed zipping his lips and took a smart step back.

Leo turned on his heel and strode toward his car, his strides long and purposeful. "Let's go."

Less than five minutes later, Leo slid into the back-seat of his car, tension rippling through him. Talos started the engine, maneuvering them out of the parking garage. Leo's fingers drummed against his thigh, his thoughts a raging storm. A random man had just chewed him out, a random single father who just happened to have a beauty mark on his neck. Leo exhaled sharply and leaned against the seat, willing himself to relax. Then, out of the corner of his eye, he saw the man again, IcXander at his side, and another man standing with them. Leo's gaze narrowed as the newcomer embraced the father and son.

Warm. Familiar.

Just like the one IcXander had given him.

Just as I thought, a scammer. Poor kid.

A dull ache settled in Leo's chest, but he ignored it, forcing himself to forget the entire incident.

CHAPTER 4
JASON

J ason hurried into the sleek lobby of DRA&D, his grip firm around Xander's small hand as they navigated the polished marble floor. His plan was simple: grab the paperwork he needed and make it home in time for lunch with the twins.

The morning had already been a struggle. Both kids refused to cooperate, clinging to him and begging him not to leave them with their caregiver, Mrs. Sing. For a moment, Jason wondered if something had happened. But he had cameras placed discreetly around the house, allowing him to check in throughout the day. Nothing had set off any alerts. It wasn't fear. Just his babies wanting him close.

And truthfully, Jason couldn't blame them. Mrs. Sing was the kindest woman he had ever met, but in the eyes of his children, no one could take his place. She had been their next-door neighbor since the day they moved in and had naturally stepped into the role of caregiver whenever Jason needed an extra pair of hands.

Mrs. Sing was Chinese-American, a widow who had lost her husband many years ago and never remarried. Though she had no children of her own, she possessed the warmth and patience of a devoted grandmother. Her gentle brown eyes, calm presence, and ability to handle even the most chaotic toddler tantrum made her a steady force in their home. And the twins adored her. She knew exactly how to manage their mischief while still managing to spoil them beyond belief.

As far as Jason was concerned, he had no complaints.

To appease the kids, something he knew he gave in to far too often, he quickly emailed his boss to let her know he would be working from home. Everything was going according to plan until he realized he needed to stop by the office to pick up some paperwork.

That was when the real negotiations began.

Just as he reached for his keys, Xander insisted on coming with him.

Jason didn't like leaving one of the twins behind, but Sera flat out refused to go with him. Since he was only running to the office and then coming straight back, he asked Mrs. Sing to stay with her. That seemed to calm his five-year-old a little too easily. Jason narrowed his eyes at his daughter but let it go for now. Still, something in his gut told him they were up to something.

They had been suspiciously well-behaved since moving to Valleywood, and if he said he wasn't worried, he'd be lying. Even if they weren't up to something, Jason couldn't help it. His little ones seemed to have latched on to a trickster gene and enjoyed pranking him for fun. He could only wonder what he'd find when he returned home.

He knelt in front of Xander, adjusting the straps on his backpack before handing it to him. "Okay, boebié, you sit here while I run up to my office, and please don't run off and cause any trouble," he said, giving his son a firm look.

"I'll be good, Daddy," Xander replied with a sweet smile, his innocence and charm making Jason's stomach twitch. But he had no time to dwell on the feeling.

Jason would have brought up his son, but his office was far from kid-friendly. It wasn't just about the chaos a five-year-old could unleash; his work was so sensitive that he needed the highest degree of security clearance, a requirement he hadn't known when he first took the job.

In the three months since starting at DRA&D, he had realized that his job description barely scratched the surface of what he actually did. The Arcadia Development Department was merely a front; Jason didn't work for Arcadia at all, but rather for Quantum Urban Intelligence & Architecture, or QUA, as those in the know called it.

Though technically a subsidiary of DRA&D, QUA operated in secrecy, focusing on advanced technology, industrial and residential development, and sustainable, next-generation architecture. Their goal? To bring Valleywood into the future. Even in a magical city like Valleywood, some of the technology resembled something straight out of a science fiction novel or TV show. Jason had never expected to be part of something this cutting-edge.

Shaking off his thoughts, he hurried to the elevator, exhaling in relief when the doors slid open to reveal an empty space.

He was thankful for small miracles.

Jason scanned his badge and pressed his floor number. Just as the doors began to close, the elevator across from him slid open. A man stepped out, and Jason's breath caught. Tall and effortlessly handsome, the stranger carried himself with a quiet authority that commanded attention. His jet-black hair was slicked back, and he wore a midnight-blue three-piece suit that matched the sharp, familiar blue of his eyes.

Jason froze.

A wave of déjà vu crashed into him, stealing the breath from his lungs. His heart raced faster.

Why do I feel like I've seen him before?

The elevator doors slid shut before Jason could take another look, yet the feeling lingered like a deep and unsettling itch at the back of his mind.

Where have I seen that guy?

And then it hit him.

The airport.

Jason grimaced, recalling his behavior at the airport, and shook his head in embarrassment. After reflecting on it and listening to his son, he realized he might have misjudged the guy. He acknowledged he was overprotective of his children and didn't give a damn what people thought about him. But what stung was the thought that a handsome man had looked down on him simply for being a single father.

Yeah, he had been attracted to the guy at first sight. *Who wouldn't be?*

The man was tall, with ink-black hair and blue eyes as clear as the sea, a sexy beard that Jason could easily imagine running his fingers through on a lazy Sunday while resting his head against that broad, muscular chest. Jason hated to admit it, but even while he was tearing into him, his eyes had been drinking him in, standing there effortlessly composed in an expensive suit that probably cost two of Jason's paychecks.

They would never fit.

Fuck, what the hell am I thinking? He and I will never meet again.

The elevator stopped, and the doors slid open to his floor. Jason shoved the man from his thoughts...for now.

WAS that who I thought it was?

Leo's steps faltered, his thoughts momentarily drifting. It had been three months since that so-called altercation with the guy, if anyone could even call it that. Still, he hadn't been able to shake the memory of that intense, heated gaze.

He gave his head a quick shake and turned to Talos.

"Have you found the guy from six years ago?" he asked.

Another unanswered mystery lingering in his life.

"No. Honestly, sir, it's like he dropped off the face of the planet."

Leo narrowed his eyes, clearly unconvinced. "In a time when everything is online, you're telling me you still can't find one person? Should I start looking for a new special assistant?"

"Try it," Talos said, without an ounce of fear. "No one else can handle your demanding ass."

Leo shot him a look. "You're real mouthy today."

Talos didn't say a word, but Leo could see it written all over his face, the silent judgment that this mess wasn't on him. And it wasn't. Leo wasn't blaming Talos because he had slept with someone and never even got their name.

Not that it made him feel any better.

Leo still couldn't find the man, despite all his resources and connections. And as much as Talos might have wanted to point that out, he had the good sense to keep it to himself.

Leo wasn't sure if the evidence had been erased on purpose or if the guy had government ties, but everything from that night five years ago had vanished without a trace. The hotel security footage had been useless, barely catching the man's face. Just another frustrating dead end in a trail full of them.

He was about to press the issue when Talos spoke, pointing ahead.

"I wonder what's going on?"

Leo followed Talos's gaze and spotted a group of women clustered near the far end of the lobby when they should have been working. Irritation twisted in his chest. His mood was already sour, and this was the worst possible time for distractions.

He strode toward them, fully prepared to demand an explanation.

But before he could speak, a small voice rose above the murmurs.

"Papa."

The crowd fell silent. Dozens of wide eyes turned to him in stunned disbelief.

Leo acted like he didn't notice.

His attention was locked on the little boy staring up at him as if he had finally found what he had been searching for.

"Come here," Leo said, his voice low and steady.

Without hesitation, the child walked over, and Leo bent down, scooping him up as if it were the most natural thing in the world. He barely noticed the collective gasps and awed whispers that followed as he turned and carried the boy toward a quieter corner of the lobby.

He spotted a nearby sofa and gently set the child down, then crouched in front of him, his gaze steady and searching.

"Why are you here?" Leo asked.

"Daddy had to pick up something and told me to wait here." "Your dad works here?" That caught Leo's interest.

"Uh-huh." The boy nodded confidently.

Despite himself, Leo found the kid undeniably adorable. He was too cute for his own good.

"What's your daddy's name?" he asked, his voice softening. "Jason Dupree."

Leo's gaze flicked to Talos. No words were exchanged, but the message was clear. Talos gave a slight nod and quietly slipped away, leaving Leo alone with the child.

Leo studied the boy, taking in every detail. He looked well cared for, healthy, bright-eyed, and strong. It might have been his imagination, but... had he grown since the last time Leo saw him?

"Why do you think I'm your papa?" He wasn't sure why he asked. The words slipped out before he could stop them. Curiosity, or something deeper, gnawed at him.

"'Cause I can feel it here." The boy pressed a hand to his chest, his expression solemn and sure.

Something inside Leo cracked just a little.

"Why aren't you at daycare?" he asked, his voice gentler now.

"Don't wanna go. It's boring," the boy said with a shrug. "So we stay with Daddy and Mrs. Sing."

Leo opened his mouth to ask who *we* meant, but Talos's voice cut in.

"Sir, I found the information you requested," he said, striding forward and handing Leo a gray-covered folder.

Talos was nothing if not efficient. It was one of the many reasons Leo trusted him and paid him the big bucks.

Flipping open the folder, Leo glanced at the photo first, and paused.

Jason Dupree.

He stared longer than necessary.

Even in a still image, Jason's presence was undeniable. Sharp eyes, firm, full lips, and the same confidence that had caught Leo off guard in the parking garage three months ago. He looked composed. Capable. Beautiful.

Leo's grip tightened slightly on the folder before he forced his gaze down to the printed details.

Jason Dupree. A young, accomplished architect working under his sister's division. Leo rarely went to the QUA department, relying on Ada's detailed email and video conference reports. No wonder he had no idea the man was even part of the DRA&D family.

Maybe it was time he started paying closer attention to what Ada was doing.

Still, he understood why the child had been left in the lobby. With the kind of sensitive information Ada's team handled, bringing a five-year-old into the workspace wasn't exactly practical.

"Do you want me to take you to your daddy?" Leo asked.

The little boy nodded eagerly.

Smiling, Leo scooped him up and headed toward the elevator —only to stop short when Mya Simpson stepped into the lobby, her gaze instantly locking onto them.

"Leo, whose child are you holding?"

Before he could respond, the boy beat him to it.

"Papa, who's this lady?"

"Papa?" Mya repeated, eyes widening as she looked from Leo to the boy. "You have a son? I... I didn't know. Your mother never mentioned—"

"He's not mine," Leo said, his tone flat. "He's the son of one of my employees."

"Oh." She let out a light laugh, her posture easing as she smiled. "That's a relief."

Leo didn't return the smile. His expression remained cool. "Why are you here?"

"We haven't seen each other in a while, and I thought maybe we could have lunch," she said, tucking a lock of hair behind her ear, her cheeks flushing as she looked up at him with a coy smile.

"I don't have time." Leo hated how cold he sounded, but he was tired of finding polite ways to tell her he wasn't interested. She wasn't listening. "Now, excuse me."

He turned to go, but Mya reached out, her fingers lightly catching the edge of his jacket, stopping him mid-step.

The contact lasted only a second. The moment he looked down, she snatched her hand back.

"Leo, don't be like this. You and—"

"Mya," he said, cutting her off. His voice was firm, leaving no room for argument. "I've told you before—I don't have feelings for you. Don't waste your time on me."

She met his gaze without flinching, her voice soft but steady. "It's my time. Why shouldn't I spend it the way I want?"

Leo sighed, his expression unreadable. "You're young, beautiful, and full of potential. Find someone who can love you the way you deserve. Someone better than I ever could."

He paused, voice quieter now. "I'm not good for you, Mya."

"But I want you," Mya said, her voice steady, a flicker of stubborn hope in her eyes. "What's wrong with us being together? It's not like either of us is seeing someone, I—"

"But that's just it, Mya." Leo's voice was calm, even. "I am seeing someone."

Silently, he thanked his mother goddess. Because in that exact moment, Jason stepped off the elevator, as if the fates had chosen to intervene.

Without a second thought, Leo turned away from Mya and crossed the lobby, closing the distance before Jason could make sense of what was happening.

"Play along, and I'll explain later," he murmured, his voice low and urgent.

Jason blinked, his brows pulling together. "What—?"

Leo didn't let him finish. He reached out, resting a firm but steady hand on Jason's arm. The contact was small, but it grounded them both.

Behind him, the unmistakable rhythm of Mya's heels tapped closer. Her presence lingered like a storm gathering in the air.

Leo's face remained composed, but beneath it, his thoughts raced. He didn't owe her anything. Not anymore. And yet, the second he pulled Jason into this, something inside him shifted. He hadn't planned to lie. He hadn't planned to make it real.

But it felt real.

Whether it was pride or instinct, he didn't know. Only that something in his chest had locked into place the second Jason appeared.

Mya stopped a few feet away, arms crossed tight. Her eyes narrowed.

"Leo, who is this?"

Jason looked between them, hesitation clear on his face. Leo didn't blink. "This is Jason. He's my lover." The words settled into the air like truth.

Jason tensed beside him, but Leo didn't give him a chance to speak. He leaned in and gently pressed a kiss to Xander's forehead. The boy had fallen asleep, oblivious to the tension building around him.

Only then did Leo turn fully to Mya.

"And I lied to you earlier," he said, voice smooth but final. "He's our son, and we're getting married."

Jason inhaled sharply. "What?" His tone was soft but stunned.

Around them, the lobby had gone quiet. Leo didn't need to look to know his employees were frozen in place. He could practically feel Talos staring, eyebrows somewhere near his hairline.

But Leo kept his focus on Jason and the warmth of the child between them.

"Moró, I'm sorry," he said smoothly, turning to Jason with practiced calm. "I know you wanted to keep our relationship a secret,

but... well, the cat's out of the bag now." Jason's

nostrils flared. "Secret? What the f—" Leo pinched his side, firm and fast.

Jason winced. "Dammit, why did you—"

He stopped himself, glancing down at Xander, who shifted slightly in his sleep.

Leo leaned in just enough for Jason to hear him clearly. "I'll explain everything. Just go with it."

Jason shot him a look. "You better—"

Before he could finish, Leo leaned in and kissed him.

Jason froze the moment their lips met, his body stiff with surprise. But the second lingered, stretching just long enough to shift the air between them. The kiss was soft, barely more than a brush, but it held something weightier beneath the surface.

Their eyes locked. Jason's were wide, stunned, his breath catching in his throat.

Leo pulled back slowly, licking his lips without thinking. A strange, quiet unease settled in his chest. It hadn't been deep or intense, just a simple, intentional connection.

But it felt good.

Too good.

And he wanted more.

Mya exhaled sharply, breaking the silence. "You really are in a relationship."

Leo arched a brow. "Did you doubt me?" He glanced at Jason, who still looked frozen, his brain clearly buffering.

"Why didn't you tell me a long time ago?" she asked, and he didn't miss the sadness in her voice.

Leo kept his tone steady. "Think carefully, Mya. Have

I ever reached out to you since we met? If my mother hadn't given you my personal number, you wouldn't even have it. I don't want to be

an ass, but you're leaving me no choice."

Her lips parted. "What does he—"

"Don't ask that question," he said, cutting her off before she could finish. He already knew what she was about to say. She wanted to know what Jason had that she didn't. But there was no point in answering. No comparison needed. It wouldn't be fair to her, and it definitely wouldn't be fair to Jason.

"Just know that he's my man, Mya. My fiancé. And now, we need to take our son home. Find your own happiness."

Without giving her a chance to respond, Leo tightened his hold on Jason and guided him, still dazed, out of the building. Talos followed closely behind. Thankfully, Leo's car was already waiting at thecurb.

He helped Jason inside, handed Xander back into his arms, and slid in on the other side. It was a cowardly move. He knew that. But seeing Jason sitting there, too stunned to speak, Leo did the only thing that felt right. He reached for Xander again, gently taking the sleeping child into his arms. It was a small gesture, instinctive and protective, but it felt far too natural.

Talos gave the driver Jason's address, which wasn't far from the company. As the car pulled away from the curb, Leo leaned back in his seat, already bracing for what was coming. By now, Mya had undoubtedly sent word to his mother about his so-called engagement.

That was a problem for later.

Right now, the real problem sat quietly beside him.

Jason.

How the hell was Leo going to convince the man to marry him?

CHAPTER 5

JASON

Did someone... kiss me?

His fingers glided over his lips, still warm and tingling with a sensation that sent a slow shiver down

his spine. The lingering trace of woody, spiced musk clung to him, rich and intoxicating, sinking into his skin like an invisible imprint.

He blinked through the haze clouding his thoughts and took in his surroundings. The low hum of the engine, the steady rhythm of tires on asphalt, and the warmth of golden sunlight filtering through the windows settled over him, anchoring him in the present.

He was in a car, moving fast, the world outside rushing past in a blur.

"What the fuck? Did we just get kidnapped?"

"I'm not in the habit of taking people by force," a deep voice murmured beside him.

Startled, Jason jerked upright, his pulse pounding in his ears. His gaze landed on the man beside him, handsome and composed, with Xander nestled comfortably in his arms.

"Like hell, you kissed me without my permission," Jason snapped, his voice sharp with indignation.

"Stop yelling. You'll wake the baby. And desperate times call for desperate measures."

Jason's gaze shifted to Xander, still curled peacefully in the man's arms, completely unbothered by the tension in the air. His anger wavered, breath unsteady, as the weight of the situation settled over him.

He exhaled sharply, lowering his voice. "That's not a good excuse."

The man hesitated, his grip on Xander shifting slightly as he adjusted to the boy's weight. His expression softened. "You're right," he said quietly. "I'm sorry."

And somehow, Jason could tell he meant it.

His mind drifted back to the lobby. The scene was still fresh. The gorgeous blonde. Her expression tight with disappointment and frustration.

"Was that lady your girlfriend?" Jason asked, lifting a brow.

The man scoffed. "If she was, do you think I would have kissed you? I'm loyal to the person I'm with."

Jason huffed, leaning back in his seat and crossing

his arms. "Then what's the deal? If you're not interested in her, tell her. Don't drag me into your mess."

The man let out a sharp breath. "I've been trying for six years, but she doesn't get it." He glanced at Jason. "Or maybe she just

refuses to accept that she's not getting what she wants."

Jason narrowed his eyes. "What does she want?"

The man raised a brow, the corner of his mouth lifting in a smug smirk. "Do you really need to ask?"

"Wow. Confidence and ego in one neat package. Must be exhausting." Jason let out a bitter laugh. "Glad I could be your prop in whatever dramatic performance that was."

Leo chuckled, low and unbothered. "You're sharp. I like that."

Jason turned his head, clearly unimpressed. "Good for you."

Leo shifted slightly, his gaze softening as he looked at Xander asleep in his arms. "Look, I know I turned that lobby into a mess, but I wasn't faking any of it."

Jason scoffed. "The kiss too?" Leo met his eyes. "Especially the kiss." What a flirt.

Now that they were close, Jason studied him, taking in as much detail as he could. It wasn't hard to see why a woman would chase him for six years. He looked like he had been carved by a master sculptor. Sharp cheekbones. A strong jawline. A body built for sin. Tall, broad, and probably packing more than just an eight pack.

His quick assessment from the airport hadn't done

the guy justice. The man was stupidly hot. And exactly his type.

Damn. Too bad he had women problems. He mentally tsked.

"Have you looked long enough?" the man asked, grinning like he had known Jason was checking him out the entire time.

Jason scoffed and rolled his eyes. "I don't see the appeal." He turned toward the window, pretending not to hear the amused chuckle that followed.

A beat of silence settled between them.

Then the man spoke again. "I need your help."

Jason turned back, skeptical. "I'm not killing anyone, nor am I helping you hide the body."

The man blinked, caught off guard. "What the hell? Why would you think it's something that crazy?" Then he smirked. "Besides, I know people who can handle that cleanly."

Jason gasped, clutching his chest in mock horror. "Oh fuck, you're in the mob. Don't kill us!" He covered his face and peeked between his fingers.

A flick to his forehead made him wince. "Are you always this dramatic?"

Jason rubbed the spot, frowning. "Not normally. Or at least, I don't think so." He paused, then shrugged. "This is just who I am. Take it or leave it."

The man chuckled again and shook his head. "You're quite interesting, Jason Dupree."

Jason lowered his hands, suspicion creeping into his voice. "Thank you?" He took a slow breath, glanced at the man who may or may not have just kidnapped him, and gave in to curiosity.

"Okay. What do you need my help with?" The man met his gaze without flinching.

"Marry me."

Jason's brain short-circuited. His ears started ringing.

"I must have heard that wrong. Say that again?"

"I said marry me. I'm being serious." His tone was casual, like he was discussing the weather. "It will be for one year. I'll pay you five million and give you a home in any district you choose." Jason blinked at him.

What. The. Flying. Fuck.

He stared at the man, completely stunned, genuinely wondering if something was wrong with him. Who offers marriage and millions to a complete stranger?

Is this guy crazy? Does he not realize this is real life and not some reality show where people get married in 2.2 seconds after meeting? Wait. Am I on a reality show and don't know it?

His gaze darted around the car, searching for hidden cameras. It was the only logical explanation for why a man whose name he didn't know would suddenly propose. That would also explain why they were in a luxury car that probably cost more than his entire salary for the year. Not to mention the two guys in the front seats; one of them had to be the director, right? He leaned forward and tapped the shoulder of the man in the passenger seat, who turned and looked at him in confusion.

"Director, which reality show are we filming, and why didn't I sign a contract?"

The driver blinked in the rearview mirror. "Sir?"

"We're not on a reality show," the man beside Jason said, his tone a mix of amusement and exasperation.

Jason narrowed his eyes. "Then do you have a few screws loose?"

The man smiled. "Last check-up said I was mentally stable."

Jason scoffed, trying and failing to ignore how sexy the man looked when he smiled. "Then why the hell do you want to marry me? A total stranger. An un... omega with kids. I know nothing about you, and you don't know me. The last time we met, I..."

He trailed off as the memory of his rant at the airport hit him like a punch to the gut. His stomach twisted. *Yeah, don't bring that up.*

"Hell, I don't even know your name."

The man gave him a long, unreadable look before speaking dryly. "You really don't know who I am?"

Jason shook his head. "Am I supposed to?"

The man didn't answer. Instead, he lifted a hand and pointed out the window.

"Look at the billboard."

Jason followed his gaze, and his stomach immediately dropped.

They were at a red light. The car had come to a full stop. Jason leaned forward, and his eyes widened as he stared at the massive advertisement looming just ahead.

Leo Devereux.

The name stood out in bold, commanding letters beside a striking photo of the very man sitting next to him. Beneath it, in clean modern font, were the words:

Devereux Real Estate and Architecture.

Jason's stomach clenched. A wave of shock and disbelief rolled through him.

Oh, fuck.

Slowly, he turned back toward Devereux, who was watching him with clear amusement. A deep flush of embarrassment crept up Jason's neck, burning hotter by the second.

How the hell did I not recognize my boss's boss this entire time?

In his defense, he hadn't seen Devereux once in the three months he'd been working at DRA&D. And he was pretty sure that billboard hadn't been there this morning. Or the day before.

So, how the hell was he supposed to know?

Jason swallowed. "Sir..."

Leo raised an eyebrow, clearly entertained. "Oh, now I'm 'sir'?"

Jason winced. "I just figured out who you are. It felt appropriate."

Leo leaned back slightly, the corner of his mouth twitching.

"You were a lot mouthier when you didn't know." Jason muttered, "Yeah, well... ignorance was bliss."

I just found out you're a fucking tycoon. You could buy and sell me with a snap of your fingers.

Devereux smirked. "Call me what you called me the first time we met. Or better yet... husband."

Jason gawked. "I didn't agree to marry you, asshole."

Devereux chuckled and gently covered Xander's ear.

"No cursing around the baby. And you will marry me. Besides, you owe me an apology."

Jason's eyes narrowed. "And what makes you think that?" "Shall we recount the airport?" Devereux asked smoothly.

Jason opened his mouth to argue, but Devereux cut him off with perfect timing. "We're here."

Jason blinked and looked out the window, only now realizing they had stopped in front of his apartment building. He lived in the Amon Island City District, at The Athens Condominiums. It was an older building that was well-maintained and fully updated. He loved it for the courtyard, the community garden, and the playground for the kids. The rent didn't drain his entire paycheck, either.

Most importantly, no one there had ever pried into his personal life, asked about the twins' father, or tried to insert themselves where they didn't belong.

He had no problem telling people to fuck off nicely, but he preferred to keep things cordial with his neighbors.

"Are you coming?"

Jason turned toward the voice and saw Devereux standing beside the car with the door open.

That's when something hit him like a brick to the chest.

Devereux had been holding Xander the entire ride.

Jason had been so wrapped up in their ridiculous conversation that he hadn't even thought about it and hadn't worried and hadn't panicked.

Fuck. He should have been in a car seat.

Jason climbed out of the car and immediately reached for his son. "I'll take him."

"Go open the door," Devereux said gently.

Jason frowned. "I can handle things myself. I've been doing it for five years."

Devereux exhaled. "Don't argue. Your neighbors are watching."

Jason glanced up at the building and, sure enough, spotted a few curious faces peering down from their windows.

Nosy-ass people.

They might not ask questions, but that didn't mean they weren't watching.

"Fine," he relented, not entirely sure why he was giving in so easily.

The elevator ride was quiet. Jason stood stiffly beside Devereux, silently praying his apartment wasn't a mess.

"You really don't have to do this," he muttered, hoping to dissuade him. "I'm sure you're busy."

"I have all day for you—and night—for you," Devereux said without missing a beat.

Sure, you have time, but what if I don't? What's stopping me from just saying no?

Jason had never been the type to keep things bottled up, and he didn't care that this man was technically his boss's boss. The only time he ever hesitated was when he found someone attractive and wasn't sure how they would react to him.

Jason, get that thought out of your head right now. He's your boss's boss. You have no business being attracted to him. Even if he does look good holding your son. And he doesn't actually want to marry you either. That alone should be reason enough to kick his ass to the curb.

Jason opened his mouth to tell Devereux to get lost, but the words caught in his throat, sticking like something stubborn and unspoken. He coughed, trying to clear it, but the feeling stayed— thick, persistent, and entirely unwelcome.

"Are you okay?" Devereux asked, his voice edged with concern.

"Yeah, my throat's just a little dry," Jason choked out, silently thanking every god in existence when the elevator finally stopped on his floor. The moment the doors slid open, he stepped out quickly, eager to put space between them.

But Devereux's long strides easily caught up with him.

Jason's apartment was at the end of the hall, and the moment he pushed the door open, he barely had time to react before his baby girl launched herself into his arms.

"Daddy, you're back!" Sera squealed, throwing her arms around his neck.

Jason chuckled, tweaking her nose. "Did you think I wasn't coming back?"

She shook her head, her tiny fingers gripping his shoulders. "I just missed you."

His heart softened instantly. He kissed her cheek. "I missed you too, boebié. Where's Mrs. Sing?"

"She went to get a book," Sera said with a giggle, snuggling closer.

"You have two kids?"

Jason turned toward Devereux and caught the rare flicker of surprise on his face.

Didn't expect that, huh?

Before Jason could respond, Sera gasped dramatically, her eyes going wide as she spotted Devereux.

"Papa, you came!"

Jason groaned. *Oh, for fuck's sake.*

Sera wiggled out of his arms, sprinted straight to Devereux, and latched onto his leg like a determined little koala.

Devereux raised an eyebrow, staring down at the girl wrapped around his leg. "And I see you've taught her the same bad habit," he said dryly.

Jason crossed his arms and exhaled through his nose. "I never teach my children bad habits," he muttered. "I don't know why she thinks you're her papa. I've never even shown her your picture." *Hell, I just found out who you were.*

"It doesn't matter now anyway. When we get married, I'll really be their papa."

"Daddy and Papa are getting married!" Sera cheered, bouncing with excitement.

"Sera, we're not," Jason said, trying to correct her, but they ignored him.

And as if it were the most natural thing in the world, Devereux stepped inside, completely unbothered, walking smoothly with Sera still clinging to his leg, standing on his foot like she was hitching a ride on her own personal chariot.

Jason gawked. "Are you seriously walking around with my daughter attached to you?"

Devereux smirked, utterly unbothered. "She seems comfortable."

Jason resisted the urge to roll his eyes so hard they'd fall out of his skull.

Roll, you fucking asshole hovered on the tip of his tongue.

"Jason, you're back?"

He looked up at the sound of Mrs. Sing's voice.

"Yeah. Thanks for watching Sera for me."

"It's no problem. She's a darling. They both are." She glanced around, then back at him. "Where's Xander?"

Jason pointed toward where Leo and the twins were sitting, and if he hadn't been paying attention, he would have missed the way Mrs. Sing stiffened the moment her eyes landed on them.

Weird.

"Well, dear, since you're back, I'll return to my place. Let me know if you need anything."

"Thank you, Mrs. Sing. I'll send your payment in a bit. And don't forget, we're having dinner tomorrow."

"Yes, yes," she said quickly, already heading for the door.

She left in a hurry, as if the apartment had suddenly caught fire.

Jason stared at the closed door, a frown tugging at his brow.

That was... odd. Mrs. Sing had never acted like that before.

CHAPTER 6
LEO

Familiar blue eyes and a head of curly blond hair. *Maybe I'm overthinking it. Or maybe it's just the kids calling me Papa that's messing with my head.*

But it was filling a hole that had been empty for a long time. That was how Leo justified it as he watched Sera. She looked so much like Athena, it was almost unsettling. His mother's blood was very strong. Leo might not have gotten her looks when she blood- and magically adopted him, but her blood skipped him and went to a little girl who might be his daughter. Leo knew the only person he hadn't used protection with was the guy he slept with six years ago. That meant the kid would be five. There was no one else afterward, and it had been years before the night he slept with the escort that might not have been an escort.

He had spent the past three hours with the twins while Jason kept himself busy around the apartment, making lunch, taking work calls, doing anything to stay in motion. Anything to avoid him.

The apartment had an open floor plan, with everything in view except the bedrooms and bathrooms. And Leo knew Jason was keeping an eye on them, quietly watching from a distance.

He didn't take offense. Jason was their father. Protecting them came first.

He could respect that. Leo knew he should have left hours ago, but he was enjoying getting to know the twins far more than he had expected. He had followed Jason home with the intention of discussing marriage, but he hadn't anticipated meeting another child.

That revelation shifted everything.

If Jason refused him, Leo would understand. He wasn't just thinking about himself anymore. He had two children to protect, and that changed the stakes completely.

Leo's gaze flicked toward the kitchen, where Jason stood with his back turned, focused on preparing dinner. He moved with effortless grace, his lean, toned body shifting fluidly with each motion. He had the kind of swimmer's build Leo liked. Not too much muscle, not too little, just enough to feel solid beneath his hands.

The thought stirred something at the back of Leo's

mind. A flicker of memory. The press of warm skin. The sound of breathy moans. A body writhing beneath him, nails dragging down his back, pleading for more.

Yeah, definitely my type, Leo thought, pinching the bridge of his nose as he tried to shake off the erotic thoughts creeping in about the twins' father.

"Papa, watching it?" Sera's small voice pulled him from his thoughts.

"Yes," he answered automatically, not even bothering to correct her. He had given up trying. Both she and Xander were dead set on making him their father, and strangely, the idea didn't scare him as much as it probably should have.

He couldn't exactly tell her that he wasn't watching Athena the Wonder Goddess, but her father. If his mother ever found out she had such a devoted fan, Sera would be spoiled beyond reason. The show was clearly her favorite.

Xander, on the other hand, looked like he was suffering.

"Can we do something else?" Xander whined. He had woken up a few minutes after they got home. "We watch this all the time." "What do you want to do?" Leo asked.

"Build my model," Xander replied without hesitation.

Leo had learned earlier that Xander was working on a model of Valleywood, a gift from Jason that clearly aligned with the boy's natural curiosity. Whether it was to encourage his love of building or to keep him grounded from his fascination with flight, it was working. Xander's imagination was big, and his focus even bigger. Maybe he would be a pilot. Maybe an architect. Either way, the potential was obvious.

In the few hours Leo had spent with them, he had to keep reminding himself that they were only five years old. They stirred memories he thought he had long buried. Their intellect was beyond their years — impressive, and just a little unnerving.

Leo wasn't sure what Sera's path would be, but Xander already showed a spark that was hard to ignore. These kids were bright, gifted, and full of promise. They deserved to be nurtured, not hidden.

Something warm stirred in his chest as he watched them, and he found himself hoping that maybe, just maybe, he would get to be there to witness their growth.

"Then go do it and let your sister watch her show," Leo said, ruffling the boy's hair. "Let me know if you need help."

Xander hesitated, his voice dropping to a softer note. "But if I go to my room, you'll leave."

Leo stilled. *So that was why Xander had been torturing himself by sitting through a show he clearly didn't enjoy.* Something in Leo's chest loosened, a quiet ache rising before it melted into warmth.

"I won't leave," Leo whispered, leaning in just a little. "I need to talk to your daddy about something important, and it might take a while."

"You promise?" Xander asked, his small face unusually serious.

Leo wasn't the only one watching him now. Sera had turned away from the television, her bright blue eyes fixed on him, studying his expression like she was trying to decide if he was telling the truth.

"When I make a promise, I never break it," Leo said firmly. "Go do your thing."

"Do you promise to be our papa?" Sera asked suddenly.

"I... I..." Leo stumbled over his words. If anyone had seen him in that moment, they wouldn't have recognized the take-no-shit CEO. The question had caught him completely off guard. And as much as he wanted to say yes, he couldn't lie to them.

"I can't promise you that," he said gently.

"Then what can you promise?" Xander asked. Again, Leo had to remind himself they were only five years old. The depth of their questions made them feel older.

"I promise I'll be here when you have dinner tonight. And I'll visit often."

Xander studied him for another moment, then gave a small nod, as if deciding Leo was trustworthy. Without another word, he jumped off the sofa and darted toward his room.

Leo stood, turning to Sera. "I'm going to help your dad in the kitchen."

Sera grabbed his pant leg, her little fingers clinging with surprising strength. She glanced toward the kitchen, then back at him, like she was weighing his words. After a long pause, she finally let go.

Leo walked into the kitchen, his gaze landing on Jason, who was focused on adding seasoning to the pot. At some point, he had changed out of his button-up shirt and slacks and into a black Tshirt and soft-looking sweats. His blond hair was slightly damp and tousled like he had just rolled out of bed after being thoroughly fucked. The faint blush on his cheeks, likely from the rising steam, made his skin glow and drew more attention to the mole beneath his left eye and the one just barely visible on his neck.

Leo's breath caught in his throat.

An image surged through his mind, sharp and impossible to ignore. His mouth moving over flushed skin, his teeth grazing that same spot on Jason's neck, fixated on that beauty mark that had tempted him all night long. The déjà vu hit so hard it left him off balance for a second, his fingers twitching at his sides.

The longer he stayed near Jason, the harder it became to control his thoughts. It was as if his mind had already figured something out and was urging the rest of him to catch up.

No. Why the hell didn't I realize it before? Could he be the man from that night?

Leo's gaze flicked between Jason's face and the small mole on his neck. His heart pounded as the truth clawed its way to the surface.

Is this a joke? Is this the Fates screwing with me just because I'm the child of a god?

There was no way. No fucking way he had been standing in front of the man he had searched for over the past six years, completely clueless. His chest tightened with a sharp, sinking ache, twisting deeper with every breath.

He could already hear the mockery. Every demigod.

Every immortal. They would never let him live this down.

The great Daedalus. The arrogant, brilliant inventor. Brought low by a single night of passion and a five-year-long blind chase.

Even he had to admit it. It was almost funny.

Almost.

"I thought you didn't break promises."

Leo barely registered Jason's voice at first, still reeling from the weight of realization.

"What?" His voice came out quieter than he expected.

"You told the kids you don't break promises," Jason repeated, one brow lifted. "But what about me? You said you'd help me cook. So far, all you've done is stand there like a statue, staring into space."

Leo swallowed hard and reached for the edge of the counter to ground himself. Six years of searching. Six years of frustration and dead ends. And now, the man he had been looking for was standing less than a foot away.

Fuck, get it together.

Snapping out of the fog, Leo rolled up his sleeves and stepped into the kitchen. He washed his hands at the sink, then turned to Jason.

"What do you need me to do?"

Jason handed him a cutting board and a few carrots. "Cut these. Not too big. It's for the kids."

"Got it."

Leo got to work, settling into the simple rhythm of slicing vegetables. It had been a long time since he cooked for anyone, even himself. Between his schedule and constant travel, eating out had become routine. But this? Standing in a warm kitchen, helping make dinner for two kids who had already claimed him as their father —it was unfamiliar, but not unwelcome.

He glanced at Jason, who stood focused at the stove, gently stirring the pan. There was something calming about the way he moved. He worked with quiet confidence, the kind that came from doing it countless times before. It made Leo wonder just how much Jason had handled on his own over the past few years. Had it been hard with the twins? Had he struggled?

Leo thought, his chest tightening, *if only I had found you sooner.*

But I can make it right now.

"What are you making?" Leo asked.

"Chicken satay skewers and pineapple rice," Jason said, smiling. "It's the kids' favorite. Mine too, if I'm being honest. We ate it all the time where we used to live."

Leo remembered seeing that detail in Jason's file. He had completed his postgraduate degree there.

"Is the kids' father from Singapore?"

The question slipped out before Leo could stop it. *Am I their father?*

Jason looked over at him. "How do you know I was in Singapore?"

"I read it in your file after I found out you worked for my company," Leo answered truthfully.

Jason gave a small nod. "Oh. That makes sense."

Jason paused, then exhaled slowly. "No. They were the result of a one-night stand. One I don't regret."

He set the knife down and met Leo's eyes. "Other than their father, I've only been with one other person. If you can even call it that."

His voice stayed calm, but there was something else beneath the surface—a quiet vulnerability, a truth long buried.

"As for the kids' father, I don't know who he is. No name. No contact information. I don't even remember what he looks like."

He gave a small shrug. "It could be you for all I know." Silence settled between them, heavy and full of possibility.

"What I'm saying is... if you still want to marry me, you must decide whether you can accept another man's children. Because they're mine, they come first." *They might be mine.*

"I—" Leo began, but Jason cut him off.

"I don't know if I'm going to regret this, but I always follow my gut." His smile was small but real. "I get that we're not doing this for love, and yeah, it's a pretty dramatic way to get your mother off your back. But I'm not after your money or your properties."

He looked down at the cutting board, then back up at Leo. "I want to give my kids something they've been asking for."

Leo set his knife down. "And that is?"

"A papa," Jason said quietly, his voice softer now. "I might be foolish for going along with this. Maybe I do spoil them too much. But like I said, they come first. They're all I have, and I want to make them happy."

His fingers curled around the edge of the cutting board as he drew in a breath.

"I won't go into details, but my family and I don't get along. It's just us. For some reason, my babies like you. And while most parents might say their kids are too young to understand what's happening, I think Sera and Xander are different. I don't know how to explain it. If I believed in reincarnation, I'd say they've been here before."

He looked up, steady and clear. "You made them a promise.

Now I'm asking you to make one to me."

Leo nodded once. "What is it?"

"Don't hurt them."

Leo's eyes flickered. "And what about you? Am I allowed to hurt you?"

Jason didn't hesitate. "I know what I'm getting into. They don't."

Leo took a step closer, his fingers brushing the back of Jason's neck only to freeze for the briefest moment when he felt the knot beneath his touch. He masked his reaction instantly, pretending he hadn't noticed.

An unbound omega.

Interesting.

Unbounds were rare. They had the power to choose their alpha instead of being claimed by one. Leo had only encountered a few in his lifetime, and he knew how deeply their emotions were tied to their knot and their magic. It wasn't noticeable unless touched. Some possessed healing abilities, others unmatched intelligence. He was certain there were more gifts, ones no scholar had dared to document.

That night... a vivid image surged forward in his mind. His teeth at the base of a lover's neck. The scent of heated skin. The sound of soft breathless moans that still haunted his dreams.

It had to be him.

The thought dug in deep, raw and possessive, stirring something that had remained buried for years.

I can't let you go, now.

The resolve coiled tight in his chest. His grip on Jason firmed as he pulled him closer until their bodies were nearly flush. His gaze locked on Jason's stormy gray eyes, sharp and guarded, but hiding something deeper beneath the surface.

"Don't you want to be happy?" Leo murmured, his voice low and steady. "You're committing yourself to me, Jason. Shouldn't you want something out of this too?"

"Seeing my babies happy will make me happy," Jason replied softly.

Leo's fingers rested at the back of his neck, careful not to touch the knot. He didn't want to startle him or risk making Jason second-guess everything. Not when Leo had already made up his mind.

"I know I said I wanted to marry you because of Mya and my mother," he continued, watching closely as Jason's breath caught. "But what if I've changed my mind? What if this is just an excuse to be with you?"

Jason's voice dropped to a whisper. "Don't tell me you've fallen in love with me."

Leo's eyes didn't waver. "What if I have?"

Jason's lips parted, but no words came. He looked dazed, caught between fight and surrender, as if something inside him resisted the pull between them. Like he didn't trust it. Or maybe he didn't trust himself.

"You fascinate me," Leo said, his tone steady and quiet. "And when something fascinates me, I have to make it mine."

Jason swallowed hard, his throat working around the emotions crashing through him. Leo saw the exact moment his words sank in. It showed in the quick, nervous flutter of Jason's pulse just beneath his skin.

Leo's lips curved, his smile small but sure. "I think that makes twice today I've left you speechless."

Jason's brows pulled together. He opened his mouth, searching for words, but they slipped through his grasp. "You don't... I don't..." He trailed off, lost in the flood of thoughts he couldn't untangle.

Leo's hand steadied him, his grip firm but gentle. Then, without hesitation and without fully understanding why, he leaned in and pressed a slow, deliberate kiss to Jason's forehead.

The scent of him washed over Leo in a heady wave. Warm spice and something deeper, something rich and grounding that made his blood hum. His body tensed as he fought the instinctive reaction, a pull that felt far too familiar. It was as if his very soul recognized something in Jason.

He lingered a second longer than necessary.

"We'll take our time getting to know each other, Jason," he said, his voice quieter now, threaded with something even he couldn't quite name.

Jason gave a small nod, and they stepped apart, returning to the rhythm of preparing dinner. Neither of them spoke, but the air between them had changed. It was thicker now. Charged. Every movement felt more intentional, every glance more meaningful.

Several minutes passed in silence before Jason finally spoke.

"So... does that mean you don't want to marry me?"

Leo smirked, not looking up from slicing the carrots. "That part we'll need to do as soon as possible. If I know Mya, she's already off complaining to my mother, and my mom will want proof. I don't know when she'll show up. It could be tomorrow, or it could be months from now. So it's better to be prepared and get married now." He paused, then looked over at Jason. "How about tonight? Runaway Chapel?"

Jason froze mid-stir. "Fuck, I never thought I'd be eloping with a guy I've only met twice. And I'm not even drunk."

"We can fix the sober part real quick," Leo said, flashing a devilish grin. "It'll make a great story when my mother asks how we met."

Jason narrowed his eyes. "Are you serious? Do you always do what your mother says?"

"Not usually, but if I don't, she'll keep setting me up on blind dates. I can't take another one. And besides..." Leo shrugged. "I want to make her happy. She's done a lot for me."

Jason scoffed and shook his head. "She sounds delightful."

Leo chuckled. "You'll like her. I promise."

Jason arched a brow. "I'm holding you to that."

Leo's gaze lingered on him, a slow smirk tugging at his lips.

You can hold me to anything you want, he thought, watching Jason move through the kitchen like he belonged there. Like he belonged with him.

$\sim$

"Leo and I have something to tell you both," Jason said, looking at Sera and Xander.

He and Leo had talked about it, but he felt the kids deserved to know what was happening. This was a major moment in their lives, and they had a right to be included.

"We're getting married," Leo announced before Jason could even finish gathering his thoughts.

"Yes!" the twins shouted in unison.

"Your plan worked, Sera," Xander said proudly.

Jason blinked. "Plan? What plan?"

"Nothing, Daddy," Sera said sweetly. Too sweet. The kind of sweet that practically screamed guilt. Her honeyed tone dripped with mischief, and in that moment, Jason's suspicion snapped into sharp focus.

Oh no. Oh, hell no.

He narrowed his eyes at his daughter, who was now glaring daggers at her brother. "Sera Marie Dupree, what did you do?" She huffed and muttered, "I told Xander to bring Papa here." Jason's head snapped toward his son, his mouth falling open. "You what?"

"Well," Sera said, arms crossed like he was the one

who messed up, "Xander got to meet him, and I didn't. He showed me Papa on TV and said he works at your company. Plus, I know it here." She touched her chest above her heart. "I got happy when I saw him. So when you had to go into the office, I told Xander to find him and bring him home."

Jason turned slowly to Xander, who was casually munching a carrot and looked completely unbothered by being outed as an accomplice.

"Xander, do you have to do everything your sister tells you?"

"Yeah," he said without hesitation, as if the question itself was ridiculous.

Jason pinched the bridge of his nose as the full weight of the chaos settled on his shoulders. They were five. Just five. Not fifteen. Not twenty-five. Not undercover masterminds disguised as children. And yet, that was exactly how they acted. It worried him that they were so sharp, sneaky, and terrifyingly effective when they worked together.

And if they really had pulled this off, then Sera—sweet little Sera—was definitely the ringleader who would lead her brother by the nose.

I'm in trouble. I need a parenting manual. I need coffee. I need to lie down. No, scratch that—I need a drink.

A soft snort dragged him from his spiral. He looked over to find Leo trying, and failing, to hold back laughter.

"Laugh it up," Jason muttered. "You're marrying me, and they come as a package."

Leo leaned in and kissed his cheek. "I can't wait. By the way, I need a raise."

"Huh?" Jason blinked.

"I work for your company. Sera said so."

"What the—" Jason started, but Leo clapped a hand gently over his mouth.

"No cursing in front of the babies. Or I'll let Sera punish you." "Punish Daddy, yay!" Sera cheered.

What the hell is happening right now? Jason mentally shouted.

I MUST BE out of my mind.

Jason kept telling himself this was for the kids. For Sera. For Xander. To give them the family they kept asking for.

But no matter how many times he repeated it, the uneasy feeling in his chest wouldn't go away.

It lingered quietly beneath the surface, whispering that there was more to this than he was willing to admit. Something deeper. Something he couldn't quite name.

He trailed behind Leo and followed him into the infamous *Runaway Chapel*, his heart pounding with a mix of nerves and disbelief. He'd heard plenty of gossip over the years, celebrities sneaking in for quick, secretive *I-dos*, paparazzi lurking outside hoping to catch a scandal. He had laughed about it more than once.

Never in a million years did he think he would become one of them. They had left the kids at home with Mrs. Sing, wearing simple clothes, nothing flashy. Just two men on the verge of doing something completely insane.

Once inside, Jason noticed a familiar face—the guy from the car earlier.

"Sir, I have the documents you requested," the man said, handing a folder to Leo.

"Thanks, Talos," Leo replied smoothly before turning to Jason. "Oh, let me introduce you. Jason, this is my assistant, Talos. If you

ever need to reach me and can't, you can contact him."

Jason extended a hand. "Nice to meet you, Talos."

Talos started to shake it, but before their hands could meet, Leo cleared his throat and swiftly grabbed Jason's hand instead with a firm grip.

Jason raised an eyebrow at him. Talos, on the other hand, merely nodded in silent understanding.

"You too, Mister Dupree," Talos replied politely.

Jason grimaced. "Just call me Jason. Mister Dupree makes me sound like my father."

"Call him Mister Devereux," Leo interjected firmly.

Jason shot him a look. "Seriously?"

Leo ignored him. "Come with me. There's something I want to discuss before we get married."

Jason exhaled but followed him without protest. "Alright."

They moved to one of the benches, and Leo handed him a covered folder. Jason opened the cover, his eyes landing on the bold title of the first document: Marriage Contract.

His stomach twisted.

"What does this mean?" he asked, his voice tinged with suspicion as he glanced up at Leo.

"I understand what I'm asking of you: marriage for convenience. However, there's something you should know first." Leo's tone was steady and firm. "I've waited a long time to get married, and I don't plan to divorce once we say those vows. But I would never keep anyone in a relationship they don't want to be in. So, if we don't develop feelings for each other after a year, we'll go our separate ways. No hard feelings."

Jason watched him closely as Leo gestured to the contract. "Everything listed on page three will remain yours."

Curious, Jason flipped to the third page, his eyes widening with each line he read. Money, cars, properties, a trust fund set up for the twins.

His stomach twisted. "Mister Devereux, I don't ne—"

"It's Leo," he corrected smoothly, pressing a finger against Jason's lips.

Jason stiffened at the touch, heat prickling against his skin.

"I'm not just looking for a marriage in name, Jason," Leo continued. "And I know this probably isn't how you imagined your wedding day would be— sneaking into a chapel in the dead of night, dodging gossip rags. But if we end up madly in love in a year, I'll tear up this contract, and we'll do it all over again, properly, with all the bells and whistles." His voice dropped lower, more intimate. "And don't try to tell me you don't want this. You're not just signing a contract; you're giving up something you probably never thought you would. This isn't just compensation; it's deserved." A slow, knowing smile played at his lips. "Because if we do fall in love, half of everything I own will already be yours."

Jason searched Leo's face for any sign of deception. But Leo was serious. Too serious.

It made Jason wonder if the man was being overly generous for his own good. However, despite the recklessness of this whole situation, there was a strange, undeniable logic to it.

Jason took a steady breath and said, "Okay."

Without another word, he signed the contract and handed it to Leo, who did the same before passing it to Talos.

"All right," Leo said, standing up with a decisive air. "Let's go get changed."

"Changed?" Jason echoed, confused.

"Yeah," Leo replied casually.

"But I didn't bring anything," Jason said, glancing down at his slacks and shirt.

"Did you think I would let you get married in just anything?" Leo asked with a crooked grin as he took Jason's hand and led him toward the back room.

Two suits—one dark blue and the other off-white—hung neatly on racks. Leo gestured to the off-white one. "I had Talos pick these up for us."

Jason stepped closer and took the offered suit. From a distance, it looked simple, but up close, he noticed silver threads delicately woven into the lapels and sleeve cuffs.

"How did you get my size?" Jason asked suspiciously, eyeing Leo with a raised brow.

Leo smirked and shrugged. "I have my ways. Are you impressed?"

"Nope," Jason replied flatly, though he was absolutely impressed by the perfect fit.

"You're going to be hard on my ego," Leo said, chuckling under his breath.

"Someone has to keep you grounded," Jason quipped, lips twitching.

Leo reached out and tapped him lightly on the nose. "Last chance to turn and run."

Jason didn't hesitate. He shook his head. "Let's go."

"I love a man who is decisive," Leo said with a wink, then turned and left the room, giving Jason a moment to himself.

Jason drew in a deep breath and held the suit to his chest. "No turning back now," he murmured.

CHAPTER 7
JASON

I'm married. Wow.

He never thought this day would come, and yet, in the blink of an eye, it had. Jason stared out the car window, watching the city lights blur past as they drove home. His mind was restless, a storm of thoughts swirling inside him, but his heart had settled into a quiet acceptance about marrying a man he had only met twice.

Most people would be freaking out and panicking, doubting every choice.

But Jason?

He felt like this was meant to happen.

It was strange.

Then a thought struck him. Could they be fated mates?

No. That's impossible.

He was an unbound omega, a rarity among their kind. Unlike others who were fated to be with a destined alpha, he had the unique ability to choose. But what were the odds that he would be the one to defy nature so completely?

His fingers drifted to the back of his neck, recalling that moment in the kitchen when Leo's hand had lingered there. His knot had been tingling since the slight touch. The memory sent a ripple of unease through him. He wasn't sure whether to feel relieved or unsettled that Leo had not said anything about what he felt.

Jason had never talked about his knot. Not even his closest friends knew he had one, and he planned to keep it that way. But depending on how close he and Leo became, that secret would not stay hidden forever.

Jason sighed, pulling his hand away and shifting his gaze back to the scenery, his eyes landing on the massive billboard of his now undeniably handsome husband. Leo was an alpha, a dominant one at that. The kind of man who should have been drawn to an omega bound by fate, someone meant for him, not an unbound anomaly like Jason.

And yet, Leo had chosen him.

It didn't make sense. Unbounds were rare and often overlooked, viewed as unpredictable or complicated. Jason had spent most of his life hiding what he was, guarding his secret like it was something shameful, something dangerous. But Leo had looked at him with purpose, with desire, as if Jason was exactly what he wanted.

Jason had always promised to give the twins stability, not risk their hearts too. And yet, here he was, teetering on the edge of something real, something that could change everything.

A part of Jason wanted to believe that. Another part feared it.

Because if this was real, if Leo truly meant it, then everything Jason had built to protect himself would have to come down. The walls. The doubts. The distance.

And that was terrifying.

"You fascinate me, and when something fascinates me, I have to make it mine," Leo had told him. *What was so intriguing about me?*

Jason didn't believe Leo had fallen in love with him that quickly. Love at first sight wasn't real. But lust at first sight? That, Jason believed in. Completely.

Am I overthinking this?

Jason had grown up believing that only certain alphas and omegas had fated mates, like his brother and sister. That was what his parents told him, and he had never had a reason to doubt it. According to them, he would never have a mate. And Jason, never one to chase after dreams he didn't think belonged to him, had simply accepted it. He had never researched it. Never asked questions. Never looked deeper. The whole concept felt like a romanticized fantasy, something pulled from novels or whispered in stories about extraordinary people. It was a myth for others, never for him.

But this was Valleywood, a city steeped in magic,

where the impossible often became reality. Maybe he should have questioned their words. Jason might've been an omega, but he had always seen himself as a normie. No magic. No shifting under full moons. Hell, he couldn't even heal himself. The moment he got sick, he was buried under blankets, miserable, and had to be forced to take his medicine like a child. The twins were more mature than him.

He hated to think his parents telling him he wouldn't have a mate was another way to hurt him, but he couldn't deny that he was a novice when it came to intimate relationships that didn't last longer than a couple of hours. Not counting Leo, he'd never been in a relationship. Except for the twins and his career, everything else had been a wash.

So why wouldn't he believe what his family had said?

And then there was his knot.

A useless, ridiculous thing. It wasn't a good luck charm.

He had considered having it removed once, had even scheduled the appointment. But at the last second, he had chickened out. The thought of being cut open sent his body into shock, as if it was reacting to a traumatic effect. So he was stuck with a knot that did nothing.

Maybe that was why his family had treated him like he was defective.

A disappointment.

Despite everything, Jason had always pushed forward. He had tried to stay positive, to carve out a place for himself in a world that had already decided he was less-than. He had spent his entire life proving himself, throwing everything into his career, into building a future for his kids. He showered them with love, encouraged their creativity no matter how insane it sounded to him. Maybe he was overcompensating, but he wanted to make sure they never felt the way he had growing up.

And getting married and finding a mate was never part of the plan.

But now he was married.

Not just to anyone, but to Leonidas Devereux. A tycoon. An exceptional man who could one day break Jason's heart when he found an omega who fit him better than Jason ever could.

Maybe that was why their vows had been so simple. No elaborate declarations. No grand gestures.

Just words spoken with quiet certainty.

Yet...

His breath softly hitched as he exhaled, fingers grazing his lips. His skin still tingled with the ghost of their kiss, lingering like an unshakable memory.

"I won't make promises of love, but I promise to be faithful to you and to us," Jason said as he slid the simple silver wedding band onto Leo's finger.

He hadn't expected anything more, so when Talos pulled out a small burgundy ring box and handed it to Leo before the ceremony, Jason's breath hitched in surprise.

Leo took Jason's hand, his grip firm yet gentle, and slipped the ring onto his finger, his gaze steady. "I do the same. I will care for the twins as if they were my own and give the three of you a life of happiness," he murmured, his voice quiet but certain.

"With the power vested in me by the state of Pennsylvania, I now pronounce you husbands. You may cement your vow with a k—" The officiant didn't finish.

Leo's hand curled around the back of Jason's neck, pulling him in before the final word could leave the officiant's mouth. Their mouths met, the kiss beginning as a soft brush, but the moment their lips touched, heat surged through Jason's body. A memory flickered across his mind, one so familiar it sent a shiver down his spine. Before he could linger on it, Leo swept his tongue over Jason's lips, coaxing them apart and awakening a craving so deep it nearly unsteadied him.

The light scrape of Leo's beard heightened every sensation, the contrast between rough and soft making Jason gasp. Instinctively, he rose onto his toes, gripping the front of Leo's jacket as if to anchor himself, needing more.

Leo's arms tightened around his waist, drawing him flush against his solid frame. The warmth of his embrace wrapped around Jason with such fierce protectiveness that it felt dangerously close to safety. It thrilled him. It unraveled him.

A moan slipped between them, his, Leo's, he couldn't tell. Their kiss deepened, turning into a battle of want. A claiming for all to witness. Something deep inside Jason sparked, a fire he could no longer ignore.

Leo's lips softened between each teasing bite and lingering press, but he never let go for long. Every return was more intoxicating than the last. Jason lost all sense of time, lost himself in the heat, in the kiss, in Leo.

If not for the pointed clearing of a throat, he wasn't sure they would have ever stopped.

Breathless, they pulled apart, eyes locked. Something

unspoken passed between them, weighty, silent, but deeply understood.

"Well," the officiant said, breaking the moment with a smirk, "I think that just set the chapel's record for the longest kiss."

Jason's face flushed. He ducked his head, pressing his forehead to Leo's chest. His heart pounded, not with uncertainty, but with the overwhelming realization that his entire world had just, irreversibly, changed.

"What are you thinking about? You've been quiet since we left the chapel," Leo asked, his voice low and searching as he slipped a finger under Jason's chin, gently tilting his face toward him. The warmth of his touch sent a shiver down Jason's spine, but it was the concern in Leo's eyes that held him captive. "Are you having second thoughts about marrying me?" "No," Jason whispered.

"Then why are you so quiet?"

Because I want to kiss you again, but I feel like I'm being too greedy if I ask for it.

Instead, he forced himself to say, "I was thinking about work."

Leo frowned slightly. "What about it? Is my sister working you too hard?"

Jason blinked. "Sister? Who's your sister?" "Ada. Or, as I like to call her, pain in my ass." Well, damn.

"No, she's a good boss. I'm just worried about how things might change now that we're married." Jason reached for Leo's wrist, turning in his seat to face him fully. "People saw you kiss me in the lobby today, and no doubt it's already spread all over the company. Will everyone think I slept my way into my position? I might not be the head of a department, but my work is very important to me."

Leo's expression softened as he shook his head. "You don't have to worry about that. I've already handled the kiss and anyone who might have recorded it."

"When? You've been with me and the kids all day." Jason frowned. He recalled Leo taking a phone call or two, but they were quick, no more than fifteen minutes.

"What do you think I pay Talos for?" Leo said.

"Oh," Jason replied. "Wait, please tell me you didn't fire them?" "Nothing like that," Leo said. His voice was calm but firm. There was a quiet finality in his tone that made Jason believe him, at least for now. "But trust me, no one will treat you any differently just because you're the CEO's husband."

Jason wanted to press him, to ask exactly what Leo meant by "handled," but something in the man's tone told him he wouldn't get a straight answer. He would figure it out when he got back to work.

"Can I say that sounds weird?" Jason said.

"What?"

"Being called the CEO's husband." "Get used to it," Leo said with a smile.

Jason was going to say it was temporary so why should he, but held back. "If that's the case, can we not broadcast our relationship?"

Leo's brows pulled together, his displeasure clear. "What do you mean? Are you ashamed of being married to me?"

"No... no... no..." Jason said quickly, shaking his head.

"Then why?"

Jason exhaled slowly. "Like you said, until we figure out our feelings for each other, it's best if we don't spread it around the company."

Leo's lips curved into a smirk. "You want me to be your secret lover?" he teased.

Jason blushed and glanced away, but gave a small nod.

"Look at me," Leo said softly. His voice was low but steady.

Jason hesitated before lifting his eyes to meet Leo's.

Leo chuckled, clearly enjoying himself. "I'll agree under two conditions."

Jason swallowed. "What are they?"

Leo leaned in close, their lips just a breath apart, but he didn't close the distance. Instead, he held Jason's gaze, his tone soft yet firm. "You never take your ring off. It might look simple, but it's my promise to you."

Butterflies fluttered in Jason's stomach at the words. The thought filled him with warmth, and for a fleeting moment, he wondered if Leo really had feelings for him. He wouldn't deny the instant attraction he'd felt from the moment they met at the airport, but that was all it was... wasn't it?

"What if someone asks me about it?"

"Tell them the truth. You're taken," Leo said, never looking away. His gaze locked in place like his words were aimed straight at Jason's heart. The message landed hard, making it beat faster before settling into a slow, steady rhythm.

"Okay," Jason agreed after a quick thought. "And what's the second?"

Leo's eyes flicked to Jason's lips, then back to meet his. "I can kiss you whenever I want."

Jason's breath caught, but he managed to keep his voice steady. His heart, which had just begun to calm, slowly picked up its pace. "As long as I can do the same to you."

Leo grinned, tilting his head slightly. "Like I said, this is not a marriage in name only. We are legally wed."

"Does that mean we'll also...?" Jason let the words trail off, lifting a brow, hoping Leo understood his meaning.

Leo smirked. "Most definitely. But not until you're sure of your feelings for me." He brushed a soft kiss against Jason's lips before leaning back, a mischievous glint in his bright blue eyes. "Go on upstairs before I kiss you again."

Jason blinked, realizing they were already in front of his apartment building. At some point, Talos had put up the partition, granting them privacy.

"Aren't you coming up?" he asked.

"Not tonight. Besides, you haven't asked me to move in." Leo arched a brow, amusement dancing in his expression.

Jason scoffed, turning to him with a grin. "Says the man who barged into my house uninvited." "That was a special case."

"And what about now? You just told me we're married. Shouldn't that be a given?"

Leaning in, he cupped the back of Leo's neck,

rubbing their cheeks together in a slow, intimate caress. "It's not good for newlyweds to sleep apart," he murmured, feeling the warmth of Leo's breath against his skin. "What would the kids think if they didn't see you in the morning?"

Leo's lips brushed his ear as he whispered, "Only the kids?"

Jason swallowed hard, nodding as he pulled back just enough to meet Leo's gaze, his breath coming in soft pants. He didn't know why, but the thought of Leo being away from him, even for a second, felt unbearable. A shiver ran through him. Was he in heat? That didn't make sense. He hadn't been intimate with anyone since his night with the twins' father, and after that, he'd never missed a dose of his suppressants.

So why did Leo's presence feel less like a want and more like a need?

Leo exhaled, his voice husky. "I was trying to be good, Jason."

Jason smirked, feeling uncharacteristically bold. "Who wants you to be good? I haven't had sex in five years, and I'm a newlywed. How long do you expect me to wait?"

A low growl rumbled in Leo's throat before he pulled Jason onto his lap, gripping his wrists and securing them behind his back. Their bodies pressed together, heat crackling between them, the charged air making Jason's skin prickle.

Leo's breath ghosted over his lips, his voice dark and full of promise. "This is your last chance to get out." His grip tightened slightly. "Because if you stay, our first time as husbands will be right here. In the car."

Jason's chest rose and fell rapidly, his breath unsteady. Leo's blue eyes burned with desire, glowing like embers in the dim light, making Jason's cock twitch in his pants.

"Your lips say one thing, but your actions say another." He shifted slightly, testing Leo's hold on his wrists, a teasing challenge

in his voice. "So what do you really want?" Leo didn't answer. He acted.

His mouth crashed against Jason's in a hard, bruising kiss. Possessive. Unyielding. Leaving no room for doubt. Jason gasped against him, the faint taste of copper mingling on his tongue, but he didn't pull away. He leaned in, meeting Leo's hunger with his own, deepening the kiss, surrendering to the fire that had been burning between them since the chapel.

The car wasn't small by any means, but in that moment, it felt suffocating. The air was thick with heat, the space between them nonexistent. The world outside faded into oblivion. Nothing else mattered.

All Jason could feel was Leo. His warmth. His strength. His undeniable claim.

And Jason took it all. Willingly. Recklessly. Desperately.

LEO RELEASED JASON'S WRISTS, his hands immediately sliding around him, pulling him close in a desperate embrace. Their lips moved in sync, the kiss all-consuming, ravenous, as if Jason was his salvation, his oxygen. They only broke apart to gasp for breath before Leo's mouth traveled down Jason's neck, trailing open-mouthed kisses, sucking and nipping at the sensitive skin.

When he reached the birthmark, he lingered, teasing the spot with slow, deliberate strokes of his tongue before grazing his teeth over it, savoring the way Jason's body tensed beneath him.

"Leo," Jason whispered, his voice breathless, needy, wrecked.

"Call me Husband," Leo ordered.

"Husband," Jason moaned, jerking his hips, searching for friction, begging without words.

"Fuck," Leo growled, the sound guttural, primal. So this was what it felt like. He finally understood why his friends lost their minds when their lovers called them mate.

Hearing Jason call him Husband sent fire coursing through his veins, an intoxicating rush that tightened his grip, darkened his hunger, burned away any remnants of control.

His teeth scraped over that sweet patch of skin as he tore Jason's jacket off, barely sparing it a second thought before his hands moved between them, hungry, determined, unstoppable.

With one sharp movement, he had Jason sprawled across the plush leather of the luxury car's backseat, a vision of debauchery waiting to be taken. He grabbed

Jason's shirt and ripped it open, buttons scattering across the interior.

But nothing mattered except the man beneath him, spread out like a feast, waiting to be devoured.

Jason reached for Leo's jacket, but Leo caught his wrists, locking them above his head, pinning him in place.

Jason gasped, his pupils blown wide, stormy gray eyes darkening with need. Their pheromones flooded the car, thick and intoxicating, dragging them both down into an abyss of lust.

And Leo had no intention of escaping.

He licked his lips, watching Jason's chest heave, his breath coming in ragged pants.

Something deeper than lust coiled between them, something raw and irrevocable.

He didn't know if Jason was being honest about them getting married so quickly, but tonight, Leo was going to make his little husband understand exactly who he belonged to.

"Who am I?" Leo asked.

Jason's breath hitched. "Leo..." The name came out hesitant, like he knew it wasn't the right answer.

Leo leaned down and bit Jason's neck where the mole was, his teeth sinking in just enough to leave a mark. Jason's body tensed beneath him, his breath stuttering, chest rising faster.

"Wrong answer," Leo murmured against Jason's flushed skin. "Try again."

Jason sucked in a sharp breath. "My... boss," he rasped, his throat bobbing.

Leo dragged his teeth down, his mouth closing over one pebbled nipple, biting just enough to make Jason's entire body jolt beneath him.

"Try again."

Jason's lips parted, his wrists flexing under Leo's grip, but instead of giving in, he smirked.

"My secret lover," he said, as if daring Leo.

Leo stilled. Then, with a dark chuckle, he dragged his tongue over the now-sensitive nipple before taking it between his teeth and biting down. Harder.

"You enjoy being tortured, I see," Leo whispered against his skin, moving to the other nipple, torturing it far more and longer than he did the other.

Jason twitched, thighs clenching, his entire body tightening beneath him. "Please, Husband, no more," he gasped, his voice breaking, utterly wrecked.

Leo pulled back, meeting his gaze, hungry, commanding, unwavering. "Don't ever forget it again."

Jason didn't speak. Didn't dare. His lips parted, his gaze glassy with need, body taut, breath ragged. And then he surrendered, surging up and crushing their lips together in another searing kiss, shattering whatever was left of Leo's restraint.

He needed to taste Jason, every inch of him.

The last time he'd felt this feral, this unhinged, this completely undone, was five years ago, cementing one undeniable truth in his mind.

He had found the man from that night.

It had been Jason all along.

And fuck, he wasn't letting him go. Not this time.

Leo's mouth traveled lower, hot, wet kisses tracing

Jason's smooth chest, stopping at each nipple to lavish attention on the sensitive pink nubs.

"Oh damn," Jason whimpered, his body arching into Leo's mouth, thighs tensing beneath him.

Leo smirked against his skin. "You like that, baby?" he teased, flicking his tongue over the tight bud before sucking it deep into his mouth.

Jason's fingers twitched, gripping at nothing. "Why are you asking stupid questions?" he muttered, voice thick with pleasure.

Leo chuckled darkly. "I like hearing you beg."

His fingers moved lower, dragging Jason's pants down at a maddening pace, slow and teasing, until Jason's cock sprang free, slapping against his stomach, thick and leaking. Leo groaned, rubbing his still-clothed chest against Jason's cock, grinding against him, smearing the slick heat between them, marking him.

"You're not fair," Jason grumbled, his voice wrecked. "Why are you still dressed?"

Leo leaned in, his breath hot against Jason's ear. "Because tonight is for you," he murmured, his voice a seductive promise. "I want to prove I can take care of you. That I can be a good provider."

Jason sucked in a sharp breath, his fingers digging into Leo's arms.

Leo wanted to ruin him. Completely.

Sliding lower, he gripped Jason's ass, lifting him effortlessly, bringing that beautiful cock to his mouth.

He didn't hesitate.

He swallowed him down in one slow, indulgent glide.

"Husband," Jason howled, his back bowing, his hips snapping up, fucking into Leo's mouth, desperate, lost.

Leo moaned around him, utterly drunk on Jason's taste, his heat, his essence.

Leo ignored his own aching cock, the throbbing heat pressing against the seam of his pants. His sole focus was on Jason. On his pleasure. On owning every sound, every shudder, every gasping breath. And he wasn't stopping until Jason completely unraveled.

Leo pressed a finger inside Jason's slick, welcoming heat, searching for that spot that would drive his little husband into madness. Jason jerked, his back arching, thighs trembling, a choked cry ripping from his throat as pleasure shattered him. Leo groaned at the sight, his own arousal pulsing in response to Jason's wrecked, desperate unraveling.

Leo smirked against his skin. "That's it, baby. Give in to me." And Jason did.

Leo lifted his head, licking his lips slowly, savoring the taste.

"You taste like sin," he murmured, voice dark with promise.

"And one I would go to the underworld for."

And he would never let Jason go. Not in this life. Not in any.

CHAPTER 8

LEO

"Papa, do you have to go on this trip?" Sera asked, pulling a freshly packed shirt from his suitcase without hesitation.

"Yes," Leo answered, sighing as he placed the shirt back inside. "I'll only be gone for a few days."

"But that's too long," she whined, flopping onto the bed with a dramatic huff, so much like Jason sometimes that it made him chuckle.

Leo smiled, brushing a hand over her hair. "I'll be back before you know it."

She peeked up at him with big, hopeful eyes. "Will you bring me something back?"

"What do you want?"

Sera tapped a finger against her lips, clearly giving it serious thought. "Hmm..." Her expression brightened. "A spear."

Leo huffed a laugh, shaking his head. She was definitely Athena's grandchild.

"Do you want your dad to kick me out of bed?" He scooped her into his arms, kissing her cheek as she giggled. "No spear. Think of something else while I'm away, and if I can find it, I'll get it for you. How's that?"

She sighed dramatically, clearly unimpressed with his compromise. "Okay, I guess," she mumbled. "But I really want a spear."

Leo had no doubt she meant every word.

It had been six weeks since he and Jason got hitched. The only ones who knew were Talos and the kids, who had been so ecstatic they refused to leave his side. Leo had taken a full week off just to spend time with them, a decision that had apparently shocked the staff, according to Talos.

In the weeks since their marriage, he had learned a few things. The twins had Jason wrapped around their little fingers, but Jason was also a good father, one who knew when to discipline and when to let things slide. Leo had also come to realize that, despite being inseparable, the more time he spent with them separately, the more their unique personalities shone through.

One thing was certain: Xander was fiercely protective of Sera. Together, they were downright mischievous, and every day felt like the start of a new prank war. Like the other morning when Leo had stumbled out of bed, still half-asleep, and walked straight into a Saran-wrapped doorway. That had definitely been Xander's idea. Or the night Jason had to work late, and the kids filled the bathtub with soap, creating a mountain of bubbles that flooded the entire bathroom. That one had Sera's name all over it. Leo had barely managed to call a clean-up crew in time before Jason got home.

Jason.

His little husband.

Their relationship was evolving. And now that Leo had confirmed Jason was the man he had slept with five years ago, he no longer needed a DNA test to know the twins were his. Jason had basically told him without even realizing it.

But Leo hadn't told Jason.

Jason never seemed to think about that night, and every time Leo tried to bring it up, they were interrupted, either by work or the kids. He had Talos quietly reinvestigate the group of college students who had been at the hotel that night celebrating, and it confirmed what Leo already suspected; Jason had been among them. With a few pointed questions and some careful digging, Leo had pieced the rest together.

He had come close to telling Jason just a few evenings ago. They had been sitting on the couch, watching the twins play, talking about life and the mystery of the twins' father. The moment had been almost perfect.

"So when you got to Singapore, that's when you found out you were pregnant?"

"Yes, but not right away," Jason admitted. *"I was there for*

almost two and a half months before I even got morning sickness."

Leo's fingers twitched, but he kept his voice neutral. "You must have been shocked," he prodded carefully.

Jason exhaled a laugh, though it held no humor. "I completely freaked out in the doctor's office. It was not a pretty sight." He paused, his gaze growing distant for a moment before he sighed. "But after a couple of weeks, I worked things out mentally and settled with the whole 'going to be a father' thing."

Leo studied him hesitantly before asking, "Did you consider contacting the other guy?"

Jason shrugged. "For about two-point-two seconds. It was a one night stand. Nothing more. Nothing less. So I scrapped the idea. It wasn't worth the hassle. What if he didn't want kids?"

Leo swallowed the words on the tip of his tongue, an ache settling in his chest. "I'm sorry you had to go through that alone," he said softly.

Jason smiled, brushing it off. "Why are you apologizing? I know the kids call you Papa, but you're not the guy that got me pregnant."

Leo's mouth moved before he could stop it. "What if I am?" Jason stared at him for a few seconds, then barked out a laugh.

"Wouldn't that be crazy?"

Leo tilted his head. "Why would it be?"

"Think about it. And I don't want to hurt your feelings, but none of the kids look like you. You and Zander have the same hair texture, but it's also the same texture as my mom and grandfather."

Leo glanced at Xander. Jason's words were true, but Leo knew in his heart that the kids were his.

"Besides," Jason said, shaking his head, still amused. "Leo, seriously. You're good-looking. I doubt you've ever had trouble finding lovers, much less pay for one. You had a woman chasing you for five years. The kids' father was a one-night stand. He was an escort my friends paid for me. A birthday-slash-going-away present."

He snorted before adding, "And get this, when I woke up the next morning, I dropped a twenty-dollar tip on his face. He had terrible stroke game as far as I can remember." Leo nearly choked.

What... What?!

I have never had a single complaint about my skills in bed, Leo mentally fumed. And I was drugged that night. His jaw clenched. My technique wasn't that good? Oh, he would show Jason. When the time was right, his little husband would beg him all night.

"Maybe he had an off night," Leo said mournfully.

Jason sighed, then smiled and leaned in for a quick kiss on his cheek.

"I can guarantee you would be better than him."

Leo didn't know whether to feel smug or personally offended.

He opened his mouth to tell him, finally tell him, but then Jason's phone rang.

"Hold on," Jason said, answering the call.

It was Ada who had called. Leo realized that as soon as Jason switched to speaker and immediately focused on work again. Leo had a nagging suspicion that his little sister might have a crush on his man. Ada was an even bigger workaholic than he was, which was saying something. Maybe he should ask Athena to set her up on a few blind dates.

He didn't know the full extent of the project they were working on, but he knew Jason was deeply involved. Leo had considered talking to Ada about it, but Jason wanted to keep their marriage a secret.

Ada clearly liked Jason. That much was obvious.

She had mentioned him before, praising the young architect in her department whose models felt so viscerally real that it was like stepping inside them before they were even built. *Soul-changing* was the word she had used. She also raved about how Jason picked up coding and tech effortlessly, able to analyze a program and work through it faster than most professional techs. He was a hacking genius, something he had been doing since childhood, just for fun.

Who the hell does that?

That made Leo suspicious.

Was this yet another layer of Jason being an unbound omega? Were his abilities subtly influencing his work? Was he unknowingly enhancing his designs with his omega nature?

Leo needed to find out.

But first, he needed time with his husband and kids before the rest of his family found out. They were still in the honeymoon stage, even though they hadn't formally gone on one, something Leo fully intended to rectify soon. Jason didn't seem to mind, but it bothered Leo that he hadn't been able to romance his husband the way he should have.

If his mother sensed their bond was not genuine, accepting Jason into the family would be difficult. Athena valued honesty and love, and Leo didn't want Jason to miss out on experiencing his mother's unfiltered affection. He knew how Jason had grown up, and he wanted the man to understand just how much he mattered. He wanted Jason to know, without a doubt, that Leo cared for him.

And while Leo had gone into this marriage for strategic reasons, he couldn't deny that real feelings had started to take root. Or maybe they had been there from the beginning. He hadn't been lying when he told Jason he was interesting. He had spent five years searching for him, and now that he finally had him within reach, there was no letting go.

How could he?

Jason was alluring in every way, in looks, humor, and heart.

He wanted to tell his mother and sister about their relationship, to make it real in every sense. But Jason had asked for time, and Leo would respect that.

Oddly enough, he hadn't seen Athena. They had texted back and forth, but neither had mentioned his marriage. Leo wanted to tell her in person, not over the phone. But her not popping up unannounced was troubling.

His mother always knew everything. She was the goddess of knowledge, after all. If she hadn't reached out yet, it could only mean one of two things. Either she truly didn't know, or she did and was waiting for him to say something. And that was odd.

Athena never waited unless she was planning something.

The last plan she had hatched was Mya.

One small blessing was that Mya hadn't reached out yet either. Leo knew she and Athena had grown close over the years, dinners and brunches, always keeping each other in the loop, so he wasn't sure what to make of his mother's silence. Maybe Athena was hurt that he hadn't liked Mya the way she had hoped.

Perhaps Athena was living her best life and had finally fallen in love, leaving Leo to live his own life. He would love to see the person who could make the goddess lose all reason. Whatever the case was, it still made him wonder why she wasn't around. But for now, he would put that aside and focus on building a strong bond with Jason and the kids.

"Are you all packed?" Jason asked, stepping into the room.

"Just about," Leo said, tickling Sera. "Except this little monster keeps distracting me."

"Sera, let Papa pack his suitcase," Jason said, scooping her up and setting her down. "I made you a snack. It's on the table." Sera nodded and ran off, leaving them alone.

Leo stretched an arm out and pulled Jason against him. "Are you going to miss me?"

Jason pushed him away, folding the clothes Sera had taken out.

"I'm not one of the kids. I can manage with you gone."

Leo circled his arms around Jason, burying his face in his neck. "Then look at me when you say that."

Jason hesitated, but his fingers clutched Leo's shirt when he turned. "Maybe I'll miss you a little."

Leo smirked. "What a shame," he murmured, tilting Jason's chin up. "Because I will miss you a lot."

He brushed their lips together, just a taste, before pulling back, leaving Jason breathless.

Jason stared at him, lips slightly parted, eyes dark with something he wasn't quite ready to name.

Leo found Jason's lips were like a drug. One hit, and he wanted to devour the man whole.

"Go out with me tonight," Leo said.

Jason arched a brow. "Don't you have a plane to catch early in the morning?"

Leo smirked. "I own a private plane. It leaves when I tell it to."

Jason shook his head. "We can't. Mrs. Sing went to visit a friend, which means we have no one to watch the kids."

Leo's forehead twitched hearing Mrs. Sing's name. The sweet neighbor was quite strange to him. It was as if she had two personalities, one that would speak to him and another that didn't want to look him in the face. He'd thought about bringing the whole thing up to Jason, but he wanted to observe her a bit more.

Leo pulled out his phone and dialed Talos. "You're on babysitting duty tonight."

"Sir, I—"

"Four thousand dollars an hour," Leo cut in.

"...What time? And I need an allergy list."

"Be here at seven. For each second you're late, I deduct one thousand dollars."

He hung up and smirked at Jason. "We have a babysitter." Leo knew he was looking smug and didn't care. "Now go get ready for our date."

Jason chuckled, shaking his head. "You're unbelievable. Is it that easy to throw money around?"

Leo shrugged. "When you have it like we do, you can."

Jason rolled his eyes. "Must be nice."

One day, Jason would realize it wasn't just Leo's money anymore. It was theirs. He had already given Jason a credit card with no limit, and he knew for a fact Jason hadn't used it. Stubborn man.

Leo still hadn't told Jason about his life as Daedalus or the fact that he had been around for over three thousand years. Though he had built an immense fortune, he didn't just hoard wealth. He invested it back into the world, funding magical communities, rebuilding what had been lost, and helping ensure their survival in an ever-changing society. His business trip wasn't just about securing another deal. It was about negotiating with Armand Dracul, the current President of the United States, to fund affordable housing for supernatural beings.

Building more magical communities wasn't just important to Leo. It was necessary. As belief in the gods waned, so did their power. Athena, like the rest of the pantheon, was affected by the world's dwindling faith. The fewer people believed, the weaker they became. But if magic flourished again, if supernatural communities thrived, belief would follow. And the more belief flooded the world, the more power the gods could reclaim.

That was why Leo couldn't shake the feeling that Odin had deliberately set plans in motion using Loki's powers and Valleywood as a catalyst. The city was a hub of supernatural influence, a melting pot of myth and magic where belief could be rekindled. It was too perfect, too well-placed, for it to be a coincidence. Odin was always several steps ahead, playing a long game no one else could see until it was too late.

Or maybe this wasn't a game at all. Maybe, for once, Odin was truly punishing Loki for his many crimes, hoping the trickster god could find redemption.

But Leo had his doubts.

Jason sighed. "What if Talos had something to do tonight?"

Leo smirked. "Then he can reschedule. He gets paid more than you, you know."

Jason's eyes widened. "You're kidding."

Leo shook his head. "He's been with me for a long time. I take care of those I see as family. He also knows most of my secrets."

"I'm kind of jealous," Jason admitted, his voice quieter now, almost hesitant.

Leo cupped Jason's face, his thumb brushing over his cheek. "Don't be. One day, you'll be the person I trust the most."

Jason searched his eyes for a long moment before he scoffed, shaking his head. "Then maybe I should become your special assistant."

Leo grinned. "I'd never get any work done."

"Why?"

"Because I'd be too busy convincing you to let me fuck you across my desk."

Jason groaned and pushed at Leo's chest. "Lustful old man."

"You married me."

"No regrets," Jason whispered, pulling Leo into a slow, deep kiss.

~

"WHAT DID MY BROTHER WANT?" Ada asked as she leaned in to kiss Talos on the cheek.

"I have to work for a few hours," he replied, setting his phone down on the nightstand.

"What?" She sat up abruptly and punched the sheets with a pouty expression. "You promised we'd go to the movies today." She huffed in frustration. "I'm going to kill my brother."

Talos sat up beside her and gently cupped her cheek. "I'm sorry, baby, but you knew what my job was like when we started this relationship."

"Still, I think my brother is taking advantage of you. I'm going to talk to him."

"If you do that, does it mean you're ready to tell your brother about us?" he asked with a small grin.

"Um..." she murmured, suddenly hesitant, and Talos smiled knowingly.

When he and Ada first started their relationship, it was supposed to be nothing more than sex with benefits. But somewhere along the way, feelings crept in, and because of their public status, they had decided to keep things a secret for now. He had to admit he was nervous about telling Leo he was in love with his sister. Everyone in the company, and any associate with common sense, knew just how overprotective Leo was when it came to Ada.

Talos knew firsthand how ruthless Leo could be when it involved Ada. He had personally conducted background checks and watched his boss threaten or scare off enough men to know Leo didn't play games when it came to his baby sister. Most guys folded at the sight of Leo Devereux. Talos didn't want to be another name on the list of those sent away. Not only was this a good job, but he was falling hard.

"Let's hold off on telling him for now," Talos said, kissing her forehead. Ada gave a soft nod, and they laid back in bed together. He didn't have to leave right away. They could steal a few more moments of peace.

"I don't like keeping secrets from my brother," she whispered, curling closer to him.

Heh, he's keeping a big one from you and your mother. "I know," he murmured, brushing her hair back from her face.

"Wait," she said suddenly, sitting up straight. "Why do you need an allergy list? You already know what my brother likes to eat." Her eyes widened. "Is he going on a date and needs you there?"

"Um..." Talos looked away, trying not to give anything away with his expression.

"Tal, what are you hiding from me?" she asked, straddling his legs and leaning forward, her tone demanding.

As much as he tried to focus on her question, his eyes betrayed him, drifting to the swell of her breast peeking from the neckline of her silk nightgown.

"Tell me. What's my brother up to?" she insisted, her voice sharper now.

Talos swallowed hard. "I... I... can't," he stammered, then suddenly flipped her onto her back, pinning her beneath him, a gasp escaped from pretty pink lips. "Let's make a deal."

"I'm listening," she said cautiously, her eyes narrowing but amused.

"No talking about your brother when we're in bed or when you're dressed like this," he said, his hand sliding up her side to cup her breast, his thumb teasing her nipple.

"You're cheating," she whimpered as her body arched toward his touch.

"I know," he murmured, leaning down to kiss her hard, hoping to distract her, hell, hoping to distract himself too. He hated that he had to leave her for the night, but it was his job to come to his boss's aid no matter the time of day. Plus, he wasn't an idiot to pass up four thousand dollars an hour.

CHAPTER 9
JASON

J ason leaned against the passenger seat, watching the thick forest blur past as Leo navigated the winding driveway. The canopy of towering trees suddenly parted, and Jason gasped. When he'd agreed to the date, he had expected Leo to take him to some fancy restaurant with a list of dishes he'd never tried or heard of.

Who would have thought he would bring him to a mansion in the Greenstone Heights community, a part of the Jade district known for having mansions and elegance instead of houses and the exclusive Verdant Court Country Club that was open to anyone who could afford the astronomical membership fees, no matter how basic the package might seem. Although he was born into a semi-wealthy family, Jason was never into flaunting wealth the way his parents and siblings did.

Still, Jason found himself fascinated as a breath-taking mansion came into view. As an architect, he took in everything, from its light-colored stone facade bathed in the golden hues of the setting sun, which gave it an almost otherworldly glow, to the steep slate roofs, symmetrical design, and elegant dormer windows. To Jason, it looked like something straight out of a historical novel. The two towers flanking the structure made it all the more dreamlike.

He noticed the floor-to-ceiling windows reflecting the landscape like mirrors, even from a distance. The grandeur would make anyone envious, and that was just the outside.

Leo slowed the car as they approached the circular driveway, the tires crunching over gravel. Jason took in the fountain that stood proudly at the center, water cascading down its four tiers. Perfectly manicured gardens framed the estate, the hedges trimmed into pristine shapes and flowers blooming in soft, muted colors.

His eyes traveled to the imposing entrance, where massive double doors were framed by tall white columns. Above them, an arched transom window hinted at the elegance waiting inside. He was so absorbed in taking everything in that he hadn't realized the car had stopped until he heard Leo chuckle and speak beside him.

"Are you impressed?"

Jason cleared his throat and looked at Leo. "It's alright."

Leo scoffed and touched his chest as if wounded. "You seriously hurt a man's ego, Jason Dupree-Devereux."

"How? You know what, don't answer that." He was too busy trying not to blush at Leo hyphenating his last name. He couldn't deny it sounded good. "Anyway, what are we doing here? I thought you were taking me on a date?"

"This is part of it," Leo said, taking Jason's hand in his. "This is my home."

Jason choked on his breath and looked back at the mansion. He felt a bit ashamed of himself. Since their wedding night, Leo had been living at his place. He had never asked where Leo's home was and had assumed he had a place closer to the company. "You...

you live in this? By yourself?"

"I do." Leo smiled. "It was my very first home design when I moved to Valleywood."

Wow, Jason thought. As much as they had talked in the weeks since getting married, Jason realized he was the one who had done most of the talking. Not because he had intended to, but because Leo always asked, and Jason answered.

It wasn't that he wasn't interested in Leo, because he was. Leo was intelligent, sweet, gorgeous, wealthy, and most of all, he loved Xander and Sera as if they were his flesh and blood. But in Jason's case, he felt he wasn't good enough for Leo. With the kind of money Leo had, Jason shouldn't have had any worries, but he did. He was an unbound omega, and there was nothing fated keeping them tethered to each other.

So what if one day Leo found an omega that was worthy of him? One with money and class. Jason knew there were rumors of omegas wanting to jump into Leo's bed because they thought he was single. As rushed as it was, he didn't regret marrying Leo. Because for however long they would last, he knew what it felt like to be cared for. Leo was nurturing, and the last six weeks had made him feel special.

"I get it, you know," Leo said quietly, breaking into his thoughts.

Jason looked over, his voice low with curiosity. "What is it that you understand?"

"You're not comfortable with my wealth," Leo replied gently. "I won't push you into accepting it. The longer we're together, the easier it will be for you. The credit card I gave you is to use whenever you're ready, for whatever you need."

It was the truth. He wasn't comfortable with it. His parents had told him countless times that anything they owned did not belong to him, just his sister and brother. That was why Jason always prayed in thanks to his late grandfather, who had set up an inheritance for him. There were many times he thought he was adopted, but it still didn't explain why they treated him like he didn't matter.

"I'm sorry," Jason said softly.

Leo tilted his head. "Why are you apologizing?"

"Honestly, I'm not sure."

"Let's make a rule," Leo said, his tone warm. "If we

apologize, let's make sure it's for something meaningful."

"Okay." Jason smiled, his chest warming at how patient and understanding Leo always was. "So, is there a purpose for you bringing me here? Don't tell me there's a five-star restaurant in there."

Leo smirked and shrugged. "If you want me to add one, I will."

"That's not necessary," Jason said with a blush, eyes darting away for a second.

Leo reached out and cupped the back of his neck, guiding him closer with care. As always, his fingers never wandered too far, never touched the knot.

"Are you sure?" Leo asked, his voice soft but steady as he looked into Jason's eyes.

Jason blinked, his stomach twisting with heat, the urge to crawl into Leo's lap and recreate parts of their wedding night rising like a tide.

"I will do anything to make my husband happy," Leo murmured, his voice dipping low with intention. The promise in his tone made Jason's breath catch. It wasn't just words, it was truth. It was more.

Jason didn't answer. He didn't need to. Instead, he leaned in and brushed their lips together in a tender kiss.

"Same," he whispered. "And thank you."

I don't know how long this will last, but I'm going to hold onto it for as long as I can.

～

LEO LED him around the house, taking him from one room to another: the kitchen, the family room, the entertainment room, the library, the dining room, and the living room. Each space reflected both elegance and comfort, and Jason could tell it had been carefully curated, not just by money but with thought.

"These bedrooms," Leo said as they passed a hallway, his voice quieter now, "I hope they'll belong to the kids one day."

Jason paused at the doorway and glanced inside but didn't comment. The rooms were spacious and filled with natural light, empty but full of possibility.

Leo watched him closely before guiding him forward again. He had saved these two rooms on the second floor for last. As they walked, memories stirred in Leo's mind. He remembered the first time he had designed this house, back when the Aegis community was little more than a scattered plan with only a few estates built. At the time, neighbors had to trek across wide plots of land just to greet one another. It had been quiet, isolated.

But things had changed.

Over the years, more homes had been added, and with them came life, a bustling community full of magic, ambition, and carefully protected peace. Athena had partnered with the god Yu Huang Da Di also known as the Jade Emperor and purchased the land and the surrounding area, claiming it as a legacy project. Gifting land to him and Ada, pieces of a future built to last.

She had asked him and Ada for three designs detailing what she wanted, and like dutiful children, they did what their mother asked. Leo knew Athena loved extravagance and elegance, so he hadn't asked many questions when she requested a home design with multiple rooms, bathrooms, spas, and all the other luxuries. Who could have predicted that years later, it would blossom into the Aegis community, with her rarely visited personal home becoming the Verdant Country Club.

"I take back what I said," Jason remarked, coming to a stop in front of him.

"And what was that?" Leo asked, tilting his head with interest.

"I'm starting to be impressed. This is a beautiful home."

Leo smiled at the admission. When he had built this estate, his only intention had been to make something for himself. Throughout his long life, he had designed homes for everyone else, but never for his own comfort. He hadn't imagined that one day he'd bring a husband and two children into it. Truthfully, he hadn't spent much time living here. The silence echoed too loudly, the emptiness a reminder of a heart he had long thought would remain alone.

Bringing Jason here was his way of changing that. Slowly. Carefully. Introducing him to this part of his life, this piece of himself that not even his mother or sister had fully seen.

"Beautiful enough to move here with the kids?" Leo asked, his voice carrying a hint of hope.

"I said I was a little impressed, not blown away," Jason replied with a smirk.

"Then I guess I need to bring out the big guns," Leo

said, reaching for his hand with a playful smile. "There are two other rooms I want to show you."

"Is one of them the master bedroom?" Jason asked, arching a brow with a knowing look.

"Was there ever a doubt I would take you into my lair?" Leo teased, his tone low and suggestive.

He fought the urge to circle an arm around Jason's waist and pull him close. Since their night in the car, Leo hadn't pushed for intimacy. But gods, it was getting harder and harder not to take his little husband right here and now.

"I can't wait," Jason said, his voice soft but full of anticipation.

Leo gently squeezed Jason's fingers and guided him down the hall. As they walked, Leo's eyes drifted to a framed photo of Ada and Athena at the beach, a memory that pulled a small smile from his lips. That had been a good day. A peaceful day.

The walls were lined with artwork and paintings collected over the years, carefully chosen and lovingly preserved. But this hallway was different. This one was filled with photographs. Moments frozen in time, captured with friends, family, and places that had meant something to him.

Just before they reached their destination, Leo noticed Jason had stopped. He turned back and found him standing still, staring at a large portrait at the end of the corridor.

It was Athena.

A replica of a statue Leo had sculpted lifetimes ago,

brought to life in brushstrokes of gold, ivory, and shadow.

Leo slipped his hands into his pockets and stepped up beside Jason.

"She's beautiful," Jason murmured in awe, his gaze locked on the painting.

Leo nodded slowly. "She is."

Athena looked radiant in gold and white, her expression serene, her posture commanding. Everything about her screamed grace, strength, and quiet power.

"Tell her that when you meet her," Leo said casually.

Jason's head tilted slightly. "Who is she?"

"Some call her the goddess Athena," Leo replied, watching him carefully. "But I call her Mother."

Jason blinked, startled, then gave a small laugh. "I can see why people would think she's a goddess. Her beauty is flawless." He looked between the portrait and Leo. "Don't take this the wrong way, but you look nothing like her. Ada, now that I think about it, doesn't either."

"That's because we were adopted," Leo replied with an easy shrug.

"Ah, that makes sense." Jason nodded, then stepped closer to

the portrait. "She looks—" He paused, shook his head, and took a step back.

Leo didn't need to ask what he was about to say. He saw it too.

The resemblance between Athena and Sera was undeniable. Blue eyes, blonde hair, rosy, full lips. Traits that could have come from Jason, yes, but more likely, from her grandmother.

Jason chuckled, rubbing the back of his neck. "I must be really tired or hungry," he said. "You don't have a brother, right?"

He looked at Leo, his tone light, but something deeper flickered in his expression. Was it worry? Or hope?

For a moment, Leo was tempted to tell him the truth. All of it.

The gods. The immortality. Who Jason really was to him.

But the time wasn't right.

Their relationship was still new, still fragile. Too many truths, too soon, might shatter everything they were trying to build.

"No," Leo said softly. "It's just me and Ada."

Jason let out a slow breath and nodded. "Oh." He glanced back at the portrait, then shook his head, trying to brush it off.

Leo reached for his hand again. "Come on," he said gently. "There's still something I want to show you before we go to dinner."

Leo wrapped an arm around his shoulder and guided him to one of the most precious places in his home, which he had paid a lot of money to keep secure because of all the valuable objects inside. When they reached the door, he opened a latch and pressed his hand to the pad, waiting for it to recognize his DNA. Once that was done, a door slid open, but he didn't enter immediately. He turned to face Jason. Leo wasn't sure why, but he was nervous about showing Jason what was inside.

"What's wrong?" Jason asked, cupping his cheek and staring worriedly in his face.

"Nothing," he said softly then turned and pulled Jason inside and watched as his eyes widened.

Behind protective glass, on display were the drafts of every first that made him who he was, from Daedalus to the present. From his sculptures to the temples, his most notable and first commissioned work was the Labyrinth, which he did for Minos. Most believed the whole mino-taur and labyrinth was a myth, but it was all true.

"Welcome to my sanctum," he said, getting Jason's attention. "In this room are drafts of some notable archi-tects, sculptors, inventors, and engineers."

"This is wonderful," he said, looking around with a bright smile.

"Are you impressed?" Leo joked.

"A little," Jason said, ducking his head, but Leo could tell he had made an impression on him by the look in his eyes. "Come on, let me show you around."

"These are marvelous," Jason said after an hour of looking around the collection room, as Leo liked to call it. "How did you get your hands on them?" "Auctions," he lied.

"I can't believe you found drafts going so far back in ancient Greece. And this labyrinth, it looks so real. I've always wanted to visit Greece. I hear the beaches are beautiful."

"They are, and I'll take you for our honeymoon. I haven't been back in many years."

"You don't have an accent," Jason commented.

"It slowly disappeared over the years," Leo said.

"I can see that." Jason leaned over the case, studying the Labyrinth model he'd recreated years ago. The blueprint was locked away in a safe with a few other drafts. The Labyrinth was one of his greatest joys and heartbreak simultaneously.

"It's like I entered a museum," he said. "I noticed you have a lot of work done by someone with the initials D. I wonder who the architect was."

"Daedalus, the inventor," Leo quickly responded.

Jason was silent for a second. "You've got to be kidding me. Isn't that guy a myth?"

Leo stared at Jason intensely. "What if he was real? What do you know about him?"

"Let's see, brilliant inventor, but he fucked around with the gods and got his ass burned, basically."

"Some part of what you just said is true, but he was more than just an inventor. He was an architect first. Designed many buildings that brought Greece and many other countries into the twenty-first century. Some try to recreate what was lost, but they can't capture the spirit he had. That's what I was told anyway," Leo shrugged.

"And that's why you bought so many of his works? Let's hope you didn't get scammed. He wasn't real, Leo. Next, you're going to tell me gods are real, too. I thought you were a smart man, Husband," Jason said with a shake of his head, his voice tinged with amusement.

Leo remained silent, watching Jason drift toward a tall, unfinished statue at the back of the room. His gaze softened, and something unreadable flickered in his expression. He had no intention of ever completing that sculpture. It was more than just a relic of the past. It held memories, pain, and the weight of someone he had never fully let go of.

Jason admired the figure, unaware of the emotions stirring in Leo's chest. "Wow, the physique on this statue is so perfect," he said in awe, his fingertips gently grazing the ridges of smooth marble. His tone was light, almost teasing. "You wonder if the carver and the model had a love affair."

Leo swallowed hard. He knew the truth.

We did, or I thought we did. The statue had been a gift he would have given to Minos, but after what happened between them, he had no desire to finish it. Leo knew he should have thrown the damn thing out, but he couldn't bear to see any of his work destroyed.

Like this room, he had taken time to curate what he wanted, and everything was displayed as if he were telling a story. That was how he felt about the statue. It was meant to be the story of their love, one that was, by all rights, forbidden. At the time, he had been unsure of himself, unsure of his talents and his worth as an alpha, let alone a dominant one. He had become ensnared by the powerful aura of a king.

Yet the very man he had been willing to give everything to betrayed him without a second thought and then imprisoned him. It had taken Athena's guidance and healing to bring him back from the depths of despair. That was a time in his life he never wanted to revisit.

"I've thought of being a sculptor," Jason murmured,

his voice thoughtful as his fingertips traced the lines of the statue.

"I can teach you," Leo offered, his voice low.

"Really?" Jason turned to him with hopeful gray eyes, then looked back at the statue, curiosity flickering in his gaze.

"Yes," Leo said, stepping behind him and gently sandwiching Jason between his chest and the cool marble. He took Jason's hand and brought it back to the statue, guiding it slowly over the ridges of the stone. He leaned in, his voice close to Jason's ear. "It's all about knowing your model."

Their joined fingers glided around the statue's chest, circling the nipple before trailing down over the muscled abs, then back up. "It's like making love for the first time and wanting to memorize every inch, every breath they take," Leo murmured.

Jason let out a soft laugh. "The way you describe it makes it sound like every sculptor has slept with their model." "Maybe," Leo replied, his tone unreadable.

Jason tilted his head, eyeing the unfinished statue again. "I wonder who the model and artist were. Except for the head, everything is so detailed."

Leo stepped away, just slightly, enough to create space but not distance.

Jason turned, sensing the shift. He cupped Leo's cheek gently.

"What's wrong?"

"Why would you think something's wrong?" Leo asked, his tone steady but quiet.

"You suddenly looked sad," Jason whispered. He

kissed Leo's palm, then took his wrist and drew him close until they were pressed together.

"Right now, I'm the happiest man in the world."

Jason smiled. "Oh really? Why's that?"

Leo didn't answer right away. Instead, he leaned in and brushed his lips across Jason's with soft reverence. "How could I not be, when I have you in my arms?"

"You really are a charmer," Jason said with a playful roll of his eyes. He stepped back and looked around the room, admiration in his voice. "Thank you for showing me this. I can tell it means a lot to you."

"You don't find it weird that I collect blueprints? Even if I might have gotten scammed."

"No," Jason said, shaking his head. "It says a lot about who you are and your dedication to your craft. It also gives me insight into how deeply you love." He leaned up, brushing his cheek along

Leo's jaw, his voice softening. "I find it sexy."

Leo's breath caught in his chest when Jason's fingers trailed down the front of his shirt, brushing against his nipple before continuing lower, tracing the ridges of his abs. Just as his hand neared the waistband of Leo's pants, Jason stepped away, pulling back with a teasing gleam in his eye.

But he didn't get far.

Leo growled low in his throat, a sound of pure want, and grabbed him by the back of his neck. He turned Jason around and crashed their mouths together, claiming his lips with a kiss that was hot, hungry, and filled with intent. He swept his tongue between Jason's lips, tasting him deeply and giving him everything he had been holding back.

Jason responded instantly, melting into the kiss as Leo slowly backed him up against the nearest wall, not giving him a chance to catch his breath. The cool surface met Jason's back, grounding them both. Behind them stood the unfinished statue, silent and still, yet it felt as if it were watching. Leo could almost feel the weight of nonexistent eyes boring into them, and instead of discomfort, the idea thrilled him.

A wicked thought flickered to life.

The statue had once represented love and betrayal. Maybe now it could bear witness to something entirely different.

I've found a new muse who has captured his heart in ways Minos never did.

CHAPTER 10

JASON

Intoxicating, sweet, domineering, consuming.

The words played continuously in his mind, and Jason felt as if he were being swallowed whole. Leo's hands, his mouth, his entire body surrounded him, consuming him in waves of heat and desire. Every touch burned through the fabric of his shirt, leaving trails of fire skimming his skin, setting every nerve alight.

His heart pounded hard against his ribcage, as if trying to match the rhythm of their kiss. He clung to every last touch, every breathless second, holding on as if the moment would slip away too soon.

Just when Jason felt like he might lose himself entirely, Leo broke the kiss, releasing his lips with a final, lingering pull. They both gasped for air, their chests rising and falling as they struggled to catch their breath, the heat between them thick and undeniable.

No, don't stop, he mentally cried, opening his eyes and chasing Leo's lips for more, but he was stopped by a finger pressed against his lips.

"If we continue to do this, you won't get to eat, and I'm sure you're hungry."

Jason opened his mouth to protest that he didn't want food, but his stomach growled loudly, betraying him. Heat rose to his cheeks as Leo chuckled under his breath.

"Come on, let me take you out to eat," Leo offered with a gentle smile, brushing his fingers over Jason's arm.

Seeing that he had no choice, Jason sighed and nodded in agreement, though a question tugged at the edge of his thoughts.

How can I get this man to sleep with me?

For weeks, they had danced around each other, drawn close through long conversations, heated kisses, and intimate touches. Blow jobs. Hand jobs. Everything but what Jason truly wanted. He was ready for more.

Leo was waiting, that much was clear. Waiting for Jason to develop feelings. But Jason already had them. Maybe it wasn't love, not the full-blown, soul-deep kind, but it was close. Close enough that his chest ached from wanting more.

And he was tired of being teased.

Did Leo even know how sexy he was? How Jason's breath caught every time he caught him playing with the twins or washing dishes with rolled-up sleeves? Or the way Jason couldn't look away when Leo cooked barefoot in pajama pants, leaning against the counter like some domestic dream?

Even the way Leo held him at night was seductive. Wrapped in his arms, head resting on those strong muscles, Jason felt as if he were being folded into something safe and sacred.

He knew sex wasn't everything, but his heat was coming soon, and he wanted Leo. Not just out of instinct, but because he craved every part of him. His presence. His touch. His voice. Everything.

Suppressants would help, but they wouldn't satisfy the yearning that had settled deep in his bones.

And right there, in the middle of that thought, a plan began to take shape. A very tempting, very effective plan. A sly smile pulled at his lips. He would stop taking his suppressants and let his heat happen naturally.

"What's with that smile?" Leo asked, pausing to open the passenger door for him.

Jason stepped out and met his eyes with a soft shrug. "Just thinking about how much of a good time I'm having," he said.

"Really?" Leo asked, amused by his expression.

"Yes," Jason replied with a nod. "I haven't dated much, but I'm enjoying this."

Leo leaned in and gave him a quick kiss. "I'm glad to hear that."

They got into the car, and Leo took him to Vanis, a

charming Greek restaurant tucked into the city's quieter side. There, Jason ate far too much delicious food and laughed until his sides hurt at Leo's stories—some about success, others about embarrassing failures that made him seem even more human.

It was the best low-key date he had ever been on. He appreciated that Leo didn't try to flash his wealth or overwhelm him with expensive gestures. Jason knew he would have to come to terms with Leo's status eventually, but for tonight, he was grateful that it felt simple. Comfortable.

"I had fun tonight," Jason said sincerely as Leo parked the car in front of his apartment building. He turned in his seat and looked at him with a warm smile. "Thank you."

"I'm glad, but I don't think that's how you should be thanking me," Leo replied with a playful grin.

Jason shook his head at how silly he could be, but decided to indulge him just a little. He leaned over and pressed a gentle kiss to Leo's cheek, then pulled back, his eyes meeting Leo's steady bluegaze. "Is that thank you enough?" Jason asked, teasing lightly.

Leo cupped his cheek with one hand and leaned in closer, his voice low and full of intent. "No, it's not."

Before Jason could respond, Leo's lips captured his in a kiss so intense it stole the air from his lungs. His hips were pinned, the world fading as their mouths moved together, heat unfurling between them like a match striking dry tinder.

Why does this man always consume me with every kiss?

LEO WALKED into the hotel lobby that would be his home for the next three days, Genice, his secretary, walking beside him. His first day meeting with Armand and a few senior staff members had gone well, and he didn't foresee many issues getting the project off the ground. What weighed on him more heavily was the unusual concentration of magic in the area. Was it tied to an object? Or a person, the way Loki was bound to Valleywood?

Leo didn't want to believe his theory was true. The idea that Odin would go so far as to imprison his son's power within a city was hard to accept. But if that were the case, what would happen to Valleywood if Loki ever regained full access to his magic? The town's magical structure could shatter under the pressure, and there was no telling what form Loki's wrath might take in the aftermath.

He hoped he was wrong. Still, the unease had only grown since his meeting with Armand. Leo wasn't the paranoid type. Not after living as long as he had and witnessing events that most would call fantasy. But even he knew better than to ignore instinct. So he prepared. Quietly. Strategically. In case anything went wrong, he would protect himself, his family, and the magical communities he had helped shape.

And if nothing happened, then he would still stand firm in his resolve to strengthen Valleywood and every other enchanted town across the map.

"I'll go check us in," Genice said, brushing a lock of hair behind her ear as she stepped toward the front desk.

Leo gave her a short nod. They had come straight from the airport to the White House. There had been no time to stop at the hotel, no chance to regroup. But now that the day's meetings were behind him, he was ready to unwind, if only for a few moments.

Moving to the far side of the lobby, he was just about to sink into one of the plush sofas when his phone vibrated in his breast pocket. He pulled it free, and the corner of his mouth lifted when he saw Jason's name flash across the screen.

He answered with a chuckle, lowering his voice. "Miss me already, Moró?" he teased, settling into the cushions, ready to hear his young husband's voice.

"Papa, when are you coming home?" Xander's small voice came through the speaker.

Leo straightened slightly. "In a day or two. Why, sweetheart?" he asked with a fond smile.

"Can you come home sooner?"

The question made Leo sit forward, tension creeping into his spine. "Is something wrong?" he asked, his voice firmer now.

"Where is your dad?"

"I miss you," Xander said quietly. "And Daddy is sleeping." *Sleeping?* Leo glanced at his watch and saw that it was after six. He couldn't recall if Jason had taken a nap so close to dinner in the six weeks since he'd moved in. *Did he have a hard day? Is he sick?* Leo hated that he wasn't there to take care of him. Just as he was thinking of calling a doctor to check on Jason, he heard the man's voice in the background.

"Xander, who are you calling?" Jason's voice filtered faintly through the background.

"Papa," Xander replied simply.

Leo heard a bit of shuffling before Jason's voice came more clearly through the phone.

"Did he disturb your meeting?" Jason asked.

"No, I'm at the hotel," Leo replied, his tone light.

"Don't allow any strange men into your room," Jason said with a teasing edge in his voice.

"Not unless it's you," Leo answered with a quiet chuckle. He paused for a beat, then added more gently, "You sound tired."

"I was, but the nap helped," Jason said, his voice tinged with a yawn.

"Is Ada giving you too much to do?" Leo asked with concern. "I can talk to her."

"My workload is the same as it has always been. I just got a little tired. Nothing to worry about," Jason assured him, his tone soft but steady.

"Alright," Leo said, though he still felt uneasy.

"Sir, I have your room key," Genice said, stepping up beside him and handing it over.

"Moró, let me get settled and I'll call you back," Leo said into the phone.

"Okay," Jason replied before ending the call.

"I remember the days when you used to call me Moró," a voice said from nearby, smooth and familiar.

Leo froze for a moment, forcing himself to remain calm. He turned to find the speaker already approaching.

"May I join you?" the man asked with a smile.

"No," Leo said firmly, surprised at how steady his voice sounded. He knew, however, that the man would not listen. As expected, he ignored the refusal and took a seat across from him.

"Sir, you..." Genice started, clearly prepared to intervene, but Leo raised a hand to stop her.

"It's okay, Genice," he said evenly. "You can go rest for the night."

"As you wish," she replied, though her eyes narrowed at the man seated across from Leo. Genice was loyal and perceptive. She might not know all the details of Leo's past with this man, but she had worked for him long enough to read his reactions. It also did not help Minos that Genice was a werefox and could smell bullshit from miles away.

With a last, lingering glance in Minos's direction, Genice turned and walked away, her steps deliberate and slow. She was clearly irritated, and Leo could not blame her. The last person he expected to see here was his former lover and king...Minos.

"I don't think she likes me," Minos said with a wry smile.

Leo did not bother denying it. Instead, he studied him in silence.

Time had been generous to the former king. It was as if the years had barely touched him. His thick, wavy brown hair, once wild and tousled as if he had just rolled out of bed and raked his fingers through it, was now neatly cut and slicked back, held in place with an excessive amount of product. There was not a strand of gray in sight.

His vivid green eyes were just as piercing as ever as they swept over Leo from head to toe. Once, Leo had thought that gaze was filled with desire. Now he knew better. Behind those eyes had always been secrets—not longing, not love, just manipulation and betrayal.

Minos was still undeniably handsome. His sharp cheekbones and square jawline remained striking, and his full lips had not lost their appeal. Those same lips had once whispered words of devotion, had kissed every inch of Leo's body, had begged him to make love until the world disappeared.

And it had all been a lie. It had shattered his heart into so many pieces it took centuries to repair.

The memory of being chained and dragged into court before the nobles and advisors, declared a danger to Crete, never left his thoughts. Yet, what hurt more was not being labeled a traitor or accused of theft. It wasn't even being blamed for seducing the king away from his queen's bed —especially when everyone knew the queen kept a harem and only interacted with Minos for ceremonial appearances. What truly cut deepest were the words that came from Minos's own mouth. Words spoken coldly, while his sharp gaze sliced straight through Leo's soul.

"You are just like the tools you use, Daedalus. Easy to break and replaceable."

It was like a knife cutting through Leo's heart. While he had given Minos everything, the other man saw him as nothing more than a useful idiot. Leo had been so hurt that he hadn't even pleaded his innocence. When he was thrown in prison, he refused to eat, couldn't sleep, and didn't speak a single word. He allowed his soul and body to wallow in despair.

Then, one day, a goddess appeared before him and told him she had heard his call.

Leo couldn't recall if he had actually cried out, but when she offered him a new life, he took it. He knew that he would have died in that cell if it hadn't been for Athena. She only asked him to become her devoted son in return. From that moment on, Leo learned to read people and promised never to open his heart to another.

Until Jason came along.

He wasn't in love with Jason, at least not yet, but he knew deep down that Jason would never hurt him. Unlike Minos, Jason was transparent. His heart was honest and open. That was why Leo had no regrets about asking Jason to marry him so quickly. It was why he wanted to spend every waking moment by his side and allow himself to fall in love at his own pace.

Leo studied Minos for a moment and realized the man was speaking, but he hadn't heard a word. Once his mind turned to Jason, nothing and no one else existed.

"You look good, Dae," Minos said with a soft smile, his voice almost nostalgic. "I know I hurt you in the past, and even though it was so long ago, I have an explanation."

Leo didn't want to hear it. He didn't want apologies, or excuses, or anything from the man who had once shattered him. Without saying a word, he stood, adjusted his suit jacket with slow precision, and turned away.

"I'm moving to Valleywood," Minos added, his tone casual as if it were just another update between old acquaintances.

Leo didn't flinch. His steps remained even as he walked toward the elevator. If Minos expected a reaction, he wouldn't get one. Not anymore.

When the elevator doors slid open, Leo silently thanked every god in existence. He stepped inside, scanned his room key, and waited. Only when the doors shut firmly and the elevator began to move did he finally exhale, his breath releasing slowly, like a weight dropping from his chest.

"Let me get this right. You've been married for almost two months, and you're just now telling me?" Tracy asked, his brows lifted in disbelief.

Jason nodded as he stuffed a fry in his mouth. He had taken the afternoon off to have lunch and go shopping with his best friend, who had just returned from a business trip. The first thing Tracy noticed was the ring on Jason's finger. Tracy worked for Valleywood PD as a training officer and missed nothing.

"Who is it? Is it the little ones' father? Did you find him?" Tracy asked, his voice sharp with curiosity. "And why the secrecy? The last time I checked, you weren't seeing anyone. Or is that another secret you're keeping from me?"

Jason had expected this. When he decided to tell Tracy about his marriage to Leo, he knew there would be a flood of questions, and rightfully so. Tracy knew him well, knew he wasn't the type to do anything impulsively. He took time with every decision, sometimes days or even months, weighing all outcomes. But with Leo, it had only taken hours.

"No, it's not the kids' father. I told you I don't want to find him. He's living his life, and I'm doing the same with mine. Keeping our marriage a secret was my idea. And before I tell you who it is, you have to promise not to overreact or draw attention to us."

"Now you have me worried," Tracy said, leaning in to whisper. "He's not the head of the mafia, right?"

Jason scoffed and shook his head. "That's where your mind goes?"

"Well, what am I supposed to think?" Tracy huffed in defense. Then his eyes widened. "Wait. Is he a celebrity? Who is it? Is it Dio or Rheon? I'll be pissed if you're married to one of my crushes."

Jason chuckled, amused despite himself. "No, it's not one of your crushes."

Still, he couldn't deny that Leo was indeed a celebrity. And he kicked himself for not realizing it sooner. Ever since they got married, Leo's face had been everywhere. Magazines. Television. Billboards. Leo had even been named Valleywood's sexiest man alive.

Jason couldn't believe he hadn't recognized just how influential Leo really was. He had seen countless videos of Leo at parties and movie premieres, either alone or on the arm of some stunning date, mingling effortlessly with the Hollywood elite. It made Jason wonder if he'd ever be ready for that kind of world. A part of him felt jealous watching Leo be so effortlessly charming, sweet, and public with others. But he had to remind himself those moments were in the past. That was before he entered the picture.

Their marriage was supposed to last one year. That was the deal. And as patient as Leo had been, Jason doubted he would want to keep it all under wraps for that long. Still, Jason couldn't deny the quiet fear inside him, the part that didn't want it to end at all.

"So who is he?" Tracy asked again, nudging Jason's arm.

Jason leaned in closer, ready to share his secret, but before he could say the name, an image on the restaurant's television caught his attention. There, on the screen, was Leo standing beside Armand Dracul.

Jason reached out, turned his friend's head toward the screen, and whispered, "Him."

"The President," Tracy gasped, his voice rising with disbelief. "But he's married."

Jason rolled his eyes and pointed toward the screen. "No. The handsome one stepping up to the podium with the sexy-as-fuck smile," he said softly, shaking his head.

Tracy turned to stare, eyes widening with realization. "Wait, that's L—"

Jason quickly covered Tracy's mouth with his hand before he could blurt out Leo's name. He could feel his friend buzzing with excitement, practically ready to stand on the table and shout.

"I have so many questions," Tracy said once Jason

lowered his hand. "Like, how did you two meet? Is he good in bed? Does he have an eight-pack? Do you love him? Was it love at first sight? Is he good in bed?"

"You asked one question twice," Jason pointed out with a laugh.

"Because it's important enough to ask twice. Now, come on. Answer it."

Jason smiled and leaned back. "First, I won't answer all of your questions because there are some things I don't know yet."

"Fine," Tracy said with a dramatic sigh. "Just tell me what you can."

"Alright. We met because of Xander. Remember I told you about the asshole at the airport?"

Tracy blinked, then his mouth dropped open as it clicked.

"Don't tell me that guy was..." He pointed subtly toward the screen. Jason nodded. "Yeah, it was him."

"Oh, that must've been weird when you met again," Tracy said, already grinning.

He sipped his drink and told Tracy what happened during his and Leo's second meeting and what quickly led to their marriage. He also stressed that he was worried about meeting Leo's mother and how close they had gotten, even though they had only been married for a few months. Leo's mom hadn't shown up. He was glad his friends didn't look at him any differently. Tracy, like Jason, wasn't one to hold his tongue, and since they'd been friends since college, there had been many tough talks where anyone listening would think they were trying to hurt each other's feelings.

"The kids love him," Jason said, his tone softening. "And the feeling is mutual. When he's home, they're attached to his hip."

"What about you?" Tracy asked, giving him a pointed look. "I'm sure you're attached to him too."

Jason hesitated for only a moment before nodding. "Even though we got married in a flash, I can't help but want to be. I know I shouldn't feel greedy for wanting his eyes and attention on me all the time... but I do."

I want him to do things to me that I'm afraid to ask for.

"I'm afraid to tell him I'm an unbound omega, but I'm sure he knows," Jason admitted, his voice low as he swirled the last of his drink with the straw.

"Why? Being an unbound is not a bad thing," Tracy said, leaning forward, his brow furrowed with confusion.

"I know, but my parents..."

"Fuck your parents," Tracy snapped, his voice sharp with anger. "I hate those bastards. I'm sick to death that they have this mental hold on you. Every time you mention them, I want to..."

"Alright, alright, don't get upset," Jason interrupted quickly, lifting his hands in a calming gesture. "Let's not talk about my parents. Fuck, forget I mentioned them."

Tracy narrowed his eyes but backed off. He knew everything about Jason's upbringing, had witnessed the verbal abuse firsthand on more than one occasion. The topic always ignited something in him, something protective and fierce.

"Are you falling in love with him?" Tracy asked suddenly, shifting gears with a more thoughtful tone.

Jason's eyes drifted back to the restaurant's television screen, where Leo stood at the podium, addressing the press. He looked confident and at ease in the spotlight. Jason couldn't help but admire him. He knew why Leo had gone to Washington, and he respected him for it. Leo donated both time and money to help develop magical towns across the country. Although the word "magical" was never explicitly used in public statements, those within the magical community understood the signals.

Leo was wrapping up his meetings and would be back in Valleywood later tonight. Jason already felt the absence weighing on him. Sleeping without Leo beside him had been harder than expected. He missed the warmth of his arms and the comfort of waking up in his embrace. Their late-night phone calls were sweet but not nearly enough to make up for the physical closeness he had grown used to.

"By the look on your face, I'd say yes," Tracy said, interrupting his thoughts.

Jason blinked and turned to him. "What look?" "The look of love," Tracy replied with a knowing smile.

"I'm not sure we're there yet," Jason admitted, though the blush on his cheeks betrayed him.

Tracy sat quietly for a moment, his expression pensive. Jason could tell he was about to say something serious.

"Can I give you some advice, friend to friend?" Tracy asked.

"Have I ever stopped you?" Jason said, smirking softly.

"No, you haven't," Tracy replied with a grin. "So here

it is. Let go of your fear and embrace this new phase in your life. I can see you're stressing about how much money he has, even though you haven't said it out loud. Learn to live a little. If it wasn't for me, you wouldn't even have the twins."

"Do you have to remind me of that every time we talk?" Jason groaned.

"Yes, I do," Tracy said unapologetically. "I love my little ones, but Jason, seriously, it's okay to enjoy life. The world isn't going to fall apart just because you're happy. And be greedy, Jason. Don't hold yourself back. You have a fine-ass man at home who, I'm sure, has wrapped himself around your finger trying to get you to love him."

Jason looked down at the table, letting the words sink in. He couldn't deny that Tracy had a point.

"And for fuck's sake, tell the man you're an unbound. If you think he already knows, then spill it. It's not good to have secrets in your relationship, Jay, especially one as fragile as yours."

"I know," Jason murmured with a sigh, dragging his fingers over the rim of his glass.

"Okay, since we got that out of the way, answer my question. Is he good in bed? He looks like he has a big di—"

"Didn't you mention wanting to go shopping?" Jason said quickly, standing from the table and tossing a few bills down for the tip since Tracy was covering the meal.

"Don't you dare walk away from me! Jason Dupree, you get your ass back here and answer my question," Tracy shouted, his voice rising above the restaurant chatter.

Jason kept walking, a smile tugging at the corner of his mouth as he waved him off.

Whether Leo was good in bed or not, he had no intention of

spilling that secret. That was something sacred, something meant to stay between him and Leo. Always.

He would never kiss and tell.

CHAPTER II
LEO

In Washington

L eo sneezed just as he got into the car and paused, rubbing his nose with a puzzled look. Someone must be talking about him. The thought made him smile. It had to be Jason.

He leaned back against the seat, the last flashes from the press conference still buzzing in his ears. He had just wrapped things up with Armand and didn't bother sticking around for any meaningless chit-chat or back-patting. As soon as it was over, he made a beeline for the car and climbed in without a second glance.

"Airport. Now," he told Genice as he settled into the seat.

"Yes, sir," she replied, adjusting her earpiece and guiding them smoothly into traffic.

Leo glanced out the window, his smile deepening. The thought of going home stirred something in him. Not to an empty house or just a place with his name on the deed, but to something real. To Jason. To the twins.

A family.

It still amazed him how quickly things had changed, how, in such a short time, he had everything he had spent centuries longing for. A home. Love. Laughter. A future.

And it was waiting for him.

He grinned brighter, chest warm and full. He had a family now, one he never believed he'd get in this lifetime, and for once, he wasn't looking back.

A couple of hours later, Leo was getting off the plane. It didn't take long for him and Genice to take care of the formalities before they walked out of the airport.

"Take the next two days off," he told her, his tone warm but firm.

"Thank you, sir," Genice replied, giving a respectful nod.

Leo was about to say something else when small hands suddenly wrapped around his leg, and a wave of déjà vu washed over him.

"Papa!" came the cheerful voice.

Leo looked down, and this time, instead of Xander, it was Sera clinging to his leg.

"Little girl, I think you have the wrong person," Genice said gently, glancing between them.

"Nu-uh, this is my Papa," Sera insisted, lifting her chin with pride as she looked up at Leo. "Right, Papa?"

Leo smiled and gently unhooked her arm before scooping her up into his arms and planting a kiss on her cheek. "That's right," he said, ignoring Genice's shocked gasp. "What are you doing here? Where is your brother? Where is your daddy?"

"Xander is home with Mrs. Sing," she explained, then pointed across the terminal. "Daddy is over there dealing with the bad auntie."

"Bad auntie?" Leo repeated, frowning in confusion.

Sera pointed again, and this time, Leo spotted Jason standing a short distance away, locked in what appeared to be a heated argument with a woman Leo didn't recognize.

Without wasting a second, he strode toward them, Sera still perched on his hip, just in time to hear the woman hiss, "I knew you were a cheap slut. I bet you don't even know who the little bastard's father is."

"Who says he doesn't?" Leo growled, voice low and dangerous.

"Leo," Jason breathed, turning toward him. The look in his eyes was hurt and exhausted, and it made Leo's blood boil.

"Who the hell are you?" the woman demanded, eyes narrowing.

"None of your business, Willa," Jason snapped, stepping forward protectively.

The woman turned her attention to Leo, and after a

moment of scrutiny, realization dawned on her face like a slap.

"You're Leonides Devereux," she said, stunned. Her eyes flicked between him and Jason, filling with disbelief. "Why would someone of your status want someone like him? I doubt my brother is smart enough to keep your attention. Are you paying him to sleep with you?" *Brother.*

Leo now noticed the resemblance between Jason and his sister. They both had the same hair and eyes, but he was going to be biased and say Jason was the better-looking of the two.

Before he could say anything, a loud crack rang out, and Leo watched as Jason's sister cupped her cheek, eyes wide in disbelief.

"You fucking bastard," she snapped. "You hit me!"

"Why are you so damn surprised?" Jason bit out. "Isn't that how we were brought up? A hit for every insult spoken." He stepped closer to her, his voice rising with each word, causing her to stumble back, though she didn't fall. "A punch for every wrong answer, a kick for every fight lost, an arm broken, a leg, for every infraction, there must be pain! But it wasn't you or Ian who had their bones constantly broken. I was in the hospital so much it was a wonder I graduated from high school or was able to do the job I love. For all the shit you bastards put me through, a slap doesn't cover it."

"Watch yourself, Jason," she hissed, her eyes narrowing.

"Or what?" Jason shot back. "What will you do to me that you haven't already done?"

"I can still ruin you," she said, her gaze flicking to Leo as if expecting backup.

Jason laughed, loud and unrestrained. Leo, standing silently beside him, felt a surge of pride and protectiveness. This fire in Jason reminded him of their first encounter. He was bold, sharp, and unrelenting. A part of him wished he could see those blazing eyes now, but Jason had his back to him.

"Try it, Willa. I'm not the weak kid who sat by and let you and Ian beat and insult me because I wanted you to like me. The man standing in front of you is not the old Jason. Valleywood is a big city, so I'd advise you and your family to stay the hell away from me and mine. Put yourself in front of me again, and every bit of dirt I have on you will be front-page news. And trust me, it could bring down that sweet little life you're so used to living."

Jason stepped beside Leo, who immediately wrapped a steadying hand around his shoulder. Jason was trembling, and Leo could feel it in the tension of his body. He hoped the gesture grounded him.

"Now, you have the fucking day you deserve," Jason said coldly.

Leo shot Willa one last look before turning with Jason. He already planned to have Talos investigate the entire family. Jason rarely spoke about them, and now Leo fully understood why. His baby had been hurt deeply, and anyone who broke someone he cared for would pay dearly.

When they reached the car, Leo gently set Sera down. Jason knelt in front of her, his voice soft.

"I'm sorry, baby. I didn't mean to scare you or use such bad words," he said, pulling her close.

"It's okay, Daddy. That bad auntie was rude," Sera said, hugging him and patting his back like she was the one comforting him.

Jason leaned back and pressed a kiss to her forehead. He helped her into the car and buckled her into her seat before turning back to Leo. His voice dropped to a whisper.

"That's not how I wanted to surprise you," he said, eyes cast downward. "I'm sorry you had to witness that." *Don't hide from me, Moró.*

Leo cupped Jason's cheek, raising his face to meet his gaze.

"Thank you. I'd rather see you than Talos."

"You mean that?"

Leo leaned in and kissed him softly. "I do." He kissed him again, wrapping him in his arms, holding him close. He would have continued if a certain little girl hadn't spoken up, making them pull apart quickly.

She was watching them between her parted fingers, pretending she had covered her eyes.

"Papa and Daddy kissing, ew."

Jason and Leo both chuckled, the tension between them easing as the moment shifted.

"I know you have questions," Jason said, his voice quieter now. "I'm not ready to talk about it."

Leo pressed their foreheads together, gently touching him. "I will be here whenever you're ready," he murmured. "I won't run, no matter what you tell me. I know it might be too soon, but..."

He didn't get to finish the thought because Jason placed a hand over his mouth.

"Don't say it yet. Not yet."

Leo gently removed Jason's hand from his lips, his tone steady. "I have to so that you have no doubts about where I want this to go. I don't want one year anymore, Jason. It's not enough for me." He stared deep into Jason's trembling eyes. "I want forever. I won't force you, but if you want to walk away right now... I don't think I can let you go."

They stood there in silence, the world quiet around them, caught in each other's gaze until Jason finally spoke.

"I'm not perfect," he said softly.

"I know," Leo replied. "I make mistakes, too."

"I'm not rich."

"Everything I own is yours."

"I'm an unbound omega," Jason confessed, biting his bottom lip like he was bracing himself for heartbreak.

"I want you even more," Leo said without hesitation.

"What if you meet your fated mate?" Jason asked.

"Who else would be more destined for me than you?" Leo responded, unwavering.

"Then don't let me go," Jason whispered.

"Never."

Leo held Jason in his arms for a few minutes longer. It wasn't what he'd expected when he got back home, but he wasn't complaining. It wasn't an outright admission of love, but it was something just as meaningful, something real.

IN THE AIRPORT'S private lounge, a figure leaned against the window, a cocktail glass in hand, watching the two men embrace on the private runway. Anger and jealousy surged inside him. The glass in his hand shattered, shards slicing into his skin as liquid spilled across his fingers, clothes, and the floor. He didn't flinch. Instead, his fingers curled into a tight fist, grinding the splinters deeper into his palm as he stared, unblinking, at the scene below.

You can only be mine, Daedalus. I've given you enough time and space now it's time to come back to me.

"Oh my gods, are you okay?"

He looked up when a beautiful woman touched his bleeding hand.

"Um," Minos muttered, watching as the beauty with dark hair and enchanting gray eyes wrapped his bloody hand in a napkin.

"You should get this looked at. You don't want your hand to get infected."

"I will. Thank you," Minos replied, though he wasn't worried. His hand would heal in a few minutes.

He observed her as she brushed a lock of hair behind her ear, her gaze shifting out the window. She scowled.

Minos followed her line of sight and saw Daedalus and his companion parting ways, each getting into their car.

A sharp tsk drew his attention back to the woman.

"Do you know them?" Minos asked.

"Sadly, I do. I bet he's just playing him to be his fuck boy," she grumbled, her lips curling in irritation.

"I'm not following."

The young woman shook her head. "It's a family problem I don't want to discuss."

"I know we just met, but I can listen while I wait for my ride," he said, offering her a charming smile as he watched her cheeks flush.

She sighed and turned her gaze back to the window, eyes trailing the car as it pulled away.

"I'm not sure telling a stranger my family problems is a good idea."

"Then how about we change that?" He extended the hand that wasn't injured. "I'm Elias."

She hesitated for a few seconds before sliding her hand into his. "Willa."

"It's nice to meet you, Willa. Now that we know each other, how about you tell me what's bothering you?"

"Not yet," she replied, sidling up to him with a teasing glint in her eye. "You haven't bought me a drink yet. And since I have a couple of hours before my plane takes off, I think I can fit at least two in."

What a nuisance, he thought, but instead, he smiled smoothly. "What's your pleasure, my lady?"

JASON SIGHED as the hot water cascaded down his body, soaking into his skin and relaxing his tight muscles. He pressed his forehead to the marble tile, breathing deeply, trying to calm the fire rippling under his skin. He couldn't say it was unexpected, but his heat was rising fast, and nothing was helping, not the shower, deep breaths, or even the distractions of the day.

And what a day it had been.

After shopping with Tracy, picking up the kids, and getting them settled, he had called Talos to say he'd grab Leo from the airport himself. Everything had been going fine until Willa showed up at the terminal like a ghost from his past, her words laced with venom. Jason had figured his family knew he was back in Valleywood, but clearly, their spies hadn't told them about the kids. If Jason could go his entire life without seeing any of them again, it would be a fucking blessing.

But after the disaster at the airport, they'd finally said what needed to be said. And ever since they had returned home, Jason had been fighting the urge to shove the kids aside and throw himself at Leo like a man starved.

"Gods, I'm jealous of my own kids," he muttered with a soft chuckle.

"What's so funny?" came the familiar, deep voice behind him.

Jason glanced over his shoulder and smiled as Leo stepped into the shower, the space easily fitting them both.

"Are the kids in bed?"

Leo circled his arms around Jason's waist and buried his face against his slick neck. "Yeah," he murmured against Jason's heated and sensitive skin, which was getting hotter with every touch. "Three stories later, they finally passed out."

Jason tilted his head, giving him better access. "They missed you."

Leo lifted his head and turned Jason's face by the chin, his blue eyes glowing with warmth and hunger. "What about you? Did you miss me?"

Jason's voice dropped to a low whisper. "Do you really need me to answer that?"

Leo smirked. "Yes."

Jason turned and circled his arms around Leo's neck, then licked a slow line up Leo's Adam's apple and grazed it with his teeth. Leo shivered visibly, groaning when Jason repeated the action until he was breathless, pulling Jason's head back by the hair.

"You know what you're doing?"

Jason raised a challenging brow. "I wouldn't start something I couldn't finish."

"Remember you said that."

Leo picked Jason up with one hand under his knee, and Jason tightened his hold on the taller man. With his free hand, Leo shut off the faucet and, with no hesitation, carried him to the bed. He tossed him onto the mattress, and the air left Jason's lungs with a gasp. The show of dominance lit his nerves on fire.

Jason crawled to his knees, running his palms over Leo's wet abs, then up to his broad chest, never breaking eye contact. Leo cupped the back of his neck, his fingers drifting over his knot at Jason's nape. The touch sent a pulse through Jason's core, his cock hardening instantly.

He moaned as Leo pressed the tip of his thick cock against Jason's lips. "Make me hard," Leo ordered, his voice like silk wrapped in steel.

Jason hesitated only a second, his eyes dropping to the semierect length in front of him, licking his lips. Until Leo, he'd never sucked a man's cock before, and with his husband's guidance, he had learned what Leo liked, but that didn't mean there wasn't room for improvement. The truth was, Jason loved feeling Leo's thick, hot, long cock moving between his lips, now being caressed by Leo's thumb.

"I love your pretty mouth."

Jason didn't say anything and leaned forward, kissing the head of Leo's cock. His husband moaned, holding the back of his head with one hand and grasping his shaft with the other, tapping the tip lightly against Jason's parted lips, smearing precum on his jaw and mouth before sliding it inside just enough to wet it. The contact drew a groan from them both. Leo continued to tease and stimulate Jason's overheated senses, making him whimper with need at each slide of his cock, brushing the back of his throat.

"Fuck," Leo groaned, and Jason looked up at him, enjoying his lover's reaction. "Baby, shit, your mouth..." He bit on his bottom lip as if stopping himself from saying too much, but he couldn't hold back. "Feels so good."

Jason preened with pride and began to move slowly, deliberately, alternating between gentle strokes and hollowing his cheeks as he sucked Leo deeper. He closed his eyes and slackened his jaw, breathing through his nose, letting spit drip and coat Leo's cock until it gleamed. Leo's hands threaded through his hair, guiding him, rolling his hips forward, pushing deeper until Jason gagged and his eyes watered.

"That's it," Leo growled. "Lick my balls."

Jason obeyed instantly, massaging Leo's balls while continuing to suck, then licking his shaft before dragging and swirling his tongue down and taking Leo's balls into his mouth. He moaned around them, and Leo's entire body jerked in response. Jason grasped Leo's cock, massaging it from the root to the tip while rolling his balls on his tongue.

"Fuck," Leo hissed, his nails digging into Jason's neck, pressing into his knot. The touch sent Jason's body into overdrive. His cock twitched, desperate for attention, but he refused to touch himself.

He didn't want to come yet.

He wanted Leo to hear him scream his name as he exploded in his mouth.

Jason released Leo's balls, kissing his legs, moving to his pelvis, then the root of his cock, and finally the head to pull it back into his mouth. But Leo pulled him back by the hair. Jason blinked, dazed, lips swollen, eyes half-lidded.

Leo cupped his cheek, brushing a thumb across his mouth. "Do you know how sexy you look right now?"

Jason's gaze dropped to Leo's cock, wet and flushed from his mouth. He wanted it inside him. Not his mouth, but his body.

"Want to suck me more?" Leo asked, already knowing the answer.

Jason shook his head.

"Then what do you want?" Leo pressed.

Jason didn't speak, too turned on to form words.

"I won't give you what you want unless you ask," Leo murmured, his fingers pressing into the knot at the back of Jason's neck, making Jason whimper and grow even hotter. "Tell me."

Jason swallowed hard. "Fuck me."

"Why?"

He hesitated. He couldn't admit it; he couldn't say he was in heat because he skipped his suppressants or that he planned this.

He wanted to feel Leo pounding deep and hard inside of him, taking him and putting his mark on him. As an unbound, it shouldn't be something he wanted or needed, but with Leo, he craved it with every ounce of his being. That was why he had forced himself into heat. He couldn't wait anymore. He didn't want to tell Leo that even with their earlier promise, he was afraid the man could leave him after their year was up. He needed to find a way to keep Leo devoted to him. Jason wasn't normally the scheming type, but he wouldn't be upset if he got pregnant with Leo's child.

"Talk to me," Leo said, low and demanding, squeezing his neck.

Jason choked on a whimper. "Please. I'll do anything you want."

Leo smirked. "Then call me Husband."

Jason crawled up, brushing kisses along Leo's chest, stopping at his throat to speak against his skin. "Husband... make me yours."

Leo growled, tightened his grip on Jason's hair, and

pulled his head back. The look in his eyes made Jason's breath hitch. "Say it again."

"My husband, I want you to fuck me," he whispered.

Leo slammed their mouths together, kissing Jason like he needed to consume him. He laid him back on the bed with his weight on top. Tongues tangled, teeth clashed. Jason wrapped his legs around Leo's waist, grinding against him as their cocks pressed and rubbed together, their slick precum making it all hotter, messier, and needier.

Their moans filled the room, feral and desperate.

Jason gasped as Leo peppered kisses down his throat, biting and sucking his way to his nipples. He licked and teased each one until Jason was trembling. Then a finger pressed into him, slow and sure, and Jason cried out.

His knot throbbed, and the heat flared even higher, making him want more.

Fuck, this man is going to turn me into a love addict, and I have no regrets.

CHAPTER 12

LEO

The air was thick with consuming need. Their pheromones were sweet, heady, and filled with an intoxicating blend. The scent clung to Leo's body, seeping into every breath. Their bond was still fresh, but their life and soul threads pulsed like a live wire. He could feel it thrumming under his skin, breathing life into him. He could not resist the pull and wanted to bite and claim Jason.

He liked how Jason's skin flushed, glowing with need, his pupils blown wide as he writhed beneath Leo's touch. He looked drugged, so drunk on lust it made it easy for Leo to slip another finger into his slick hole, moving it with care before beginning to scissor him open. He added a third, and Jason moaned, a sweet, broken sound that spilled from his throat.

Leo captured his swollen lips in a bruising kiss, then dragged his mouth down to lick the sweat clinging to the curve of Jason's throat. Jason arched, desperate for every brush of Leo's fingers, every teasing scrape of teeth. Leo could feel Jason's pulse thrum against his tongue. He listened to the breathy pants and the moans that poured out of him and felt sharp nails digging into his back.

Jason dragged those wicked digits down his spine, scoring red lines into his skin. The scent of blood mingled with their pheromones, making Leo feel wild, feral, unrestrained, and so fucking hungry for more.

"Please," Jason whispered, his voice wrecked and trembling. "I need you."

Leo groaned low in response, the sound vibrating between them like a promise. One hand tangled in Jason's dark hair, tugging his head back to expose the vulnerable length of his neck. The marks on Jason's skin screamed taken and claimed, but the dominant in Leo wasn't satisfied. He wanted every part of Jason to belong to him.

"Who do you belong to?" Leo rasped, his lips brushing against Jason's skin as his tongue flicked out to taste the salt and heat.

"I'm yours," Jason whispered, breath hitching. "Tie me to you and never let me go."

Leo growled and captured Jason's sweet mouth in a hungry kiss. He slowly withdrew his fingers, then grasped his shaft and pressed the head against Jason's hole before easing it inside. A moan tore from their joined lips. Leo didn't move right away. He wanted Jason to have a moment to adjust to his girth. He kept kissing him, their tongues tangling, bodies flush, breath hot and ragged as they melted into each other.

When he felt Jason's muscles loosen around him, Leo pulled back slightly and pushed in deeper, feeding more of his cock inside. Jason groaned, his body yielding, opening for him without hesitation. Leo sank in fully, pelvis flush against Jason's ass. He gripped Jason's waist and began to move, fucking him with slow, deliberate thrusts that pulsed with tenderness and heat.

"So hot," Jason whispered, "...burning up."

Leo groaned, low and hard. He buried his face in Jason's neck, biting and sucking the slick skin as he ground into him, driving deep.

"Fuck, so good," Leo moaned, his voice thick with need.

"Husband, please," Jason whimpered. "Need more."

Leo knew exactly what he wanted. He was trying to be gentle, remembering the last time they had sex and how rough he'd been. But it was a fucking challenge. His little husband felt so good, so hot inside, it took everything in him not to lose control.

"I'm trying to be gentle, baby," he murmured against Jason's ear.

"Who asked you to be?" Jason snapped, nails digging into Leo's back.

Leo lifted his head and crushed their mouths together in a bruising kiss. "Remember your words."

Before Jason could respond, Leo withdrew and

flipped him onto his side, facing away. One hand slipped beneath him to hold his chest, the other lifting his leg. In a swift, fluid motion, Leo thrust back into him with a snarl of pure, raw need. He pressed forward until Jason's back was flush against his chest, their bodies locked tight. He could feel Jason's heartbeat pounding through his skin, steady and frantic beneath his palm.

His thrusts were slow but relentless, each one caressing Jason's prostate with careful, deliberate precision. Jason whimpered with pleasure, incapable of forming any complaints. His body trembled against Leo as the pace deepened. The bed rocked beneath them, keeping rhythm with their pleasure, while the room filled with the sound of desperate cries.

"Fuck me, Husband... yes, right there," Jason babbled, his voice wrecked with need. "Make me yours. Make me cum."

Leo buried his face in the curve of Jason's neck, biting down on the beauty mark he loved, letting the scent of his mate flood his senses and stoke the fire already burning in his blood. He dragged his tongue over the knot pulsing just beneath Jason's skin. His hand found Jason's cock, jerking it in perfect sync with every thrust. Their bodies moved in tandem, the friction and heat wrapping around him like a drug. The string of fate binding them stretched tight. The pressure coiled deep inside him, ready to snap.

"Cum, baby, cum for me," he ordered, voice thick and raw.

Jason cried out his name and spilled into Leo's hand. His body clenched, walls tightening around Leo's cock.

But Leo didn't stop. He kept thrusting, kept jerking him off, using his little omega's cum as lube to stroke him deeper.

When he felt the swell of his knot beginning to form, he grazed his teeth across Jason's trembling knot and then sank them into the salty flesh. Jason came a second time, shuddering, crying out as Leo followed, spilling inside him, knotting them together and sealing their bond forever.

If Leo had been sensible, this wouldn't have happened. Jason was an unbound. But that was a matter for another time.

Right now, all Leo wanted was to fuck his man again and claim him as many times as Jason's body and the night would allow.

THE FOLLOWING MORNING, Jason groaned and rolled over in bed. The dull ache in his waist felt familiar, like the morning he woke up five years ago. He reached over to the other side of the bed and found it empty.

Slowly, he opened his eyes and realized something was stuck to his face. Reaching up, he pulled it off and stared in confusion when he saw it was a twenty-dollar bill with something written on it.

Return to sender.

"What the hell does that mean?"

"You're awake."

Jason looked up and saw Leo entering the bedroom, carrying a tray. His bathrobe hung open, and Jason could see every bite mark and hickey he'd left on his lover, from his neck down to his chest and stomach.

Jason's face burned with heat as the memories came rushing back. He'd taken Tracy's advice and let go, letting himself enjoy the moment without overthinking. The proof of that decision was now scattered across Leo's skin. But it still didn't explain the money.

Then it hit him.

He had once told Leo that the twins' father left him a twenty dollar tip after sex like it had been transactional. That had been a lie. The truth was, the guy had rocked his world and then some, but Jason hadn't been able to admit that to Leo.

Now he sat there, staring, heart thudding in his chest.

Was Leo trying to tell him he wasn't good in bed?

"Are you saying I'm bad in bed?" Jason asked, his voice low and direct. He didn't want to say it out loud, but a small part of him ached at the idea that he might not have pleased his husband.

Leo stepped into the room, nudged the bedroom door shut with a gentle kick, and carried the tray to the bed. He set it down and sat beside Jason, eyes steady.

"Far from it," he said, his voice low and sincere. "You are the antidote I've been searching five years for."

Jason frowned, clearly confused. "What? What are you talking about?"

Leo smiled, the expression soft but weighted with something deeper. "Five years ago, I was at the Luxe Horizon Hotel celebrating with a couple of my friends.

While I wasn't paying attention, someone drugged my drink with an aphrodisiac."

His fingers brushed lightly against Jason's knee as he continued, "I got out of there before the drug could fully kick in. I told Talos to call for an escort. It was a fucking struggle just to make it to my room, but then, out of nowhere, this beauty with gray eyes

bumped into me just as I opened my door."

Jason blinked, his mouth parting in surprise. Leo leaned in slightly, his tone growing rougher. "Long story short, we spent the entire night fucking. And when I woke up the next morning, he was gone. All that was left was his scent and this twenty-dollar bill on my face."

Jason stared at him, the weight of Leo's words sinking in. "That night... it was you?"

"Yeah," Leo said, his voice low. "I spent the past five years looking for you. Not because I wanted to relive what we did, but because there was blood on the sheets." He cupped Jason's cheeks gently, his eyes serious. "It killed me to think I might have hurt you."

"No, you didn't hurt me," Jason replied quickly, and Leo immediately pulled him into his arms.

"Then why was there blood on the sheets?" Leo asked, his brows drawing together in concern.

Jason groaned, shifting uncomfortably. "I don't want to talk about it."

Leo leaned back slightly, but he didn't let go. "Did I take your virginity?"

"Not really," Jason admitted, avoiding his gaze. "The last person I'd had sex with was on prom night... and let's just say he wasn't... you get what I mean."

Leo smirked, and Jason immediately wanted to pinch the grin right off his face.

"No, I don't know what you mean. Break it down for me, sweetheart. Stroke my ego."

"Didn't I do that last night?" Jason shot back, raising a brow.

"I'm greedy for more. Besides, I seem to remember someone saying they would never fuck me, even if I were the last man on Earth."

"Oh my gods, did you have to bring that up?" Jason groaned, burying his face in Leo's muscled chest and muttering against his skin. "The guy wasn't as endowed as you are."

"What was that? I didn't hear you."

Jason looked up at his husband with a scowl. "He didn't have a big dick, alright? Did that make you happy?"

"Yes. Yes, it did," Leo said with a grin that only grew wider. "So,

I guess I did take your virginity that night." "Asshole," Jason grumbled. "All I hear is that I have a big dick." *Cocky bastard.*

"Wait." Jason suddenly pushed Leo back and stared at him, his expression shifting. "How long have you known it was you I spent the night with? And... that means you're the twins' father?"

"I've known for a couple of weeks," Leo admitted, his voice quieting as his expression turned sheepish. He looked just like one of the twins when they got caught doing something they knew was wrong. Jason might have found it cute if he wasn't feeling so upset.

"You kept something that important from me? Why, Leo?"

"In my defense," Leo said, raising his hands slightly, "you said you didn't want to know. And you said I wasn't good in bed."

"That's your reason for not telling me?" Jason snapped, eyes narrowing.

"No, I just..." Leo sighed, the bravado slipping from his voice. "I wanted to be sure before I told you."

Jason heard what Leo said, but what kept looping through his mind was that Leo had known he was the kids' father for weeks and had still chosen not to tell him. He didn't know if he was overreacting, but he knew one thing. He needed space to think.

Pushing the covers back, he climbed out of bed.

"I need to get ready for work," he muttered, not looking back.

"I thought you were taking the day off to spend it with me," Leo said, his voice quiet. Jason could hear the sadness behind it.

"I need to be away from you right now," Jason replied, each word clipped with frustration.

Before he could walk away, Leo's arms wrapped around his waist and held him still.

"I get that you're upset with me," Leo said gently, refusing to let go. "And you have every right to be. But don't shut me out, Jason. I..."

He turned Jason around to face him.

"Don't hide from me," he continued, his voice thick with emotion. "I'd rather you yell, scream, even hit me than pretend like I'm not here. I should have told you the second I suspected the twins were mine. But I was scared. You were so resistant to the idea of finding their father. And you didn't even know where we stood yet."

Jason looked at him, his brows drawing together.

"So when you said you wanted to be sure," he said quietly, "it wasn't just about the twins. It was about us."

"Yes."

Jason sighed, and the edge of his anger began to fade. He understood where Leo was coming from. He had also held back from telling Leo that he was an unbound omega, and Leo had taken that in stride. Jason reasoned that he should do the same with this, but not without setting some conditions.

"No more secrets, Leo," Jason said firmly.

Leo sighed. "There are some things I need to tell you, but now... or today... isn't the right time."

"You promise?" Jason asked, eyes narrowing slightly.

"I do," Leo replied with a small smile. "So, does this mean you forgive me?"

"I feel like I'm going easy on you for this. I should let you suffer a bit, but I find your puppy-dog looks hard to resist."

"That's because I'm irresistible," Leo said smugly. He leaned in and brushed their lips together. "And admit it. I'm great in bed."

Jason smirked. "Hmm... you're not bad."

"Not bad?" Leo's brows shot up. "Do I need to remind you who was chanting, 'Husband, please let me cum, don't stop,' right th—"

"Alright, alright," Jason cut in quickly. "No need to give a replay of what happened last night."

"I feel like we should, just so I can get a higher score," Leo teased.

He scooped Jason into his arms, making him shriek in surprise. Just as Leo was about to toss him onto the bed, a knock came at the bedroom door.

"Daddy and Papa, are you two playing?" Xander called from the hallway. "I wanna play too!"

Jason's eyes widened in horror as the door handle began to turn. He was still completely naked, and the last thing he needed was his curious child walking in and asking questions he definitely wasn't ready to answer.

"Put me down," Jason hissed, pushing at Leo's shoulder.

Leo growled low in his throat but pressed a quick, heated kiss to Jason's lips before setting him down.

"Go before the kid comes in and sees you," Leo warned, grinning. "I'll rock your world again tonight."

"You promise?"

"That's one promise I will never break," Leo said, voice full of certainty.

Jason chuckled and rushed toward the bathroom.

Leo shook his head and turned just as Xander opened the bedroom door and peeked inside.

"Papa, where's Daddy?" Xander asked, his eyes wide as he looked around the room.

"He's taking a shower," Leo replied, scooping him into his arms without hesitation. Now that Jason knew the twins were his, Leo finally felt like he could relax a little more.

"Oh," Xander said softly, resting his head on Leo's shoulder.

"Did you finish the model you were working on?" Leo asked, rubbing gentle circles on Xander's back.

Xander shook his head and pouted, his lips pushing out in that exaggerated way that always made Leo want to laugh.

"Is it giving you problems?" Leo asked, tilting his head to catch his son's eyes.

Xander nodded slowly, his frown deepening.

"How about I give you a hand?" Leo offered with a small smile.

"Okay," Xander said, his voice barely above a whisper as his fingers curled into Leo's bathrobe.

Since Xander loved to draw and build things, Leo had invested in a wide range of model block kits, including homes, animals, and buildings. Some were a little advanced for his age, but with Xander's intellect and enough time, Leo was confident his son would figure them out. He always did.

Leo didn't just invest in real estate. Over the years, he had partnered with Avery to open a few restaurants. He also owned a couple of jewelry stores and boutiques and had invested in several expansion projects at Valleywood General. If everything went according to plan, he would soon own a law firm.

That law firm meant more to him than any other business venture. It was personal. It didn't talk about it much but there as a time he studied law and could even practice law in twenty-five states. He'd kept up with the law for a just in case he wanted to do something else for a while. A law degree wasn't the only thing he had, but he had degrees, certificates, and masteries in many different areas. Living for over three thousand years he couldn't do the same thing every day. He needed to change careers sometimes. But architecture was and will always be his first love.

When they reached the kids' bedroom, Sera was already seated at her desk, quiet and focused on her work. Her concentration was razor-sharp, and Leo didn't want to disturb her. He brought Xander over to his side of the room, where a half-assembled model lay on the table surrounded by tiny scattered pieces.

Leo helped him into his seat, then lowered himself onto the floor beside him. "Alright, little architect. Show me where it's giving you trouble."

Xander pointed with a dramatic sigh. "This piece won't fit, and the roof keeps falling."

Leo leaned in and inspected it closely. "That's because you need this support beam first. See?" He handed the correct piece to Xander, who accepted it with furrowed brows.

"Thanks, Papa," Xander said, already focused again. "You're kinda smart."

Leo chuckled. "Kinda? I'm hurt. I'm brilliant, thank you." "You're Papa-smart." Xander grinned.

Leo reached out and ruffled his hair, a fond smile tugging at his lips.

The kids shared a room, and although they each had their own little corners, Leo had been thinking about bringing it up to Jason. It was time to move to a bigger place where the twins could have their own rooms. The current setup worked, but only just.

A tall shelf divided the space, filled with books and personal touches that subtly marked the contrast between Sera's structured genius and Xander's wild imagination. Neutral walls and warm wood furniture gave the room a calm, upscale feel, but Leo couldn't help imagining how much more they could flourish with spaces of their own. Somewhere they could stretch out their brilliance and grow even more.

He also needed to talk to his little husband about enrolling the twins in kindergarten. They were ready. It was time they spent more time around kids their age instead of staying home all day with Mrs. Sing.

Granted, Mrs. Sing seemed like a lovely lady. But Leo had started to wonder if she truly wanted to spend her days babysitting. More than that, he was beginning to suspect something wasn't right, which left him uneasy.

Sometimes, she could recall a conversation they'd had word for word. Other times, she avoided eye contact or refused to speak, as if she were afraid of him. And just last night, the moment he and Jason walked into the apartment, she had practically run out the door like it was on fire. Maybe it wasn't an illness. Maybe she was hiding something.

Leo wasn't sure, but he figured it was time for the kids—and for Jason—to create some distance. He didn't want to wait too long and risk her becoming a danger to the children.

Just as Leo started thinking of ways to talk Jason into

moving, his cellphone vibrated in his pants pocket. Shifting to the side, he pulled it out and frowned when he saw an unfamiliar number on the screen.

He hesitated for a second before answering. "Who is this, and how did you get this number?"

"I have my ways," the person on the other end replied, and Leo instantly recognized the voice.

Minos.

"What the hell do you want?" he growled.

"Is that any way to talk to me after all we've been to each other?" the voice replied, a tinge of disappointment slipping through the smugness.

Leo stood and walked out of the kids' room. "Cut the shit. What the fuck do you want?"

"Have dinner with me?" Minos said with a soft sigh. "I have a business proposition for you."

Leo didn't respond. He hung up and blocked the number without a second thought.

What the fuck? Who the fuck does that bastard think he is? And how the fuck did he get my private number? Only friends and family have this number.

"Hey, who pissed you off?"

Leo looked up at the sound of Jason's voice.

"Who says I'm mad?" he asked, trying to play it off.

"If you frown any harder, your brows are going to get stuck together," Jason said, pressing a finger between Leo's eyes. His touch softened the tension instantly when he caught his husband's reluctant smile. "Tell me what happened. The kids didn't prank you again, right?"

"No. Just something from work," Leo lied smoothly. He knew it wasn't fair, but he wasn't ready to tell Jason about Minos. He had hoped never to mention that name again. But the past had a habit of clawing its way back. It never let him live in peace for long.

"Do you need to go into the office?"

"No. I told Talos to handle it."

He tried not to grin when he caught the slight twitch in Jason's brow at the mention of Talos's name.

"Oh," Jason said quietly, looking down.

Leo slid an arm around Jason's waist and pulled him in close. "You don't have to be jealous of Talos. He's not my type."

"Who says I'm jealous of him?" Jason muttered, still avoiding his eyes.

Certainly you, Leo thought, but instead said, "I think he's seeing someone."

Jason's head lifted immediately, his eyes lighting up. "Who?

How do you know?"

"I don't know who," Leo admitted. "But he can't hide the hickeys on his neck no matter how hard he tries."

"Really? Interesting. Well, there goes my plan." Jason tsked and shook his head.

Leo narrowed his eyes. "What plan?"

"Don't get mad, but I thought about setting him up with Ada. But now that I think about it, I remember seeing a hickey on her neck yesterday."

"You what?!" Leo stepped back and stared at him. "Why are you just now telling me this?"

Jason shrugged. "With everything that happened yesterday, it slipped my mind. What's the big deal? It's just a hickey. Maybe she's dating someone."

"My sister does not date," Leo snapped. "She will only date whom I deem worthy of her."

"Do you hear yourself? Ada is a grown-ass woman and can do whatever the fuck she wants!" Jason shouted back, his eyes narrowing.

"I won't argue with you about this," Leo said, his voice dropping into something firm and final.

"Who's arguing? I'm simply stating a fact. Ada is an adult. She's a badass boss, smart as fuck, rich, and gorgeous. Who wouldn't want to be with her?" Jason threw his hands up, his tone laced with disbelief.

"She's not ready for love," Leo insisted, his jaw tightening. He had seen what her last relationship had done to her. Granted, it had been over twenty years ago, but Leo refused to let her go through that kind of pain again.

"Who is?" Jason replied without hesitation. "Love is complicated, but it's a beautiful thing." He stepped in closer, wrapped his arms around Leo's waist, and rested his head against his chest. "And when we find it, we should hold on to it."

"I..." Leo faltered, completely caught off guard. He didn't know what to say. As much as he wanted to stay angry, the fire inside him fizzled out. Jason always knew how to disarm him with just a few soft-spoken truths. He could turn Leo inside out.

Fuck. Am I being tamed by my little husband?

Jason leaned up and gently kissed his neck, and the tension from their argument melted away.

Yeah. I'm putty in his hands, and I have no regrets.

CHAPTER 13

LEO

"The contract for Kyre Corporation is ready. It just needs signatures. Our lawyers have acquired the Stetson Law Firm."

Leo nodded. He listened as Talos went over the details, but his mind was elsewhere. Ada. Even though he'd talked to Jason about it a month ago, he still couldn't let it go. He needed to know who his sister was seeing.

"Good. Have Alexander and his people investigate all the firm's employees."

"Anything or anyone in particular he should pay attention to?" Talos asked, raising a brow.

"Why did you ask me that?" Leo shot back.

"I've worked for you a long time. Buying a law firm is out of the norm."

"Willa Dupree," Leo said, his voice sharp. "She's Jason's sister. Investigate the father as well. He's a partner in the firm."

"Okay."

Leo leaned forward. "I need you to investigate two people before you leave."

Talos paused, tilting his head. "Who are they?"

"Elias Crete. Find out what the hell he's doing in Valleywood."

"Alright," Talos replied, pulling out his phone to make a note.

"And the other?"

Leo's jaw tightened. "Ada is seeing someone."

Talos blinked. "How... how do you know she's seeing someone?"

Leo opened his eyes and fixed him with a glare. "Jason said he saw hickeys on her neck. Find the bastard who did it."

The pen in his hand snapped clean in half as his fingers clenched around it.

"Sir, don't you think we should stop scaring off her suitors? What if she finds out?"

"So what if she does?" Leo snapped. "I will not have some asshole break her heart."

"So you plan to find her a man that she might not even like," Talos shouted, frustration clear in his voice.

"Why are you getting upset about this? Just do what the fuck I pay you to do."

"Yes, sir," Talos said sharply before storming out of the office.

Leo stared after him, confusion tightening in his chest. What the hell had gotten into him? They'd fought before. That was one of the reasons Leo trusted him. Talos never hesitated to tell him when he was being an idiot, no matter the paycheck. But this was different. This was the first time Talos had paused before following a direct order.

He acts like he's the one dating her.

Leo pushed the thought aside. There was no way Talos would go behind his back like that. Not with Ada. Not when he knew how protective Leo was of her. Still, the doubt stuck with him, the same way it did whenever he thought about Loki and Odin. That nagging suspicion wouldn't let go.

From now on, Leo decided he would keep a close eye on the two of them.

Right now, though, he had a meeting to get to.

Since learning that Jason was an unbound omega, Leo had been searching for a doctor who could explain what that meant. He was on his way to the car in the parking garage, his phone in hand, blocking another unknown number like he had so many times before.

Then he collided with someone and froze the second he saw who it was.

Mya. He hadn't seen or heard from her since that day.

"Excuse me," she said softly, stepping around him as if she had no earthly idea who he was.

Leo was about to go after her but stopped himself. Maybe ignoring him or pretending she didn't recognize him was her way of letting go. If that was the case, he would respect it. They weren't the same people they had been a few months ago.

He turned and walked to his car, never noticing the soft eyes that lingered on him. She didn't look away until his car disappeared from view.

Leo had just sat down when Doctor Kevin Pace, entered the office. Kevin was a doctor of science who studied omegas and their development.

"Did I keep you waiting?" Kevin asked, offering a brief smile as he approached the desk.

"No, I just got here myself," Leo replied, adjusting his suit jacket as he met the other man's gaze.

"Good. Then let's get down to business. You said you were interested in finding out more about unbound omegas."

"Yes," Leo said with a nod. "I'll be upfront with you. I'm married to one, and even though he hasn't said much, he doesn't seem to know a lot about what being unbound actually means. He wears it like a stigma."

Doctor Pace smirked. "Probably had a traumatic experience or someone drilled into him that being unbound is taboo." He leaned forward, steepling his fingers. "Has he exhibited any abilities?"

"None that I know of."

"Then maybe it's hidden," Pace said thoughtfully. "Or maybe it's something he uses every day without realizing it."

That was when Leo remembered something Ada had told him. He explained it to Pace, recounting the strange detail.

"Are you saying they envision themselves in the drafts?" Kevin asked, his brow furrowed in confusion. Leo didn't blame him for being skeptical.

"Not exactly. According to my sister, it's more like she felt as if she were walking around inside the drafts."

Pace leaned back in his chair, his expression dazed. "It can't be."

Leo narrowed his eyes. "What are you thinking?"

Pace stared at him in silence for several long seconds. Just when Leo thought he wasn't going to respond, the doctor finally spoke.

"I might be wrong, but I think your husband is a dimension transporter."

"A what?"

"A dimension transporter. They're rarer than us unbound." "Wait, you're an unbound?" Leo asked, his eyebrows lifting.

"Yes, but that's beside the point. Your lover can create and move between dimensions. They're able to pull themselves into one or send others elsewhere, as long as they've been there before. Depending on certain factors, they could remain in a dimension for extended periods. Combined with his transporter ability, he could travel freely between dimensions and realms. In essence, his power is limitless if he learns to control it. I think your husband unknowingly creates dimensions and imprints them into his drafts. When others touch them, they're not just seeing themselves in the drafts. They're actually being transported inside. But if they're able to leave, it means he hasn't yet accessed his full potential. If he'd shown this ability as a child, we could've trained him to harness it. It's not too late, but it will be more difficult now. Do you understand what this means? Now that he's aware, it will be harder for him to control the urge to create or transport at will. With proper training, he could become the most powerful unbound—"

"Wait. Hold up," Leo said, lifting a hand to cut him off before the conversation turned into a scientific rant he couldn't follow. "I need to understand a few things first. Will understanding his ability hurt him?"

"No. Our abilities are our strengths, not weaknesses. The only ability every unbound has in common is healing, which we never discuss. We keep it quiet because we don't want to be used. So instead, we let the world believe only one unbound is born with that ability."

"And what's the weakness?" Leo asked, leaning in slightly.

"Falling in love."

"What?"

"Let me explain," Pace said calmly. "There's a reason unbounds are told not to mate. It's because mating with a human could kill them. Unbounds don't need to tie themselves to one person, but if they fall in love, they risk death. For example, if they're bonded to a normie, their life thread becomes connected to that person. And when that person dies, the unbound dies too. It's not like most omegas, who could find another alpha to mate with."

Leo's eyebrows pulled together. "But not needing a mate... wouldn't that make them less of a target?"

"You'd think so. But not having or needing a mate is exactly what makes unbound omegas highly valuable on the black market," Pace said grimly. "But we also crave the touch of others. You've probably noticed that the more attention you give to his knot, the easier he is to influence, especially during sex. Most alphas, and even some betas, don't want an unbound for love.

They want them for control."

"That's sickening," Leo growled, his voice low and tight.

"Very. But that's the world we live in. Our knot makes us strong but vulnerable at the same time."

"What if they're mated to a shifter?" Leo asked. He kept the word *immortal* to himself.

Pace snorted. "Name one alpha shifter who wants to be mated to an omega who might be stronger than them. It's not exactly a fantasy they dream about." His tone turned sarcastic. "Besides, an unbound finding a true mate is about as likely as meeting a god. People see the knot on the back of our necks as a defect. They don't understand that not all omegas are petite and cute. Some are just as big and muscular as an alpha."

Leo couldn't argue with that. He knew what the world expected from omegas, but this wasn't about changing the world. It was about understanding his little husband.

"You said his lifeline is connected to mine," Leo said, his voice quieter now.

"Yes, he'll live as long as you do, but only if you bite his knot. If not, then he could live for over a hundred years, depending on what his body can handle."

That was a weight off Leo's back. Since he was immortal, it meant he and Jason could share a long life together. It was just one more thing he would need to explain to his little lover.

"Do you have any information I can read on transporters?" Leo asked.

"There is some," Pace replied, rubbing his jaw. "But it'll take me some time to dig it up. Can I meet your husband?"

"Let me talk to him first," Leo said, keeping his tone even. "Like I mentioned, I doubt he realizes he has any abilities."

"Maybe that's for the best," Pace said, nodding slowly. "If people knew what he could do, they might come after him. Not just for his power, but for what he could offer as a lover."

"Who would dare?" Leo growled, his voice dropping with menace.

"Then protect him," Pace said, his gaze steady. "Make sure he knows how important he is to you. Tell him not to listen to anyone who doesn't know shit. Like I said, transporters are rare. Just imagine being able to travel through this world and into other dimensions and realms. And if his abilities are developed the right way, he could trap people and objects in a dimensional space. He could keep them there forever or release them whenever he wants."

Leo took in everything the doctor had said. He stood, adjusted his suit jacket, and was about to leave when he stopped.

"Would I be imposing if I asked what your abilities are?"

"No," the doctor replied and snapped his fingers,

producing a small flame in his palm. "Not glamorous, but I think it's cool as hell. Pun intended."

Leo chuckled. "One more thing. This conversation stays between us."

"I'm not in the business of outing other unbounds."

"Thank you," Leo said, then left the doctor's office with only one thing on his mind. He needed to see his husband.

JASON WAS LEANING over a drafting table, making changes to a project Ada had requested. They were scheduled to meet with the client later that day, and if the revisions weren't made in time, he knew he wouldn't hear the end of it. Since the design was for a smart house, Jason had to adjust the layout to better accommodate the upgraded automation system the client wanted.

The home had all the charm and elegance of a restored Victorian, complete with ornate crown molding, carved wood archways, and stained-glass accents. But behind the walls, everything was state-of-the-art. He shifted the wiring closet for easier access, reworked the wall spacing to include hidden panels, and adjusted the kitchen island to integrate the voice-activated system seamlessly.

"I think you should move the control panel here," said a deep, familiar voice, warm breath brushing the outer shell of Jason's ear. A finger traced the wall between the kitchen and dining room without touching the paper.

"You think?" Jason glanced at Leo, then back at the blueprint.

"This client is particular. I don't want to mess it up."

"Do you trust me?"

"Always," Jason replied, locking eyes with his husband.

"Then trust me on this. Your client wants it to be easily accessible, but they don't want it completely hidden. Think of my secret room."

Jason immediately pictured the panel that opened the entrance to Leo's treasure room. It wasn't hidden, not really. It blended perfectly with the decor. Jason hadn't even known it was there until Leo placed his hand on the exact spot. He nodded in agreement, made a quick note on the blueprint, then turned to face Leo.

"What are you doing here?"

"Can't a man come see his husband?" Leo asked with a faint smirk.

"Sh... shh..." Jason pressed a finger to his lips. "Don't say that too loud. These guys have bionic hearing."

He glanced around, checking to see if anyone was paying attention. Fortunately, everyone seemed caught up in their own tasks. Jason had his own office, but the drafting tables were part of the shared community space.

"Baby, don't you think it's time we announced our relationship?"

"Are you getting tired of being my secret lover?" he whispered.

"Never."

"Well, this is a surprise. What are you doing here?" They both turned at the sound of Ada's voice.

"What's with that question? I own the company. Shouldn't I be allowed to check things out?" he asked with a raised brow.

"Jason, do you see what I have to deal with?" Ada said, crossing her arms.

"Are you kidding me? Do you know how much trouble you give me?" Leo shot back, pointing a finger at her.

Jason watched as the two bickered, catching glimpses of a miniature version of Xander and Sera in the way they snapped at each other. Their voices weren't loud, but they were starting to attract attention.

"And now I find out you're seeing someone. Tell me now, who is it?" Leo demanded.

"Why should I tell you?" she huffed. "Do you think I want you to pay him off like you did the others?"

"If they love you, they wouldn't take the money," Leo shot back.

"You two, stop it," Jason said, stepping between them. "Remember where you are and who you are."

They both quieted and looked at him, but Jason turned to Leo first. "I get that you want to protect her, but she's an adult. She can make her own decisions. If she's not ready to tell you who this new person is, then wait until she's comfortable."

"But—"

"No, Leonidas. I love that you're overprotective, but try thinking about Ada's feelings first."

"Okay, I'll listen to you," Leo said, smiling softly.

"And you," Jason added, turning to Ada, "your brother cares about you more than he knows how to say.

He's trying to protect your heart from assholes who only see dollar signs. Granted, he's been handling it all wrong, but that's how you know he gives a damn. Now both of you need to grow the fuck up. My kids are more mature than you two."

"You're right." Ada let out a breath, then smiled. "Do you see why I love him, Leo?"

"Yeah, it's why I married him," Leo replied.

The entire workspace fell into silence for a beat, until Ada finally spoke.

"Leonidas!" she shouted, then turned to look at Leo. "Married?"

"Ah, hell, cat's out of the bag now," Jason muttered, covering his face with one hand.

"You two are really married? How? When? Does Mom know?" Ada fired off questions in rapid succession.

"Let's take this elsewhere," Leo suggested, glancing around.

"Now you want to talk privately," Jason quipped, narrowing his eyes.

"I'm sorry," Leo said, and he had the nerve to smile sexily. "I'll make it up to you."

"How?" Jason asked, folding his arms across his chest.

"I'll cook dinner for a week."

"Deal." Jason stretched his hand toward him.

Leo took it without hesitation and pulled him in, flush against his body, before kissing him on the lips. They held each other's gaze for a moment, smiling softly.

"You two are sickening," Ada groaned, then disappeared into her office.

"Is it me, or does she sound a little jealous?" Leo asked, raising an eyebrow.

"No teasing her," Jason warned, then smirked. "But yeah, maybe just a little."

They both chuckled and walked into Ada's office, still holding on to each other. Jason had been hesitant to announce their relationship, but now that it was out, he felt nothing but relief.

"LET ME GET THIS STRAIGHT. You two met six years ago, had a onenight stand, found each other... no, scratch that, your son found you, and now you're married?"

"That sums it up," Leo said, glancing over at Ada. He had told her the whole story, though he realized he'd forgotten to explain why he asked Jason to marry him.

"Does Mom know?"

"Not yet," Leo replied. "Or maybe she already does. I just haven't spoken to her. I sent her a message, but she hasn't responded. Have you heard from her?"

"Nope," Ada answered, crossing her arms. "You know how she is? She's probably off causing trouble, annoying the hated grandmother who doesn't want to be called a grandmother, or saving the world."

"Why don't you two sound worried?" Jason asked, jumping in. "What if your mom's been killed or kidnapped or something?" "No one would dare try to kidnap our mother," Ada said flatly.

"They'd send her back without even asking for a ransom." Leo nodded without hesitation.

199

"She might give off a damsel-in-distress vibe, but our mother is far from weak," he explained.

"What I'm more interested in is meeting my little niece and nephew, and whether there's any more on the way," Ada said with a teasing smile.

"Calm your ass down," Leo told her. "We've only been married for a short time. We want to spend more time together before adding any more kittens to the litter. How about you tell me who you're sleeping with first?"

"We're not talking about me, big brother," Ada replied, crossing her arms.

Leo opened his mouth to say more, but Jason pinched his arm, and he decided to let it go. "You can meet the twins this weekend." He stood and pulled Jason up with him as they walked toward the door. "We're going home."

"Wait, I have a meeting later," Jason said, glancing back.

"No worries. Your new sister-in-law can handle it, right? Unless she wants to reveal who she's dating. Then Jason can stay."

"Can Jason decide for himself?" his little husband asked, raising an eyebrow.

"Not in this case," Leo answered without hesitation.

"Can't you just drop it?" Ada snapped. "Who I date is none of your concern."

"And when they break your heart, should it be my concern then?" Leo argued back.

"Leo, that was a long time ago," Ada said. "You act as if I'm the only one who's had their heart broken."

"That's true, but I'm only concerned with your heart." Leo sighed. "I get that I can be overbearing, old-fashioned, and a tyrant in your eyes, but I'm just trying to protect you."

"I know," Ada said softly, stepping forward to hug him. "I appreciate it. And I promise, when I'm ready, I will tell you who it is."

Leo wrapped his arms around her and held her close. "It's going to be hard, but I'll wait. But if he makes you cry, come to me immediately." He pulled her back gently so she could see his eyes. "Because nobody, no matter their status, will hurt this family,

Duchess."

"Thank you." Ada smiled.

"I love you, Ada. Never doubt that."

"I know."

He hugged her again, feeling her body relax in his embrace.

He was still worried about who she was dating, but for now, he would back off.

"You're a good big brother," Jason told Leo as they walked hand in hand through the park.

"Really? I'm impressive, right?"

"Narcissistic is more like it," Jason mumbled under his breath.

He had watched Leo and Ada interact with a quiet jealousy stirring in his chest. It was clear Leo loved his sister and would do anything to protect her from heartbreak. Jason was certain that if the law allowed it, Leo wouldn't hesitate to kill for Ada. The thought made something ache inside him. None of his own siblings had ever shown him even a fraction of that kind of love.

"I don't just care about Ada's heart," Leo said, stopping in front of him. "I care about yours as well."

"Why?" Jason asked, eyes narrowing.

"Why shouldn't I?" Leo took Jason's hand and pressed it gently against his chest. "You are my husband. The man I plan to spend the rest of my life with. Your heart is now mine to protect."

"Why are you so good to me?"

"I think it's the other way around," Leo said, his voice low and honest. "You've changed my life, Jason."

"I hope it's for the better."

"Most definitely." He smiled warmly.

"I know you tricked me, by the way," Jason said, his tone shifting.

"What are you talking about?"

"Your little slip-up about telling Ada that we're married," Jason said, quirking a brow.

"You caught that?"

"You weren't slick about it."

"Are you angry?" Leo asked as he wrapped his arms around Jason and pulled him close.

"No. I think it's time we announce our relationship." Leo smiled and kissed his little husband.

"Come on, let's go home and get the kids. It's early enough for us to take them to the amusement park."

"Okay," Leo agreed, taking Jason's hand as they started walking again.

"You have something on your mind," Jason said a few minutes later.

"How can you tell?"

"I'm starting to know better." Jason lightly squeezed his fingers.

"Talk to me."

Leo didn't hesitate. "I went to see a scientist today."

"Why?" Jason stopped walking and looked at him seriously. "Are you okay?"

"I'm perfectly fine." Leo cupped his cheek gently. "I went to see him about you."

"Me? Why?"

"I wanted to know more about unbounds. More about you."

"Oh, there's nothing special about me," Jason said, starting to walk away, but Leo stopped him with a firm hand.

"That's where you're wrong, baby. You are extraordinary."

"How? I've heard that other unbounds are born with abilities, but what about me? Hell, I can't even heal myself."

"All unbounds are born with the ability to heal themselves," Leo said.

Jason's eyes widened. "No. But I've never..." He paused as the realization slowly sank in. After being kicked out by his family, he hadn't been in constant pain or rushed to the hospital like before. The scars that once covered his body had faded, especially the one on his back.

He had never been ashamed of them, but he remembered the night he lost his virginity. He hadn't wanted to take off his clothes completely, and he refused to let the lights stay on. Maybe that was why it had gone so badly.

"I'm such an idiot," he whispered. "I had the ability all this time and just chalked it up to being away from my family and time doing the healing. I've spent so long blocking out my own existence that I never even connected the dots."

"Don't blame yourself," Leo said gently, his voice full of quiet reassurance. "It's a secret between unbounds. Once your parents realized what you were, they should have guided you and explained everything."

"That definitely didn't happen." Jason let out a bitter chuckle. "What else did the scientist say?"

"The doctor seems to think you're a dimension trans-porter," Leo said.

"A what? And how would he think that without knowing me?"

Leo took his hand, guided Jason over to an empty bench, and explained everything. He told him what the doctor had said, what Ada noticed about his blueprints, and how it all connected to his possible ability.

"Wait, so you're saying people are being transported into my drafts when they touch them?"

"Yes." Leo studied Jason's face. He could tell he was still trying to process it all.

"I know it sounds complicated, but you have an ability."

"How did you know?" Jason asked after a few minutes of silence. "How did you know I was worried about not having one? I never shared that fear with you."

Leo smiled and pressed a kiss to Jason's forehead. "You don't have to say the words. You're not the only one who can tell when something's bothering the person they love. You worry that you're not my equal. But Jason, you are in every way. I'm not with you because you're an omega. I'm with you because I like you."

"Really?"

"Yes."

Jason smiled and wrapped his arms around Leo's neck. "You think you know me so well."

"I want to know everything about you," he whispered. He leaned in and brushed his lips softly against Jason's. "Never be afraid to open up to me."

"Okay." He smiled. "What else did the scientist tell you? Can I meet this person? And when can I start training?"

"Yes," Leo chuckled, then gave more details. He watched Jason closely, especially when he mentioned unbounds dying with their lover.

"So I will die when you die?" Jason asked quietly.

"That's if I die," Leo replied.

"What do you mean?" Jason looked at him, clearly confused.

Leo hadn't expected today to be a day full of revelations, but he knew it was better to be honest than to keep things hidden.

"Remember I told you a while back that there were things I wasn't ready to share?" Jason nodded.

"Before I tell you, I need you to promise to keep an open mind." "I can try," Jason said, and Leo could see he meant it.

Leo glanced around and realized this wasn't the right place for the conversation. "This isn't something I want to discuss out here." "You're scaring me," Jason admitted.

Leo gently cupped his cheek. "Don't be. I promise, it's all good. This is just another part of me. I hope you'll understand." He pressed a kiss to Jason's forehead. "Call Mrs. Sing."

Jason nodded and pulled out his phone, making a quick call home. Leo remained silent, offering a quiet prayer to his mother.

Mother, if you're listening, don't let me lose the man I'm falling in love with.

A second later, he felt a soft, comforting brush across his cheek. He knew it was from Athena, and some of the worry in his heart began to ease.

Maybe I'm making this out to be more than I should. We live in Valleywood, after all.

"WHY DID YOU BRING ME HERE?" Jason asked, looking at the familiar scenery leading to Leo's home.

"Because it's more private," Leo answered.

"Oh."

Leo had held his hand the entire drive. They didn't speak, and the silence was killing him. But it also gave him time to think.

He had been told he was useless for most of his life, and eventually, he'd believed it. Meeting Leo changed that. It gave him a whole new outlook on life. He couldn't wait to learn more about being a transporter. To think he had been using his abilities all this time without even knowing it made something flutter in his chest.

It might've sounded cliché to some, but Jason could

always remember what he was thinking about when he worked on his blueprints, whether they were for a family or a business. Realizing he had been leaving behind more than just his impression or vision on paper made him excited, but it also left him a little unsure of how to move forward.

"We're here," Leo said beside him as the car came to a stop. "Come on."

Jason nodded, got out of the car, and met Leo on the other side. Leo took his hand, and together they walked up the stairs and entered the grand foyer. This time, there was no tour as they headed straight to the second floor, where Leo's home office and private museum were located.

"The last time we were here, I only gave you part of the reason why this room is special to me."

Jason watched as Leo went through the security measures. When the doors slid open, the familiar scent of aged books reached him. He didn't wait to be invited in. Taking a step inside, he was just as awestruck as before. Blueprints, drafts, and ancient machinery were displayed behind glass cases, each one carefully preserved, each one telling its own story.

The room was the largest in the house and gave off the feel of a museum. Jason wondered if Leo had used magic to expand it. He might not act like it, but he loved this room just as much as Leo did, and it was only his second time being here.

Jason walked over to one of the sculptures, the only one that looked complete compared to the others. It was a statue of a man, posed with one foot in front of the other, his back heel lifted as if he were about to run or walk away. His arms were raised at his sides, head lifted, and his gaze fixed on something in the distance, or maybe on Jason himself, since he was standing directly in its path.

It seemed lifelike, as if it could come alive at any moment.

The naked statue was carved with careful detail, and Jason noticed a single letter etched into the figure's hip —the letter D, written with a flamboyant flourish.

"I remember when I sculpted this," Leo said, approaching him from behind. "I didn't know what the fuck I was doing." He chuckled. "Most of what you see in here came to me in a dream, and I had no choice but to make them, draw them, create them, and get others to appreciate them for what they were. My life's work."

Jason turned to look at Leo. He didn't speak or ask questions. He just listened, trying to understand the weight of what Leo was saying.

"I was not born Leonidas Devereux. That was a name I gave myself, like all the others. I was born Daedalus of Athens, over three thousand years ago."

Jason gasped, his eyes widening at Leo's words. He wanted to ask if Leo was pulling his leg, but the serious expression on his lover's face told him this wasn't a joke. Still, he had to make sure Leo wasn't sick or slipping into some kind of delusion. He reached up and pressed the back of his hand to Leo's forehead, then placed his other hand on his own forehead.

"What the hell are you doing?" Leo asked, grabbing his wrist.

"Checking to see if you're getting sick."

"I asked you to be open-minded, not make jokes," Leo snapped.

"I'm sorry... I just... are you a vampire?" Jason asked, blurting out the only thing that made any sense to him.

Leo chuckled. "I like the taste of your blood, but no. I'm a demigod."

"A demigod? As in the child of a god?"

"Yes."

"So gods are real," Jason mumbled.

"Yes. Some of them live in Valleywood. Others live in magical towns and cities around the world. And some choose to remain in the realm of the gods. Athena, the goddess of knowledge, adopted me. One of her gifts was immortality. It means I cannot die. And Jason, although you can live a long time as an unbound, being with me makes you even more invincible."

"You're starting to sound like one of Sera's cartoon characters," Jason joked.

"Baby, listen to what I'm saying," Leo said. "We are now one. Maybe not as mates, but as lovers for life."

Jason stared at Leo waiting for the punchline but the serious expression on his face told him differently, as his husband's words sank in slowly. His knees gave out beneath him, but before he could fall, Leo caught him and held him close.

"I know it sounds strange. I know this is a lot to take in," Leo said, his voice steady but gentle. "But I didn't do this to trick you. I didn't keep it from you to hurt you. I just... I know you might not want to be with someone like me for all eternity. So if you ever want to walk away, I..."

"You don't want me?" Jason shouted, shoving Leo back. "You made me fall for you, and now you tell me you don't want me?

How dare you, Leo?"

"You're falling for me?" Leo asked, stunned.

"Isn't it fucking obvious by now?"

Leo smirked. "I will always want you, regardless of the day, the year, or the century." He stepped forward and cupped Jason's cheeks. "You have become my every breath, Jason Dupree."

"You know what doesn't scare me?" Jason asked, his voice softening.

"What?"

"Death."

"They aren't scary to look at. In fact, they're quite handsome and gorgeous," Leo said with a teasing smile.

Jason had a dozen more questions building inside him, but he knew that would have to wait for another time.

"Anyway, what scares me is losing you and the kids. Speaking of which... if you're a demigod, does that mean they are too?"

"Yes. There's a reason Sera is fascinated with having a spear, and why Xander thinks he can fly. Even though I was adopted, it was done through blood and magic. I may not look like Athena, but I have her eyes, and so does Sera. That's how powerful her bloodline is."

"Holy fuck," Jason muttered, backing up and placing a hand over his chest. "My kids are demigods."

"You're taking the kids being demigods a lot harder than me being three thousand years old."

Why does it look like he's pouting? I've never seen a six-foot-four baby.

"Of course, I'm taking that a bit harder. Don't you understand why? It explains so many things," Jason said, pacing around the room. "Like why they seem so smart at five. Hell, even before that. I never told anyone this, but when the kids were around one, they slept in separate cribs. And every morning for a month, I'd wake up to find Xander next to Sera."

He stopped and looked at Leo, frustration and disbelief in his voice.

"Then one night, I checked on them and saw Xander floating over to Sera's crib. Do you know how crazy I felt thinking my apartment was haunted? So I moved them into my bedroom and had them sleep beside me. It stopped happening after that, but then other weird things started up again. Floating toys, stuff disappearing and reappearing. Shit that would just go boom out of nowhere."

Jason recalled the times he thought he was losing his mind. Electronics would flicker on and off, toys would move on their own, and that was just the beginning. The memory made him start pacing again.

"I moved four times, and it never stopped. I figured the ghost liked us, so I just stayed put. Not only is Xander adventurous, but he's strong, too. And Sera... she's brilliant. I know most parents say their kids are smart, but she's like a genius mastermind. She bosses her older brother around, and somehow, he just follows her lead without question. I don't even know if that's a good thing."

He turned sharply to face Leo. "Tell me, who did they get that from?"

Jason gasped. "The kids knew. They knew you were their father. How did they figure it out before I did? Is that some kind of demigod thing? Like you just recognize each other right away?"

"It's..."

"They say the gods can hear our thoughts and see everything we do. So does that mean your mother knows about me and hates me? Is that why she hasn't come around?"

LEO GRABBED Jason and pulled him into his arms before he could start another round of ranting and pacing.

"Calm down," Leo told him gently.

"How can I relax at a time like this?"

"First, when I asked Xander why he was so sure I was his father, he told me he felt it in his heart. I didn't realize it then, but a bond had already started forming between us. At first, I wasn't sure what to believe, but deep down, I hoped he was mine. I kept thinking about the boy and his father at the airport. It wasn't until I saw Sera that I knew for certain. She resembles my mother. And no, she doesn't hate you."

"How do you know that?" Jason asked, still unsure.

"Mother, do you hate my husband?" Leo called out.

"Of course not," Athena said, appearing in the room without warning.

Jason stiffened in Leo's arms.

"It's okay," Leo whispered in his ear.

"Are you sure?" Jason asked softly against Leo's chest.

"Yes," Leo replied, then gently turned him to face her.

"Finally, you call me and tell me you got married," Athena said with a dramatic sigh. "Do you have any idea how hard it was for me to stay out of your relationship?"

"So that's what you've been doing?" Leo asked, raising an eyebrow.

"Yes, and other things," she replied.

"What other things?"

"Later, we'll talk about that later," Athena said offhandedly, pulling Jason away from Leo. "My, you are so handsome. You are the perfect man for my son," she gushed.

"I... I..." Jason stuttered.

"He's so adorable." Athena wrapped him in her arms, crushing him against her chest.

"You're going to suffocate him," Leo snapped, stepping in to pull his husband away.

"Don't be selfish, Daedalus. You have to share him," Athena said, pulling Jason right back into her embrace.

"Stop it. You two are making me dizzy," Jason snapped, then immediately covered his mouth. His eyes went wide as he stared at Athena, as if waiting for her to smite him for speaking out.

Instead, she burst into laughter. "Yes, he will fit right in," she said, still chuckling.

"Are you sure she's a goddess?" Jason whispered to Leo.

Leo smiled. "You'll find the gods aren't what you were told. They make mistakes and act like idiots just like humans."

"You said other gods live in Valleywood. Who are they? Or can't you tell me?" Jason asked.

"You and Ada had a meeting with the mayor last week, right?"

"Yeah, but what does..." Jason's eyes grew even wider. "Are you saying Mayor Loki is actually *Loki*, god of tricks?"

"Well, he's more of a demigod right now. He got his powers taken away. It's a long story," Leo told him.

"This is all so fucking much. You're Daedalus, a man said to be

a myth. Your mother is Athena, goddess of knowledge and so much more. My kids are demigods who might be powerful little troublemakers. Our mayor is a demigod of sorts, and I can't die.

Did I sum it up nicely?"

"Let's not forget that you're pregnant," Athena added.

"What... what did you just say?" both Jason and Leo said at the same time.

"What, you didn't know?" Athena asked, as casually as if she were commenting on the weather. "You're a month pregnant." "Holy fuck," Jason said, then promptly fainted.

Leo caught him before he could hit the floor.

"You could have broken the news better, Mom," Leo said, cradling Jason. "Are you sure?"

"Yes," Athena replied with a smile. "A new demigod is growing inside of him."

Fuck, Leo thought and tried not to stumble. He was elated; he was more worried about Jason. *I'm going to be a father again.*

"It's better to rip the bandage off now," she said with a shrug and stepped closer to Leo and Jason. "Hm... so that's how he was able to hide from me the first time. He masked both his presence and the children's. Very smart young man."

"What are you talking about?" Leo asked, looking down at Jason, who was still knocked out in his arms.

"He is a very special unbound, because he wasn't born as one but made."

"What?"

"The knot he has was implanted in him, maybe from birth. Until he met you, his abilities remained dormant."

"How can you tell?" Leo asked as he carried Jason over to the sofa and gently laid him down.

"His abilities are blocked. Besides being a dimension transporter, he can also mask his presence. I doubt he even realized he was doing it." She touched Jason's forehead and whispered an incantation Leo had never heard before. A golden glow spread across Jason's entire body.

The light grew so intense Leo had to turn his face away so it wouldn't blind him. A few minutes later, the light faded.

"This poor child has been through so much."

Leo looked at Athena, noticing the sadness in her expression. "Did you just read his mind?"

"It's the only way to unblock his potential. Consider it my welcome-to-the-family gift," she said with a soft smile. "I added a little something more. Since the abilities weren't originally his, it will take time for him to learn how to control them."

"What do you mean? Someone implanted the knot?"

"I'd say his parents, specifically the mother. Don't worry about her. Let me handle Valencia Dupree."

"What are you talking about? Isn't she a pharmacologist?" "No." Athena sighed. "She's the kind who likes to play god. Valencia Dupree is a geneticist. And the worst kind. She used her own son as an experiment for her personal ambition. She manipulated his DNA and gave him a knot that was removed from another unbound, without even knowing what their abilities were."

"She experimented on her child?" Leo growled, his anger building quickly. "Yes. And she abandoned him emotionally when he showed no signs of ability. He craved her attention. What child wouldn't want their mother's love?" Athena gently caressed Jason's cheek. "You and he have no idea what kind of torment he endured as a child."

"How do you know this?"

She shook her head slowly. "I saw it through the memories buried deep inside him. I won't force them out, so don't worry. They were hidden for a reason, and I would never let him relive that trauma again. But I can't let her get away with this. We can't let the entire Dupree family escape the consequences of what they did to him."

"Are you sure?" Leo asked, fully aware of the strict rules surrounding gods and their interference in mortal lives.

"I won't break the rules. They've hurt him far more than just physically, and no one hurts my family. You know that."

"I do. Thank you, Mother."

"There's nothing to thank me for. You're fulfilling my wishes. The least I can do is make sure you and your family are safe. Over the years, I could sense the children's presence, but they vanished every time I tried to find them. Then, a few months ago, I came across a kind woman caring for a twin boy and girl who looked an awful lot like me. When I found out they were neighbors, I took on the role of nanny to get to know them better. And once I did, I couldn't spend just one day. I needed more time. Our little ones are so cute and smart. They're curious, brave, and full of life. I'm excited to see how they change the world."

"Don't tell me you're Mrs. Sing."

"Only on even days," Athena admitted with a mischievous smile. "I fooled you good, didn't I?"

"Do you know I thought that woman had dementia?" Leo snapped. "You're the reason she kept forgetting our conversations, wouldn't look me in the eye, and ran off every time she saw me."

"I'm sorry. I just wanted to get to know Jason and the kids. When you showed up at the apartment and later got married, I knew staying out of your relationship was the right choice. I made that mistake with Mya and didn't want to repeat it."

"Speaking of... did you erase her memory? I bumped into her earlier today, and it seemed like she didn't recognize me."

"I did. But there might still be a lingering trace of her feelings. That will fade with time."

Leo opened his mouth to respond, but Jason groaned, stirring awake.

"Hey, are you okay?" Leo asked, shifting his attention.

"Leo, I had the strangest dream. I met your mother, and she told me I was pregnant."

"It wasn't a dream, baby. You're pregnant."

Athena conjured a glass of water and handed it to Leo, who gently sat Jason up and helped him sip it slowly.

"Are you sure? Maybe she's mistaken?"

"I'm not wrong, dear," Athena said with a knowing smile. "But you should still take a test to confirm it. Well, I must be off." She turned to leave, then paused at the door.

"Oh, and Daedalus... be careful of Minos. I don't know what he wants, but I cannot interfere with him. He has the protection of a god."

"Thanks, Mother."

She gave a short nod and vanished just as suddenly as she had appeared.

Jason blinked, still trying to process. "What is Athena talking about? Who is Minos?"

"A blast from the past," Leo said. "Let's not worry

about that right now." He touched Jason's stomach. "You're pregnant."

Jason smiled. "If it's true, it's not as scary this time as it was the last time." He placed his hand over Leo's. "Because you're here with me."

"Always." Leo leaned in and kissed him, slow and deliberate. The kiss wasn't rushed or hungry, but it held something deeper. It was comfort, reassurance, and love without condition.

Jason let his fingers slide into Leo's hair, holding him close, his breath catching when the kiss lingered. There was a heat building, quiet but real, not born from lust alone but from the depth of knowing they were no longer alone in this.

When their lips parted, Jason leaned his forehead against Leo's. His voice dropped to a whisper. "I never thought I'd feel this again. This... hope."

"You don't have to go through it alone this time," Leo said. "I'm here. Every step of the way."

Jason closed his eyes, holding Leo's hand tighter. "You want this baby?"

"I want everything that comes with you," Leo said without hesitation. "A child, a life, a future. I want it all."

Leo pulled Jason onto his lap. Jason went easily, resting with his legs curled to the side, his head tucked beneath Leo's chin. He breathed in deeply, the familiar scent of Leo grounding him in the moment.

"Do you think they'll be okay? Xander and Sera?" Jason asked softly. "With all of this? The bloodlines, the powers, the gods?"

Leo rubbed slow circles along his back. "They'll be

more than okay. They're strong, smart, and loved. That's more than most kids ever get."

Jason nodded but didn't look up. "I just want to do right by them. And by this baby. I want to get it right this time."

"You already are," Leo said, pressing a kiss to his temple. "You're showing up. You're loving them. That's everything."

Jason's voice trembled, barely audible. "Promise?"

Leo tilted his face up and kissed him again. "With everything I am."

Jason let out a slow breath and closed his eyes. For the first time in a long while, he allowed himself to feel safe. He allowed himself to believe.

CHAPTER 15
JASON

J ason strolled through the mall, searching for the perfect birthday present for Leo. He had found out from Ada that his husband's birthday was in a couple of days, and even though Leo didn't make a big deal out of it, Jason wanted to celebrate him in a way that truly mattered.

It had been a couple of weeks since he discovered everything about himself, about Leo, and about the kids. His abilities were slowly revealing themselves, and he was adjusting to them more each day. He had met with Doctor Pace, who gave him deeper insight into what it meant to be a dimension transporter. The idea that he could move from one place to another instantly with just a thought was both fascinating and a little terrifying. They had decided to wait a few more weeks before starting his training to help him control it.

In the meantime, Leo had been helping him explore his limits carefully, making sure he didn't push too hard or accidentally harm himself or their baby. They hadn't told the twins about the pregnancy yet. They'd agreed to wait until after his first doctor's appointment, which was scheduled for the day after Leo's birthday.

Jason still couldn't bring himself to call Leo *Daedalus*. It felt too new and too surreal. But even if the name caught in his throat, he couldn't be prouder of the man he had married. Knowing that Leo had contributed so much to the world, to history itself, filled him with a quiet, overwhelming pride.

Over the past few weeks, Jason had asked question after question. Luckily, Leo hadn't lost his patience. He answered every single one.

Ada and Athena had met the children, and Jason was still shocked to learn that Athena had sometimes pretended to be Mrs. Sing just to spend time with them. He had also found out about Ada's past as a duchess and was thoroughly impressed to discover that all his bosses had made meaningful contributions to society. He had even stopped the goddess from gifting Sera a spear— three times.

He smiled at the memory and realized he had been doing that a lot lately. As unconventional as his life had become, he had a family. And it was far better than the one he grew up in.

He had just stepped into the jewelry store when his phone rang. Pulling it from his pocket, he frowned at the screen. The name *Sperm Donor* lit up across the top.

Jason didn't know why his father was calling. He debated whether to answer, finger hovering over the screen, before finally giving in and tapping it with a sigh.

"Hell must have frozen over if you're calling me," Jason said once the line connected.

"Watch how you speak to me," Jackson Dupree growled.

"What do you want?" Jason asked flatly, not bothering to lean into his father's anger.

"Your mother wants to see you for her birthday," Jackson said.

"Her birthday was two weeks ago. Try a different lie, and maybe I'll believe you," Jason said, the words slipping out before he could stop them.

"We want to meet the children."

"No," Jason snapped. "I will never let my children around you people."

"You cannot keep our blood away from us," Jackson shouted.

"I'm your blood," Jason growled. "Yet you stood there like a coward while I was beaten and broken."

"It was to strengthen you. You know how people view us omegas. They think we're weak," Jackson argued.

"What the fuck do I care what other people think?" Jason yelled, his voice carrying through the store. He didn't give a damn about the gasps around him or the eyes that turned his way. "You were supposed to protect me. You were my father. And I was a fucking kid. *Your* kid. And you kicked me out without a single goddamn penny, just the clothes on my back. Now you think I'd let you anywhere near my children?"

He paused just long enough to make sure every word cut deep.

"So you can poison their heads with the same bullshit you tried to feed me? Or break them down piece by piece the way you did me? Fuck no. That will never happen. I don't care what title you hold or what blood runs through your veins. You are nothing to me. So do me a favor and rot in hell, Jackson Dupree."

Jason hung up and blocked his father's number, cursing himself for answering the call in the first place. He should have known better. As much as he wanted to believe that would be the last time he heard from his family, deep down he knew it wasn't. He had already come face to face with his sister and now his father. His brother would be next. They always worked in patterns, saving their queen for last. Because they knew he had a soft spot for her.

Or at least he used to.

After seeing how Athena, Ada, and Leo loved one another, how they supported each other without conditions or shame, whatever warmth he had left for Valencia Dupree shriveled into ash.

She had never stood up for him. Not once. She never stopped the abuse. Never told his father to back the fuck off. She just watched. She watched him cry, bleed, and break and never said a word. But she was quick to fight for others. A brilliant scientist. A celebrated figure. A goddamn miracle worker saving strangers across the globe while letting her own son rot beneath her roof.

She turned a blind eye when he needed her the most.

And maybe, just maybe, that was the point. Maybe she had never liked him. Maybe she never wanted him. Maybe she resented the life she had built. Valencia Dupree was a strong alpha with a mate who would have torn the world apart for her. And if she told him to hurt their son, he would do it without hesitation. And in Jason's case, he did.

Jason didn't want to associate with them. Not now. Not ever. He didn't want their shadows anywhere near his kids. He didn't even want them breathing the same air.

They weren't good people. They never had been.

He exhaled, long and slow, and pushed the weight of them out of his mind.

That's when he saw it.

Something gleamed in the storefront just ahead, catching his eye.

A slow smile crept across his face.

The perfect birthday present for Leo.

A gold lion lapel pin with a chain attached to a ruby star caught his eye. His smile grew when he noticed the matching gold upper arm sleeve cuffs displayed beside it. Jason loved seeing Leo in a suit. Sometimes Leo wore harnesses, which were sexy as fuck, but Jason especially liked it when he wore those upper arm cuffs to keep his rolled-up sleeves in place. It showed off his thick, muscular forearms, and the look always left Jason staring a little too long.

"Can I help you?" the jewelry clerk asked, stepping closer.

"Yes," Jason said with a grin. "I'd like to buy this set."

He handed over his credit card without even glancing at the price tag.

Damn, Leo is rubbing off on me.

"Sure." The clerk smiled, took his card, and stepped away to collect the items he was purchasing.

"Excuse me, I want this set," said a very familiar and very irritating voice beside him.

"I'm sorry, but this is the last set, and it has already been claimed," the clerk replied, maintaining her professionalism.

"Did they pay for it?" Willa snapped.

"Yes," the clerk said, this time with a touch of unmasked annoyance.

"Since it's been bought, let's make another purchase."

Jason looked up as a voice, smooth and steady as warm silk, slid across the space. A tall, striking man stepped into view. He had short blond hair, piercing hunter-green eyes, and wore a dark blue suit tailored to perfection. He stood just a couple of inches shorter than Willa, and nearly a foot taller than Jason. His hand reached for Willa's chin, guiding her face up to his. His touch was gentle in motion but hard in presence.

There was no love in it. No tenderness. Just control.

Jason felt it immediately. That cold, calculated energy. The kind that made you watch your back.

Willa, however, looked like she would dissolve if he so much as smiled at her.

"But—"

"Don't make a fuss," he said, calm but commanding. "There are other pieces. Find one you think I'll like."

Willa nodded instantly, then turned toward Jason with a sharp glare and a scoff before strutting off in her heels, leaving Jason alone with the stranger.

"I'm sorry if she offended you," the handsome man said smoothly.

"You don't need to apologize. I'm used to her attitude."

"You know Willa then?"

"We share the same blood," Jason replied, not bothering to clarify further. Since Willa didn't claim him, he sure as hell wasn't going to claim her.

"I'm Elias Crete," the man said, extending a hand with a smile that didn't quite reach his eyes.

"Jason." He accepted the handshake, giving it a quick squeeze before trying to pull back. Elias didn't let go.

"Just Jason? No last name?"

"Here is your purchase, Mister Devereux," the clerk said, stepping in before Jason could respond.

Elias tightened his grip just enough to make Jason hiss, and Jason yanked his hand back, rubbing at the sting.

"Sorry, did I hurt you?" Elias asked, reaching for his hand again.

Jason took a step back, giving the man a sharp side-eye. "No."

He snatched his package and credit card from the counter, jaw tight.

"Your last name is Devereux," Elias said casually,

though his smile faltered. "Any relation to the real estate magnate?"

Why does this guy seem so fake when I just met him? That's not for me to ask nor care.

"Yes, he's my husband," Jason said, trying not to blush as if he hadn't referred to Leo as his husband before. His worry about others at work finding out he was married to the owner was in vain. No one seemed to care or treat him differently, but admitting it to a stranger made him want to giggle madly, but he held it together.

"Pity. Here I thought I could ask you out to dinner," Elias said with a smile that looked too smooth to be real.

"What about Willa?"

"We're just acquaintances."

Jason snorted. "Does she know that? The way she clings to you, it's like she wants to wear you like a second skin."

Elias let out a quiet laugh, but it sounded forced.

"Anyway, it was nice meeting you, but I have to go," Jason said, stepping back.

"I hope we get to meet again."

I doubt it, Jason thought, offering no reply. He turned and walked out of the store without a second glance.

He didn't see Willa watching him from the corner, her glare sharp with irritation. Nor did he catch the flicker of something darker in Elias's expression as he followed Jason's retreat with narrowed eyes.

～

Leo stretched his arms above his head and sat back, working out the kinks from leaning over the draft board for the last hour. He had been stuck in the office working on a new project and got so into it that he hadn't realized it was already past lunchtime.

He glanced toward Ada's office, hoping to pull his sister-in-law and boss into taking a break. The rooftop had tables, chairs, and a decent view that made for a peaceful spot to eat.

One thing Leo liked about DRA&D was how much effort they put into employee comfort. There was a game room, a gym, a cafeteria that stayed open all day with a few professional chefs, and soon they'd be opening a daycare. It made long days feel a little more human.

After grabbing something quick from the cafeteria, he headed

up to the roof and found a comfortable spot. He was halfway to taking a bite of his sandwich when a voice stopped him.

"I'm not ready to tell him about us, Talos." *That's Ada's voice.*

"We can't keep hiding this forever, Ada. He has me investigating myself. If I don't produce results, I don't know what your brother will do," Talos said.

"I know. He's not that scary, is he?" Ada asked, and Jason could hear a slight tremor in her tone.

"He can be," Talos said.

"Wait, I know," Ada added quickly. "What if we get Jason on our side?"

"What can Jason do?"

Yeah, what can I do? Jason thought dryly.

"You see how easily my brother bends to Jason's will. What if we get him to talk to Leo for us?"

"You think that would work?"

"Of course. My brother loves Jason, the same way I love you," Ada said, and Jason touched his chest, totally not feeling like a third wheel while listening to their confessions. "Plus, I've seen with my own eyes how easily he bends when Jason pushes."

"I love you too, but I'm still scared of what Leo's going to do when he finds out I got his sister pregnant," Talos admitted.

Pregnant! Jason mentally shouted. Holy shit, Leo is going to kill him.

"Yeah, that part we might need to wait a little longer to tell him. And my mother, too, since they just found out about Jason and the twins."

"Maybe we should wait a little longer to tell them everything. I can keep stalling for a bit," Talos offered.

"You'd do that for me?" Ada asked, her voice soft.

"I'd do anything for you, Duchess."

Aww, they are so sweet, Jason thought with a small smile. Not wanting to listen in any longer, he quietly gathered his uneaten lunch and hurried back to his office, already wondering how he could help Ada and Talos without them ever knowing it.

Leo walked up behind Jason, who was in the kitchen, and gently circled his arms around his waist. He buried his face in the curve of Jason's neck, pressing a kiss to the beauty mark there and inhaling his scent. The moment he did, the tension of the day began to melt from his body. He had spent it moving from one pointless meeting to another, dealing with incompetent idiots who made his headache throb behind his eyes.

"Rough day?" Jason asked, his voice soft.

Leo groaned. "Don't ask." He didn't want to talk about the the conversation he had overheard.

Jason turned in his arms and brushed his lips against Leo's.

"Did that help?"

"No. I need more."

Leo cupped the back of Jason's neck and pulled him in for a kiss that was anything but gentle. He pressed their mouths together with need, letting every ounce of frustration bleed out through the contact. Touching Jason. Holding him. Tasting him. That was all he needed right now.

He deepened the kiss, tilting his head to align them perfectly. Jason's lips parted with a quiet sigh, and Leo took full advantage, sliding his tongue into the heat of his mouth. The second their tongues met, the tightness in Leo's chest cracked and gave way to a slow-burning hunger.

Jason's fingers fisted the front of his shirt, tugging him closer, desperate to keep the space between them nonexistent. Their tongues moved in long, sensual strokes, savoring and teasing, the rhythm building into something that burned hotter with each breath. Leo groaned low in his throat, the sound lost in their wet, eager kiss as his grip on Jason's neck tightened slightly, holding him in place.

He pressed Jason gently against the counter, anchoring them both. Jason opened for him completely, meeting every stroke, every soft pull and teasing suck with equal hunger. Leo's other hand slid down the length of Jason's back, needing to feel him, to hold him, to ground himself in the one thing that had ever truly calmed the chaos inside him.

When he caught Jason's bottom lip between his teeth and gave it a soft bite, the sharp inhale against his chest sent a jolt through his entire body. He kissed him slower after that, drawing out every taste, letting the warmth linger between them, chasing the quiet moan that slipped free like a secret meant only for him.

Pulling back just enough to breathe, Leo kept their foreheads pressed together. "That helped," he murmured, voice low and raspy.

Jason looked up at him, lips flushed and kiss-bruised, his eyes heavy with affection and dark with something deeper. "Then how about we call your mom and have her watch the kids," he whispered, his tone soft and laced with invitation. "And you can do anything you want to me."

Leo smiled, brushing his thumb slowly across Jason's cheek. "I love being married to you."

∼

JASON SMILED against Leo's lips, a low hum escaping him when his husband grabbed and caressed his ass.

"Are you sure you're over three thousand years old?" he whispered.

Leo chuckled and gently bit his bottom lip. "Did I wear you out?"

Smug bastard. But Jason couldn't deny Leo had the energy and stamina of a much younger man.

The second Athena disappeared with the kids, Leo had pinned him to the wall and made him cum within minutes. Then came round two in the bathroom. And finally, the bed for round three.

"Let me rest for a few minutes," Jason murmured, pressing a hand lightly to Leo's chest.

Leo sighed, kissed him again, then rolled onto his back, pulling Jason with him. Jason sprawled across his chest, limp and satisfied.

"You comfortable?" Leo asked, his arms tightening around him.

"Hmm..." Jason nodded, rubbing his cheek into Leo's chest like a lazy cat soaking up warmth.

They lay in comfortable silence, the steady rhythm of Leo's heart slowly lulling Jason toward sleep—until Leo spoke again.

"I saw Ada and Talos kissing on the roof today."

Jason blinked, his eyes opening slowly. He looked up at Leo but didn't say a word.

"You don't seem shocked." Leo shifted beneath him, watching him closely. "You knew, but you didn't tell me. How long have you known they were together?"

Jason sighed and rested his chin on Leo's chest. "I wasn't hiding it. I overheard them talking a few days ago.

I wasn't supposed to hear it, and they've been trying to figure out how to tell you."

Leo frowned. "You still should've told me."

"I know. But they're not trying to hurt you. They're scared. Talos is terrified of how you'll react. Ada too."

Leo let out a dry laugh and leaned back against the pillows. "What, do they think I'm going to smite them?"

"Maybe not smite. But you've got serious protective big brother energy, and it scares the shit out of people when you're pissed."

"I only scare people who piss me off."

"And how do you feel about Talos and Ada?"

Leo's voice dropped to a quiet sigh. "Hurt. That they didn't trust me enough to come to me."

Jason pushed himself up on his elbows and looked down at him gently. "You love them. They love each other. If you want them to open up to you, you've got to give them the space to do it on their own terms."

Leo said nothing for a long moment, just stared at the ceiling in thought. Jason didn't push—he knew Leo needed time to work through it in his own head.

Then, in a low voice, Leo muttered, "Talos got her pregnant."

Jason blinked. "Yeah. I know."

Leo turned sharply toward him. "What?"

Jason gave him a sheepish, guilty smile. "I may have overheard that part, too. Kinda cool, though. You're going to be a daddy and an uncle around the same time."

Leo groaned and pulled the covers over his head. "I'm surrounded by traitors."

Jason laughed and tugged the blanket down enough

to press a kiss to his cheek. "Not traitors. Just people who love you... and are really scared of your wrath."

Leo peeked at him with one eye. "You're lucky you're cute."

"I'm lucky you're obsessed with me," Jason said with a grin, only to yelp when Leo suddenly flipped them, pinning him to the bed again.

They play-wrestled beneath the sheets until Leo rolled off, both of them catching their breath. Jason settled half on top of him, warm and loose-limbed, his fingers drawing lazy patterns across Leo's chest.

"You know," Jason said after a moment, "this is the first time we've been home without the kids since we got together. I hope they're not too much for your mom."

Leo smiled. "I wouldn't worry about Athena. She's probably running circles around them. Let's worry about when it's time to bring them home."

Jason's gaze softened. "You never talk about your adopted father. Was he human or a god?"

"Neither," Leo said, shaking his head. "Athena never married."

Jason propped himself up on one elbow. "Why not? She's gorgeous, smart, and fierce."

"Her choice. She had admirers, like Aries, Achilles, Selene, and the craziest one of them all Ishtar to name a few, but never returned the affection."

"So why does she want you and Ada to find love?"

"Because she believes in it. Just because she chose to be alone doesn't mean she doesn't want happiness for the people she loves."

Jason nodded slowly. "I admire that. I can see why you want to make her proud."

"Athena brought me out of a dark place," Leo said quietly.

Jason reached up and cupped his cheek, gently turning Leo's face toward him. "Do you want to talk about it?"

Leo placed his hand over Jason's. "Not tonight." He leaned in and kissed him, soft and slow. "I'd rather focus on something more important."

Jason moaned against his mouth. "It hasn't been that long."

"How can I not want you every second we're alone?"
"You have a point," Jason whispered, smiling.

"That's more like it." Leo kissed him again and rolled over, pressing him down into the mattress with a groan of satisfaction.

They made love twice more before falling asleep, wrapped in each other, the world outside quiet for once, and everything exactly where it should be.

CHAPTER 16

LEO

L eo stood at the floor-to-ceiling window of his office, staring at the Valleywood sign, his thoughts miles away.

He caught his reflection in the glass and noticed the lapel pin Jason had given him for his birthday.

He usually didn't celebrate or put much thought into the day. But Jason had made it a mandatory day off in their home.

That morning started with a birthday blow job that left him breathless, gripping the sheets while Jason worked him over like a man possessed. Leo could still feel the warmth of his mouth, the way Jason moaned around him, hungry and filthy and perfect. It had set the tone for the entire day. No meetings. No calls. Just their little family tangled in laughter and joy.

Breakfast in bed came next. Sticky syrup on fingers. Jason licking it off slowly, his eyes dark with promise.

The kids gave him handmade cards that hit him right in the chest, and dinner had been his favorite meal. But honestly, Leo barely remembered the food.

What stayed with him was the way Jason looked that night. He had come into their bedroom in nothing but that silk robe Leo loved, the deep green one that clung to his body like a second skin. Jason didn't even tie it. He climbed onto the bed, onto Leo, and rode him like he was claiming every inch for himself.

Slow. Deep. Fucking spellbinding.

Jason moved like he was savoring him. Every grind of his hips, every gasp, every "I love you" was deliberate. Soft hands on his chest. Lips trailing over his throat. Leo had tried to stay in control, but Jason didn't let him. He teased. He made Leo beg. He smiled like the smug little brat he was and kissed him so sweet it almost hurt.

Even now, thinking about it made Leo's cock twitch, and a lazy grin spread across his face.

That man would be the death of him.

And Leo would go down smiling.

Things were changing fast, but Leo couldn't say he was disappointed. He had finally found someone who would love him for all time. Jason had given him a family, stirring up memories of his own childhood, both the good and the ugly.

Now they were expecting a third.

Jason was almost seven weeks pregnant, and their first doctor's appointment was later today. Leo was excited and nervous as hell. This would be his first time experiencing it all from the start. He had missed everything with the twins—every appointment, every craving, every moment Jason had faced alone.

That shit haunted him.

He hadn't been there when Jason needed him, and it ate at him. But this time, he had made a promise. He would be there for every step. Every back rub, every craving, every sleepless night.

Whatever Jason needed, whenever he needed it.

And Leo wasn't the type to break his word.

"Sir, I have the information on the law firm," Talos said, interrupting Leo's thoughts.

"Put it on my desk. I'll read through it later," Leo instructed without looking at him. "What about the other thing I asked you to look into?"

"I don't have a lot to go on about Elias Crete. A businessman from Greece, moved to Valleywood a few weeks ago. Last seen cozying up to Willa Dupree, but that's about it."

Leo didn't care about who Minos was fucking, nor was he surprised who it was. He'd spotted them a few weeks ago having a romantic dinner. Although by the look of it Willa Dupree was going to get her heart broken.

"I'm not talking about that. You'll have to dig deeper for his information. I meant Ada's love interest."

"I..."

Leo turned, eyes fixed on Talos, waiting.

"I don't feel comfortable looking into your sister's private life," Talos said, his voice lower, cautious.

"Is that right?" Leo quirked a brow, the corner of his mouth twitching like he wasn't sure if he should be amused or pissed.

Leo had told Jason he would wait until Ada and Talos came to him and admitted their relationship, but he was growing tired of waiting.

Thanks to Jason, he had learned how to suppress his need to overreact and offer support instead. That didn't mean, however, that he wouldn't test the man's love for his sister.

Not by a long shot.

"What if I told you I already know who the person is?" Leo asked.

"You... you do?" Talos stuttered.

"I do."

"Who is it? What do you plan to do to them?"

Leo huffed, already realizing his assistant should never consider playing poker. He walked over to his desk, picked up a check, and slammed it into Talos's chest. He hit him hard enough to make sure he felt it, but not enough to do damage. He wasn't trying to send the man to the hospital.

"This twenty million dollars is yours if you leave my sister and never show your face in Valleywood."

Talos took the check, stared at it, then looked up at Leo while still holding the paper in his hand. Slowly and deliberately, he tore it in half.

"You think this is some kind of performance? Some melodramatic bullshit being played out? How many times have I watched you pull this exact move on idiots who only want Ada for her money?" he growled. "Fuck, do you think so little of me? Dammit,

Leo, I love Ada. I'm not leaving her."

Leo remained calm and stared at Talos for a long moment. "It's a lot of money. Are you sure you want to turn it down?" "I'm certain," Talos said, his voice firm.

Leo nodded. "Then you're fired."

"What?"

"I said you're fired." Leo didn't raise his voice. He sat behind his desk, casual as hell. "I don't need you as my special assistant anymore." He shrugged like it didn't matter.

"You're firing me after everything I've done for you? For this company?" Talos snapped. "I've given up hours. Days. I missed birthdays, holidays, seeing my parents, just to be at your fucking side. Fuck, I could send your ass to jail for all the shit we've done over the years. And now you fire me the second I grab a little happiness? How the fuck could you, Leo?"

He let Talos rant on, ignoring the fact that the man had just threatened him. Leo didn't interrupt, didn't flinch. Instead, he reached for a folder and tossed it to the edge of the desk the moment Talos finally paused for breath.

"Read that," Leo said.

"I don't want to read anything from you," Talos growled.

"Suit yourself," Leo replied, turning his attention to the file Talos had dropped on his desk earlier. Still, out of the corner of his eye, he caught Talos hesitating, clearly debating whether to take the bait. And just as Leo expected, curiosity got the better of him.

Talos snatched up the folder with an angry huff, flipping it open out of spite. His hands froze a second later. There it was.

A new contract for Chief Operating Officer.

Leo had fired the last guy months ago for fucking around and not doing his job, leaving the position open until the right person came along. He had always known Talos was the one for it.

"Is this for real?" Talos asked, flipping through the pages.

"Have I ever lied to you?" Leo replied, just as Talos slowly raised his head, meeting Leo's sharp and unreadable gaze.

"Let's get one thing straight. I'm not giving you this position because of Ada. You've come a long way from the hacker who tried to extort money from me."

Talos had the nerve to blush.

"You've earned the right to run this company with me." "I'm not sure what to say," Talos admitted, his voice low.

"Say you'll love her and make her happy. Say you'll never break her heart. Say she's the most important person in your life. And say yes to the position."

"Then I say yes to all those things."

"Sign the contract," Leo instructed, smiling when Talos followed through without hesitation. "And before you take over your new position, train Gencia. She's taking over as my special assistant."

"Is it fair to call you a bastard?" Talos asked, raising a brow.

"It's better than what most call me," Leo replied with a shrug.

Talos extended his hand, but Leo pulled him into a firm hug instead.

"Welcome to the family."

"I agree," came Athena's voice from behind Leo, her tone regal and unshakable. Her presence was magnetic, and both men instinctively stepped apart as she entered the room.

Talos turned quickly, blinking. "How? When? I just saw you... you materialized." He looked from the door to her, visibly rattled.

"What are you?"

Athena smiled, the answer already shining in her eyes. "Finally, you ask the important question, young Talos. I am a goddess. And your new mother-in-law."

As she spoke the words, Talos's body dipped, and Leo caught him before he could hit the ground.

"Can you stop making people faint in my arms?" Leo growled.

"But seeing you go into hero mode is so fun," she said cheerfully.

"Not funny, Mother," Leo snapped.

"Oh well, I'm off."

"Wait. Where are you going?" Leo asked.

"I'm off to cause havoc, my son."

"Whose life are you planning to ruin now?"

"Jason's mother, of course. I'm leaving the rest to you, dear."

Leo wasn't sure why she sounded so damn eager, like she was heading off to war with a smile on her face.

"I haven't told Jason about what his mother did yet. Give me a couple of days to tell him, and then you can do whatever you want to them."

"Fine," she replied, sounding very disappointed.

Leo placed the still-unconscious Talos into his office chair, then turned to his mom. "We have our first doctor's appointment today. Let's focus on that first."

"Ah yes, this is a joyous occasion. Then I will wait, as you asked."

He leaned in and kissed her cheek. "Thank you, Mother."

"Then I'm off."

She vanished, and Leo turned to look at Talos, who still hadn't stirred. He shook his head and muttered, "I guess it's time to reveal some family secrets."

Life is truly becoming more entertaining lately.

LEO HAD ALREADY READ through the pamphlet on the end table three times. Jason watched him from the exam table, amusement tugging at his lips as Leo flipped it over again, like the words might have magically changed since the last time.

"You know," Jason said, his voice warm with laughter, "if you read that any harder, it might burst into flames."

Leo looked up, caught. "I just want to be prepared."

Jason tilted his head, fondness bleeding into his

smile. "You brought a list of questions, didn't you? So I'd say you're prepared."

Leo hesitated. "It's a short list."

Jason laughed. "Hubby, you printed it on both sides."

Leo huffed, but came to stand beside him, fingers brushing over Jason's knee like he needed the contact. Jason felt the quiet nerves humming under Leo's skin, the way his husband leaned in just enough to draw strength from touch.

"It's just... you're almost seven weeks. That's a big deal, right?

The heartbeat, the first scan... I just..."

Jason reached up and pressed a finger gently to Leo's lips.

"It is a big deal. But you don't have to worry. I'm healthy."

Leo's eyes searched his, uncertain and tight with emotion. "I don't know how you're so calm."

Jason smiled. "Because I've been through this before. But this time, I've got you." He nudged Leo's side lightly. "Besides, I know you downloaded three different pregnancy tracking apps on your phone and ordered a stack of books on male pregnancies after we

confirmed I was pregnant with three positive tests."

"Am I going overboard?"

"No." Jason reached up and tugged Leo down for a soft kiss. "You're doing what you need to do to feel helpful, and I love that about you."

Jason leaned in to kiss him again, but the door opened, and someone stepped inside, prompting them to pull apart. She had her head down as she looked through the paperwork Jason had filled out earlier.

Jason took her in quickly. Milk-chocolate skin, a curvy figure, and long, beautiful micro locs. She was stunning.

"Hello, I'm..." She raised her gaze, paused mid-sentence, and smiled. Her eyes locked on Leo.

Jason almost gasped. Her smile lit up the room.

"Hello, Goddess Ra," Leo said.

"What is this 'Goddess Ra' nonsense? After all the battles your mother and I have fought against each other, and the ones we fought side by side, it's Auntie to you." She grinned. "Come here and give me a hug."

Leo stepped forward without hesitation, wrapping her in a hug as she laughed.

"You've grown, Daedalus. Or should I call you Leo?"

"You've just stopped growing," Leo said with a smirk. "And either works."

"Maybe," she replied with a playful glint in her eyes. "Now introduce me to your young man."

"Jason, I'd like you to meet a family friend, Goddess Sekhmet

Ahket-Ra. Auntie, this is my husband, Jason Dupree-Devereux." "It's nice to meet you," Jason said, feeling awestruck.

"You're married? I'm going to kill Athena for not telling me or inviting me to the wedding."

"Actually, Jason and I eloped," Leo told her.

"I see. You young people always rush off to get married without wanting us parents involved. I would kick Nefertum's ass if he went off and got married without telling me. Then again, he's too busy enjoying being a big star. The only thing I'm worried about is that bad boy image of his. Maybe I should have a talk with Anubis. What do you think?"

"Ah..." was all Leo managed to get out before Sekhmet spoke again.

"Well, don't forget to send me an invitation to the reception." Her eyes lit up with excitement. "Maybe it can double as a baby shower."

Leo turned to Jason. "That's an idea. What do you think?"

"It could work," Jason responded. Then he looked at Doctor Ra, wanting to ask a question that had been burning a hole in his head. He hadn't believed in gods before meeting Leo, but since learning they were real and living in Valleywood, he had started doing research whenever he found the time.

Like Athena, he found Sekhmet, the Egyptian goddess of war and battle, especially fascinating. While Athena was a strategic genius and an inventor, Sekhmet embodied war, medicine, healing, destruction, and divine retribution. She earned the title of lioness goddess because of how fiercely she protected and how completely she could destroy her enemies.

"Are you really a goddess?" Jason blurted out, immediately wanting to crawl into a hole for asking such a stupid question.

"Yes, but today I'm your doctor." She chuckled. "Let's get you checked out."

Jason nodded and shifted to get comfortable as

Doctor Ra dimmed the lights and turned on the ultrasound machine.

"Your vital signs look good. Your blood work isn't back yet, and that's something we can't rush, not even with magic. Once we get the results, I'll let you know if we need to tailor your diet. But since you're giving birth to a demigod, I don't foresee any problems.

Your record says this is your third child?" "Yes, the twins are five," Jason answered.

"This should be warm enough," Doctor Ra said as she squirted

gel onto his stomach, then gently pressed the probe against his skin. "And that was a healthy pregnancy?"

"Yes. I didn't know I was pregnant until close to my third month."

"That happens," the doctor said with a smile.

Leo gripped Jason's hand tightly. Jason didn't flinch. He gave Leo's fingers a light squeeze and murmured, "Relax. We're good."

A soft sound filled the room, and then a tiny flicker lit up the screen.

"There it is," Doctor Ra said, smiling. "One little heartbeat, strong and steady."

Jason heard Leo gasp and turned to watch him. "Are you okay?" he asked.

Leo nodded slowly, his eyes glued to the screen. "That's... real."

Jason rubbed his thumb over Leo's knuckles. "Yeah. That's our baby."

Leo blinked fast, his long lashes fluttering as if he

were trying to hold back tears. "You knew it would be like this?"

"I did," Jason said softly, his voice dropping. "But seeing it again... with you, it hits differently." He smiled. "It's better."

Leo didn't speak for a long time. He just stared at the screen like it held everything he didn't know he wanted. "I'm gonna be insufferable, aren't I?"

Jason chuckled. "I'm glad you're self-aware."

Leo leaned down and kissed Jason on the forehead. "Thank you," he said. "You've given my dull and boring life so much meaning in the past few months."

Jason couldn't argue. It was the same for him. What had started out as a way to give his children a father had turned into a love that felt unmanageable.

"Hmm... hold on a second," Doctor Ra said, breaking into their moment. Both he and Leo turned to look at her. She had her head tilted, eyes narrowed slightly as she stared at the screen, a faint frown forming on her lips.

Jason sat up a bit. "Is everything okay?"

"Oh yes," Doctor Ra said, adjusting the probe a little to the left, then to the right. "Everything looks great. I just... see another flicker here." She moved the probe up, then to the left. "And... one more there."

She pointed at the screen.

"What flicker here and one more there?" Jason squinted, a bad premonition crawling up his spine.

Doctor Ra adjusted the screen so he and Leo could see it more clearly. "Count the flickers with me," she said. "One, two, three."

"What are you trying to say?" Leo asked, his voice trembling.

"Three," Doctor Ra said, flashing a wide grin. "You're having triplets." Then she glanced back at the screen. "Well done, Athena. You've won this round."

Jason wasn't sure what she meant by that. He was too busy trying to stay calm, but the panic was quickly taking over.

"You... you... you and your fucking super sperm," he stuttered and growled, grabbing Leo by the lapels and yanking him down. "Can you not be so fucking grand in your delivery? First twins, now triplets. You will never fuck me again!"

"Shouldn't you be telling me this when you're in labor?" Leo asked, clearly dazed and confused.

"You asshole!"

They both looked at Doctor Ra when she burst out laughing.

"You two are hilarious." She pressed a few keys on the keyboard, and the sonogram photos printed. "Congratulations, you two. I'll leave your prenatal prescription with the pharmacy. Pick it up on your way out," she said, handing them the images before leaving the room.

Leo took the pictures, and as Jason watched the wonder spread across his face, the shock he'd felt began to melt away, replaced with joy.

Gods, I love this man.

Leo sat in the chair beside the exam table, muttering, "I'm going to need more pregnancy apps."

Jason reached over and gently squeezed his wrist. "I

guess now is a good time for us to move to that bigger house."

Their eyes met, wonder mixing with disbelief, and then laughter bubbled up between them, rich with joy and surprise.

Jason leaned closer to Leo and pressed a kiss to his cheek. "Are you ready for this?"

Leo took a shaky breath, smiled, and said, "I wasn't ready to fall in love, but with you by my side, I'm ready for anything."

"Sweet talker."

"Yours."

Their lips met in a soft kiss.

"How about we go home and tell the kids they're about to be big brothers and sisters?" Leo said. "Okay."

CHAPTER 17

JASON

J ason sat in the hospital waiting area, gazing
lovingly at the sonogram images while waiting for
Leo to return. He had gone to pick up Jason's
prescription. Neither of them could stop smiling.
Triplets were unexpected, but Jason wasn't as freaked
out as he had been with the twins. This time, he had his
lover by his side.

"What the hell are you doing here?"

Jason looked up from the images, and the smile
slipped from his face at the sound of his brother's gruff
voice.

"For a doctor, you ask the dumbest questions," Jason muttered, rolling his eyes and trying to ignore him.

Ian Dupree resembled their father in every way, from his height to his sharp features. Six feet tall and muscular, with a head full of blond hair and cold gray eyes. When his brother was conceived, there had been no question who was doing the heavy lifting.

Ian didn't say anything, and before Jason could react, he reached down, snatched the images from his hand, and stared at them in horror. Jason wouldn't deny that a small part of him was still a little afraid of Ian. After all, one of the biggest tormentors of his childhood was standing right in front of him. The fact that this man had become a doctor? The irony wasn't lost on him.

"You're pregnant?" Ian snapped, scowling. "Who would dare to fuck you?"

"You sound angry that I get fucked and you don't," Jason shot back. "Give those back to me." He snatched the images from Ian's hand and wiped them off like they were covered in filth.

"You've gotten real mouthy since you moved out." Ian stepped in close and whispered near his ear. "Don't think I can't kick your fucking ass like I did when you were a kid."

Jason smirked. "You can try, but I promise you won't live to see another day if you lay a hand on me."

"Are you threatening me?" Ian asked, stepping back.

"If it sounds like it, then I guess so." Jason shrugged.

Ian opened his mouth to respond, but Leo's deep voice cut through the space between them. "Is there a problem?"

Jason stepped around Ian and walked straight over to his husband. "Are you ready?" he asked Leo, who was now staring hard at Ian.

"Who are you?" Ian growled. "And what are you to my bastard brother?"

"You know what, I'm getting really tired of you Duprees asking who I am," Leo said, his voice flat with exhaustion. "Pick up a fucking magazine, for crying out loud."

"Leo, don't engage with this rabid dog. You might get rabies," Jason said.

"Who the fuck are you calling a dog?" Ian seethed.

"The very man who's foaming at the mouth," Jason answered coolly.

Ian snarled and stepped toward Jason with his hand raised,

but Leo moved fast. He lifted his leg and kicked Ian hard, sending him sprawling backward and knocking over several chairs.

Jason glanced around and could have sworn the waiting room had been full of people just a moment ago. Now it was empty and silent, except for the sound of Ian's heavy breathing.

Ian tried to get up, but Leo was already there, pressing him back down with his knee to stop him.

"Get the fuck off me," Ian shouted.

Jason was sure people would come running at the noise, but no one came. It was as if they were the only ones left in the waiting room. He found it strange, but Leo's voice cut through his thoughts before he could investigate the oddity.

GIOVANNA REAVES

"You see this?" Leo said, his tone cold. "Your brother gave me the perfect space to kill you."

Gave him the perfect space? Jason thought.

"But your death won't be at my hands. It belongs to someone who already called dibs." Leo leaned in closer, his voice dropping lower. "Curiosity is killing you. I know it. But don't worry. You'll meet them very soon."

"What the fuck are you talking about?" Ian raged. "He's—" "Shut up," Leo said, snapping his fingers.

Ian choked on his next words and grabbed at his throat, gasping for air. Leo didn't look bothered in the slightest. Jason found that he couldn't move. He simply watched and listened.

"For a doctor, you're damn annoying. Send this message to your parents. If they come anywhere near Jason or my children, I will cut the line and ruin you Duprees myself. And tell your father and Willa to hire a very good lawyer. From all the evidence I've collected, I'd say they're looking at fifteen years plus each."

Leo crouched lower, his voice like ice. "Or should we talk about your crimes? But do you know who I will happily leave for last?"

Ian didn't answer. He was still struggling to breathe, his face turning purple.

"Your mother."

Leo leaned in closer and whispered something in Ian's ear. Jason couldn't hear what he said, but the terrified look on Ian's face told him everything he needed to know.

My mother? What did she do to me besides not raising a hand to stop the abuse?

"Now be a good lapdog and do as I ordered. Do not miss a word," Leo said, leaning back before standing and dusting off his clothes.

He snapped his fingers, and Ian sucked in a huge gulp of air. Leo ignored him and walked over to Jason, pulling him into his arms. "Did I scare you?"

Jason circled Leo's waist with his arms and buried his face in his chest. "No. You're hot when you're threatening someone."

Leo chuckled. "I don't use my powers often, but it felt good." His arms tightened around him.

"What did my mother do to me?"

Leo leaned back and stared into his face. "She turned you into an unbound."

"What?"

"You weren't born an unbound, Jason. You were born a beta with latent omega genes. Your mother manipulated your DNA with magic and science. She forced your omega traits to emerge, then gave you the knot of another unbound who had been killed."

"What?" Jason said again, unable to believe what he was hearing. "Why didn't you tell me?"

"I planned on."

"When?"

"After... Shit, this is not how it was supposed to happen. Baby, listen to me. I didn't want to tell you, especially not on a day like today. Not when we just found out about the triplets," Leo explained.

"When? When did you find out?" Jason asked, tears welling in his eyes.

Leo was silent.

Jason's anger surged. Secrets. Why was everyone keeping secrets from him? First his parents, and now his husband. He couldn't trust anyone.

Jason closed his eyes, screamed, and shoved Leo away with everything he had.

When he opened his eyes again, he was alone in the empty waiting room, feeling lost and confused.

LEO TURNED left and then right in a frantic motion in the waiting room, no doubt looking like he had completely lost his mind.

Jason. Jason, where are you? No, this is not happening.

He had known the instant Jason pulled them into a space. Leo had seen the room shift, and the people who had been sitting in the chairs disappeared.

"What the fuck?" Ian Dupree shouted, pushing himself off the ground while everyone else stared at them in shock. "What the hell just happened?"

"Shut the fuck up," Leo growled, not wanting to hear a single word from the man. "This is all your fault."

"My fault?" Dupree looked confused, but Leo didn't pay him any attention.

He had to figure out how to get to Jason, who had shut him out and locked himself in his own space. Leo didn't know much about transporters and needed help.

Grabbing his cellphone, he dialed Jason's number, but the call went unanswered. It didn't even ring in the waiting room. That meant a couple of things. Either Jason had left the waiting area and was somewhere else entirely, or there was a magical block preventing any connection once he entered his space.

He dialed Doctor Pace's number. As soon as the call connected, Leo said hurriedly, "I need your help."

"What's going on?"

"Jason used his dimensional ability, and now I can't find or get to him."

"When and where did this happen?"

"Hospital waiting room. I was pushed out maybe five minutes ago."

"Depending on his frame of mind, he's likely still in the hospital. What were you doing? We agreed not to let him test those limits until he understood the basics. Why did he push you out?"

"We encountered some problems, and he created the dimension without realizing it. Then we had a misunderstanding, and he got agitated," Leo admitted.

"I think he'll show up in the waiting room, so wait. But you need to know that time in his dimension might move differently than in ours. What feels like minutes to him could be hours for us, or the other way around. Like I said, it all depends on his state of mind. That's all the information I can give you for now."

Leo pinched the bridge of his nose and leaned back against the wall. "Okay. Thanks for helping me."

"I didn't do much, but keep me updated on what happens."

"I will."

They hung up, and Leo made one more phone call.

"Ada, I need you to take care of the kids for me tonight."

"What? Why?"

"Jason and I had a minor disagreement, and we need to work it out before coming home."

"How did that happen? Isn't today your first doctor's appointment? What did you do?"

"Why is it automatically me? He overreacted about something and didn't even give me a second to explain," Leo grumbled.

"Well, I don't care whose fault it is. Just fix it," Ada snapped. "If you run my brother-in-law away, I'll kick your ass. He's the best thing that's happened to you." She hung up before Leo could say anything.

Leo growled and nearly threw his cellphone in frustration, but stopped himself when he remembered where he was. He tightened his grip around the device, going through a whirlwind of emotions—worry, anger, and then back to worry.

He understood why Jason believed he was hiding something. But he wasn't ready to share what he had found. Not yet. He wanted to hold on to the magic of their baby news just a little longer and protect Jason from the truth buried in that file.

Valencia Dupree had never loved her youngest child. That much was clear. Yet she knew everything that had happened to him. Her notes had been clinical, cold, and horrifically detailed. Leo could still see them in his mind, each line etched with sterile cruelty. He owed Talos a large bonus for tracking it all down. He finally understood why Athena hadn't been able to uncover the memories she'd sensed.

Valencia had documented everything, from the

moment she decided on using IVF to the day she discovered her son carried a rare, dormant omega gene. The lengths she had gone to in order to fulfill her twisted desire had been monstrous.

Some of the pages had made his skin crawl.

He remembered one entry clearly. *Initiated a tibial fracture to test regenerative capability. No anesthesia was administered. Subject unresponsive.*

Jason was five at the time.

Leo had to stop reading that night. His hands had been shaking too badly, and the bile crawling up his throat refused to settle. But he kept going, because he had to know.

And what he found had been worse than torture.

No one, not even her research team, knew what she was really doing. On the surface, her work sounded revolutionary. Valencia had secured government funding by claiming she wanted to enhance betas and omegas, to give them strength, autonomy, and resilience. But the deeper Leo read, the more obvious it became. This was not about empowerment.

She hadn't been working to protect them. She wanted to prove a point. To fulfill a twisted desire. To steal the body she believed should have been hers.

She wanted to be an omega.

Valencia had been born an alpha, but she had never accepted it. She didn't want dominance or authority. She didn't want to be seen as a leader. Valencia wanted the freedom to choose, not to have fate make that choice for her.

She envied unbound omegas, not for their lack of

bonds, but for their freedom. The ability to love without fate interfering. To walk into someone's arms without being bound there. To leave when the feeling was gone and carry no guilt.

Valencia couldn't hide her dominating aura and wanted the softness of an omega's intimacy and the vulnerability they carried, but she didn't want the strings. Fate had bound her to an omega who loved her obsessively and did everything she asked. That kind of love made her feel caged. And she couldn't reject him without dying.

She loved Willa and Ian, but it wasn't enough. She had planned for a third child, one she could cultivate and control. And according to her notes it was the only child she insisted on not carrying, like she did with Ian and Willa. She was afraid her alpha dominance would change the baby's DNA and had Jackson carry Jason, where she was able to observe and manipulate his growth. Her obsession turned darker when she decided to blend science with something forbidden.

Soul magic.

Not the romantic kind told in old stories of sweet love and passion. This was ancient and brutal, a fusion of alchemy and spirit that demanded balance and blood. She had studied for years, and later, after countless failures, realized that weaving metaphysical theory with genetic design might be the answer.

But even before that, Valencia had focused on Jason's embryo. It had been altered before he was even born. Every medical procedure had been layered with ritual.

Every hospital visit, shot, scan, and lab test that was supposed to be routine had a hidden purpose.

When an unbound omega died shortly after Jason's birth, Valencia harvested the knot and grafted it into her son to trigger the omega gene.

Leo was sick to discover that Jason wasn't the only omega she had experimented on. There had been other children. Other attempts. And unlike Jason, they hadn't survived. They were failures. They were actual deaths.

Jason was the only one who made it out alive. In some ways, Leo was glad Jason couldn't remember what had been done to him.

He couldn't believe Valencia had gotten away with her sick obsession for so long. Afterward, she waited impatiently for Jason to show signs of his abilities. When he didn't, she trained the rest of the family to reject him. She kept him isolated, starved him of affection, and taught them to see him as a burden or a mistake, hoping that constant emotional abuse would trigger his abilities.

And once she got what she wanted, his body, she planned to leave them all behind.

Her entire life had become the experiment.

When she finally found a shaman powerful enough to perform the soul transfer, he refused. He told her the truth she didn't want to hear. That changing her body would not change her soul. That her fate would still follow her.

But rejection had only fueled her obsession.

Leo could still picture the parts of the file that had made him want to scream. The broken bones. The bruises left behind by Willa and Ian. The surgeries performed without anesthesia. All of it done to force Jason's abilities into the open. When nothing happened quickly enough, she discarded and kicked him out like he had never mattered.

He rubbed his face hard, pressing his palms into his eyes. His head ached from the memories. She had been evil—not misguided, not broken, but evil. And everyone in that house had helped her hurt him.

But she had missed something.

Jason had healed, which was why no scars were left on his body. His body had restored itself slowly over time. The ability had always been there; she had just refused to see it. And now, Jason was more than an omega. He was a hybrid, shaped by science, soul magic, and something deeper.

Leo couldn't stop thinking about the way he wanted to bite and knot him. That ache lived under his skin, raw and insistent, every time they touched.

It wasn't just instinct. It was the gene Valencia had awakened. And it was more powerful than she had ever understood. In every sense, Jason was his mate.

Valencia had overlooked a critical rule about soul magic. If she had succeeded, the Phantasm Grim Reaper Clan, the keepers of soul memories, would have marked her for death. Not only that, but a soul-switching ritual required one hundred pure soul coins. It wasn't something that could be forced or faked. And when it failed, the consequences were devastating.

Souls could fracture. Consciousness could merge. Identities might twist into something unrecognizable.

One mind could consume the other until nothing was left but a shell, a body that appeared alive but screamed inside with no way out.

Leo didn't have to wonder if Valencia would have gone that far. He knew she would have. She had created a child to steal his life. After learning everything, Leo wanted to give Jason the happiness he never had growing up.

But in order to do that, Jason needed to come back.

Come back to me, love. Please don't hide from me, baby.

"Dae, what are you doing here?"

Leo turned when he heard a familiar voice and thought the fates were really fucking with him.

I don't have time for this shit.

No, he definitely didn't have time for fucking Minos.

MINOS WALKED over to where Daedalus was standing, hoping to close the distance between them and finally have a real conversation. But Daedalus had been avoiding him like the plague. Every attempt Minos made to reach out had gone ignored. He just wanted to talk, lay everything out, and figure out how to get back to what they once were.

By sheer luck, he'd been visiting a friend at the hospital when he passed this waiting room and caught sight of him. Daedalus. Or Leo, as he was calling himself now.

Minos clenched his jaw. He'd been trying to reach him for weeks, but the man hadn't returned a single call or message. He wouldn't even agree to meet with him.

"What I'm doing here is none of your concern," Leo growled, his voice sharp and low.

"Why shouldn't it be? You're in the fucking hospital." Minos stepped closer, reaching out to touch him. "Are you hurt? Have you seen a doctor?"

"Minos, stop," Leo said, pulling back. "I don't know what the fuck you think you're doing or what you want, but leave me the fuck alone."

"I can't do that," Minos replied, frustration tightening his tone. "I left you alone before, and you disappeared. Now you won't even see me. I just—"

"I don't want to hear what you have to say. Fuck, I don't even care." Leo cut him off with a glare. "You had your chance before you had me thrown in prison."

"That's what I want to explain," Minos said quickly. He could feel the pressure building in his chest. "You don't know the whole story. I had to protect Crete. I accepted the goddesses' blessing and power to stop the Minotaur. But I didn't know they were tricking me. I didn't know I'd end up a servant for centuries."

He looked directly into Leo's eyes. "Everything is not how it seems."

"I don't care," Leo answered coldly. "Let me say it here and now. Whatever we were before is in the past. That was a long fucking time ago. It's dead. Just like you are to me."

Minos gasped and stumbled back, clutching his chest as Leo's words hit him like a punch. Tears stung the corners of his eyes. "You don't mean that," he said, his voice cracking.

Leo didn't respond. He pushed off the wall he had been leaning on and walked to the other side of the room without so much as a glance back.

A sudden figure appeared out of nowhere, rushing toward him.

"Leo!" the voice called out.

"Jason," Leo breathed, immediately opening his arms and pulling the man into a fierce embrace. He held him tight, burying his face in Jason's shoulder. "I'm sorry. I'm so fucking sorry, baby." "I was so lost without you," Jason cried, clinging to him.

"It's okay. I'm here," Leo whispered, his voice low and comforting.

Minos remained frozen, watching the two of them wrapped in each other's arms. He didn't know what the hell had happened between them, but the jealousy that surged through him burned hot, wild, and violent, like an inferno consuming everything in its path.

Those arms should be wrapped around me. I will get you back, Leo.

With one last look at the couple, he left the waiting room.

CHAPTER 18
JASON

A few minutes earlier

J ason stood in the empty waiting room, staring down at his hand. He'd pushed Leo, but the man had disappeared.

How? Why? Did I do something to him? Where the fuck did he go?

Jason dragged his fingers through his hair, feeling angry, confused, and completely lost.

What the hell is going on?

He glanced around the room. All the chairs were knocked over, and a storm raged outside. He closed his eyes and took deep, steady breaths, trying to figure out what the hell had just happened.

Jason sat in the closest chair and forced himself to go over everything. He and Leo had confronted his brother, Ian. Then he got angry—pissed that Leo had kept something important from him.

He hadn't been born an unbound. He was a latent omega.

Jason hadn't known what his mother was up to, and knowing that Leo found out and didn't tell him fucking hurt. He could admit there were parts of his life he had forgotten. There were no good times, no family fun he could recall. Most of his childhood had been spent in school getting his ass kicked, or in the hospital with some broken body part.

Most of the doctors he saw were in the emergency room. He never met the surgeons who operated on him. All he knew was that things got taken care of because his mother worked for the hospital.

He was just so fucking angry and needed time to think. But Jason hadn't intended to push Leo away. Leo knew what had happened to him as a child, but Jason had never gone into detail about the treatment he endured. He had never told anyone that his mother was an alpha and his father was an omega, or how neither one had ever sympathized with him for being an omega. All he ever said was that they never got along or saw eye to eye.

Jason's family always had a way of ruining a good day, showing up out of nowhere like they had a fucking tracker on him. Today was supposed to be different. He'd just found out he was having triplets, and he and Leo hadn't even had the chance to fully appreciate the moment.

Why the hell couldn't his family just leave him alone? He hadn't bothered them since they kicked him out. He built his own life, his own safe space, created friendships, found family, and excelled in his career without ever relying on the Dupree name.

Although it hadn't started with love, he'd married a man who gave him the freedom to grow and just exist without fear or judgment. That was something he had never seen in his parents. His father was the one who gave, while his mother only took. Even as a kid, Jason had questioned whether she ever truly loved Jackson. She clearly favored Ian and Willa, but something about the way she treated Jackson had always felt off.

Maybe it was because she was an alpha female and he was an omega male, a pairing that wasn't common, and definitely not equal in her eyes.

Then it hit him. Leo had said something about space to Ian.

"Your brother gave me the perfect space to kill you, but your death will not be at my hands; it belongs to someone who called dibs."

Space? Did I bring them into another dimension? If that's the case, how the fuck do I get out?

Jason stood and looked around, the reality starting to sink in. Now, it made sense why no one else was here but him.

His thoughts raced. *Am I still in the waiting room? Am I*

still in the hospital? Where the hell is Leo? Is he still waiting for me?

He walked around the room, then bolted out the door, only to find himself standing in a perfect replica of the same waiting room. It was like he was stuck, unable to escape whatever realm he had created. A wave of fear rolled through him.

How the hell do I get out? I need to find Leo.

His fear turned into a frantic pounding in his chest. He forgot all about being angry at his husband. None of that shit mattered now. He tore through the space, running from one room to the next, calling Leo's name and thinking only of him.

Leo would fix it. He always did.

Please, Leo. Find me.

And just as he stumbled into another duplicate of the waiting room, Jason saw him.

"Leo!" he shouted, sprinting into his husband's arms.

The world snapped back into focus.

Jason clung to him, breathing hard, overwhelmed. He knew right then he couldn't live without Leo. The man was everything.

His anchor. His lifeline.

"I'M SORRY," Jason said for the umpteenth time since they were reunited.

"Stop apologizing," Leo murmured, pressing a kiss to his forehead and pulling him into his arms.

They had returned home, choosing to put the chaos of earlier events on pause and instead focus on the kids. Following their typical routine, they had dinner, conversed, played with the children, and prepared them for bed. However, they had yet to mention the triplets. Jason wanted to wait until he felt emotionally grounded, and Leo respected that decision. Now, with the children asleep, the weight of everything he'd been through hit Jason hard.

"I wasn't going to keep it from you, Jason," Leo said softly. "I just wanted to find the right way to tell you. It's a lot to take in."

Jason sat up, his eyes narrowing slightly as he looked at Leo. "Is it that bad? I know my family doesn't like me, and I was always the one they targeted with their bull-shit, but I gave as good as I got."

Leo reached up and cupped Jason's cheek with his palm. Jason leaned into the touch, letting the warmth ground him.

"That was by design," Leo said quietly.

"What do you mean?" Jason asked, his brow furrowing in confusion.

Leo exhaled and sat up beside him, brushing another gentle kiss across his forehead. His voice was low, almost reluctant. "Are you sure you want to know now?"

Jason looked up at his face. "I won't be able to sleep if I don't get answers."

Leo gave a small nod, then turned, opened the drawer, and pulled out a thick folder. He handed it to Jason. "This is all the information we could get our hands on."

Jason took the folder, his gaze flicking between Leo

and the weighty file in his lap. "How did you get this?"

"Talos."

"Huh?"

"There's a reason I pay Talos more than most of my staff. He wasn't just my special assistant. He has a degree in cybersecurity and is one of the most sought-after hackers in the world. He goes by the name IronFeather."

Jason gasped. "No way."

"What? Have you heard of him?"

"Are you kidding me?" Jason said, climbing up onto his knees with a rush of energy. "That guy is a legend. I've never gone up against him, but I've heard stories, he used to break through the most secure firewalls in minutes. But then he vanished a few years ago. No one knew what happened. People thought the authorities finally caught him. How the hell did you two meet?"

Leo gave a dry chuckle. "He hacked into my company files and threatened to expose my secrets. So I turned the tables and hired him. That was over ten years ago. That's why it bothered him so much that he couldn't figure out who or where you were."

"Wow, who knew the world's best hacker has been your assistant this entire time?"

"He's no longer my assistant," Leo said, his tone calm but firm.

"What? You fired him?"

"I promoted him. He's now the new COO." "Really?" Jason blinked in surprise.

"Yes." Leo tapped the thick file. "This was the last job he did for me as my special assistant."

Jason looked down at the folder in his hands, biting

his bottom lip as apprehension coiled in his gut. As much as he wanted to know why his family hated him, the idea of actually reading the truth made his nerves spike.

"You don't have to read it tonight," Leo said gently, his gaze steady with concern.

"No." Jason shook his head, voice low but resolute. "I don't want to delay it." He glanced up at his husband, eyes shadowed with unease. "Is it weird that I might already know why my family hates me without reading what's in here? Growing up, I was always jealous of other kids. Their parents doted on them. Their siblings spoiled them. I remember my senior year, one of my classmates made the top five of our graduating class and his brother bought him a sports car. Want to know what I got? Kicked out of the house in nothing but my underwear."

Leo didn't interrupt. He listened, his expression unreadable but attentive.

"My parents never gave a damn about anything I did. It didn't matter that I graduated with a 4.00 GPA. Or that I got full scholarships to some of the most prestigious colleges and universities. What mattered most was my chosen degree. They couldn't stand that I went into architecture instead of law or medical school. But that was all on my father's end."

He took a deep breath, collecting his thoughts.

"My mother didn't even look in my direction or say a word of comfort. I always felt this visceral hate coming from her, like I wasn't what she wanted me to be. It's like I ruined her life just by being born. I think that's why I overcompensate with Xander and Sera. I don't ever want them to feel the way I did growing up." He touched his stomach. "I don't want our children to feel unwanted or unloved."

"They won't," Leo said, cupping his cheeks with both hands. His voice was firm but filled with tenderness. "I wanted to protect Sera and Xander before I even knew they were mine." He laid one hand over Jason's, the one resting gently on his stomach. "And I'll do the same with these three. You and the children are my life. Nothing in that file has changed that. Keep that in your heart while you're reading it. I want you. I need you. I love you."

"Do you?" Jason whispered, a tear slipping down his cheek before he could stop it. "Yes."

"I love you, too." He wrapped his arms around Leo's neck, pulling him close as their lips met in a deep, passionate kiss. The warmth of Leo's touch stripped away the day's anguish, reminding Jason of the love he felt before everything came crashing down.

Their lips slowly parted, and Leo rested their foreheads together, his warm breath ghosting over Jason's damp lips.

"Can you stay with me while I read through this? I might need you to hold me after."

"I never planned on leaving you alone," Leo said softly.

"Thank you."

Leaning back, Jason picked up the file. He settled between Leo's open legs and rested his back against Leo's strong chest. The steady rhythm of Leo's breathing calmed him. Leo wrapped his arms around him, holding him close, grounding him as they began looking through the information together.

"Would I be as evil as my mother if I wanted them all to die horribly?" Jason asked, his voice flat, too calm for what he felt inside.

It was nearly three in the morning. They hadn't even made it through half the folder, and the night had become a relentless loop of reading, breaking down, and trying again. Jason would read a page, go quiet, then snap. Cry. Scream. Shake so violently that Leo had to wrap his arms around him and hold him together.

Leo had never seen rage look so much like grief.

He sat beside Jason now, watching the tightness in his jaw and the tremble in his fingers. He wasn't crying anymore, and that worried Leo more than the tears ever had.

Jason's hand hovered over the next page but didn't touch it.

"My body hurts," he muttered.

Leo turned toward him, voice low with concern. "Where?"

Jason shook his head. "Everywhere. I don't remember anything, but... I feel it. Like ghosts under my skin." He swallowed, his throat working around the pain. "There's this one surgery she wrote about—bone fracture. No anesthesia. I couldn't stop staring at it."

He pulled his hand away from the folder and curled it into a fist. His nails pressed into his palm, sharp and unrelenting.

"She said I didn't scream. That I didn't respond at all.

Like I wasn't even human. Just a body on a slab. But I can feel pain now."

His voice cracked, not with tears but with something sharper. Leo had seen him cry. This was different. This was rage building beneath the surface, slow and dangerous, too hot and steady to be soothed.

"I don't remember any of it," Jason continued. "I thought the dreams were just nightmares. Childhood shit. But they're real. She cut me open, over and over, and I didn't even know." He looked at Leo, eyes red but dry. "I want them to hurt." "You're not evil for that," Leo said, his voice low and steady.

Jason's body trembled once, a shudder that barely broke through his restraint. "I want them to beg," he whispered. "I want them to feel everything they made me forget."

Leo reached for him. Jason didn't pull away, but the tension in his spine remained. Leo wrapped one arm around his waist and the other around the back of his head, holding him tightly. Jason allowed himself to be pulled close, his breathing jagged and shallow.

"Then I guess we think alike," Leo murmured. "Because I want to hurt them just as badly as you do. But don't worry. We won't have to get our hands dirty. Plans are already in motion."

Jason let out a slow breath, then looked up at him. "She gave birth to me just to take over my body," he said. "Is it really possible?"

Leo couldn't lie. "It is. But it would take more than a few chanted incantations to replace one soul with another."

"Do you think she would have succeeded?"

"No," Leo answered honestly. "If she had gotten the chance, you both would have died, and I wouldn't have met you."

Jason burrowed into Leo's arms, clutching the fabric of his shirt like an anchor.

"Do you want to confront them?" Jason didn't respond.

"Don't worry, you have all the time in the world. They will be behind bars for the rest of their natural life."

"That's not it," Jason said quietly.

"Then what is it?"

"I'm afraid that if I stand in front of them, I might actually kill them. Then what will happen to us? We're just beginning. What about Sera and Xander? I can't let them grow up with me in jail for the rest of their lives. And what about the triplets? As much as I want to hurt my so-called family badly, I don't think I could live with the guilt," he said, his voice tight with conflict, the weight of every possibility pressing down on him.

Leo grabbed his face gently. "Do you think I would let anything like that happen? If you kill them tomorrow, their bodies would never be found."

"You would do that for me?" Jason asked in shock.

"Of course I would."

"But you could go to jail. I don't want that," Jason said, his voice tight with worry.

"I wouldn't get caught. I'm over three thousand years old, Jason. I wasn't kidding when I said I have people who could take care of things. I'm well connected."

"You're sort of scaring me." His body stiffened in Leo's embrace.

"Don't be," Leo said, then kissed him gently. "All you need to know is that you and the children will never have to worry or be separated. You don't need to worry about living with guilt either, because death would be too easy for them. Your family needs to

suffer for everything they've done to you."

"What do you have planned?"

"They made your life a living hell growing up, and I will make theirs even worse. They will beg for death, but none will come."

Jason stared at him for quite some time before he spoke. "As long as you don't get arrested. I can't live without you."

Leo smiled. "And you never will." He hugged Jason tighter. "I will always protect you, baby."

"Same. I might not be as connected as you are, but I will do everything in my power to keep you safe."

"That's everything to me." Leo held him even closer. "Don't worry, their downfall will be public. Your father, the top-notch lawyer, and his daughter, who brokered million-dollar deals, and let's not forget the young doctor who's saved more lives than most. But beneath the glitz and glamor are snakes who bribe, manipulate, hurt, and steal from their clients."

"I remember a couple of months before I was kicked out of the house, I saw my father meeting with Felix Calderon. I don't know what they were talking about, but it looked like a heated conversation. A few days later, Calderon was arrested for insider trading, but not even

279

twenty-four hours later, the charges were dropped and Calderon walked free."

"Your father got him released. He paid someone to take the fall," Leo said, voice low and certain.

"What?" Jason sat up and looked at his husband. "How do you know this?"

"Talos," was all Leo had to say, and Jason understood.

"Oh." He lay back down beside him.

"Anyway, soon Calderon, your father, and your sister won't be able to get away with what they've been doing these past few years. We gave the information to the authorities, and they need

time to investigate. Just hold on tight."

"How bad is it?"

"Let me put it this way. The next time your dad blinks his eyes, he'll need to ask the guards for permission." "Damn," Jason whispered.

Felix Calderon, a career criminal with fingers in many pots and pies, from arms dealing, medical smuggling, and insider trading to underground biotech experimentation, wasn't the type to get his hands dirty. He always had a fall guy waiting in the wings. Later, he would pay off the family or kill them, depending on his mood.

Calderon was calculating and charming. He presented himself as a legitimate businessman, building a network of complicit professionals like doctors, lawyers, and even senators. He once tried to recruit Leo into his merry band of criminals, but Leo turned him down without even attending the meeting.

He didn't want to be associated with a man like Calderon.

Leo rubbed his temples, thinking about all the evidence he had on Calderon. It was enough to put him, along with the father and daughter Dupree, away for a very long time. But Talos had found something else. Leo didn't know how he did it, but Talos located phone record transcripts of a conversation between Calderon and someone referred to only as K.

Since it was typed up, Leo couldn't tell the gender or location of the other party. He hadn't wanted to put the bullseye on Dupree and Calderon just yet, but he wanted Jason to have his revenge against his family. Besides, with Calderon behind bars, the silent partner might unearth themselves.

Leo couldn't say why he was so invested in this whole thing, but he always trusted his gut when something kept nagging at him. Until then, he would continue to live his life.

Jason whimpered, and Leo looked down to see that while he'd been wrapped up in these thoughts, Jason had fallen asleep, letting out soft snores. Leo brushed his hair from his face, noticing that it had been a few weeks since his lover had gotten a haircut.

I like it.

Scooting back just a little, Leo propped up the extra pillows behind him. He did it all without waking Jason. Once he was settled, he kissed his little husband on the forehead and closed his eyes for a short nap. Whatever else had to be taken care of could wait. All that mattered was protecting Jason and his children.

CHAPTER 19
FELIX

Felix Calderon blinked his eyes open when he felt a presence in his bedroom. He remained still as he saw a figure standing at the foot of his bed. He knew who it was, since they had been business acquaintances for many years. They had made a lot of money together. It was still early in the morning, and the sun was trying to peek out through the clouds.

Felix had been running the Valleywood underworld boldly and openly for the past few years. It wasn't until ten years ago, on a trip out of state, that he met the man now standing in front of him. Felix had first noticed his gorgeous appearance and had tried talking him up, hoping to spend the night with him. But the man had turned the tables and offered to become his silent partner.

He was never one to pass up money for ass, so he listened to what the gorgeous man had to offer. It was right up his alley and a direct path into the international market. It was easier to launder money through shell companies overseas than it was in the United States. It was also better to trade organs and bodys internationally and force them to work for nothing, yielding higher profits.

For ten years, he had gone from small time to big time. During those years, his silent partner would slip in and out of Valleywood like a thief in the night. Felix wouldn't see him often when he was in town, but lately, it felt like he saw the man every day. As much as Felix liked the guy, he also valued his privacy and his sleep.

"Are you done pretending to be asleep?" The calm, warm voice washed over him.

"Who's pretending?" Felix turned over and sat up. "What are you doing here? Didn't you say you were leaving for a few days?"

"I've changed my mind. There are a few things I need to clear up."

"And that is what?"

"I think it's time we end our arrangement," the man said, shocking Felix.

"What? Why?" He jumped out of bed, not caring about his state of undress. His companion didn't flinch or move; he simply stared at Felix, whose anger was rising.

"You have become a liability to me."

"What are you talking about?" Felix shouted.

"The authorities are looking into your recent activities, and I cannot have my business meddled with."

Felix scoffed. "The cops are always harassing me, and I always get off. You've met my lawyer, Jackson. He's good at what he does. You don't have to worry."

"Oh, I'm not worried." The handsome man quirked a perfectly sculpted brow. "However, I have grown wary of you."

Before Felix could utter another word or phrase, he felt a slice at his neck as the scent of blood filled his nostrils. He grabbed his throat, trying to stop the bleeding, gagging as blood filled his mouth. He swung left, falling to the bed. As his vision blurred, he saw the man disappear from his sight.

Felix rolled over onto his back and stared at the white ceiling. *What's the fucking use of trying to stay alive? I knew this day would come sooner or later. Dammit, I never even got the chance to fuck him.*

He removed his hands from his throat just as a handsome face appeared. His eyes were a dark green. He had jet-black hair and an alabaster complexion that emphasized the black suit with purple embroidery he wore. The man didn't speak. He simply leaned against the door with his hands in his pockets, looking so cool it made Felix jealous, as if he were waiting for time to pass, or for Felix to die. That happened in the next minute, as Felix felt his soul lift from his body.

"Are you the grim reaper?" Felix asked.

The gorgeous man nodded. He was not the stereotypical depiction of the grim reaper Felix had read about in novels. He didn't even have a scythe. Who knew death was stylish, tall, and muscular, looking like an actor or a model? But then again, after living among magic and whatnot, Felix knew things were never the norm, and death wouldn't be either.

Felix looked down at his naked, lifeless body on the bed surrounded by red-stained sheets and shook his head.

"Fuck, I didn't even get to smoke my last cigarette," he mumbled, and was surprised when a cigarette appeared in front of him. Felix nodded, taking it and putting it between his lips just as a flame came into view. "Thanks."

The man didn't speak and only nodded. Felix sighed, looking at his naked spirit, then stared again at his body as he took slow drags from the cigarette. *I should have worked out more*, he thought, staring at his rounded stomach. He reflected on his life and realized he regretted nothing.

Although he might not have died going out guns blazing with a catch phrase of his lips, he had lived exactly how he wanted, without apology. He had a few kids but never claimed them. Why should he? He had always been upfront with his bed partners. If they got pregnant, he wouldn't support or care for them. The mothers and fathers never came after him, but now that he was dead, his money was open season.

A glorious smile crossed his lips. He wished he could watch the play-by-play of which kid got the most of the inheritance. Once the cigarette burned to the nub, he flicked it onto his lifeless body and turned to the handsome man.

"I've heard people say death is beautiful. I see what they mean," Felix said, and as he'd already learned, the man didn't comment. "Alright, I'm ready. Take me to hell."

For the first time since Death entered the room, he smiled, charming the hell out of Felix.

Dammit. What a pity I can't fuck Death.

VALENCIA DUPREE SAT at her desk, sifting through her notes. After years of waiting, the day had finally come. It had taken much longer than she wanted, but it didn't matter. Jason was still young and strong, as far as her reports told her. It had been a surprise to her when Ian told her about Jason's abilities. Valencia had given up on the little bastard, but he certainly knew how to surprise her in the end.

What a good mama's boy. She smirked.

Valencia leaned back in her chair, putting her foot on her desk. A few obstacles were in her way, namely the man Jason was currently tied to, but as an unbound, she was certain their lives weren't linked.

Once their souls were switched, Valencia planned on moving far away from Valleywood. She had taken precautions to make sure her family couldn't track her down, but her plans would have to wait until after the ritual. Valencia wasn't worried about the child Jason was carrying; that was an easy fix.

All that matters is that I'll be young and free again.

Valencia couldn't deny Jason's handsome, almost androgynous beauty, which he had gotten from both her and her husband. She ran her fingers over her face, feeling the fine lines that had cropped up over the years due to the stress of her job. But once her soul was switched with Jason's, she wouldn't have to worry about aging for quite a while.

She had earned enough money to live in leisure, combined with her husband's shady dealings, which had resulted in millions of dollars. There was no way she would go broke. A pleasant smile graced Valencia's lips. Soon she would be able to leave all this shit behind.

Better days are coming.

She picked up the photo of her so-called grandchildren and sneered. She didn't know how to word it properly, but there was something off about the kids. She hadn't considered doing soul magic with them, although Valencia was certain they still had value for her needs. She threw the pictures in the trash and closed her eyes, thinking about the day she could start a new life as an omega.

"Goo Mor'ng, Papa."

Leo smiled when he saw Xander walking into the kitchen, holding a stuffed whale, still in his pajamas with bedhead and barely open eyes.

"Good morning, baby." Leo put his coffee down and held his arms open for his son. "Come here."

Xander eagerly hopped into his arms and laid his head on Leo's chest.

"Are you hungry?" Leo asked, gently rubbing his back. Xander had become quite clingy over the past couple of days. Leo wouldn't complain; he liked that his kids sought comfort from him. They hadn't told the kids about the triplets yet. A lot had happened in the past two days that had taken up both his and Jason's time.

Felix Calderon had been found dead by his assistant two days ago. The police were seriously investigating what could have happened or who might have killed him. They believed magic was involved, since there was little evidence left at the scene, just a cigarette butt with Calderon's DNA on it.

Leo was peeved that someone had taken Calderon out before he could. He had been interested in finding out who the mysterious "K" was. He was certain someone had leaked to K that the authorities were about to arrest Calderon for his crimes and eliminated him before he could talk.

"Can I have pancakes?" Xander asked, breaking into his thoughts.

"Sure." Leo smiled and tapped his son's cute nose.

A second later, Sera walked in, yawning and rubbing her eyes. "Good morning, Papa," she said between yawns.

"Good morning, sweetheart." Just as he had with Xander, he opened his arms. Sera jumped into his lap, pressing her face into his chest. Leo held his two treasures close, silently thanking his husband for them. He loved mornings like this, when it was just him and his babies.

"Your brother wants pancakes for breakfast. What about you?" he asked Sera.

"Can I have blueberry pancakes?" "Sure." Leo smiled again.

"Can we help?" Xander asked, looking up at him with those puppy dog eyes that always reminded him of Jason.

"Yes," Leo said, chuckling softly.

That woke them up, and they jumped off his lap, running to the sink to wash their hands. Leo didn't move. He just watched them giggle and splash water on each other.

Yup. I love mornings like this.

JASON GROANED, reaching for his annoyingly ringing cellphone.

"Whoever you are, go away."

"Is that any way to talk to your mother?"

Jason snapped his eyes open and sat up in bed. He looked at his phone screen and saw the number, but no name. "I don't have a mother," Jason said, bringing the cellphone to his ear.

"You've grown cheeky," Valencia mocked. "Come to the park.

We need to talk."

Jason smirked. "Which park? If you haven't noticed, Valleywood has quite a lot of them. Besides, do you really think I would drop everything I'm doing to meet with you? Especially after everything you've done to me?"

Valencia was silent on the other end of the phone.

"You have no dominion over me, Valencia. Let's continue to live the way we have been. For years, I asked myself why you gave birth to me if you were just going to ignore my existence. I was a fool, trying to get you to see me, to love me, but now I know your real purpose. So you can go and fuck yourself, Valencia. After all, you see me as just an experiment."

Jason hung up the phone and blocked the number. He flopped back on the bed and stared up at the ceiling, blinking a few times to stop the tears that threatened to fall. He wouldn't care about the Duprees. He wouldn't cry over them or imagine what they could have been as a family. They didn't love him, so why should he care about them?

Laughter from the other room reached his ears. Jason got out of bed, ran to the bathroom, and took care of his morning routine. He was thankful he hadn't had any morning sickness and prayed to every god that was listening that he wouldn't. Then he headed to the living room.

He leaned against the wall and watched his husband, dressed

in a black tank top and gray sweatpants, showing their two little ones how to pour batter into the pan. They were whispering and smiling, a happy scene that made Jason feel like he belonged. For once, he wasn't an outsider. He was part of something warm, something real.

He hadn't experienced happy moments like this growing up. He had been pushed to the side, made to feel unwanted. Quietly, he ran back to the bedroom, grabbed his cellphone, and returned to the living room to capture the sweet moment. Jason pressed a hand to his stomach and smiled. Soon, they would be a family of seven.

"Daddy!" Xander and Sera shouted, then ran over to him.

"Good morning, my babies." He kissed them on the cheek.

"Do I get one of those, too?"

He smiled and wrapped his arms around Leo's neck, greeting him with a big kiss. "Hello, handsome."

"Oh, I love it when you wake up in a good mood." "It wasn't so good." He pouted.

"What happened?" Leo asked, his brows furrowing.

"You weren't next to me," Jason whispered, brushing his lips against Leo's.

Leo chuckled and pulled him close. "I'll make it up to you tonight."

Their lips were about to meet again, but they froze and looked at the twins, who said, "Ew, gross," giggling and covering their mouths.

"Gross? I'll show you gross." Leo bent down and scooped them both up before they could run off. Jason stayed where he was and watched Leo handle them both, and their laughter brought him more joy than he had realized he needed.

This is what family is all about.

~

"So, your Papa and I have something we want to ask you," Jason said, looking at the twins. They had just finished the breakfast that Leo and the kids had made.

"What do you two think about moving to a bigger place?" Leo asked.

"Can Grandma Sing come with us?" Xander asked.

"Um..." Jason stuttered. The kids knew all about Athena being Mrs. Sing, but that didn't stop their affection for their neighbor, whom they called Grandma. "I don't think she'll want to leave her home. But we can still visit her."

"Why are we moving?" Sera asked.

"Well," Leo said, taking Jason's hand in his, "you're going to be a big sister."

"I'm already a big sister," Sera said.

"No, Sera. Jason was born before you, so that makes you his little sister," Jason explained.

"That's because I told him to go first," she stated proudly.

"You..." Jason stared at his daughter, unsure of what to say. He looked at Leo, who was smirking as he stared at their daughter adoringly. Jason shook his head and looked back at the children. "What I mean is," he tried again, "you're going to be a big sister again." He touched his stomach. "I'm going to have a baby. Well, three to be exact."

The twins were silent for a few seconds, which made Jason nervous. He wondered if they felt some type of way about having more kids in the house since they were the apples of his and Leo's eyes.

"Are they boys or girls?" Xander asked.

"I... I... I don't know," Jason stuttered, feeling like he was being interrogated.

"I hope they're all girls," Sera said, a bright smile spreading across her face.

"No, all boys!" Xander declared. "That way I can be a big brother."

Jason was about to correct him again, to remind him he already was a big brother, but Leo squeezed his hand and shook his head, stopping him.

"What if it's a mix of both?" Leo asked. "Boys and girls. Would that make you happy?"

The twins looked at each other for a few seconds, as if mentally communicating. Jason had noticed they did that often. He wasn't sure if it was something new or something they'd always done, but he found it cute. After a moment, they both nodded and turned back to Leo.

"We can deal with that," Sera said, then looked at Jason.

"Daddy, you must have a boy and two girls."

"I don't have control over that, sweetheart. That's all up to science."

Sera hopped off her chair, walked over to him, and pressed her face to his stomach. "Listen up, babies. I am your big sister. One of you must be a boy, and the other two girls." She looked up at Jason. "Daddy, can you make another one so it can be two girls and two boys? That way, it's even."

"Baby, I don't control science," Jason said, trying to explain with a small laugh.

"Papa, can you fix it?" Xander asked, looking at Leo like he was a superhero.

"I'll do my best, Son." Leo reached over and ruffled his hair.

"Yay! We're going to have two brothers and two sisters!" they shouted excitedly, then ran over and hugged Jason, who had no earthly idea what had just happened.

"I guess we have more work to do," Leo whispered in his ear.

Work my ass. You will never get to fuck me again, was what Jason thought, but later that night, when Leo had him pressed down on the bed with his legs wrapped around his trim waist, there was no way he could deny the sweet pleasure.

"MY MOTHER CALLED ME YESTERDAY," Jason said a few hours later.

They were sitting in the living room watching a movie, and the kids were in their room, probably plotting to take over the world with Sera leading the charge. After telling the kids about the triplets, they'd talked about kindergarten, which they were both excited for. Jason mentally groaned, knowing he was going to get a phone call at least once a week that his daughter was leading a revolution. Those would be fun days.

"How did that conversation go?" Leo asked.

"It went as well as could be expected." Jason shrugged as if it was nothing, but it had taken everything in him not to go off on his mother. "She made demands, and I told her to fuck off. Fuck, I don't know why my family is suddenly showing up. I lived years without seeing them, and now, from my sister to my mother, who never cared about me, they want to have conversations. Well, they can kick fucking rocks!"

"Good." Leo's arms tightened around him.

Jason knew there was a lot he needed to work through. He wasn't putting his feelings aside and planned on getting some help. After reading what his mother had done to him, Jason knew it would be foolish to ignore his pain. He had done that when he was younger, but now that he was a husband and father, he couldn't afford to do the same. The only problem was that Jason didn't like asking for help. After being alone for so long, he had learned to depend only on himself. But at the same time, he couldn't lose who he was.

"Don't worry," Leo whispered, kissing the top of his head. "I won't let you fall into despair."

"How do you know what I was thinking?"

"How much of your anger did you hold back when you spoke to your mother yesterday?" Leo gently grasped his chin and lifted his head. "Baby, don't hide yourself away. If you're angry, show it. Your mother and everyone in your family deserves your wrath. All you need to know is, when it's over, I'll be there to catch you."

"I know. I don't want to burden you," Jason admitted.

There were so many things he had overcome in their short time together—Leo's wealth, making their relationship public at work and with friends. Leo had been patient, waiting for Jason to fall in love, and now that they were moving forward, it seemed even more things were surfacing.

"You are not a burden, and you never will be. We have a lifetime together, Jason. That's all we need to focus on. After the

babies are born, you'll be the one taking care of me."

"What are you talking about?"

Leo gently pushed him to sit up, then got off the sofa, walked into his office, and returned with a folder in hand. He handed it to Jason.

"What is this?"

"Open it and see," Leo encouraged.

Corporate Appointment & Share Transfer Agreement

"Leo, what's all this?" Jason asked, completely confused.

"One year from now, you will be the CEO of DRA&D."

"But, I don't..."

Leo pressed a finger to his lips. "Don't doubt yourself. I've seen clips of you running meetings and taking charge. I've watched you close deals and finesse clients into signing with our company."

"You've been watching me?"

"Of course. Jason, you brought something to DRA&D that was needed. And Ada agrees. You're brilliant and will take the company to new heights."

Jason didn't know what to say. No one had ever spoken so highly of him.

"What will you be doing in the meantime?"

"Raising our kids and being your boy-toy, arm candy,

whatever you want. That's what I'll be doing in the meantime." Leo smiled.

"I also have other businesses that need my attention."

"How about husband?"

"I'll be that too."

Jason looked through the contract and saw that Leo had given him forty-three percent of the shares and kept nineteen percent for himself. The rest were divided between Xander, Sera, the triplets, and Ada, Talos, and their kids.

"Why are you doing this?"

"I'm being selfish and a little petty."

"What? What about?"

"I know it's not anyone's fault it happened, but I'm jealous that you got to raise Xander and Sera for five years. I want to do the same with the triplets. I don't want to miss their first moments. I promise you won't either, but this is what I feel in my gut I need to do."

"That's not selfish or petty. I understand. But are you sure you want to give me this much control of your company?"

"It's no longer my company. It hasn't been since the night we got married. It's ours, so yes, I do."

Jason stared at his husband and smiled. No one had ever believed in him this much. He knew the company's worth and how much it meant to Leo.

"I'll do this if you promise me something," Jason said.

"Anything."

Jason smirked. "You call me boss in bed."

Leo chuckled, then whispered deep and low, "Boss."

Jason shivered and fanned himself, feeling flushed with heat.

Gods, this man is deadly. "I promise not to run it into the ground."

"I trust you." Leo handed him a pen, and just like the night they got married, Jason signed his name on the dotted line.

"I'll get this to my lawyers in the morning." Leo set the contract aside and pulled Jason into his lap. "Since I'll be unemployed pretty soon, how about I interview for my next position?"

"I've been told I'm difficult to work for. Do you think you can handle the hard questions?" Jason straddled Leo's legs, grinding against him.

"I can take anything you throw at me, boss." Leo licked Jason's neck, moving up his chin.

Jason moaned. "I like the way that sounds." He kissed Leo's lips. "Call me boss again."

Leo kissed him deeply, then sucked on his lips as he laid him back. Jason wrapped his legs around Leo's hips. "Boss."

Jason jerked his hips upward, grinding his semi-erect cock against Leo and capturing his mouth in a sweet, lingering kiss. They didn't take things too far, knowing the kids were still awake, but they savored the intimate moment together.

CHAPTER 20

LEO

"I can't believe you've been married for months, with kids and more on the way, and you're just now telling us," Julien said, handing him a drink. They were in Draycott's, an exclusive bar with leather chairs and expensive drinks.

"But he looks happy," Avery added.

"Maybe we should think about getting married," Julien said.

Leo quirked a brow at his friend, who had a contemplative expression.

"Are you interested in someone?" Leo asked.

"Interested? Yes," Julien said. "Want? Yes. Desire? Yes. We've only met once, but I can't stop thinking about him."

Leo looked at Avery, silently asking if he knew who it was, and his friend shook his head no.

"Who is it?" Leo asked, giving up pretense.

"You guys have seen him but might not know him. He's just starting in the entertainment industry. He's a singer and acted in a

couple of guest roles, but he already has a reputation." *A celebrity*. Of course.

"He's fucking gorgeous and smells so good, I want to bury myself in him." Julien sighed.

"Damn it, now you have me curious," Avery mumbled.

"It's Kairo Ra," Julien said, and Leo almost spat out his drink but started choking instead.

"What's wrong with you?" Avery asked, slapping him on the back. "Don't tell me your guy is the one he's mooning over?" "No," Leo said, stopping Avery's hand from hitting him again.

"Then what's the problem?" Julien asked, brows furrowed.

Leo knew who Kairo Ra was. His real name was Nefertum Ahket-Ra, the god of lotus blossoms. He looked at Julien and shook his head, already feeling sorry for him. Nefertum wasn't going to be easy to get. The god was beautiful, and despite his public bad-boy persona, he was very guarded.

"You'll need to come up with something real just to get close to him." Leo sighed.

"You know him?" Julien and Avery said together.

"Yeah." Leo chuckled. "We're family of sorts. Our mothers are friends and like to compete against each other."

"Damn, what a small world," Avery said. "So you can help our friend here?"

"Not really," Leo replied. "I make it a point not to interfere with other people's relationships. But I'll give you a suggestion. His mother wants to rein in his bad-boy image. You know who heads his PR team, you're rich, and you've got a good public persona. Any mother would love to have you as a son-in-law. Why—"

Before Leo could finish, Julien stood abruptly, grinning as he rubbed his hands together. "You're fucking brilliant," he said, then dashed off.

"Where the hell is he going?" Avery asked, pointing. "And what's with that diabolical look in his eyes? He's scaring me." Avery shivered.

"He's off to play fake boyfriend to catch his husband."

As Leo's words sank in, Avery's eyes widened. Then he burst out laughing, slapping his leg. "What a devious plan." Avery raised his drink in the air. "Good luck, my friend."

Leo followed suit, and they both took a sip. He stayed and talked with Avery for a bit longer, then stood to leave when someone called his name.

"Leo."

He turned, scowling at the other man. "Why is it you?" "Can we talk?" Minos said.

"Haven't we said all that needed to be said?" Leo asked.

"No. You had your say," Minos growled. "I just..." He sighed.

"Um..."

They both turned when Avery spoke up. "You two seem like you need to talk, so I'm heading out."

Avery didn't wait around, nor did he ask who Minos was, and he left. Leo looked at the former king, who was staring at him pleadingly.

"You have five minutes." Leo sat down and crossed his legs with leisure.

"What I have to say can't be done in five minutes," Minos said.

"You're wasting time." Leo looked at his watch, then back at Minos.

Minos sighed and sat down. "I'm sorry." It was the first thing he said as he took a seat on the same sofa. As much as he wanted to, Leo didn't interrupt.

"What I did to you back then was wrong, but I had my reasons. I was under a lot of pressure from Congress to deal with the Minotaur, and as much as I believed your labyrinth would work to capture it, they didn't. Other factors also came into play. Everyone knew Pasiphaë and I were married for political reasons, but children were important, and society wasn't as open as it is now. Sure, having a male lover was fine, but if they weren't being fruitful, it was seen as a waste. And men getting pregnant back then wasn't seen as a good thing. So, my back was against the wall."

Minos ran his fingers through his hair, a tell Leo

302

knew well. The man was hiding something, but Leo wasn't going to call him out because, frankly, he didn't care.

"You have two minutes," Leo said flatly.

"Leo, I still love you. I've always loved you. Imprisoning you wasn't my plan. Congress did that on their own. After you were taken away, I pleaded with them to release you. I begged them just to send you away from Crete, but they refused to listen. At the time, I had no power, even as their king. But I planned on rescuing you, only to find out you were gone."

Minos leaned closer, and Leo immediately pulled back.

"I want you back. I want what we had. I miss your brilliance, your smile, the way—"

"Your time's up," Leo said, standing and brushing lint from his pants. "You say you still love me, but Minos, I don't love you anymore. I've moved on and found my own happiness, and I hope you can do the same. You have a good day."

"Leo, wait." Minos reached for his arm, but Leo was faster and moved away. "You don't understand, if..."

"What don't I understand? Fuck, how many lies are you going to tell, hoping I'll believe them?" Leo growled low. "I might have been young and, in your eyes, foolish, but I knew the kind of man you are. You wouldn't have thrown me to the wolves unless they or someone more powerful offered you something. What did you give me up for, Minos? It couldn't have been gold. You already had more than enough. Or maybe it was more land? You think I didn't know who Pasiphaë was? The Minotaur?

You wanted it built to protect her, not the people of Crete when she shifted. You and Pasiphaë didn't care what happened to them. She was just as bad as you are. Her father must be proud of the goddess he raised.

"What? You think I wasn't aware of all the shit you plotted and

did behind my back just to keep your lapdog at your side? What about your other lovers? I ignored them because I foolishly

believed you'd see I was right there all along one day." As he spoke, Minos's eyes widened.

"If you knew all of that, then why?" he asked softly.

"Why what? Why did I stay? Or why didn't I say anything? Or why did I let you play me for a bloody fool, believing you would protect me? I did what I did because I loved you," Leo sneered. "You had everything you wanted, even my heart, and it still wasn't enough. But it was me you were willing to sacrifice, and I hope it was fucking worth trampling over what we had."

Minos looked away, and Leo took the moment to leave. He had said all that he needed to say and hoped never to see Minos again. But considering the man was now living in Valleywood, that was fucking unlikely.

"You're disappointing me, Minos."

Minos sat at the bar and didn't bat an eye when the sexy, voluptuous woman with dark wavy hair and brown almondshaped eyes slid onto the stool beside him. Eyes that even Aphrodite would envy. The air shifted. Her scent, rich with rose and wine, wrapped around them and refused to let go. Her voice was melodic, smooth as sin, and she matched his drink order without hesitation.

Minos didn't need to look to know every man and woman in the bar had their eyes on her. He could feel it. Of course, they were staring. She wasn't just beautiful, she was power incarnate. A goddess who inspired love, envy, war, and destruction, all while wearing desire like a second skin.

"You haven't lived up to your end of the bargain either, goddess," Minos sneered. "I've been your loyal servant for thousands of years, and yet, Daedalus isn't warming my bed, nor am I having his children."

"You will never have his child, Minos. That was something you gave up when you took my deal," Ishtar replied coldly, her voice laced with venom.

Minos looked at her with a mix of malice and a flicker of regret. He had been dying from tuberculosis, given just three months to live. That was when she appeared, a vision cloaked in divine seduction, promising salvation with a smile that could twist the world. All he had to do was serve her and deliver Daedalus into her hands. Get him to Crete.

Keep him there. Break the young man who was quickly becoming one of the greatest inventors and architects of the age. Ishtar didn't care how he did it. She wanted it humiliating. Painful. A betrayal so deep it would leave Daedalus crawling. She wanted to be the only one he could turn to.

In exchange, she cured Minos and granted him immortality. It had seemed like a simple deal. He was afraid of death then, just as he still was now. But what he hadn't expected was to grow attached. He fell for Daedalus, and later amended the agreement with Ishtar, demanding that he also get to keep Daedalus as his lover.

I should have known better.

He should have seen it coming when she agreed without hesitation. It was too quick, too smooth, too damn perfect. The truth came later, buried beneath her beauty and those honeyed words. Her conditions were so well-hidden that no magnifying glass would have helped him catch them in time.

The sad thing was, Minos was just like Ishtar. He didn't want Daedalus out of kindness or love, but to use him and own him. In the years and centuries since he'd been cured, Minos had quietly built a new empire, forged through violence and debauchery. He was seen as a king of the criminal underworld and didn't believe in second chances. If someone fucked up his business, that was it.

No warnings. No forgiveness. If only those who followed him so loyally knew there was someone even more powerful above him, someone who could destroy everything he had built without blinking.

Minos had slinked into Valleywood more than once, sometimes to conduct business, other times to spy on Daedalus from the shadows. But it wasn't until he lost the bid on prime real estate and noticed Daedalus getting close to Jason that he made the decision to move to Valleywood permanently.

I shouldn't have waited to take back what was mine.

"I'm not in the mood for you tonight, Ishtar," he

muttered, voice low and bitter. "I've truly lost him. He's really in love with that man."

"Then get rid of him," she said, taking an elegant sip of her wine as if she were discussing the weather.

"You're a goddess of love. Shouldn't you be encouraging me to find love?"

"Isn't that what I'm doing? If you want your love back, then fight for it." She turned her head slowly, meeting his gaze with a calm, dangerous smile. "No one said you had to get your hands dirty. He has enemies. You should know that already."

She slid a file across the counter, the folder crisp and deliberate. The name on the tab read: Valencia Dupree.

Minos had met Valencia once. She struck him as cold and distant, like being near family was more of an obligation than a choice.

"If I do something to Jason, won't Athena come after you?" he asked. In all the years he had worked for Ishtar, he'd never dared to make a move on anyone tied to Athena.

Ishtar's grip on her napkin tightened. Her nails sliced clean through the fabric before she snapped, "Leave Athena to me." She shredded the napkin in her hand without flinching. "This is about balance. I'm simply reclaiming what was supposed to be mine."

He's not yours. He's mine, Minos thought, screaming the words in his mind.

Ishtar leaned in, her eyes glinting. "Daedalus should've been mine," she said, her voice low and cutting, as if she already knew what Minos had been thinking. "All those buildings, those monuments... they should've carried my name, my sigil. I'm more beautiful than her. More powerful. Why do they fall at her feet? Why does she get someone like Daedalus? Loyal. Brilliant. Committed."

Minos tilted his head slightly, his smile curling with contempt. "Still carrying that grudge because she turned you down? Are you

mad that she won't let you fall and worship at her feet?"

"Fuck you, Minos," she hissed, her voice sharp and cold.

"Been there, done that," Minos replied with a smirk. "She turned you down. Move on. Why hold on to that shit for

centuries? Or is all of this just your way of getting her attention?"

"Have you looked in the mirror lately?" she shot back, arching a brow.

He ignored the jab and fixed his gaze on her, his expression darkening. "I've always wondered why you targeted Daedalus. If you really wanted him, all you had to do was swoop in and claim him before Athena. So why didn't you?"

"That's none of your fucking business." She grabbed her glass and downed it in one gulp, then slammed it down hard enough to crack the glass on the bartop. "When I take Daedalus from her, she'll finally understand what it feels like to be unwanted."

She leaned in closer, her voice low and full of menace. "So do your damn duty, Minos. Deliver him to me, or I take my blessing back. And you know what that means. Death. Ugly. Slow. Unclean. The grim reapers would gladly auction off your soul to the highest bidder. And you know how much unclean souls bring in."

Minos didn't answer. He knew about the auction she was talking about. Each year, a grim clan put on an auction with cursed objects, but their headliners were souls, both clean and unclean. Not to mention Ishtar's threat. She would do it if he failed her again. She would take away his blessing and watch him succumb to his greatest fear.

Fuck. This is what the great King Minos has been reduced to. A lapdog to a love-brained goddess.

He stared at the unopened file, his fingers tight around his glass, watching the last inch of whiskey glint in the dim light.

"Daedalus," he whispered to no one, as if the name itself could grant absolution.

His jaw clenched. He wasn't lying when he said he'd loved him. Even knowing that, in the end, he would betray him, Minos had loved Daedalus in the purest way. He missed how they used to coil around each other from night into the morning light. Laughing. Creating. Dreaming. He liked how Daedalus used to look at him like he was enough. Now, everything he used to have belonged to someone else.

Minos downed the drink, pushed the glass aside, and muttered under his breath, "Too late to regret the past now."

He stood, took the file, and walked out without a single word to Ishtar. Their relationship was nothing like Athena and Daedalus. There was no warmth. No trust.

Just debt. Master and servant. Obsession wrapped in poison.

~

A Few Minutes Later

MINOS STOOD in the shadows near DRA&D, watching Daedalus step out of the car and greet Jason, pulling him into his arms. Their affection was casual, intimate. Real. Minos could see the love between them like heart-shaped fog in the air. The trust choked him. He had never been given that kind of honest trust, despite all the love he once shared with Daedalus.

He had gone into everything with eyes wide open, but he couldn't deny he had been lost and wrapped up in the feelings he had gained for Daedalus. And now he understood. That was why Ishtar wanted him. That was why she had to have him. That kind of love, the kind that didn't ask to be worshipped, was something she couldn't understand. Something she had never had.

Their separation was his fuck-up, but what happened to the man who had a forgiving heart? Minos tightened his grip on the file. If anything in it could tear Jason away from Daedalus, he'd use it. Because if he couldn't have Daedalus's heart, he could still ruin it.

He pulled out his phone and dialed Willa Dupree. If Daedalus could fuck a Dupree, why couldn't he? She was a beta, and he didn't mind fucking her as an omega. She would do to help relieve his frustration.

The line connected. "Let's meet up," he said flatly. "You know the hotel and the room. Be there at eight."

He hung up before she could speak and disappeared into the alley. He didn't see the second set of eyes watching him from the shadows.

ISHTAR STAYED at the bar long after Minos left, sipping slowly on her whiskey. She sat with one leg crossed over the other, swirling the last of the crimson liquid in her crystal glass, which caught the soft bar light like rubies. The room was quiet, exclusive, dipped in low music and shadowed intimacy. Her expression was unreadable, gorgeous, and distant, like a statue carved to seduce gods and terrify mortals.

A soft hum of divine energy shifted the air. Her glass stilled mid-sip.

"Still chasing shadows, Ishtar?"

She didn't turn, but her smile curled like the edge of a blade. "And here I thought you only appeared in courtrooms, war rooms, and libraries filled with dust and self-importance."

Athena stepped forward, dressed sharply in a burgundy suit. Her dark hair was pulled back into a high ponytail, every movement poised and purposeful.

"Even your rose-scented ass can't cover up Minos's stench of desperation," she said coolly. She ordered a drink and slid onto the stool beside her.

Ishtar gave a soft, amused laugh. "Tell me, which

goddess had kings and queens burn cities just to get a whiff of her ass?"

"Delusional people who weren't loved enough by their mothers," Athena replied smoothly. Her gaze dropped to the shredded napkin beneath Ishtar's hand. "What did that poor napkin do to you?"

Athena leaned in, close enough for her words to land like a slap wrapped in silk. "You seem tense, dear. Not getting enough loving? Or just bitter that you never got the one thing you actually wanted?"

She grabbed Ishtar's face, tilting it toward her. "Jealousy doesn't look good on you, dear." Athena released her roughly.

Ishtar blinked once, then turned to face her fully. Her composure cracked, if only for a second. "You stole him from me."

"Stole him from you," Athena growled. "Ishtar, what delusional world have you been living in all these centuries? I was there when Daedalus was born from his mother's womb and placed my mark of protection on him. But did you stand by the agreement all we divine make not to touch one who is protected? No. You found a way to circumvent the situation. You manipulated Minos, stoked his desire, pushed him into seducing Daedalus, just so you could sweep in, play savior, and bind him to you like all the others."

"He was supposed to honor me," Ishtar snapped. "To build in my name. Statues. Cities. Devotion carved in stone." *And then you will see me.*

Athena arched a brow. "You wanted a monument to feed your ego. Did my rejection hurt so badly that you've orchestrated this whole thing? Daedalus is not a fucking pawn. What you fail to understand is that Daedalus doesn't belong to any god or man. Do you think I could let you abuse and diminish his brilliance just to make him one of your mindless servants?"

Ishtar's eyes flashed. "You don't get it. You never have. You've had loyalty thrown at your feet, and you pretend like it means nothing. You turned me down, Athena. You didn't even consider what I offered you."

"I can't love you the way you want, Ishtar," Athena said quietly. "And I've also seen how you love. You don't know how to give, only how to take from others. You wonder why your lovers and worshipers abandon you. It's because, even though you are a goddess of love, you don't know how to love."

Ishtar's laugh turned bitter. "You self-righteous bitch. What have you given him? Isn't he doing for you what I want him to do for me? How would he feel if he knew that you were aware of what

I was up to?"

"Freedom," Athena replied. "Respect. Space to become who he was meant to be. I have kept nothing from him, and I've never asked Daedalus to build, invent, or dedicate anything to me. It was all his choosing. And who says Daedalus doesn't know about you and your schemes? Unlike you, Ishtar, I don't have fine print in who gives me devotion."

Ishtar's mask cracked again, just enough for the ache beneath to shine through. "I just wanted someone who would stay. Who would choose me without being pushed."

"Isn't Minos loyal to you?" Athena didn't blink.

Ishtar's voice dropped, quiet and dangerous. "Loyal. He does what I want to survive."

"But that is human nature, Ishtar," Athena said calmly. "They love, they hate, and they crave survival."

"I see that as a weakness. And now I know for sure what yours is." She stared at Athena, her gaze unwavering. "You say I don't know how to love, but the one person who has ever made me want more in this existence doesn't want me. So the only thing I can do is make them feel the very pain I'm feeling."

She reached out and touched Athena's cheek, her fingers soft but charged with intent. "I know we've never had anything between us but words, but everything about you makes me want to give you the entire world."

She leaned in and kissed Athena, long and deep, moaning in delight when the other woman didn't pull away. Slowly, their lips separated, and Ishtar pressed her forehead against Athena's. "So sweet. If only you would give yourself to me."

"I can't, Ishtar," Athena whispered. "I am not meant to love you or anyone else the way you want. I will hurt you in the end."

"And you aren't hurting me now?"

Athena leaned in and kissed her again. "I'm sorry, Ishtar. It is the curse of who I am."

"So stubborn," Ishtar hissed, tears welling in the corners of her eyes, her heart breaking. She had loved Athena for so long, but it hurt worse not to have her. So in the end, she would destroy those she cared about.

"Then don't blame me for what happens to your family next."

Athena leaned back, her voice like steel. "Touch my family, Ishtar, and I will end you."

Athena disappeared, leaving Ishtar with her burning lips and a belly full of rage.

Hold on tight to Daedalus a little longer, because when I get him, you will be begging for my love and to be with me just to save his life.

CHAPTER 21

LEO

Athena was sitting in front of Leo, slowly sipping on her favorite tea. He was a bit surprised when she'd appeared in his office.

"Are you going to tell me what's with your visit today, or should I guess?"

Athena sighed and set her tea down. "There's something I've been keeping from you."

"I'm listening."

"Remember when I rescued you?" Leo nodded.

"Well, I knew it was going to happen."

"I figured. But you're leaving something out, aren't you?"

"I am." She stood and walked over to the window. "Have you ever wondered why I've never dated?"

"All the time," Leo responded truthfully. "I always figured it was by choice."

"In part. The other reason is that I'm cursed."

Leo's eyes widened. "By whom?"

"By the only goddess who can," she said, turning to look at him. "Hera."

"Why?"

"Jealousy. I am a child born from my father's thoughts. He made me in the image of himself, gave me wisdom, strength, and power. I proudly wear the moniker of being my father's favorite child, and Hera has never forgiven Zeus for not involving her in my birth. So she cursed me to never fall in love or experience the passion of love. I've tried to go against it, but the side effects are too much to bear, so I remain alone. Don't get me wrong, I could have sex and have tried, but when there's no feeling of affection behind it, I grew not to want it."

"So that's why you reject all your admirers," Leo said gently.

"Yes. If I dare to fall in love, I would lose my divinity. And I know this sounds selfish, but I was born a goddess and I will forever be one."

"Why doesn't Zeus tell Hera to remove the curse?"

Athena tsked and shook her head. "Has Hera ever done anything Zeus asked of her? He told her to leave Hercules alone and she made his life a living hell for centuries. It wasn't until he was made a god that she finally got over her grudge. With me, I'm not sure what

would change her mind. But there was one thing Hera never accounted for in her curse, and that was children." She walked over to Leo and gently touched his cheek. "I might never have been or will be in love, but I know what it feels like to have the love of a child. You and Ada might not have been born from me, but you are mine in every other way."

Leo wrapped his arms around her waist, pressing his head to her stomach. "Thank you, Mother, for telling me."

She hummed and ran her fingers through his hair. "I'm sorry,

Leo."

"What are you sorry for?" He looked up at her. "I've put you and your family in danger."

"What do you mean?"

"Ishtar. You know I rejected her advances, and she didn't take it lightly. She's been plotting with Minos to take you from me all these years."

"Well, they can't have me," he said, holding her tighter.

"You're not angry?"

Leo chuckled. "What would be the reason for my anger? I'm not so oblivious to what's happening. It's not my fault Minos didn't love me more than power."

"So you knew he was plotting against you even then?"

"Not in the beginning," Leo responded. "But it was after I was thrown in prison that something clicked. I didn't know about his connection to Ishtar until you just told me. Want to know what's bad? If you hadn't

rescued me, I would have forgiven him and been their pawn."

"My son," she said softly, burying her face in his hair. "I will never let that happen."

"I know," he told her. "I trust you. And it's not your fault you were born beautiful."

That made her chuckle. "You were always a sweet talker." Athena stepped back and pulled out a large jewelry box. "I made these for you, Jason, Talos, Ada, and the kids."

"What are they?" he asked, opening the box to see matching plain gold bracelets.

"Protection and tracking talismans. I don't know what Ishtar and Minos are up to. Once you put them on, not even a god can take them off."

"Thank you."

"Anything to protect my family. But as your mother, I'll give you some sound advice. Tell Jason about Minos. I have a feeling they will use him to get to you."

Leo sighed and leaned back. "I want to, but I don't know where to start."

"The beginning is always best," Athena responded. She leaned down and kissed his forehead, then disappeared.

Leo stared at the bracelets and sighed. *Life is about to get really interesting.*

JASON SMILED and cupped Ada's cheek. "Babe, you're worried about the wrong person. Or should I say, the wrong people. There's no love lost when it comes to me and them."

"So you're not upset about your dad and sister getting arrested?" Avery asked.

"No." Jason looked at the handsome man. "They did the crime. They should do the time."

"They're asking to see you," Tracy said, stepping closer and wrapping his arms around Jason, pulling him gently away from Ada.

Jason hid a small smirk. His best friend was a little territorial. All day, he and Ada had been low-key competing for who got to be closer to him. He didn't expect them to start a full-on contest the second they met, but he could tell it was all in good fun. Truth be told, he liked the attention, even though he knew he should probably shut itdown.

"Well, they can keep asking," Jason told him. "Right now, the only thing I want is pizza."

"I'll buy it for you," Ada said, sliding up to his side and resting her head on his shoulder. "What kind of meat do you want?"

"Why do you need to buy it? I'm his best friend. I'll get it for him," Tracy countered.

"He's my brother-in-law. Why shouldn't I buy it for him? Besides, since we're both pregnant, maybe he and I can share a pizza." Ada stuck out her tongue at Tracy playfully.

"What the hell is wrong with you two? Stop fighting over my husband." Leo stepped in and pulled Jason away from both of them. "If he wants pizza, I'll get it for him. Any questions?"

He glanced around the room, daring anyone to respond.

"I didn't say anything," Avery said quickly.

"Me neither," Julien added.

"You really are stingy," Tracy grumbled, then looked back at Jason. "Are you alright?"

"Yes. They never considered me their son or brother, so why should I care what happens to them?"

"Fair enough. I'll contact the station and let them know not to bother you anymore." Tracy stepped out, and Avery, who had been inventing excuses all day to be near Jason's best friend, excused himself as well.

"I'm going to see if he needs any help," Avery said, already moving.

"Alright, place your bets," Julien said with a grin.

"My bet is he won't even get a date," Leo said.

"Date? You're aiming too high, big brother," Ada chimed in.

"What are we betting on?" Talos asked, stepping back into the room.

"Avery and Tracy," Ada explained. "Date or number."

"I say neither," Talos replied.

"I bet you all five bucks that neither of them stays for dinner," Jason said, pulling a five-dollar bill from his pocket.

Everyone looked at him like he was being dramatic. But Jason knew his best friend. Avery was exactly his type, the kind of guy you fucked a few times and moved on from. He could tell neither one of them was in the mood for commitment. Still, he wouldn't mind if something came of it.

"You're on," they all said, tossing five-dollar bills into the pot.

Minutes later, Tracy returned. "I gotta head out. I need to get back to the station."

"I thought you had the day off," Jason said, pouting slightly. He already recognized the look in Tracy's eyes.

"Training never stops, babe. I'm always on the go in my position."

"Ah, I see," Jason replied, clearly not buying it.

"Alright, I'll see you guys later," Tracy said, hurrying out.

Seconds later, Avery returned. Even though he didn't leave right away, Jason counted the minutes. Not long after, his excuse came in the form of a phone call.

"Shit, I gotta go."

"Work?" Leo asked.

"Yeah," he said with no further explanation as he dashed out the door.

"I wonder if he remembers we drove together," Julien muttered, shaking his head.

Jason rushed to the front of the house, the others following close behind as they all watched Avery climb into Tracy's car.

"Pay up," Jason said, hand extended.

He chuckled at their grumbling handing him the bills from earlier.

"Can I give mine in kisses?" Leo asked.

"Hell no. I won this fair and square." Jason wiggled his fingers and laughed when Leo rolled his eyes but paid him anyway.

"We knew this day was coming. But tell me truthfully, how are you handling your father and sister being arrested?" Leo asked when everyone else went back to the kitchen.

Jason smiled. "Honestly? Relieved. Although I've long cut ties with them, there was always this feeling in the back of my mind that they'd pop up and stir up trouble just because they could. But now, I don't have to worry." He wrapped his arms around Leo's neck and gave him a quick kiss. "Because my hero slayed the evil dragons."

Leo's arms circled his waist. "What will I get when I slay them all?"

"That's a surprise," Jason whispered.

"I..." Leo began but was interrupted by the kids.

"Daddy! Papa! We're hungry!"

"Your aunt is ordering pizza," Leo said. "Go see her in the kitchen and tell her what you want."

They ran off, and Athena came down the stairs.

"I'm glad you two finally decided to move here," she said. "Now the kids can attend school, where I'm the director."

Jason looked at Leo, then at Athena. "Really?"

"Yes. Although I haven't visited in a few months, I'm sure I'll have a lot of work to catch up on. But my staff is competent enough to carry on without me for a while."

"So I take it you're sticking around more now?" Leo asked.

"Yes." She nodded and touched Jason's stomach. "With Ada and Jason both pregnant, I think it's important to be around. Speaking of Ada, when will young Talos propose?" Her eyes lit up.

"Maybe we'll have a double wedding."

"Mom, Jason and I are already married," Leo reminded her.

"Yes, but I wasn't there. So you'll have to do it again." She pinched Leo's cheek, then headed toward the kitchen, her energy shifting from warm to whimsical in a flash.

Jason turned to Leo and said, "Sometimes I wonder if you guys are really adopted."

"What do you mean by that?" Leo asked.

"You guys are more alike than maybe you or Ada realize." He leaned in and kissed his husband. "Like mother, like son. It makes me hopeful for the future."

"Good." Leo pulled him into his embrace, and they stayed for a while before joining everyone in the kitchen, where, instead of ordering out for pizza, Athena volunteered to show off her cooking skills, which were so good that it had Avery begging her over and over to be his mom.

JASON SAT at the Whisperleaf Coffeehouse sipping on ginger tea, thanking the gods that his nausea was finally passing. He had started to get morning sickness and couldn't handle certain scents, but the smell of coffee seemed to calm his stomach. He found the blend at Whisperleaf Coffeehouse to be the best. Jason didn't know why, but he took it as a strange perk of being pregnant.

He scrolled through his phone, scanning the news report on his father and sister's arrest. Jackson and Willa had maintained their innocence, claiming they were being targeted by a rival law firm they had beaten in court multiple times. Jason didn't realize just how delusional his father and sister were until now, believing all the evidence against them was fabricated. What wasn't surprising, though, was that Valencia and Ian had remained silent through it all.

Jason sighed and put his phone away, enjoying the quiet. It had been about two weeks since the move, and they were finally settled in. The kids were adjusting to sleeping in a new place, though there were a couple of mornings when he went to wake them up and found Xander in Sera's bed, or the other way around. One night, they'd even crawled into bed with him and Leo.

With all the extra open space, accidental abilities had become a common occurrence, not just with the kids but with Jason as well. At any random time of day, something would blow up, go flying from one room to another, or lights would flicker. Then there was Jason, who got so wrapped up in a project that he would unintentionally create a dimensional space and have to find his way back.

He had met with Doctor Pace, and they were set to begin his training in a few days. Jason looked down at his wrist and admired the bracelet gifted to him by Athena. It was a gold braided cuff, simple in design, yet the gold shimmered in a way that suggested it was worth far more than it looked.

"Can I join you?"

Jason looked up from his wrist and saw Elias Crete standing there. He glanced around the coffeehouse, noting that there were plenty of empty tables and chairs. That meant one thing. This guy wanted to talk to him. About what, Jason didn't know. They didn't even know each other.

"Not to be rude, but what do you want?"

Elias Crete smiled. "I heard you were a direct and to-the-point kind of man."

"I'd rather not waste people's time." Jason set his phone down, eyes steady on the man. "So I'll ask again. What do you want?"

"How are you handling your father and sister's arrest?" "If they're guilty, they should do the time. What about you? Aren't you concerned about Willa?"

"Willa knew she was a passing moment until I got the person I actually wanted."

Jason blinked. He didn't know what to say at first, so he just asked the question for the third time hoping for an answer. "What do you want?"

"Can't I just want to talk to you while we enjoy a nice cup of coffee?"

Jason chuckled, but there was no amusement in it. "We don't know each other. And I've been told I'm not that friendly."

"I see why you caught his attention," Elias said, chuckling softly.

Jason tilted his head and studied the man. "Who are you referring to?"

Elias sat down just as a server passed. He ordered a coffee and turned back to Jason. "Can I tell you a story?"

"I'm a little old for stories, don't you think?"

"You're never too old. But humor me," the handsome man said with a smile.

Jason sighed, just as the server returned with Elias's coffee. He thanked her, then took a graceful sip and set the cup down. Jason wasn't sure why he was watching the man so closely, but there was something captivating about the way he moved, even in the simplest gestures.

"Many years ago, long before you or most were born, there was a king who became infatuated with a beautiful man. Not just because of his looks, but because of his brilliant mind. The young man could build, create, and imagine the most wondrous things." Elias smiled faintly. "Once, he created artificial wings made of feather and wax because he wanted to fly."

"Did they work?" Jason asked, intrigued.

Elias smirked. "Almost. He had the sun working against him."

"The sun melted the wax," Jason said quietly.

"Yes. But he didn't give up. He tried many other ways to fly because he knew he could do it."

Jason lowered his eyes, thinking of Xander, who was back on his flying obsession. Now that they had a large backyard, Jason had caught the kid climbing trees more than once. Leo wasn't any help. He had privately suggested getting Xander a jetpack, his expression wistful, like he was remembering something from the past.

"Their love affair was known by all," Elias continued. "But the king had a problem. His congress was pressuring him to have offspring with his queen."

"Wait, so the king was openly cheating on his wife?" Jason asked, eyeing him.

"Not in the way you're thinking. The king and queen were childhood friends and had an open agreement. They both had lovers, but no illegitimate children could be born. Although the queen later broke the agreement."

"Oh," Jason said, annoyed at how interested he was becoming in the story.

"Anyway, the king refused to impregnate the queen."

"Why? That seems like an easy fix."

"The queen was against it as well because she had a special bloodline." He leaned in and whispered, "She was a Minotaur and did not want to pass that gene down to her offspring. One of the reasons the king sought out the young man was to build something to protect the queen on the nights she shifted. During those nights, his people were in danger for days. And the queen would be wracked with guilt afterward. The king couldn't bear to see her that way."

"It sounds like he loved her," Jason whispered.

"In his own way he did, but he wasn't in love with her, and vice versa." His eyes grew soft as he took a sip of his coffee.

"So what did the king and his lover come up with to keep the Minotaur from harming his people?"

"Something so marvelous that it took one year to construct." He paused and stared at Jason. "He built a labyrinth. It kept the queen trapped on those nights and busy. He was so ingenious and built traps and games."

Jason's thoughts instantly flashed to the labyrinth in Leo's showcase room and the look of joy on his face when he was describing it. He looked at Elias as a sinking feeling settled in the pit of his stomach.

"Is that the end of the story?" he asked.

"No. Soon after the labyrinth was built, the king had to throw his lover in prison."

Jason's eyes widened. "Why? I thought he loved him?"

"He did, but he had no choice. The congress threatened to kill him," Elias explained. "So he bargained with the congress to let his lover be imprisoned, but in truth, it was for his lover's protection."

Jason stared at Elias Crete, feeling like there was more to the story. "I don't think that's true," he said. "The king had many choices. He simply chose not to use them. So I'm under the assumption that the king wasn't really in love with him. It was a possessive infatuation. He wanted what the builder could create, not who the builder was."

"Is that how you see it?" Elias asked.

"Let me ask you something. Why tell me this story?"

"To prepare you," the man responded.

Jason's brows furrowed. "For what? Am I going to war with a king?" He might have said it in jest, but the steel in the man's gaze made him think twice.

Elias Crete stood. "I lied to you, Mister Dupree."

"It's Devereux. I've dropped the Dupree," Jason corrected.

"Very well. Before I became Elias Crete, I went by a different name." He extended a hand, but Jason didn't take it. The man didn't seem offended and gave a smirk, one that seemed more genuine than any he had given since they met. "I used to be known as Minos, King of

Crete." He leaned down and whispered in Jason's ear, "And I'm here to reclaim my lover."

He leaned back, still smirking, as if he had said something profound and earth-shattering.

Jason sighed and stood. "Should I be afraid?"

"Don't you even want to know who my lover is?" he asked, raising a brow.

Jason shook his head. "No. Your love life, past and present, is of no concern to me."

"Even if that person is someone you love?"

"Yes," Jason responded. "Because whatever you had with him was in the past. If you loved them as much as you told yourself, then you wouldn't have let them go. You see, what makes us different is that I would fight for the people I love. Your kind of love and protection makes them forget you ever existed." He smirked. "Your kind of love is the worst kind of affection, something no one would crave or be jealous of. It actually makes me sick that you believe what you did justifies getting him back. I'm here to tell you to give up, because you're fighting a losing battle."

He grinned, watching Elias Crete's face shift from smug satisfaction to simmering anger. "Now, you have the fucking day you deserve."

He turned and walked away, not bothering to look back at Minos, Elias, or whatever his name was. All that concerned him was getting home to Leo. His heart ached for his lover. Knowing that Leo had loved someone before him didn't hurt as much as realizing he hadn't been loved enough. That hurt worse than anything else.

CHAPTER 22
LEO

Leo had been in his study, sitting on the couch going over contracts, when Jason's scent drifted in, followed by the warmth of his arms circling around Leo's neck.

"I love you," Jason whispered next to his ear.

Leo turned and looked at his lover. "I love you, too." He studied his face for a second. "Did something happen while you were out?"

Jason nodded, then released him and walked around, taking the smart pad from Leo's hand and setting it on the table before

sitting on his lap. "I ran into an old friend of yours."

Leo furrowed his brow. "Old friend?"

"I should say your ex-lover."

Leo froze and stared into Jason's eyes. What he saw wasn't anger, but sadness.

"What did you see in that fucking jerk?" Jason growled, grabbing the collar of Leo's shirt and pulling him down. "He didn't love you."

"What did he tell you?" Leo asked, his fingers trembling as he curled them into fists, then slowly released them. There was no need to get angry if Jason wasn't.

"He told me a story about some king who was in love with a builder. At first, I was drawn in because I didn't know who they were. But when he mentioned the labyrinth, I figured it out."

Leo sighed and slouched down on the sofa, wrapping his arms around Jason's waist. "It was a long time ago, when I was a different person. And he was, or so I thought, a magnificent king. I won't deny that I was head over heels for the man, but little did I know he was setting a trap for me."

"What do you mean?"

"You're right. He didn't love me. Maybe he had some affection, but love? I doubt Minos even knows what that means."

Jason cupped Leo's cheek. "Do you want to talk about it?"

"Not really, but I can't hide it from you forever."

"I won't look at you any differently."

Leo chuckled. "Thanks." He kissed Jason's forehead. "I'm not sure what Minos told you, but let me tell you my version." Jason nodded.

"I was young, and in some ways, Xander reminds me of myself. I was always looking for ways to make things better, create, build, and invent. But I was small-time. One day, a message came in that the king of Crete wished for an audience with me. I was impressed that the king even knew who I was. But when I went to meet him, I fell all over myself."

"You were that stunned by his looks?" Jason asked.

"No, I literally fell all over myself. Almost hit my face. I was clumsy back then. It didn't matter that I was an alpha, it was like I had two left feet."

"I can't picture it," Jason said.

"Yeah, I try not to think about those days." He smiled. "Anyway, once I picked myself up, I formally met the king and his congress.

They were welcoming and complimented me from head to toe. Held a banquet in my honor and made me feel appreciated before they told me the real reason I was there. They were plagued by a Minotaur. I should have sensed something was wrong when I suggested they kill it and call it a day. But they said they wanted to capture it, and that was where I came in. They wanted me to build something to trap it. I thought a cage would be easy until I came face to face with thething." "Really?" Jason sat up.

"On the night of my first full moon in Crete, I left the castle to find answers. I wasn't very observant back then, and the empty streets should have been a clue. But I was focused on finding the tools I needed to build the cage. Then, out of nowhere, the Minotaur came charging from a dark alley, mad as hell and ready to take my head off. I ran, but being as clumsy as I was, I tripped, giving the Minotaur a chance to close in."

Leo closed his eyes, recalling the fear. He remembered the rage and hunger rolling off the Minotaur's body. He'd truly thought he was going to die.

"And just as the Minotaur caught me, he came in like a hero and saved me." He looked at Jason. "You know in the movies when the hero rides in on a white horse dressed to the nines?" Jason nodded. "That was Minos. He looked so handsome, and I became infatuated. He distracted the Minotaur and helped me get away. He yelled at me for being stupid enough to leave the castle on a full moon, and before I could even speak, he kissed me."

"Was it your first kiss? Was he your first?"

"Yes to both. Until Minos, I'd never paid much attention to love or romance."

"You were too focused on wanting to fly," Jason said.

"How do you know that?" Leo asked, a little surprised.

"He mentioned it."

Leo chuckled. "I guess that's where Xander gets it from. My need to fly was really a need to escape the limitations I felt boxed into. It's why I love that you encourage the kids to explore and open their little minds to the vastness of knowledge. Anyway, after that first kiss, things moved quickly. Even though there was a Minotaur problem, no one seemed overly concerned that I wasn't working on a solution. And then one night, after the last round of the full moon, it came to me. Since the kingdom didn't want to kill the Minotaur but also couldn't let it kill villagers, I came up with the idea of the labyrinth."

"Did you know why they didn't want to kill the Minotaur?" Jason asked.

"Yes. She was the queen of Crete. Pasiphaë, the daughter of the sun god Helios. She is a sorceress who is now a model living in

Paris. She's powerful, but she used to mess up all kinds of spells."

"Was that how she turned into a Minotaur?"

"No. She was cursed because of the actions of her father, Poseidon."

"Is there anything in this world that is not connected to the gods?"

"No." Leo shook his head. "Our lives are very intertwined."

"Okay, so with the queen being a Minotaur, is that why they didn't want to have children?"

"Yeah. But later, the queen mated with a bull shifter and had offspring. Before that, though, the king and queen kept putting the congress off. It took me about a year to design and build the labyrinth. And during that time, I fell even more in love with Minos. When it was completed, that's when my world shattered."

He held Jason close and told him about being dragged before the congress and branded a traitor. His mind had been in a whirlwind of confusion, and Minos just sat there, not refuting a single word. Then came the moment the man finally spoke, and the words carved deeper than the silence.

"You are just like the tools you use, Daedalus. Easy to break and replaceable."

"Oh, Leo." Jason wrapped his arms around his neck and held him tight. "He's wrong. He's so wrong."

Leo chuckled softly. "I know that now. But to hear those words back then, coming from someone I was supposed to love... it hurt more than anything I could explain. I was thrown into prison where I sat for days, weeks, maybe months. And better than Minos riding in on a white horse, she appeared." He looked at Jason and smiled. "Athena. All she did was hold out her hand and say, 'Come with me, and I will make it better.'"

"I'm glad you went with her," Jason said.

"Me too. It took some time to heal, but while I was in her care, Athena explained everything to me. Minos had partnered with the goddess Ishtar to turn me into her loyal worshiper."

"What does that mean? Don't we all worship the gods in some way?"

"Yes, but having a dedicated follower who lives their life solely for one god strengthens them. Especially now. The gods are losing their powers. Granted, it may take years or even centuries before it's all gone, but the decline has already started. Having a worshiper who builds temples, monuments, statues, and offers treasures in their name gives them power. In my case, every building I construct, I dedicate to Athena. But that was my choice. With Ishtar, resisting her would have meant death."

"I never knew things were so crazy. But why is Ishtar doing this? Why did Minos agree to help her?"

"Ishtar is infatuated with Athena and will do anything to get her attention. It seems she wanted to use me because, before Minos sent for me, Athena was planning to offer me her blessing. As for Minos, I honestly don't know. That's something I've never been able to get a straight answer on. And after all these centuries,

I just don't care anymore."

"He told me he came here for you. So do you still love him?"

Leo smirked, catching the edge of jealousy in Jason's voice. He gently grabbed Jason's chin and tilted it up. "He can do whatever the fuck he wants, but there is no way I'll leave you or the children. My heart, my soul, my mind, and my body belong to you. I stopped loving Minos the day he had me thrown in prison."

"I'm sorry he did that to you."

"Me too. But it taught me a lesson. And until you, I wasn't willing to open my heart to anyone. I spent six years obsessing over where you were. The second I had you in my arms, I held on like you were my last breath. You are it for me, Jason. And no man or divine being is going to tear us apart."

"This is why I love you." Jason leaned in and kissed him hard, then leaned back and looked into his eyes. "I won't let him have you."

"Good." They kissed again.

VALENCIA SAT IN HER STUDY, going over her latest research findings. She was close to getting what she wanted, but

two things were still missing. Valencia didn't have a shaman or the proper incantation. Things were not going as perfectly as she wanted them to be.

Growling, Valencia swiped a hand across her desk, sending papers and her laptop flying. How could everything go so wrong in a matter of weeks? She should've been happy that her family wasn't around, but Valencia felt miserable. After the arrest of her mate and daughter, her eldest son ran off to parts unknown.

He had no other choice when his crimes came to light, ranging from data falsification to intellectual property theft. From the way things looked, Ian was facing thirty years in prison. Not to mention her mate and daughter were looking at life. Although her own deeds hadn't come to light, she had been let go from her research team, guilty by association. So now, she was jobless and without a family. The only one unaffected by everything happening to the Dupree family was Jason.

Funny how that worked. The one kid I hate is the only one I need right now.

Valencia slumped down in her chair, grabbing her hair in frustration. She was stuck and didn't know what to do. Without her mate close by, she was becoming even more erratic. Her thoughts were scattered, and her heart felt like it was breaking into pieces. She wanted and needed her mate, but she refused to see him. She hated being dependent on him to ease the emotional rollercoaster she was going through.

She knew if she was going through this, her mate had to be having an even worse experience. Valencia could still feel their bond, but it was strained. Jackson was her lifeline. She was always hyper focused on her work, he did everything for her, from making sure she ate and bathed to picking out what she wore to work and taking care of her needs. Now all of that was gone in a flash. It made her desire to be an unbound omega that didn't need any of those connections even stronger.

"You look and smell like shit," came a voice from the other side of the room.

Valencia raised her head and blinked a few times, clearing the haze to see Elias Crete, Willa's plaything, standing at the entrance to her study. The man was handsome, but she always had the feeling that he wasn't who he claimed to be. Still, she had made it a rule never to intervene in her children's love lives. She hadn't seen the man since Willa got arrested, so she had no idea why he was here.

"How did you get in here?" she snapped. "Willa's not here, so you can get the fuck out."

"It's funny. The child you hate the most is the one most like you," Elias Crete said.

"What the fuck do you mean by that?"

"Jason is just as brash and straightforward as you are." Valencia scoffed. "I find that hard to believe."

"Oh, it's true. And that's why I'll help you get what you want." He smirked.

Valencia looked at him seriously as he entered her study.

"I know what you want, Valencia Dupree, and I can help you. The only thing I need from you is to leave Leo Devereux to me. You can hurt Jason and his brats all you want, but touch a hair on Leo and I will end you."

Valencia gasped, feeling an unnatural power radiating from Elias Crete. She could tell he wasn't an alpha, but what he really was, she couldn't identify. If only she had met him before Jackson, would he have been able to satisfy her?

"Don't even think about it. I'm not the kind of omega you want to fuck or fuck with," he sneered, then threw a sheet of paper at her. "Call me when you have Jason in your hands." He turned his back to her. "Don't disappoint me, Valencia."

And just as suddenly as he came, he was gone. Valencia picked up the paper, and her eyes widened when she saw the incantation she had been searching for. All she needed now was a shaman which was easy to find. A giggle bubbled out of her and quickly turned into a cackle.

Finally, I am going to get what I want.

"SO YOU KNOW how you've been having me look into who this K person was that's connected to Calderon?" Talos said, walking into Leo's office.

"Yeah, did you find anything?"

Leo had been thinking about the K person a lot lately, especially after his talk with Jason. He had a feeling he knew who the person was, but he needed confirmation.

"There are shell companies set up on the island of Crete under the name Ilias Kiriti. I checked the database, and it's not a common name. We also had an Elias Crete move to Valleywood recently. Not the same spelling, but it's close enough."

Leo stood and snatched the paper from Talos, staring at the name. Fuck, how could I be so stupid. The K stood for Kiriti, or in this case, King. Elias Crete in Greek was Ilias Kiriti, or more specifically, King Minos of Crete. Leo didn't need to wonder how Minos had gotten involved with someone like Calderon. It was only a guess, but Leo was certain Minos had been the one to kill Calderon. Minos was greedy and would take out even his best friend if they disrupted his business.

"Do you have any more information on him?" Leo asked Talos.

"Here," he said, handing over the file.

"Thanks." Leo took the file and flipped through it, seeing the names of other criminal organizations connected to Minos.

The man had quietly and secretly built an empire in the underworld over the past few years. Before that, he had been silent, as if waiting for people to forget he had once been a glorious king. He sat on the sidelines, watching and waiting for his time to strike, but Leo wasn't going to let him continue. He would send Minos back into the deepest, darkest shadows where he wouldn't be able to find his way out. Leo knew there was nothing he could do about Ishtar, but Minos was fair game.

"Anonymously send it to the authorities," he instructed Talos.

"Will do." Talos didn't ask any more questions and walked out of the office.

Leo picked up his cellphone off the desk and brought up the number he had blocked months ago. He unblocked it without hesitation and pressed the call button. The second the call connected, he didn't wait for Minos to say a word.

"Come to my office. You have thirty minutes."

"I love it when you're so demanding," Minos said softly. "It reminds me of the old days when you took charge."

"Cut the shit and get here," Leo growled and hung up. He tossed the phone back down on his desk, then sent a message to the front desk and Genice that he was expecting a guest.

Less than forty-five minutes later, Minos was guided to Leo's office by Genice, who shot him a sharp scowl. "Sir, your guest is here."

"Thanks, Gen. Make sure we aren't interrupted," he said. Genice nodded and stepped out, closing the doors behind her without ever turning her back to the room.

Minos smirked and sauntered in, confidence dripping from every step. "I didn't expect your call, but I welcomed it." He reached out as if to touch Leo's shoulder.

Leo slapped his hand away without hesitation, shocking him.

"This isn't a pleasure call, Minos." Leo picked up the folder from the desk and slammed it against Minos's chest. "You've been busy. I'm sure the authorities are wracking their brains trying to figure out who Calderon's silent partner is."

Minos looked down at the folder, flipping it open

with practiced indifference. No hint of surprise crossed his face. "So, you found out about my dirty deeds." He met Leo's eyes. "Should I run and hide now?"

"I didn't think you would."

"Then what do you want?" Minos snapped, his mask slipping as irritation crept in.

"Stay away from my family," Leo said evenly. "I know you and Ishtar are scheming. She wants me to get to Athena. It won't happen. Whatever deal you made with her, it won't save you." "You've really changed," Minos said, almost wistfully.

"Unlike you, I've evolved," Leo replied, slipping his hands into his pockets with a calm that bordered on deadly. "You're still stuck in your own pathetic mess of what was our past. I was so blinded by your looks and the fact that you saved me from the Minotaur that I ignored all the shit you used to do. I had a lot of time to think, and I want to thank you, Minos." "For what?" he asked, confused.

"For putting me in prison, because it woke me up and made me realize you never loved me."

"Dae..."

"My name is Leonidas Devereux. I'm not the man you used to know."

"That's the man I want back," Minos growled. "The one who used to love me."

"Yes, I admit it, openly and freely, my heart was yours. But when you had it, you crushed it. And now you think, what? I'm going to give up everything I've built and walk away from my family? From my husband? What did you think would happen when you told Jason about our past?" Leo asked, his tone turning sharp.

Minos's jaw ticked. A tell. Irritated, but trying to hide it.

Some things never change.

"Did you think he'd divorce me? Or maybe you thought I'd come crawling back to you like some lost, lovesick pup?" Leo's smile was cold. "Pathetic."

"I'm pathetic?" Minos growled, voice low.

"If the shoe fits," Leo sneered.

"You act like he's some kind of saint," Minos snapped. "What's so special about him? He's just a useless omega who—"

He didn't finish what he was going to say. Leo moved faster than Minos could react. He grabbed him by the throat and slammed him against the wall, hard enough for the back of Minos's head to crack against the surface. The sound echoed in the room. Leo leaned in, close enough to share breath.

"You want to talk about useless?" Leo hissed. "You've spent thousands of years licking the boots of a goddess who wouldn't give two fucks if you dropped dead tomorrow. You can't even take a shit without her say-so. And you have the audacity to call the man I love useless?" His voice dropped into a venomous whisper. "Say it again. I fucking dare you."

Minos growled, rage boiling over. He shoved Leo back with brute force, snarling, "You have no idea what you're talking about. Ishtar saved me!"

Leo steadied himself. "Saved you? No. She owns you. You're nothing but her lap dog."

"I'm sick of everyone treating me like I'm something they can walk all over!" Minos roared. "I am King Minos, ruler of Crete. I am no one's to rule over."

"You could have fooled the fuck out of me," Leo shouted. "When was it, huh? When did you lose your humanity? Or maybe you never had it in the first place. I guess you've always been a heartless monster."

"You want to see a real monster?" Minos growled. His body began to twist and crack, his height rising as muscle swelled and his expensive suit tore at the seams. His voice deepened into something monstrous, guttural, and inhuman. Horns began to curl from his skull, and fur shimmered across his forearms.

Leo's breath hitched, but only for a second. Then his gaze hardened. He moved with the same impossible precision that had once outwitted gods. In a flash, he closed the distance and jabbed his fingers into the space beneath Minos's rib cage, between the first and second false rib.

Minos let out a strangled grunt, his body spasming as if struck by lightning. The shift faltered and began to recede, bringing him back to his human form. His knees buckled, but Leo caught him by the hair before he could fall, holding him up.

"You sold your soul to her, and she turned you into a literal monster. Let this little display be a warning. Stay away from my family, Minos. I might not have killed the queen because of who her father is, but you, Minos, I will not shed a tear chopping your head from your neck." He threw him to the floor. "Now, as my husband would say, have the fucking day you deserve."

Leo wiped his hands on his pants and watched Minos struggle to his feet. On shaky legs, he walked out of the office, not looking the same as when he entered. Leo closed his eyes and took deep breaths, trying to calm his emotions.

He's a fucking Minotaur. How did it happen? Has he been one this entire time? Or is this something new? What kind of deal did you make with Ishtar, Minos?

"Sir, are you okay?" Genice asked, causing Leo to open his eyes.

"Yeah, I'm fine," he told her. "Cancel my meetings for the rest of the day."

He grabbed his suit jacket from the back of his chair, slipping it on as he left. He wasn't in the right frame of mind to deal with clients. What he needed was his husband and to spend time with his family.

CHAPTER 23
MINOS

Minos crouched down, his back against the wall, holding his side, his eyes locked on the DRA&D building. He hadn't expected it: the strength, the

anger, or the threat. Minos didn't care that Daedalus had found out about his criminal dealings. If the authorities got wind of him, the charges were easy to escape.

But what he hadn't wanted was for Daedalus to find out he was a Minotaur. He had used his shifted form to scare those who would oppose him, but he had forgotten that Leo wasn't someone he could scare off easily. Now, things were far more complicated.

Daedalus was on guard.

I fucked up. Fuck! He wasn't supposed to find out yet.

There was nothing he could do now. His only hope was Valencia. Once she took care of Jason and his children, Daedalus would lose all hope in Athena and turn to Ishtar. To make sure things were done properly, he'd give Valencia a few men to help her out. Minos stood and disappeared into the darkness. He had to wait, just a few more days, and all this shit would be over. Then they could go back to the way things were, with Daedalus being his and no one else's.

❧

A Few Days Later

"Daddy, will they always follow us around?" Sera pointed at the two men walking behind them at a safe but reachable distance as they moved through the supermarket.

Leo had told him what happened in his office a few days ago, and because of the uncertainty, he hired bodyguards from Athena's divine force. Who knew the goddess had bodyguards? Not only that, but when they weren't protecting Athena, they worked for Synder Protection Services. So they were always guarding someone.

They weren't with him twenty-four seven, only when Jason went out with the kids. He and Leo hadn't explained everything to the twins about his dimensional transport abilities and didn't want to scare them, so having bodyguards was the next best and safest option.

"Only for a couple of days," Jason answered.

"Why are they following us anyway?" Xander asked.

"It's a little complicated," Jason responded.

"We're not babies, Daddy," Sera added, and Xander nodded in agreement.

Jason and the two men walking behind them chuckled. "I know you two are all grown up, but right now, your papa and I just want some security when we travel. Why don't you two go and get two snacks each," he told them.

"Okay!" they called and ran off to the front of the aisle where Jason could still see them. Without needing to be told, one of the guards followed closely behind.

Jason had just put an item into the cart when he looked up and gasped at the sight of Valencia walking toward the twins. Without thinking, he hurried over and placed the kids behind him, halting her movements. Their eyes locked. The guard who had been with the twins stepped in front to block her from view, but Jason tapped him on the shoulder, and he moved to the side.

"You look healthy," she commented.

"And you look like shit," he replied.

He wasn't kidding. He had never seen the once-prestigious Valencia Dupree, who had always been meticulous about her appearance, dressed in jeans that looked like they had seen better days. Her black T-shirt had visible stains, and her dark hair, now streaked with gray, looked like it hadn't been washed or combed in days.

"My, how the mighty have fallen," Jason sneered.

She licked her cracked lips and wiped her nose with the back of her hand, then cleaned it off on her shirt. "Well, what can I say? Someone decided to intervene in my life when they should've minded their business."

"Daddy, do you know this lady?" Xander asked.

"No," Jason said quickly. "Come on, let's finish shopping and get home to Papa." He guided the kids back to the cart, but his footsteps stalled at Valencia's final words.

"I will have you, Jason."

He turned to confront her, but she was gone. It was as if she had been a figment of his imagination. Her sudden disappearance left him deeply unsettled, and he couldn't shake the feeling that something was going to happen.

"Daddy, are you okay?" Sera asked.

"Yes," he said with a smile. "Let's finish up." He looked at the two guards. "Keep your eyes open. I don't trust her." "Yes," they said together.

Jason kept the shopping trip upbeat for the kids, but there was tension swirling around him. Lately, he had been practicing with Doctor Pace on his abilities and was finally getting the hang of things. He was confident in certain areas, while others would take more time to master. One thing he had become proficient in was creating his dimension and moving both his body and consciousness within it. However, it could only transport one person at a time.

It wasn't much, but it gave Jason a way to protect himself and his children if something serious went down. With shopping out of the way, the group made their way out of the store and to the car.

Jason kept his guard up and didn't let it down until he got home and was wrapped safely in Leo's arms. Still, the feeling of being watched came back the next day and lingered for several days after. He worked from home most of the time, not wanting to leave the house unless Leo came with him.

The good thing was that his husband didn't mock him for his paranoia. Leo simply held him through his worries. But after two weeks passed without incident, Jason finally exhaled the tension and stepped out of the house without Leo or the bodyguards at his side. He returned to work.

"Are you sure you don't want me to come with you?" Ada asked.

"I'm certain. I think seeing my mother freaked me out more than anything else," he told her. "If I don't leave now, I'll be late meeting the client."

He grabbed his bag and headed out of the office, slinging the large strap over his shoulder, careful not to put too much pressure on his stomach, which had just started to show. Luckily, he was wearing one of Leo's shirts, so it wasn't noticeable.

Just as he exited the building, his cellphone rang. He didn't need to check the screen to know who it was.

"I'm fine," he said as he answered.

"I'll drive you to the meeting spot," Leo offered.

"No, the driver is already here. But you can pick me up," Jason replied.

"You got it."

They ended the call, and Jason climbed into the car, barely acknowledging the driver. He didn't need to say anything. The man worked for the company, and Jason had already informed the staff about his meeting. It was supposed to be a simple ride. Nothing unusual.

But minutes after they pulled away from the DRA&D building, a soft clicking sound echoed through the cabin. The doors had locked.

Jason stiffened. He looked around, confusion quickly turning into unease. The partition between the front and back seats began to rise, slowly and deliberately, until the driver was completely out of view.

Something was wrong. His instincts screamed at him to act, but before he could, a sharp hiss cut through the silence. A faint mist began to fill the air. He covered his nose and mouth with his sleeve, but it was too late. The gas was already burning his eyes and coating his lungs.

A surge of fear shot through him. Jason banged on the windows, then reached for the door handle, but it wouldn't budge. He tried to focus, to channel his abilities, but his skin was already tingling and his nerves were fraying. The connection in his mind that usually brought him clarity and control was slipping fast.

He fumbled for his phone, but his fingers felt heavy, sluggish, useless. His entire body was going numb. Each breath came in short, ragged gasps. He tried to move again, to shout, to think. Nothing worked. Every second dragged him deeper into stillness.

His head dropped back against the seat. His eyelids fluttered. The edges of his vision dimmed, and even the pressure in his chest began to dissolve. The last thing he felt was the cold weight of helplessness settling into his bones.

Then everything went black.

∾

"WHAT THE HELL IS THIS SHIT?" Leo growled at one of his top executives, throwing the folder onto the conference table.

He was unexplainably irritated, and it had nothing to do with the executive's work. But he had nowhere else to vent, so his employee had to take the brunt of his anger.

"You've been working on this for three months, and this is what you bring me? Do I need to pay you less so you can finally get it done right?"

The executive opened his mouth to respond, but Ada burst into the office.

"Leo, Jason never made it to the meeting."

"What?" He stood up, eyes narrowing as he looked at his sister.

"I tried calling him, but his phone keeps going to voicemail. The driver who was supposed to take him to the restaurant came up to get him. I even called the client, and he said he's been waiting on Jason for thirty minutes. He was just about to leave when I reached him." She grabbed Leo's arm, her voice trembling. "Leo, I think something happened to him."

"Baby, calm down." Talos stepped in and wrapped his arms around her shaking body.

"Everyone out," Leo shouted at the onlookers.

No one hesitated. The room cleared in seconds, leaving only Leo, Ada, and Talos.

Leo pulled out his phone and dialed Jason's number again and again. Each time, it rang once before going straight to voicemail. He fought back the rising panic, trying to convince himself he shouldn't have let Jason go alone. He should have cancelled everything and gone with him. But he knew he couldn't keep hovering over his husband the way he had for the past few days.

"Ada, Talos, go pick up the twins from Mrs. Sing. Actually, convince her to go back to the house with you."

Mrs. Sing still watched the kids during the day while they were at work. The twins were set to start school next year, but for now, they enjoyed spending their days with her, something both Jason and Leo had no issue with.

"Okay, we'll try," they said, and hurried out the door.

Leo called Jason's phone one more time. It went straight to voicemail, just like before. He was about to try again when his phone rang, with Jason's name flashing across the screen.

"Baby, where are you?" he asked, breath catching with hope and fear.

"He's with me," came a cool voice from the other end of the line.

Leo's face darkened. "When I find you, I'm going to kill you."

"Then you better hurry," the voice drawled. "Because Valencia is itching to take over his body, and I'm honestly excited to see it. I want to watch you scramble to save your little lover. But maybe we need to delay it a bit. Gotta get rid of the brats he's carrying."

Leo snarled and hurled his phone at the wall, watching it shatter on impact. His fists clenched. The fire inside him ignited, burning hotter than ever.

He was going to kill Minos.

And that was a vow he would not break.

"Mother, I need you," he whispered.

The moment the words left his lips, Athena's arms wrapped around him. "Don't worry," she said softly.

"Jason," was all Leo could manage to say.

"I know. We will find him in time." "But," he started, and his voice cracked.

"There is someone there protecting them."

Leo looked at her, brows drawing together. "Who?"

"You will see when you get there. Now, let's hurry before Ishtar figures out what I've done." She grabbed his arms and pulled him out of the conference room. "The bracelet's protection won't last long. I can feel the magic waning."

Leo had been so out of sorts, he had forgotten about the protection bracelets. He stopped walking and pulled his arm from her grasp. "Did you know this was going to happen?"

"Not to this extent. But as warriors, we must have contingency plans. I've taught this to you, my son. You've grown too lax over the years. Now get your head out of your ass and let's go save my son-in-law and grand-children."

Leo nodded, the fog in his mind beginning to clear.

"And Daedalus," Athena added, her tone sharp.

"Don't hold back on your power. If you must kill Minos, do it. That is an order, not as your mother but as your goddess."

"That's not an order you needed to give. Minos won't get to see the sun rise tomorrow," Leo said coldly, following Athena out of the DRA&D building.

Downstairs, a small group of her divine guards, dressed in tactical gear, were already waiting.

"Lady Athena, Master Leo," one of the soldiers said. "We're all set. We tracked the bracelet's signal to the Amon Island District. I've already sent a team to scope out the area."

"Very well. Get moving," Leo instructed. "We don't have much time. I can't trace the triplets magical signatures because they're too young, so do your best. My mother and I will head directly to the Amon District."

The men and women piled into three black SUVs and sped off into the night. Athena took Leo's hand, and within seconds, they vanished from the street, reappearing in a dark alley in Amon.

Although all the districts were equal in size, none of them looked alike. The protectors had ensured that each one remained unique.

The main part of Amon was a district brimming with greenery and sleek, modern towering skyscrapers that Leo himself had designed. It had flourished under the guidance of Dio, its appointed protector, and had become a safe, thriving part of the city. It was also where the port was located. A lively hub catering to cargo ships carrying all of the supplies in and out of Valleywood. But like all places, it held its shadows. Seedy alleys, abandoned warehouses, and forgotten factories offered the perfect cover for illicit activity.

The sun was setting, casting the sky in ominous streaks of red and orange. To Leo, it looked like an omen. Someone would die tonight. The only question was who.

"Let's go," Athena said. "I can feel the trace magic near the warehouse district."

Leo didn't ask questions. He followed close behind her. As they moved, Athena's dress shimmered and shifted into black tactical gear. Her magic extended to him, transforming his suit into matching combat armor.

Leo didn't need weapons to defeat Minos. One of the blessings Athena had given him was strength rivaling Hercules. That was how he'd dropped Minos in a single blow at the office. But tonight, he wouldn't hold back.

Minos was waiting for him.

I won't let you go this time, Minos.

Jason groaned, his head pounding as he tried to sit up. Only then did he realize he couldn't move. His limbs felt leaden, and his body was sluggish, as if he had been drugged. Panic crawled up his spine like a swarm of ants. His eyes fluttered open, only to be seared by bright, sterile overhead lights. The space around him was clearly unfamiliar, not his room and definitely not his home.

What the hell is going on? How the fuck did I get here?

He turned his head to the side, blinking through the haze that clouded his vision. But it was no use since everything else but the light above his head was in complete darkness.

Where the fuck am I?

A sudden rush of memories struck him like a freight train, each one distorted and painful as it forced its way to the surface. He remembered being in a car on the way to a meeting when gas suddenly filled the cabin. He winced at the sharp sting behind his eyes and instinctively tried to clutch his head, only to realize that his hands wouldn't move.

There were no ropes or chains restraining him from his chest down, yet he was lying flat on his back, arms pinned tightly to his sides and legs held together by some invisible force. As panic began to rise in his chest, he twisted left and right, struggling harder with each breath in a desperate attempt to break free. His breathing grew faster, and his heart pounded in his chest. What the hell is happening? Where the fuck am I?

A deep, unfamiliar voice echoed through the space. "It's no use. You're magically restrained."

Jason's entire body went still, tension locking into his muscles. His eyes darted around the room, scanning and praying for any sign of movement from anywhere. He saw no shadows and no figure, but he knew the voice had been real.

"Who's there?" he shouted, trying to keep the fear from showing in his voice and failing.

"There's no time to talk. They're coming. Wait for the signal, then enter your dimensional space."

What signal? Who the hell is talking to me? Jason's

pulse thundered in his ears. "Are you still there! What signal? Where are you? Who are you?"

He strained to hear a reply, but only silence met him. Seconds later, the heavy groan of industrial doors echoed through the space, followed by a brief flood of light that disappeared as quickly as it arrived. He held his breath as the sound of heels clicked against the floor, slow and deliberate. There was no urgency in the stride, only confidence.

Maybe there was something predatory in the way she moved. Judging by the rhythm and weight of the steps, he guessed it was a woman. Jason remained still, with his muscles locked and nerves stretched thin, while dread pulsed through his body like a current. His breath caught in his throat as a familiar voice pierced the silence with chilling precision.

"You have been a pain in my ass since the day you were implanted," Valencia said coldly as her face came into view. "From having to care for Jackson because of morning sickness to making me believe you were worthless."

A jolt of disbelief and horror surged through Jason's chest. She looked exactly as she always had, composed and elegant in the most terrifying way. Her dark hair was parted neatly down the middle, bone-straight and brushing her shoulders.

She wore all black beneath a crisp white lab coat, giving her the appearance of someone ready to perform a clinical procedure. Her makeup was flawless, and her signature red lipstick painted her smile into something both striking and cruel.

"But tonight, all of my efforts will finally pay off."

She leaned in and slowly traced a red-painted nail down the side of his face, letting it skim his jaw and brush across his lips, as if she were admiring a work of art. Jason flinched at her touch, but he couldn't move. Every part of him screamed to fight, to resist, but the magic holding him down refused to release even the smallest part of him.

"I always thought you were an ugly baby. Not cute and adorable like Willa and Ian," she continued, her voice soft and filled with amusement. "But you grew into a good-looking man. I cannot wait to take over your body. But first, let's take care of those pesky brats. In my new life, children are not part of the deal." Terror spread through Jason like wildfire. His heart hadn't stopped pounding in his chest, and bile rose in his throat as her words sank in.

"No," he said, his voice hoarse. "You can't touch them." Valencia cackled. "Watch me."

He strained against the restraints, twisting and pulling with everything he had, desperate to break free. His muscles burned, and his wrists ached, but the invisible force refused to budge.

"You will never get what you want," he growled, channeling every ounce of fury and fear into the words.

Valencia tilted her head, watching him with cold amusement. "Oh, sweet boy," she whispered, brushing her knuckle over his cheek as if she were comforting a child. "You have no idea what

I've already taken."

"Is that supposed to scare me?" Jason growled.

"Yes."

"I hate you," Jason seethed.

"The feeling is mutual," Valencia said. "Your only purpose of your birth was for this day." She let out a sharp, delighted cackle that echoed off the walls. "And now that it's going to happen, there's no one here to stop me."

"Do you think my husband is going to sit by and not come after you? You have no idea of the power he has."

"I'm not afraid of some architect who knows how to spend money like it's water. By the time he finds you, your soul will already be gone." Leaning in until he could feel her breath against his skin, she smiled with mock intimacy. "Here's a secret. I have a very powerful friend helping me out. If it wasn't for him coming to my side, I would still be going crazy trying to figure out how to get you."

"Who?" Jason asked, narrowing his eyes. As far as he knew everyone had turned their backs on her because of Jackson and Willa's arrest.

"You'll find out soon." She straightened and gave a careless shrug, her red nails flashing in the light. "I have no idea why he wants to help me, but who am I to turn down free labor?"

Jason closed his eyes and forced himself to tamp down the rising fear. It wasn't helping. He didn't know who was assisting Valencia, but he was certain of one thing. Once Leo and Athena discovered what she had done, Valencia and her allies would not live long enough to see another birthday.

He was just about to speak, the words forming in his

throat, when the heavy doors groaned open again. Light flooded into the room, more intense than before, and this time the person who entered made no effort to close the door behind them.

Jason wasn't sure if his eyes were playing tricks on him or if it was his fear clouding his vision, but he saw two men dressed similarly in all black. What set them apart was the intricate purple embroidery stitched across their suit jackets. Both were handsome, silent, and focused entirely on him.

Despite the threat of his mother stealing his body and harming his children, a deeper fear crept over him as he stared back at the two strangers. But this time, there was a third person, dressed in white, slowly walking away from them.

Could they be the people helping Valencia?

His internal question was soon answered when the man in white pressed a finger to his lips and shook his head, silently telling Jason not to say anything. Jason's eyes widened in absolute shock and fear when the man walked through Valencia and over to him, careful to remain in the shadows, away from the light.

"Blink once if you can hear me," the man said softly. Jason was shaking, but through his fear, he recognized the voice from earlier.

Jason looked at Valencia, who seemed completely unaware of what was happening.

"Come on, Jason. We don't have a lot of time. I need to know you can see me and hear me," the man in white stressed. Between him and the second set of footsteps growing closer, Jason blinked.

"Good, good," the man in white whispered near his ear. "Whatever they do, try not to get riled up. It will stop you from entering the dimension."

"Haven't you taken care of the brats yet?"

Jason's attention snapped back to Valencia, who had turned to address the person who'd asked the question. Elias Crete stepped forward from the shadows.

"So it's you," Jason said, his voice low with disbelief.

"Are you surprised?" Elias smiled, as if they were sharing an inside joke.

"Why are you doing this? Why are you helping her?" Jason asked, even though part of him already knew the answer.

"That's a dumb question, Jason," Elias replied. He stepped closer and grabbed Jason's face, tilting it roughly toward him. "But I take it you want to hear me say the words. I told you I came to

Valleywood with one goal. I came to get the man I love."

Jason growled and twisted his face away from Elias's grasp. "He won't forgive you for this."

"Maybe," Elias said with a smirk. "But who said he's going to remember you?"

"No matter what you do, Leo will never forget me. He will never forget what we shared or the fact that he loves me."

"His name is Daedalus!" Elias snapped. "Not this Leo nonsense. No matter how many times he changes his name, he will always be the clumsy man who gets excited over the simplest inventions."

Despite the situation, Jason let out a snicker. "You're

so lost in the past. You think erasing me and destroying our family will bring back what you already gave away. I told you before that you never loved him, and hearing you now only proves I was right. You're a pathetic fool who will never get what he wants."

Jason's voice dropped into a cold, unshakable promise. "I swear to you, Elias Crete, or should I call you Minos, today, you will die."

"You fucking bastard!" Minos lunged forward and grabbed him by the throat, his fingers tightening with rage.

But before he could squeeze harder, a white glow exploded between them. The force blasted Minos across the room, sending him crashing into the far wall with a sickening thud.

"What the fuck was that?" Valencia yelled.

"Did you check his body for a protection amulet?" Minos gasped, standing to his feet.

"Amulet?" Valencia echoed, her voice laced with confusion. "What does it look like?"

"It could look like anything," Minos said, staring at Jason but not moving any closer. "A token, a pendant, jewelry..." He paused, then rushed toward Jason, who immediately began struggling against his magical bindings.

"Don't you dare touch me," Jason growled.

"Stop fucking moving," Minos snapped. He reached to touch him again but hesitated, clearly afraid of being blasted a second time. He pointed at Valencia. "You search his body. It seems I can't touch him."

"But you touched him earlier," Valencia noted.

"That time I wasn't trying to kill him. Whatever protection amulet he's wearing has registered my intent. It's figured out my signature."

"Damn it, why the hell is magic so complicated?" Valencia grumbled. "And stop ordering me around. I'm not your fucking lackey."

"Just do what I told you. If my guess is correct, that amulet isn't just for protection. It's probably a tracking spell too."

Jason listened to their exchange, curling his fingers into a fist to try and conceal the bracelet on his wrist. Since the blast that sent Minos flying, he had regained just a bit of movement.

Valencia approached him, her fingers trembling as she touched his chest and began unbuttoning his shirt. She paused for a second after making contact, almost as if she expected to be blasted like Minos.

Jason watched as she exhaled with relief, then smiled smugly and continued her search with renewed confidence. This time, her hands were far less gentle. She touched his wedding ring, his watch, and finally, the bracelet Athena had given him.

The entire time, Jason didn't flinch. He didn't move or struggle. He needed them to keep thinking the magical restraints were still holding him in place. What they didn't know was that he was slowly regaining full control of his limbs.

"I don't see anything out of the ordinary," Valencia said to Minos.

"How would you know what's out of the ordinary? You've never spent time with him."

"Fuck you," Valencia growled.

"Whatever," Minos muttered and started pacing. "Something isn't right. Athena wouldn't let her beloved son-in-law roam around without protection."

"I don't know who Athena is," Valencia commented. "But we don't have time to feed into your paranoia. The sun is almost done setting, and we need to set up for the soul transfer. The shaman will be here soon."

"Since you're able to touch him, do what you need to do. But be careful. Just because you weren't blasted away before doesn't mean the protection spell won't sense you trying to hurt him now."

"Okay," Valencia said, annoyed.

"I'll..." Minos began, then suddenly paused. "Fuck!" "What? What is it?" Valencia asked.

"They're here," Minos replied, his tone low and sharp. "How do you know?"

"They broke through one of my magical formations." He turned his gaze toward Jason. "If you want his body, you're going to have to do it without the shaman. This is your only opportunity." "And what will you be doing?" Valencia snapped.

"Don't worry about that. Just focus on your task."

"You're going to die, Minos," Jason said in a sing-song tone, his voice full of defiance.

"Don't be too happy. Nothing says they'll survive."

"You think you can kill a goddess?" Jason asked, cocky and unbothered.

"No. I can't kill her," Minos said calmly. "But I know someone who can. My lady Ishtar, I need your assistance."

Unlike Athena, who had appeared seconds after Leo's call, Ishtar took a couple of minutes before materializing in the room. Valencia gasped and instinctively stepped back from Minos.

"G-goddess..." she stammered, eyes wide.

The gorgeous woman who appeared carried an aura of power, her curvaceous figure cloaked in elegance and the intoxicating scent of roses. She ignored Valencia completely.

"This better be fucking good, Minos," Ishtar said, her voice like velvet and venom.

"My goddess, she is here," Minos said, a note of reverence in his voice.

A menacing smile crossed Ishtar's face before she disappeared in a shimmer of power.

Minos turned to Valencia. "Do your thing, and no one should bother you."

With that, he ran out of the room, leaving Jason alone with his deranged mother.

"See? I told you, Son. Friends with power. Now, let's get started."

She turned her back. Out of the corner of his eye, Jason caught

a flash of white moving from one end of the room to the other. He took it as the signal.

Jason closed his eyes and focused, thinking of a place where he would be safe. Just as he was about to slip into his dimension, Valencia turned and grabbed him.

They vanished.

Jason didn't think. He reacted. With every ounce of

force he could muster, he kicked her hard in the stomach, sending her flying from his space.

She screamed and disappeared into the void.

Jason closed his eyes, panting, his chest rising and falling as he tried to calm his racing heart. He placed a hand over his stomach, grounding himself.

He was safe. They were safe. For now.

He didn't know what would be waiting for him when he left his dimensional space, but one thing was clear. He would not back down from a fight if it came.

CHAPTER 24

LEO

A Few Minutes Earlier

L eo and Athena crept between the steel cargo crates, scanning the area. They'd followed the magical tracer to the ports. Leo didn't know what Minos had done, but no matter the time or day, the port was always bustling with people, ships coming in and out like clockwork, but now it was empty. When they had entered the pier, they had triggered a warning barrier woven into the very air. Not that it mattered. They hadn't come to skulk in shadows.

"I sent the guards our location. They'll be here any

minute," Athena murmured, her voice calm but alert. "Also, I just received word. Jason escaped into his dimension."

Leo's gut tightened. Relief for Jason warred with unease. He hadn't expected Valencia to follow. That added a layer of complication.

"It's good someone's with him," he muttered, though his voice held the sharp edge of concern.

Athena placed a hand briefly on his arm. "He's being guided. Right now, we focus. Minos and Ishtar are close."

"Who did you send to protect him?" Leo asked, glancing at her.

"Death, of course," she said, as casually as if she were commenting on the weather.

"Mother, seriously?" Leo pinched the bridge of his nose, trying to keep calm.

"I made a deal with Kieran. Our boy is safe."

Kieran Grimlock, the head of the twelve death clans in the Death Realm, was not a man to be trifled with, especially when it came to his favorite son, Chase. In fact, Chase was the favorite of the entire Grimlock clan. Leo had once thought about asking Chase out, but he hadn't liked the way Chase's two older brothers and three sisters had stared him down.

Not to mention Chase's three mothers. Kieran might have been older than Leo, but he looked no older than a man in his forties. Leo had no desire to get entangled in that chaos, and he had a small amount of pity for whoever Chase eventually ended up with.

"What did you give him to protect Jason?"

"Twelve pure soul coins," she answered offhandedly.

Leo stared at her. Soul coins were not easy to come by, especially pure ones, and even harder to find for a divine goddess. It was easier for a grim reaper, since they were death and controlled souls after they died. For gods, they had to convince someone to die in their name or sacrifice part of their soul to the reaper.

"Fuck, Mom... I don't even know what to say."

"Say thank you, and that's it. Haven't I already told you? You, Jason, and the kids are my family. I would do anything for all of

you. Besides, it wasn't my soul I gave up."

"Whose were they?"

"They were from followers who died a long time ago and remained among the living. And before you start worrying, I asked for their permission before handing them over to Kieran. He promised not to sell them at the coming auction. Instead, he'll turn them into revenants."

Revenants were bound to the grim clans as their servants in any capacity. They were created when a person made a deal with a grim reaper moments before their death. Leo nodded grimly, just as dark-suited figures emerged from behind the cargo containers. Their footsteps were light but deliberate. Leo's sharp eyes counted fast, fifty, maybe more. They weren't Reapers. That meant only one thing.

"We have company," he said flatly.

Athena cracked her knuckles, her smile sharp and hungry. "Let's cower in the corner," she said with a wink. "Get this done quick, then we go home."

She stepped into the open with casual confidence.

The mercenaries circled her like wolves, unaware the lioness had just bared her teeth.

Leo moved to her side, flexing his fingers. The ground beneath his feet already felt lighter. "You look happy," he said, raising a brow.

"Of course I am. How often does a mother get to fight beside her beloved son?" She beamed. "You take the left. I'll handle the right."

With matching grins, they broke into a run, diving into the fray like twin storms. Leo's punches landed with thunderous force, sending men flying into crates. He tore through their ranks, smashing rib cages and tossing bodies like rag dolls. Athena was just as brutal, snapping necks, twisting arms from sockets. It was all brute strength, no divine power needed.

Screams echoed. Metal groaned. The scent of magic and blood filled the air. And then, just as Leo hurled a man straight through a stack of steel drums, a pulse shimmered through the air. A cold silence followed. A slow, taunting clap rang out.

From the shadows emerged Minos, clad in a dark silk robe and black pants underneath, his expression smug. Beside him stood Ishtar, radiant and deadly, lips curled into a cruel smile.

"Well, well," Minos drawled. "A family reunion. How touching."

Athena narrowed her eyes. "You're late."

Ishtar tilted her head. "We wanted to let your warm-up play out first."

Leo cracked his neck, mentally and emotionally

unlocking his divine blessing, and the air trembled around him. "Then let's not waste time chit-chatting."

"I miss that about you, Dae. A man who knows when to get down to business. But before we start, let's make a bet. If I win our fight, you will forsake Athena and all she gave you, and come to me."

"And what happens when I win?" "Then I will be yours." Minos smiled.

"I don't want you," Leo said without a thought to the other man's feelings. "But if I win, you will never set foot in Valleywood, or in front of me and my family again."

Leo watched Minos nibble on his bottom lip before nodding.

"I agree."

"These foolish mortals and their games," Ishtar commented.

"I kind of like the idea," Athena said. "How about it, Ish? Want to place a bet?"

Ishtar was silent for a few seconds, then nodded. "Fine, let's do this. You already know what I want," she said. "You and him to be mine for all eternity."

Leo thought Athena was going to object, but she agreed.

"Okay. And when we win, you will give Leo, Jason, Ada, and Talos divine blessings each. Oh, and don't worry, I know the ones I want them to have."

"Aren't you asking for a bit much?" Ishtar sneered.

Athena didn't say anything, only tapped her temples as if to say she was born with brains, not just beauty.

"Okay, I agree," Ishtar said, and the moment the words left her mouth, the heavens opened with thunder and lightning. No rain followed, which only meant one thing—Zeus was watching.

"Your fucking family annoys me," Ishtar snapped.

Athena shrugged. "What can I say? He's a girl dad."

Leo lifted his gaze and saw Dio standing within the clouds. He waved his hand, and Leo guessed the god was putting up a barrier to protect the citizens of Amon from the fight. Once it was done, Dio disappeared.

"Enough chatting," Ishtar shouted, then turned to Minos. "You lose, you die."

Minos's only response was shedding his robe and shifting quickly into an eight-foot-tall minotaur. He roared, the sound shaking the air. Leo thanked all the gods that the pants Minos wore had stayed intact and conformed with his shift.

Leo licked his lips and grinned. "Athena was right. This is going to be fun as hell."

He made the first move, shooting forward like a missile, his fist cocked back. When he struck, Minos met him head-on. The sound of their collision shook the ground and toppled several of the surrounding cargo containers. Leo didn't slow down. He delivered blow after blow while ducking wide swipes from Minos's claws.

Leo growled and drove a hard punch into Minos's rib cage, smirking as he heard and felt the crunch beneath his knuckles. Minos bellowed in rage and swung his head in a sharp arc from right to left, horns aiming for Leo's chest.

But Leo was faster. He caught one of the horns mid-swing, the sheer force nearly lifting him off the ground.

Using that momentum, he twisted his body, planted both feet against the side of

Minos's massive head, and launched himself into the air with a burst of strength and agility that defied his size. He landed in a perfect crouch, grinning as he looked up at the towering minotaur. "Come on," he taunted. "I know you've got more than that."

Minos roared in fury and stomped his massive hooves, sending shockwaves rippling beneath them.

"What, you can't talk?" Leo jeered. "She really turned you into a wild animal."

Minos snorted and grunted, dropping his shoulders low and widening his stance. He took on the posture of a charging bull, though he remained upright. A breath later, Minos launched forward, horns lowered, barreling straight for Leo.

Leo dodged to the side, but Minos was ready. He twisted midcharge, catching Leo in the right side with a crushing fist that knocked the wind out of him and sent him staggering. Minos didn't give him a moment to breathe, stepping into his space and landing hit after hit.

He struck Leo in the chest, stomach, and side. With a growl, he drove his elbow into Leo's jaw, snapping his head back, then kicked him in the ribs with a hoof hard enough to launch Leo into the cargo behind him.

Leo grunted and steadied himself, using the back of his hand to wipe away the blood trickling from the corner of his mouth. A wide grin spread across his lips as he looked at the half-man, halfbull in front of him.

"Good job, bull boy, but this will be the only time you

get your hits in." He raised his hand and slowly curled a finger, challenging Minos even more. "Come at me."

Minos roared and stomped his foot before charging at Leo with his horns poised and ready to strike. Leo was ready for him. He ducked and twisted, just barely missing the horns by inches. He countered with a brutal haymaker to Minos's jaw that snapped his head sideways. Not holding back, Leo seized the moment and grabbed Minos's horns. He yanked hard and slammed the large bull head into a nearby cargo tank.

The half-bull, half-man seemed dazed, but it hadn't knocked him down. "I must admit you're a strong bastard."

Minos snarled and swung his massive arm, backhanding Leo with enough force to send him skidding across the pier. Again, doing a move that most stunt actors would be proud of, Leo rolled with the impact and came to a stop against a broken crate, chuckling as he rose to his feet, completely unfazed by what was happening.

Leo wiped away the blood from his forehead that threatened to run into his eye and flicked the excess off his fingers. He was aching all over, but his body would heal thanks to his goddess mother's blessing.

"Well done, Minos," he muttered. In the distance, he could hear the sounds of swords clashing, like thunder rolling, and he knew Athena was having just as much fun as he was. He hadn't realized how far they had gotten separated. He quickly calculated in his head how much money he would need to send to Dio for all the damage he and Athena had caused, but it would be worth it.

It had been a while since either of them engaged in a fun or competitive battle. But the reason they were there wasn't for a good time. It was to rescue his little lover, who must be going out of his mind. Although Athena said he was safe, Leo knew he had to wrap this up quickly.

He looked at the towering beast, surprised to see him still. Too still. His eyes dropped to the weapon now clutched in Minos's thick, furred hands. A massive double-bladed axe, its dark metal etched with glowing runes, shimmered with a hungry pulse.

"Well, aren't you full of fucking tricks?" Leo tsked and shook his head. "Should've pulled that out earlier. Might've stood a chance."

Minos snorted, steam curling from his nostrils. He lowered his head and pawed at the ground with a hoof, letting out a thunderous bellow. Then he charged, raising the axe high over his head. Every step felt as if the ground was shaking beneath them.

Leo grinned. *Oh, bull boy is big mad. This is going to be an easy takedown.*

Leo didn't run from the beast barreling toward him. He simply counted the seconds. Minos got close enough to swing, and just before the axe came down, Leo acted. He sidestepped with effortless speed, catching the shaft of the weapon mid-swing. The force of it rattled through his arms, and the glowing runes seared his skin. His muscles flexed as he halted the blow with sheer power. Leo tightened his jaw, grunting from the pain flaring in his palms.

But he didn't give up or let it go. He strengthened his

hold. The axe groaned under the strain, as if it were in pain too. Leo wrenched it from Minos's grip and flung it across the pier. It crashed into a stack of steel cargo containers, sending a loud clang echoing into the air. Blood dripped from Leo's fingers, but he paid it no attention.

Minos barely had time to recover before Leo lunged, ignoring the sting in his hands as he drove his fist into the minotaur's gut. The impact folded the beast with a guttural grunt. Leo followed with a savage uppercut that snapped Minos's head back, the crack of bone echoing across the darkening pier. Shadows stretched around them, the last remnants of sunset casting a crimson hue over the water.

Without pause, Leo grabbed the beast by the horns, pivoted, and with a roar, hurled him into a towering stack of cargo containers. Steel dented inward with a thunderous crash as Minos crashed through, sending crates tumbling and debris scattering across the dock.

Minos slumped in the wreckage, groaning, blood trailing from

his mouth. Leo rolled his shoulders and spat to the side. The glow of distant floodlights caught the blood dripping from his hand. "You would have had a better chance if you used the axe in the beginning."

Scanning the area, Leo saw bodies knocked out cold, followers of Minos and Ishtar, while the divine guards moved quickly, rounding them up. And a couple of grim reapers had already begun collecting souls.

A loud clash drew Leo's attention to his left. He saw Athena and Ishtar locked in combat, striking each other blow for blow, their swords clashing violently. Sparks flew with every strike, both women evenly matched in speed and power. Leo didn't worry. He knew Athena would win that fight. He took off running, heart pounding, eyes scanning every shadowed corner. He had one goal now, to find his husband.

ATHENA'S CHEST rose and fell, each breath sharp and burning through her ribs. Blood stained her jaw and shoulder where Ishtar's strikes had cut deep. Her clothes were torn in several places, fabric clinging to her skin, but she was still standing, a bloody smile stretched across her face.

Across from her, Ishtar looked just as wrecked. Her pants were slashed at the thigh, one sleeve hanging by threads. The blade in her hand trembled slightly, though her eyes still burned with fire. They didn't speak. They simply moved.

Their swords collided with a shriek of metal, sparks bursting with every blow. Athena parried a slash and twisted, her blade cutting across Ishtar's side. The goddess hissed and retaliated, scoring a shallow slice across Athena's thigh. Pain lanced through her leg, but she refused to stop.

This wasn't a battle for dominance. It was punishment and a warning to anyone who dared to threaten her family. Athena had no intention of falling. She had to bring everything, her discipline, her rage, and her precision, to win. One mistake could mean death.

"Think of all the fun we could have, Athena," Ishtar said midstrike, their swords grinding together. "We fight, then fuck."

Tempting. It really was. But even without Hera's curse binding her desires, Athena couldn't stomach a relationship that felt like a never-ending war just to earn moments of pleasure and peace. Not only that, she had a moral rule not to be intimate with someone who was trying to tear her family apart. One that she worked hard to achieve. Despite the curse, Athena loved her life, and once this fight was over, she planned on getting back to it.

"You talk too much," Athena growled, then drove her boot into Ishtar's stomach, sending her stumbling back with a grunt, but that didn't stop the goddess.

She let the momentum carry her into a backward roll, flinging her sword away. She came up low and lunged forward with a snarl, slamming her shoulder into Athena's midsection and driving them both into a steel cargo container. Before Athena could react, Ishtar grabbed her hair and yanked her head back, bringing a knee to herribs.

Athena gritted her teeth through the impact to stop herself from howling in pain. Instead, she threw an elbow across Ishtar's jaw, hard enough to knock her head back and break her hold. They separated for a breath, chests heaving, blood dripping from open wounds, soaking their clothes.

"Fuck, I knew this was going to be a hard fight," Ishtar said.

"Did you think I was simply going to grin and twirl

my hair while you try to fuck with my family, just because I'm attracted to you?"

"You're attracted to me?" Ishtar asked in shock.

"Who isn't?" Athena responded. "But I can't be with you, so just walk away now, Ishtar. Your boy is down for the count. You've lost the fight."

"Do you think I'm going to listen to you just because I want to fuck you?" Ishtar snapped.

Athena scoffed and shook her head. "You don't get it, Ishtar. Even if we could be together, after what you've done, there can never be an us."

"Don't say that," Ishtar shouted.

"Why? It's the truth. I can never be with someone who lashes out and tries to hurt people I care about because you don't get your own way. That is not how you win my affection."

"Then tell me how. I just want to build a life with you!" "It's too late," Athena whispered.

She knew this could have all been avoided long ago if she had told Ishtar the real reason for her rejection. But knowing the goddess like she did, Ishtar would have tried to find the one who cursed her, and then Hera would have done something that could hurt them both.

"Why must you always reject me? Why can't you just give me what I want?" she screamed.

Athena didn't respond. She watched Ishtar grow even more frustrated with her silence.

"You're so fucking stubborn," Ishtar growled.

Athena ditched her sword when Ishtar charged again, wild and fast, throwing a wide hook aimed to take Athena down. But Athena ducked low, letting the strike sail over her head, then surged upward with a brutal head butt that cracked against

Ishtar's nose.

Athena barely registered the blood spraying on her arm and stepped in close, slamming a fist into Ishtar's jaw and snapping her head to the side. Ishtar stumbled, her footing unstable, but Athena didn't hesitate. She grabbed the goddess by the torn shirt and yanked her forward.

"You think I don't want to love you or anyone else?" Athena snapped, kneeing Ishtar in the stomach with all the strength she had left.

Ishtar doubled over, gasping. Athena caught her in a chokehold, twisted her weight, and brought them both crashing down onto the pier. The wooden planks groaned beneath them. Ishtar coughed, writhing, trying to slip free. But Athena moved fast, straddling her chest, one knee digging into her ribs. She raised her fist and brought it down hard.

"I can't love you or anyone else," she said, punching Ishtar a second time, then a third. Each hit landed with the dull, sick sound of flesh giving way to fury. "I'm fucking cursed!" Tears she never wanted to shed trailed down her cheeks. She struck her again, and then once more, as her strength finally ran out. "I've been cursed to never fall in love."

Hearing that, Ishtar stopped moving. They stared at each other, panting heavily. Ishtar's face was swollen, battered, and far from the beauty she was known for, but Athena knew she would heal in no time. Ishtar reached up to touch Athena's cheek, but Athena slapped her hand away and stood.

"Let this be the end of it, Ishtar," Athena rasped, looking down at the goddess still flat on the ground. "I expect to see you in three days to award those blessings. And don't try any funny shit. We don't want a repeat of what happened tonight."

Athena turned and walked down the length of the pier on shaky legs. She should have been elated that she won, but she wasn't. The one secret she had tried so hard to keep from others had been revealed. Athena saw the curse as a weakness and was surprised Hera had never shouted it from the highest mountain on Olympus. Not even the vengeful, jealous goddess had said a word about it.

Athena could only hope Ishtar would keep it to herself so she could return to her regular life and prepare for her grandchildren. That thought brought a smile to her aching face, and she didn't care. She had grown used to not having the love of a partner. The love of her children and grandchildren was all she needed, and no one would ever take that away. Not Ishtar, and not Hera.

~

Back to Jason's Dimension

JASON GASPED as he stood and glanced around. This place wasn't familiar to him. It looked like an apartment, larger than the one he'd lived in with the twins. Usually, when he entered his space, it was only a fragment of what he could imagine.

"Where am I?"

"My space." He chuckled. "Well, kind of."

Jason turned, recognizing the voice of the man who had spoken to him when he was tied down. He was still dressed in a white suit and smiling at him. The man was Asian American, with a short, coiffed hairstyle, gray eyes, and about the same height as Jason.

"Who are you?" he demanded. "How did you get in here? What is this place?"

"I'm Mark St. James. I got in here because you pulled me in with you, well, sort of. And this place was once my home, just as the knot you have used to be mine."

"Wha... what?" Jason stuttered, touching the back of his neck and feeling his knot.

"You're a very loved man, Jason. I'm kind of a little jealous of that."

"How... how... how are you here?"

"Someone powerful made a deal with death, and here I am."

A *deal with death*, Jason thought. *Who would do that? So is Mark here to hurt me? Fuck, I'm seeing dead people now. I hate agreeing with Valencia that magic is complicated.*

"What are you going to do to me? Do you want your knot back? Because you can't have it."

Mark laughed. "I'm dead, and in some ways, my knot is still with me. So no, I don't want it back." "Then what do you want?" "To help you," Mark said.

"Help me, how?"

"I will teach you how to use your dimensional travel

perfectly. It will take some time, but not today. I'm here for a different reason."

"What reason? Wait, don't answer that yet," he said and started pacing. "I need time to process all of this." He stopped walking and looked at Mark. "You're dead, and the knot I have used to be yours. Someone influential made a deal with death to bring you to me, but you're not here to kill me, you're here to help me. Athena is the only person I can think of that's strong enough to do that."

Mark nodded. "Like I said, you're loved."

"Do you know what kind of deal she made?"

"No," Mark said, shaking his head. "You'd have to ask her. But I will tell you what I've learned while in the death realm waiting to be judged. The grim reaper lord wouldn't have agreed if he wasn't getting something valuable. They may work for the gods, but they have their own rules."

Jason lowered his eyes, silently thanking Athena and praying that the deal she made wouldn't bring her harm.

"You don't have to worry," Mark said, getting his attention. "The gods and the reaper clans have an understanding relationship."

"This is all so much to take in," Jason said.

"Get used to it," Mark smiled. "You think being an unbound is

the only shocking thing that will happen in your life? Think again.

You've already met death."

"Hold up, when?"

"When what? When did you meet death?" Jason nodded.

"Those two men I was standing with weren't super-models, even though they looked like it."

"Fuck," Jason said and sat down, his mind so blown he wasn't sure what he was thinking.

I saw death. Does that mean I'm going to die?

Jason went to say something, but Mark spoke once more. "Your man is here. Go to him."

"What about you? My mother? How do you know he's here?"

"I'm still connected to the grim reapers. They've been telling me what's going on. My job was to keep you hidden until the fight was over."

"Why? I can handle myself."

"I'm sure you can, but don't be stupid. You're pregnant, and you have to keep those babies safe."

Mark was right, and Jason didn't argue anymore. He couldn't put his children in unnecessary danger.

"As for your mother," he sighed, shaking his head. "She is in the arms of death right now."

"She's dead?" Jason asked in surprise.

"Who did you think they were here for? You?" Mark said. "Unlike me, you will never have to stress over being killed."

That caught Jason's attention, but before he could ask, Mark spoke.

"Now, let's get the hell out of here. You have a man to pacify, and I have shit to do until you need me."

"Wait, before you go. For helping me, do you get anything out of the deal?"

"I wouldn't have agreed if I didn't."

With that said, he disappeared, and the neat apartment dissolved into a blank space, leaving Jason no choice but to leave. Thinking of Leo, the dark, damp room where he had been captured came back into view.

"Jason," came an anguished cry as strong arms wrapped around him.

The scent of blood, mixed with Leo's masculine aroma, reached his nose and calmed any worry or questions that had been on his tongue. There was no need to speak. He circled his arms around Leo's waist, tightening his hold on his husband, silently promising to never let him go.

∾

Three Months Later

MINOS SAT IN HIS CELL, staring at the bare walls. After the fight, nothing had gone his way. First, Ishtar took away her blessings, and now he was on a slow road to death. He had been arrested at the airport while trying to leave town.

His connection to Calderon had somehow come to light, and all his former allies had turned their backs on him. Minos closed his eyes and took a deep breath, hearing the faint rattle in his chest.

He felt the presence of magic enter the room but didn't open his eyes. Even stripped of his divine blessings, he could still feel the shift in the air, the weight of power. He already knew who it was. His time was drawing near.

"You've been waiting for this day, haven't you, Kieran Grimlock?" Minos said, finally opening his eyes.

"Your escape from my clutches was heartbreaking," the reaper lord replied, his voice soft, yet edged with command and calm.

"I'm not ready to die," Minos whispered, struggling off his cot and dropping to his knees in front of Kieran. "So let me become your servant."

Kieran chuckled. "Do you think you are worthy of becoming my servant?"

"No, I'm not, but my soul is too corrupt and I will never be reincarnated," Minos wheezed. "I already know what my judgment will be. The scale won't tip in my favor. So, the only selfish way to save myself is to ask you to turn me into a revenant."

He knew he was asking for something that might not be granted, but he had to take the shot.

"You know your plight," Kieran said.

Minos nodded. "I can feel my life draining out of me. I know I'm asking for a lot, but I will do anything. Be anything you want me to be."

Silence stretched between them, each second dragging as Minos felt more of his life slipping away.

"Very well," Kieran finally said.

Minos exhaled shakily, a ghost of a smile curving his lips as his body swayed. "I have two requests."

"You may speak," Kieran allowed.

"I know you will erase my memory, but I want to keep it."

"Is that a request or an order?"

"A request. I don't want to forget what I've done. Let it be my punishment."

"And the second?"

"I want a new identity. A new name and face."

"You're asking for a great deal. However, it may be best. I plan to use you for the rest of your life, and I do not need your past appearance to interrupt my plans. This will be a pact between us. If you break it, your soul will vanish. You are not allowed to see or

speak with anyone from your past." "Yes," Minos whispered.

"Know that you will never have a normal afterlife. And the rules may change or grow as time passes."

Minos nodded, using the last of his strength. His eyes drifted shut as he felt his soul begin to lift from his body. The moment he stood in spirit form, Kieran waved his hand, and agony erupted.

Minos howled in pain, clutching at the back of his neck and collapsing to the floor as he writhed. The death mark was being carved into his soul, each stroke permanent and excruciating.

He didn't know how long the pain lasted, but the second it ended, his entire being ignited. Or at least it felt like it. His soul went up in flames as his entire structure was torn apart and remade. A new kind of magic surged into his consciousness. Throughout the entire transformation, he screamed while his physical body lay still and dead on the cell floor. No one came.

More time passed before the screaming finally stopped.

Minos lay naked and panting, exhausted, trembling as he held himself on the cold floor. But Kieran showed no concern for his weakness. Minos eventually sat up, blinking through the haze, and looked down at his new form. He was no longer spirit, no longer soul alone. He was flesh and bone again.

His gaze slid to the side, landing on the lifeless body he had once inhabited. He stared at it for a long moment, a heavy weight of regret sinking into him. He couldn't change the past, not the destruction, not the mistakes, but he had been given a chance at a different future. Being a servant of death didn't sound so bad anymore.

"From this day forward, you will be known as Caelan Vayne.

Do you accept this name?"

"Yes, master." The rush of magic washed over his skin, sealing the name into his reborn form. He exhaled in shaky satisfaction.

"Because of your combat and leadership experience, I will make you the head of my Obsidian Vanguard."

Minos—no, Caelan—went to his knees and bowed. The Obsidian Vanguard was an elite agency that answered only to the high lord grim reaper and served as the equivalent of the most powerful governmental intelligence and covert operations forces.

"I am honored, my lord reaper."

"Yes, well, don't disappoint me like you did Ishtar."

Caelan raised his head and looked up at Kieran, determination burning in his newly forged eyes. "I won't."

"Come. We have work to do," Kieran said.

Caelan rose to his feet and followed his new master, never once looking back.

EPILOGUE

"Come on, Jason, push," Sekhmet said, her tone calm and encouraging.

"I am," he strained, holding and squeezing the life out of Leo's hand.

Leo gritted his teeth, trying his best not to show he was in pain too. "You're doing well, baby." Leo dabbed Jason's forehead with a cool towel.

"This is harder than the first time," Jason said through clenched teeth.

"I know, baby. But I'm not going anywhere. I'm right here," Leo told him, his voice low and steady.

Things had gone back to normal, or what passed for

normal in their world. Minos was arrested for his crimes, and three months later, he was found dead in his cell. No one mourned his death, and no one claimed his remains, which were cremated without ceremony.

The case against the Duprees had begun and was still ongoing. Not long after Valencia died, so did Jackson, leaving Willa to fend for herself. She pleaded not guilty despite the mounting evidence, and she seemed to change lawyers every two weeks. Ian Dupree went missing after reports surfaced about his malpractice and unethical behavior. Leo doubted he would ever return to Valleywood. And while he wasn't exactly at peace with that, he was just relieved the man was far away from Jason.

Leo learned about the unbound omega spirit attached to Jason, thanks to Athena. Mark wasn't always present, only appearing to guide Jason through mastering his abilities, which he was gradually getting better at. The rest of the time, Mark vanished to gods knew where.

Ishtar kept her word and granted them blessings that enhanced the talents they were already born with, including cunning intellect, beauty, strength, divine insight, and more.

The kids had started school, meeting new friends, and enjoying things like soccer and dance classes. Jason and Leo found themselves adjusting their work schedules to drop off or pick up, laughing through chaotic mornings. Their days were full of noise and joy, and Leo couldn't be happier.

They were in the process of building another house

on the property for Talos and Ada, who, as fate would have it, was also in labor at the same time. Ada's water broke just as they got Jason to the hospital, and the staff had to rush both couples into separate delivery rooms.

"Ahhhh..." Jason screamed, snapping Leo out of his thoughts.

"Leo, are you ignoring me right now?!"

"No, I was thinking about—"

Jason grabbed him by the collar and yanked him close. "You better not be thinking about leaving me," he growled, his eyes blazing.

"What? Where would I go?" Leo asked, confused and concerned.

"Good," Jason said with a grunt, bearing down again. "Leo."

"Yes, baby. I'm here. What can I do for you?"

"Stop breathing like that. You're not helping."

"Oh. Okay. I'll stop."

"And stop talking too!" Jason shouted, clutching Leo's fingers so tightly he was sure they were going to break or be permanently deformed when this was all over.

"That's it, Jason," Sekhmet said. "I can see the head. Keep pushing."

"You can do it," Leo encouraged, his voice thick with awe and emotion.

Jason nodded and pushed. Leo grabbed the cool rag, pressing it to his face, then got some ice chips and gently rubbed them on his lips. Five minutes later, the first child was born, screaming, redfaced, and furious.

"It's a boy!" Sekhmet announced.

"A boy," Jason panted. "Xander will be happy."

Leo nodded, kissed him on the forehead, and chuckled softly.

During all of Jason's doctor appointments, they had chosen not to find out the sex of the babies, so it was all a surprise to them.

"Come on, Papa," Sekhmet said. "Let's cut the umbilical cord so we can get this baby settled, because baby number two is on its way."

Leo moved quickly, cutting the cord and checking over his son before handing him gently to a nurse.

"What's his name?" she asked.

"Theron," Leo responded.

They had come up with a list of names depending on what they had. Leo returned to Jason's side and resumed his duties.

The next forty-five minutes were a blur of more yelling, crying, and Jason swearing in impressively creative ways as he delivered Elira and Cassian. The two were not at all silent about their entry into the world.

Leo had hoped to finally name one of his sons Icarus, but just like with Xander, the moment he said the name, the baby cried loud enough to rattle the ceiling tiles. Leo quickly changed it to Cassian, and the child immediately quieted down.

JASON COLLAPSED BACK against the pillows, panting, sweaty, and exhausted.

"They are beautiful, baby," Leo whispered, leaning

down to kiss him on the forehead, only for Jason to howl in pain as another contraction struck.

"What's wrong?" Leo asked, concern flooding his voice.

"I don't know, I feel like I need to push again," Jason answered, grimacing.

"Ah… I don't know how to say this," Sekhmet said, still positioned between Jason's bent legs. "But we have a fourth one."

"Tell me you're joking!" Jason shouted and grunted, unable to stop his body from doing what it needed.

"No wonder the afterbirth hadn't come out after baby number three," Sekhmet muttered. "Jason, this is the last one, I promise. When I count to three, I want you to give it all you've got. Okay?"

Jason didn't respond. He simply did as he was told, and no more than five minutes later, a fourth child was born. Unlike the other three, she was quiet. When her big blue eyes landed on Jason, his heart melted as her name came to him.

"Hello, little Atina. You are truly a surprise. Were you hiding behind your sisters and brothers?"

Her eyes slowly closed and then opened, as if answering his question.

"She's a little underweight, but very healthy," Sekhmet said, smiling warmly. "I can't believe I missed her presence. She's going to be a special little one." She looked at the other three. "They all are. Enjoy some time with your babies before we wheel you into the family room and you're bombarded with guests. Oh, and I got word that Ada had twins. A boy and a girl. Daye and Kira.

Congratulations to you all." "Thank you," Jason said softly.

"No thanks needed. We're family."

With that, Sekhmet walked out of the birth room, leaving them alone.

Leo took Atina from Jason's arms and gently placed her in the bassinet beside her brothers and sister.

Jason was exhausted. After delivering four babies, he wanted to sleep for hours, but he couldn't close his eyes. He couldn't stop looking at his treasures.

"Thank you, baby," Leo said. He leaned in and kissed Jason's forehead, then dropped to one knee and gently took Jason's hand, pressing a kiss to the back of it.

"Leo, what are you doing?" Jason asked in a trembling whisper.

"Jason, you know that I love you."

Jason nodded, tears welling in his eyes. "I love you, too." "Then marry me," Leo said.

Jason smiled. "We're already married."

"I know, but this time we'll do it for the right reasons. Not because I was trying to get someone to stop chasing me, or to please my mother, but for us. For our love."

Jason nodded again, unable to form words. Leo stood and smiled, then kissed him soundly and hugged him tightly.

"Thank you for coming into my life."

Jason pressed his ear to Leo's chest, listening to the steady beat of his heart. He was safe. He was happy. And that was all that mattered.

❧

Six Months Later

Breaking News:
We're thrilled to announce the double nuptials
happening this Saturday!

Real Estate Tycoon **Leonidas Devereux** will marry **Jason
Dupree**, and **Talos Blacke** will wed **Ada Devereux** in a
joint ceremony celebrating love, family, and second
chances.
Mark your calendars, Valleywood. This is the wedding
event of the season.

❧

JASON SWITCHED OFF THE TELEVISION, set the remote on the
coffee table, and looked over at his husband, who was
feeding Elira. "Did you really have to make it breaking
news that we're getting married?"

"Hey, the last time we said 'I do' it was under the
cover of darkness. This time, I don't want to hide," Leo
said with a grin.

"You're shameless," Jason said, shaking his head.
"And you still want to marry me."

"That's because I'm a glutton for punishment."

Thanks to Athena, who helped him and Ada put
everything together, all the wedding preparations had
been completed. Just as Leo finished feeding Elira,
Athena appeared. Since the birth of the babies, she'd

been living with them, and Jason had to admit he liked having her around. Not just him, but the twins too, who were learning so much from her.

"Why don't you two go out for a bit? I want to spend time with my grandbabies," she said, taking Elira into her arms.

"Are you sure?" Jason asked.

Athena smiled. "Yes. Now go. It's been a while since you two had a date."

"You game?" Leo asked, looking at Jason.

"Alright."

They stood and walked out of the living room, heading off to enjoy a wonderful night together. Instead of going to a fancy restaurant, they chose a romantic evening in the backyard, where Leo had set up a tent, ordered takeout, and danced with Jason under the stars. To Jason, it was perfect.

"I think you've tamed me," Leo said. "And I like it."

Jason smiled and leaned in to kiss him, but stopped just before their lips touched. "Then how about we sneak up to our bedroom and go a little wild? I'll make sure to leave you a hefty tip and an outstanding review."

Leo grabbed his ass and kneaded it, grinding their crotches together. "Fuck, I love being married to you."

This time, there was no hesitation. Their lips met and locked in a heated kiss. They didn't make it to the bedroom right away. Leo took him to a part of the garden where no one could see and made love to him twice. Then again, in the bedroom, where they stayed most of the next day, entwined in each other, just the way Jason liked it.

THANK YOU

Dear Reader,

Thank you for taking the time to support me. I hope you enjoy reading Taming Leo. I loved reading about Greek and Egyptian mythology; stepping into a new world was enjoyable. This book also surprised me because I had been experiencing writer's block and wasn't sure how to break it. Then came Leo and Jason, and I went with it. I love writing in the Valleywood world. It's an escape for me from all that is happening in reality, and I hope it's the same for you. There will be more to come from Valleywood. With all of my thanks and appreciation,

Giovanna (Gia) Reaves

BOOKS BY GIOVANNA REAVES

Audiobooks Available on Audible

Jordan's Pryde

Ryland's Inferno

The Cowboy's Baby

Winter's Promise: Omegaverse Romance

The Drummer's Heartbeat: A Winter Romance

Protecting His Omega

BECOME A VIP MEMBER

As a VIP member, you gain exclusive access to a treasure trove of content, including exclusive one-shots with new and old characters, behind-the-scenes content, and much more. This membership is designed to provide an intimate, enriched experience for my most dedicated readers.

https://www.giareaves.com/vip-content

GIA'S VIP BACKSTAGE PACKAGE

https://www.giareaves.com/vip-content

AFFAIR

- Monthly episodes to a serialized story
- Access to the lower tiers
- Your name featured in serialized chapter
- Early access to current WIPs
- And much more not listed

$10 per month

LIAISON

- Access to my backlist
- Signed Swag or Merchandise (US only for now)
- Exclusive webinars or live Q&A sessions
- Discount on books and merchandise
- And much more not listed

$15 per month

TEMPTATION

- Early access to my WIPs
- Unlimited access to all lower tiers
- Monthly VIP Zoom chats or one-on-one interactions
- Quarterly surprise package mailed to you (US only for now)
- And much more not listed

$20 per month

See website for a full list of benefits in all levels

GET 25% OFF THE FIRST MONTH SUBSCRIPTION

MY ONE-NIGHT STAND SERIES

Book 1: My One-Night Stand, My Forever

Young and on the rise in his career, Christen Travers wanted a new lease on life. After moving to a new state and accepting the dream position he worked so hard for, Christen just needs to blow off some steam. Not

wanting a relationship, his goal is to find the perfect one-night stand, one to hit it and forget it, then go back to the life he's strived for.Special Agent

Jaxson Colvin works long hours on his cases for the FBI. On a night off and wanting to unwind, offering to buy the sexy stranger on the next bar

stool a drink turns into a night he won't soon forget. The memories of that one night keep Jaxson company when he is out on assignment far longer than he anticipated.

Sometimes one-night stands bring much more than a few hours of enjoyment and memories. When Jaxson and Christen bump into each other again, they both must learn that sometimes one night can turn into a Forever.

Book 2: Loving You

After catching his fiancé cheating, Ethan Beaumont needed to get away.

Ethan decided a spontaneous weekend in Las Vegas was just what he needs. He was not expecting on running into the dashing and sexy Tyler Hamilton, the man he'd had a crush on since the day they met.

Tyler Hamilton, known for his love 'em and leave 'em attitude, just got back from tracking a bioterrorist and needed some downtime. Asked to

go to Las Vegas to close a business deal by his

business partner and twin brother, Lucas, Tyler decided to take time to relax as well. Running into Ethan Beaumont, Tyler made him an offer Ethan couldn't refuse.

They say what happens in Vegas stays in Vegas, will that be the same for Ethan and Tyler?

Book 3: Hidden Truths

They say your past always show up when you least expect it. Brenden Smith made a promise to himself that he would never put his heart on the line again. He swore off romance after his last breakup. But what happens when the man he thought he was over shows up in his life with news he wasn't expecting?

Stephen Young broke off his relationship with Brenden over a misunderstanding and miscommunication. Working for the FBI, he knew

it was only a matter of time before he and Brenden would work together. Will they be able to cooperate and put the past behind them? Or will Stephen's secret keep them apart?

Book 4: His Lover's Vow

A budding friendship that leads to a one-night stand and a second chance at love.

After the death of his wife, Lucas Hamilton put finding love behind him, his only focus on being there for his young daughter. As the CEO of Hamilton Enterprise, Lucas has more on his plate than he could handle without adding a relationship in the mix. He promised his late wife that when love came around, he would not let it pass him by. Which is why

Lucas was shocked to find himself attracted to Tucker Stevens. Does he ignore his attraction or keep the vow he made to his wife?

Tucker Stevens has mourned the death of his wife and daughter for so long that he's forgotten what love is. As an FBI agent, Tucker used work as a way to keep himself busy, forgetting the promise he made to his wife to never give up on love. Even though most of his family and friends are in

love, married, and living their lives, he still didn't recognize or believe he had the right to fall in love. That was until Lucas Hamilton who found a way to break through the wall he built around himself.

ABOUT GIOVANNA REAVES

Giovanna (Gia) Reaves is my alter ego, who is a dreamer. I spend my days and nights dreaming and thinking of the worlds I want to create with words. I started writing about three years ago, when I was introduced to the world of fan fiction.

I loved the idea of creating a new world around characters that people already knew about. And ones that are original of my own making. I have written two novels and a few free stories.

I am a mother, wife, and a military veteran. I enjoy trying new things such as traveling, cooking, and reading. I try to incorporate some of the things I have experienced into my books.

Currently living in Newport, RI with my two favorite men. If I am not hidden in my cave writing, I love to read and spend time with my hubby and son. I love listening to R and B along with neo soul when I am writing.

When I'm not writing, I am trying to perfect my baking and decorating skills or try to pick up something new. I love spending time with my husband and son playing video games and traveling.

I love hearing from you.
Email me at GotRomance@GiaReaves.com or sign up for

my newsletter to receive updates on what I'm doing next.

Check out my website for more deals and more:
https://giareaves.com
Join my reader's group:
https://www.facebook.com/groups/GiovannasSecret OneNighters/

 facebook.com/GiovannasSecretOneNighters

 instagram.com/GiaReaves

 tiktok.com/@giarwrites

 amazon.com/Giovanna-Reaves/e/B01CKXHKRA

 reamstories.com/giovannareaves

 youtube.com/@giovannareaves5712